KATE CATERINA

KATE
CATERINA

WILLIAM RIVIÈRE

GROVE PRESS
New York

First published in 2001 by
Hodder and Stoughton, London, England

Printed in the United States of America

FIRST GROVE PRESS EDITION

Library of Congress Cataloging-in-Publication Data

Rivière, William.
    Kate Caterina / William Rivière.
    p. cm.
    ISBN 0-8021-3973-6 (pbk.)
    1. World War, 1939–1945—Italy—Fiction. 2. Physicians' spouses—
Fiction. 3. British—Italy—Fiction. 4. Married women—Fiction. 5. Italy—
Fiction. I. Title.

PR6068.I97 K38 2002
823'.914—dc21   2001046417

Grove Press
841 Broadway
New York, NY 10003

03 04 05 06 07 10 9 8 7 6 5 4 3 2 1

'. . . little more than the register of the crimes, follies, and misfortunes of mankind.'

The Decline and Fall of the Roman Empire

I

ON THE EVE

1

She had harvest-coloured hair and dark eyes, and her name was Kate Fenn, until she married Gabriele D'Alessandria and went to live in Italy, where her new family and her new friends called her Caterina. It was Mussolini's time, it was the time of jack-booted Black Shirts, and diversity of opinion was not encouraged in the country. Certainly most of the respectable citizens of Arezzo whom the bride came amongst did not expect a young lady to go in for unorthodox thinking or feeling of any kind.

Of course, her husband's friends knew he was a covert Socialist – which was dangerous. As for her father-in-law, melancholic old Luigi D'Alessandria, who these days only had antipathies for all philosophies and factions, if donkeys' years ago he had harboured any mild political sympathies, almost nobody could remember what they had been.

No one in Tuscan society suspected Caterina D'Alessandria of abstruse awarenesses, any more than her London friends had done when she had been Kate Fenn. They didn't suspect her of ambiguous loyalties either. People commented freely on how striking her colouring was – though her hair needed more ripple, young coquettes and ancient matriarchs agreed, having to find something amiss with such fairness. They commented on the straightness of her nose; on the rather too marked resolution in her mouth and chin; on the dark amber brilliance of her eyes when her enthusiasms caught fire – her too many, chaotic enthusiasms; on her figure.

The newly arrived bride was strongly built, and she would have been voluptuous, polite opinion allowed, had there not been something lamentably tentative about the way she sat, or stood, or turned. English gaucheness, clearly. The poor girl had simply never been taught how to move, and didn't have it instinctively. (But one or two of the men were fascinated by how, even when she was immobile, she appeared to be wavering. It was something in her eyes, perhaps.) Anyhow, she would always be hopelessly outgunned by her sister-in-law Esmeralda, who was the recognised beauty of those circles in those years.

Then, after not much more than a year of the marriage, Lisa was born. After that, discussion of Caterina D'Alessandria invariably commenced with how charming it was to see a young mother so joyfully devoted to her infant, before just as predictably passing to speculation about how long she would take to produce a male child. The eyes and hair which seemed to contradict each other, and the strange coexistence of resolute lips with a hesitant voluptuousness, quite lost currency in conversation.

Kate, for twenty-two years; then Caterina, in her new life. Only that, right from her entrance onto her Italian stage, she began thinking of herself as Kate Caterina. Signing her name like that when, for example, she scribbled a note for her husband to say that she'd taken the baby out for a dawdle as far as the gardens by the cathedral but she'd be back in an hour – as if that self-translation were one name, her double name. Not that anyone ever called her Kate Caterina, except Gabriele sometimes when they were playing their erotic games; so the two words came to mean licence and concupiscence and being someone slightly other for a while.

Kate Caterina. Almost as if she had already known of her deplorable capacity for self-dividedness – though not much had yet occurred to ram home to her consciousness the essential doubleness of who she had so blithely become. Not much . . . Because in '36, which was the year she and Gabriele had got married, everyone was relieved that the war that had nearly broken out over Abyssinia between Italy and Britain had not broken out, the League of Nations being all yap and snarl but no bite. Not much . . . Though the anti-English clamour in the newspapers and the anti-English clamour in the streets were hurtful to her, however hard she tried not to mind.

Kate Caterina. As if she had already been growing that keen perception not only of her inner dividedness but of her multiplicity too. That talent or weakness she had for burgeoning with selves. For putting forth not only Lisa but shadowier souls too; other lives of hers; less apparent stories. Presences she conjured up, or she met and could never quite forget.

Then came the Pact of Steel, the military alliance forged by Hitler and Mussolini. So Caterina D'Alessandria knew that her divided loyalties were going to split her in two, just as plainly as she knew, and sometimes said, that Italy was her country now.

But today it was the end of summer, and she was driving to Arezzo station to meet her brother Giles, whom she hadn't seen since her wedding. And because Giles must be offered all things, her mind was fizzing with all the lives she was living. Apparent things that she would show him, and she was desperate for him to approve of and like. Awarenesses she'd tell him the stories of.

2

‘My God, Kate, it’s wonderful to see you again.’ Grinning irrepressibly, Giles Fenn sat twisted sideways in the clanking old Fiat. He saw Kate take her eyes off her driving to flash him her old tomboyish smile. ‘Watch out, those children haven’t seen you. Thinking of which, how is my niece?’

‘Oh, she’s in terrific fettle. Stumping here and there. Saying things. Sometimes in English, sometimes in Italian. With bits of her own baby language still mixed in.’

Her quiet, merry voice unchanged, Giles heard happily – unless it rang with a contentment, even a pride, which were new. He winced with sudden jealousy of all that her Italian life had given her, reminded himself firmly that he was delighted she was happy in her marriage to Gabriele D’Alessandria, glanced at the late August sun on the houses. No, honestly they were palaces, some of them. Kate had said Arezzo wasn’t grand like Florence or Rome. But these façades with their stone gateways big enough to ride a horse through, with their handsomely carved balconies, their sculpted coats-of-arms and high windows and deep eaves . . . Still, some of those skirmishing ragamuffins had been barefoot, he’d noted with a jolt. And the tiny black-swathed old women, selling a handful of eggs or a handful of herbs. The thin men pushing carts of firewood. What was she saying?

‘Three years, since you gave me away.’ She laughed. ‘Remember how we stopped the car a couple of hundred yards from the church because we were early, and you said, What about you *not* giving me to Gabriele to take to Italy, what about you hanging on to me like we’d been before? And I said – oh Lord, are they . . . ? No, it’s all right, they’re regular troops. I said I’d always fancied Samoa. Ever since I’d fallen in love with Robert Louis Stevenson when I was fifteen and *particularly* passionate, I’d longed to sail to Samoa in a schooner. But otherwise, if you preferred, we could just bolt back to Canonbury Square and barricade ourselves into the house, though in all that bridal get-up I wasn't really dressed for barricading. Oh Giles, Giles, I don't think I'd ever loved you as much as I did that day. Only perhaps today I love you pretty immoderately. Can't wait to show you Lisa.'

That day of Kate Fenn's wedding, their mother had been dead for three years and their father had been in a Flanders graveyard since 1918. So it had been that the bride and her younger brother had found themselves having to organise her nuptials largely on their own. With damn all money. With a bit of desultory help from an aunt or two, help that just came down to fussing and interference. So of course it had been the least swish wedding there ever was, but high spirits and a submerged desperation had carried them through. All her uncles had offered to give her away. But she'd said that if she couldn't walk up the aisle with her brother she wouldn't get married at all.

Luckily, when the D'Alessandria contingent arrived in London they had turned out to be charm itself – well, all except Cosima, Giles recollected. Cosima was the elder sister and she'd married a Roman marquis. Not only that, but he was one of the potentates of the colonial service. So she was enormously grand, or she was revoltingly stuck-up, depending on your point of view. But Gabriele's mother had been nice, she'd helped Kate and him *without* seeming to be taking them over in their own house. Giles was looking forward to seeing Sonya D'Alessandria again.

They were held up by a platoon of infantry marching along.

'What do you mean, about it being all right, they're regular troops?'

He gazed at the unfamiliar uniforms, the soldiers' arms and legs swinging in unison, their glinting bayonets. So these were the men who quite likely, if the war that hadn't broken out last year over Czechoslovakia broke out this year over Poland or next year over somewhere else, one was going to have to get steamed up about enough to . . . But perhaps you did it coldly. Yes, almost without doubt you did it coldly, Giles reflected. So these were the fellows who, if Italy was idiotic enough to come into the war, and on Germany's side, he might easily find himself fighting. And Edoardo? he wondered, remembering the younger D'Alessandria brother, who

was about his own age and whom he'd liked, at the London
wedding.

'Not Fascist militia,' his sister was saying. 'Not Black Brigades. Oh, I don't mean I feel physically afraid every time I clap
eyes on them – though the shadow crosses my mind. Remember
the old saying about a goose walking over your grave? All the
same . . . Gabriele is nothing like as cautious as I'd wish him
to be. Lord, that's another thing – I'm going to have to explain
all the politics to you, or at least enough for you to get through
the wedding party tomorrow without committing some frightful
gaffe. If Esmeralda really does marry the man, that is.' And
her cheek dimpled in the way he remembered from old times
when it had just been the two of them, really, in all the world.
Harum-scarum childhood times. Then later, after their mother
died, the running-their-own-show times.

'Keeping you all guessing right up till the last minute, is
she?' he asked. Esmeralda was the dashing sister, the one Kate
enthused about in her letters – they'd clearly struck up a great
alliance. The car was jolting forward again. And although it was
for Esmeralda's wedding that Giles had come all the way from
London, and it simply hadn't occurred to him that it might be
called off at the last minute (Kate and he had only been joking
about a dash to Samoa for heaven's sake, or he'd been mainly
joking), he truly didn't care about Esmeralda and her fiancé
either way. Because here he was, still sitting turned so he could
see his sister.

She looked all right, he thought half with relief and half
reluctantly. Kate in profile, concentrating on her driving for a
change. Yes, she looked fine. Here he was, hearing her laughing
voice, when she said: 'Well, not all of us, Giles. I trust the
bridegroom and his family haven't a clue about the dance she's
leading us, or the show she's putting on, or whatever it is she's
doing. But those of us who've got her in the house . . . Mind
you, I've never known her in better form, she's enjoying life all
right. Now, we've arrived, just about. That's our church, the
Santissima Annunziata. I mean, it's the church the family have
always gone to, and where tomorrow we hope that . . . Though
possibly one or two subversive souls among us decline to hope
very fervently. Sorry, didn't see that dog. Missed it though.'

'You haven't taken to going to church, have you?' he asked, surprised by the obscure distress he felt. 'I mean, except for weddings and things.'

'Good heavens, no. My mother-in-law is the only real Catholic in this family. She converted when she got married. She's German, or she was. But of course you know that. From a little port on the North Sea. Damn, stalled again. Look, I reckon I've parked. Giles, I *know* I'm babbling, I'll try to sober up, but honestly, after three years of never seeing you! Yes, Sonya is a religious person – in the good sense. She does the praying for all our souls – yours too if you actually want to know – and we hope that does the trick.'

Caterina turned to face her brother. She put her hand on his sleeve, smiled at him with her eyes as darkly brilliant as they'd always been. 'I'm all right, Giles darling, you know.' She gave his arm a little shake. 'I haven't changed. I'm fine in Italy, and I'm still your old Kate, and . . .' She flung herself across the car, she hugged him. Her head muffled against his shirt collar, he heard the beginnings of a sob. 'Now,' she said, 'let's get out. That's the house. See the wistaria hanging over the garden wall?'

Standing between the church and the wistaria, Giles Fenn saw that the D'Alessandria family house was a family palace and no mistake. Honey-coloured plaster exceedingly shabby, even cracks in the walls, but . . . Enormous. Dozens and dozens of rooms, there must be in it. Late Renaissance, Kate had said. Instantly, he recalled Canonbury Square and their beloved but poverty-stricken house.

Kate had understood, naturally.

'Don't be impressed, it's half-ruined inside. What is more . . .' She appraised her brother with unashamed adoration. 'Very few indeed, if any, of the young men at the wedding party are going to have a hope in hell of turning the girls' eyes away from you. I did remember to tell you that there are going to be *lots* of beautiful young women, didn't I? Well, now . . . I think there are only about twenty people in the house right this minute, so I'll start by introducing you to them. Can't tell you what a scatter-brained week it's been. Splendid, and all that – but scatter-brained. So shall we . . . ? Then there's a dinner party tonight, given by the groom's family, in their hotel – just them, and us lot. Then the real show tomorrow, with far more people. Giles, what's wrong?'

Kate had been a light-hearted innocent when she'd sallied off to Cambridge, but while there she'd become rather sophisticated, moody, intellectual – or at all events, Giles had been conscious of losing her to the university, as then he'd lost her again to Italy. And now she was the young lady of this mansion. He eyed it slightly resentfully.

'No – nothing. Look, you haven't forgotten that I don't speak a word of Italian? Oh, except a man on the train told me the word for coffee was *caffé.*'

'Don't be a coward, you *know* all the D'Alessandria speak English. As for Beatrice Castiglia, ever since I showed her the photograph of you which I keep on my dressing-table, she's been practising how to be sweetly fetching in English, for an hour, every morning, in front of her looking-glass. Not to mention Rosalba D'Alessandria – she's a cousin – who's dangerous all right. Only she's awfully nice too. Come to think of it, last thing tonight, I'm going to brief you on the perils, in good older-sisterly style. Which of these charming terrors will flirt with you one day and say vile things about you the next. Which are in fact already engaged, though they won't tell you that.'

'All right.' He grinned, picked up his suitcase. Lord the sun was hot! And the blazing blue sky made his eyes sting. 'I'll be brave. But why isn't Esmeralda sure she wants to marry this fellow? And do we know he isn't just as dubious about her?'

'Oh, Esmeralda!' Most people contrived to appeal to Caterina's sense of wonder and delight so dismally little. But since their first acquaintance she had rejoiced in how her imagination could never resist being vivified by Esmeralda's.

She slid her arm through Giles's, for an instant she limpet-stuck to his side. Like limpets, we are . . . That had been one of their jokes.

'You'll see. Esmeralda is . . . Oh, she's fireworks.'

3

—⁂—

When Gabriele D'Alessandria had been a medical student in
Padua, a squad of Black Shirts had hustled him into the local
Fascist Party office and given him a bad beating, his socialist
inclinations having become known to them.

It was common enough, it was happening daily all over Italy,
that sort of thing and worse than that. A group of men, with
pistols at their belts, bludgeoning with truncheons one unarmed
man, in the comfort of a political party's office. Just a warning,
they told him, when on beating him to their satisfaction they
had forced castor oil down his throat so he shat himself, as
they turfed him out in his befouled trousers to drag his cut
and bruised body back to his lodgings.

Gabriele was a steady-minded young man, and the episode
had, if anything, stiffened his political resolve, made him less
flexible. Certainly by the time he was in London, specialising
in pediatrics, which was when he got engaged to marry Kate
Fenn, his determination to work for the downfall of Fascism
in his native land was equal to his dedication to doctoring.
Conscious of following in the great Mazzini's footsteps, who
in London a hundred years before had dreamed up the birth
of Italy, Gabriele spent a lot of time with fellow expatriates
in tea-shops scheming the overthrow of this latest tyranny.
He liked England. Not only Mazzini, but Herzen too, had
found safety and friendships there. The victorious Garibaldi
had been lionised by English society. In the British Museum
reading room, Marx had brooded, written, drawn up the new
freedoms. Possessed by a sense of exultation, Gabriele went to
read there too, and to think his straightforward, progressive
thoughts which always seemed to know where they were going
and how to get there.

It was Sonya D'Alessandria into whose mind horror seeped.
She who as a young woman had lived through the Great War as
a member of a well-regarded Arezzo family, with small children,
with her husband at the Front — but also as an enemy alien of

a sort, even though one who by then had an Italian passport. She who, in her adopted country where anti-Austrian and anti-German feeling was being whipped up every day, with her golden hair and her light blue eyes had stood out in the street. Who thus early in her marriage had already known too much about divided loyalties and about political brutality.

It was Sonya who, when she thought of her boy on the floor being clubbed, roaring with pain as they struck where they knew it would hurt, on his knees, on his elbows, in his groin, was rendered speechless, was as it were spiritually immobilised, by this way of conducting the life of a great and civilised people. Not that Italy was worse than Germany. She knew it was not. But that here, or there, or anywhere, men and women who thought themselves of good character should accept such thuggery as probably inherent in the nature of things, or anyhow as something they were not going to stand up against, was to Sonya one of the symptoms of her society's degradation. Or had it always been like this? No! She refused to think that people were irredeemable. Still, it exasperated her to the verge of despair. Kneeling in the Santissima Annunziata, she would clench her praying hands.

Now the mother and son were standing together in the hall of their house, where it was blessedly cool, waiting to welcome Giles Fenn. The inner doorway leading to the courtyard was of dark grey stone. The staircase and balustrade going up to the principal apartments on the first floor, the pediments and the coved ceiling of the hall – all were of the same sombre, grainy magnificence. Her hair had been so light a gold that it had never really gone grey, it had just paled and paled, and now was a faded aureole in the stony dimness. She stood with dignity, without moving.

Sonya knew too much about the family's impoverished condition to be proud of her house. But she was proud of her clever, successful son beside her, who was determined that he was going to make far more money than his father or his grandfather ever had, and who was so handsome with his brown hair brushed back from his high forehead, and his new waistcoat and that yellow bow-tie with blue spots. All the rest of the house was in such a merry hubbub of preparation for tomorrow, that she was happy to be secluded with him for a minute. Neither of them felt any call to break their companionable quietness. Gabriele took off his light, steel-rimmed spectacles and wiped them. Shoving his silk handkerchief carelessly back into his breast pocket, he caught his mother's glance, raised his eyebrows in a gesture of shared amusement at all this turmoil in the family.

Gabriele D'Alessandria was just as sanguine about his private life as he was when it came to his country's political destiny. Maybe Caterina had her strange moods, sometimes. But he was if anything *more* in love with her than when he'd asked her if she would marry him. (Gabriele was marvellously free about telling people this.) She had got to grips brilliantly with her new country, and if her thoughts were forever careering off in imaginative directions – well, luckily he himself was a plodding, logical sort of fellow, so they complemented one another.

So now Esmeralda was getting married, perhaps madly unsuitably? Gabriele reckoned that, with a bit of good sense all round, things would shake down. Giles's imminent arrival had meant that Caterina was over the moon, all day she'd been making absolutely no sense at all. Well, splendid! He twitched his sleeves so he could admire his gold cufflinks, he smiled to recollect how his wife had set off for the station far too early. There on the platform she'd have fretted to and fro, she'd have decided that all the clocks were wrong, she'd have decided that the train must have crashed and every single passenger been killed – and then hurled herself into her brother's arms.

4

Caterina took Giles's hand, started eagerly toward the tall four-square house. Then she smiled at her own gesture and dropped his hand. She hurried ahead, glancing back over her shoulder with bright eyes, telling him a few words of Italian to use when introduced to people.

His pronunciation was so funny, she had to stop to tease him, make him repeat after her all over again. Then she remembered a jumble of things she'd forgotten to tell him in her letters, and anyway it was wonderful to have him to herself for another minute. So they stood together in the sunny lane, and she began telling him about a few of the people he was bound to meet during the wedding festivities. She spoke quickly, lightly, one hand swinging her straw hat aimlessly against her leg, and she kept breaking off simply to smile into her brother's eyes, and say, 'Oh Giles!' or, 'My God, here you *are!*'

Well, for a kick-off there'd be Gaetano Da Durante, who was an old friend of her parents-in-law. He'd be the *real* guest of honour – not the Podestà who was the Fascist top dog in the city or the Prefect who ran the province, who of course would think they were. Oh yes, they were coming. All the top brass. Gaetano was *quite* the most enigmatic man in Italy as well as the fattest, though he'd always been sweet to her and she'd begun to see glimmerings in his mysteriousness. Then the bishop, who ran people's souls. No lesser cleric would be allowed to hitch a bride as fashionable as Esmeralda – if she subdued her spirit sufficiently to get married at all. Was she being bitchy? No, she didn't think so. Esmeralda was quite unabashed about liking to be as fashionable as all hell. Who else? Cosima's pompous husband couldn't come, luckily. Too busy helping run the Dodecanese colonies. In other words, lolling about like a satrap on Rhodes. Oh yes, Grazia Damiani was coming. She was that rare creature, a flaming Latin redhead, and they were all afraid that Edoardo had fallen for her, which would be a disaster. Giles remembered Gabriele's younger brother

Edoardo, didn't he? He was at Siena university these days, and having *all* the wrong flirtations and flings, Edoardo was.

Now, she must gather her wits. Caterina swished her hat through the air, settled it on her head. What were the potential difficulties Giles ought to be aware of? Well, for a start, the big one. Carlo Manzari, the bridegroom, was a fire-breathing Fascist, which meant that sooner or later Gabriele and he were bound to . . . Unless everyone was tact incarnate, or decided that family loyalty was going to have to be regarded as paramount. No, Manzari didn't come from a snobby old family. A self-made man, a politician, rather a successful one.

As soon as Giles Fenn found himself in the hall, shaking hands with Gabriele and his mother, it seemed to him that he had never forgotten how much he liked them. Of course, their friendship at the time of the London wedding had been superficiality itself – but all the same . . . ! Since then, Sonya had written to him every year for his birthday, asking how he was enjoying his engineering degree course, saying what fun she hoped it was for him to be lording it in the Canonbury Square house. Each year she had written to invite him to Arezzo for Christmas and Epiphany, too, and once had added that she *did* hope it didn't appear to him that they had stolen his sister away. She rather feared it must. So please would he come?

Three times, Giles had written back to say he couldn't, he had to work. Which had been true. Every vacation, he had worked, not only at his engineering books, but at all manner of odd jobs to pay his way through college, to live. That was why he had never come to see Kate. Too hard up, simply.

He flushed at the thought, standing under the stone arches of the D'Alessandria hall. He wasn't exactly lording it in Canonbury Square, either. He'd taken in lodgers. And that time he'd written to Kate suggesting she visit him, and she'd written back that she couldn't because of Lisa, he'd reckoned it was her new family liking to keep her corralled up. No, he mustn't hark back to that – and anyhow he'd probably been wrong. Yes, it was good to see Gabriele and remember their talks in London – though he'd forgotten what a dandy he was. Giles was suddenly conscious of the modesty of his own second-hand summer suit, bought from a family of Jewish traders in the Mile End Road with whom he'd become friends. They'd been kitting him out for years, the husband giving him fatherly sartorial advice, the wife then busily taking in waists and letting out legs.

This was the first time Giles had been out of England, but he'd been interested in Italy – from the engineering point of view, chiefly. How the Romans had built their aqueducts and their harbours. How the Venetians had built on their mud shoals, how they'd regulated that lagoon of theirs. And later – how Brunelleschi had worked out the dome of Florence cathedral. But Gabriele's conversation in London had kept veering back to the liberation and unification of Italy. He'd found him books in English about Mazzini the dreamer and about Cavour the master of political tight-rope-walking. He'd told him heroic stories about Manin's defence of Venice against the Austrians, and well-nigh unbelievable stories about Garibaldi's defence of Rome against the French. So one way and another . . . And now with Kate standing here and smiling at Gabriele and him. With Kate wishing them to pick up their friendship again. Kate willing it with – Giles became precipitately aware – colossal innocent force . . .

They set off on their tour of the house, amid much chat about who was where, doing what, and who would show up later. Amid chatter about the wedding preparations, too. Sonya D'Alessandria was wearing what struck Giles as a very formal dark blue silk dress and a massive brooch that glittered dully, and she did not appear to be participating in the hard work. But the responsibility for resolving a hundred different complications was weighing on her, she confessed, speaking to him in her careful English which came from a schoolroom on the coast of Heligoland Bight in the eighteen nineties.

There was the friend with vineyards who insisted he provide the wine for the wedding at a special knock-down price, but the snag was that his vintages were famous, and for consider-ably less than his knock-down price she could buy perfectly acceptable wine. Then, the butcher had quarrelled with the grazier, so they had gone elsewhere for the pork, she hoped it was going to be good. And the quantities! Merely the logistics of the commissariat! They were going to sit down to lunch a hundred strong. Could Giles imagine the numbers of flasks of wine and crates of vegetables? The quantity of loaves to be baked, puddings to be made?

Of course, by the next day he had worked out a rough plan of the house. But for that first half hour, Giles was blurredly aware of seeing grey arch after arch, and big shadowy spaces with brilliant splashes of sunlight at their far ends, and pediments everywhere. A stone newel post with its head carved as a sphinx stuck in his mind. So did an iron door handle that was a dragon, and hinges like sword blades, and intricate keys the size of his hand. Everywhere overhead there were ancient lanterns festooned with cobwebs.

'We had Cosima's wedding here ten years ago, Giles, so we ought to know how to go about it. But somehow . . . Well, for good or ill Esmeralda does not have her sister's placidity. And I hope . . .' Sonya D'Alessandria frowned. 'I hope everybody will have the sense not even to begin to talk about politics.'

They went into the walled garden, with its medlar tree and its gnarled wistaria, and Caterina told her brother about the fireflies that sparked and jinked there in early summer. They went to the cavernous kitchen, where the fire made the already hot afternoon stifling and where delicacies for next day's first course were already being concocted. Giles shook hands with the perspiring cook and her helpers. He tried out his half-dozen words of Italian politeness, to general merriment.

His head was, if anything, in more tumult not less as his introduction to the Palazzo D'Alessandria proceeded. But Giles reminded himself that he was here for a whole fortnight, and that after the wedding the household would presumably return to peace and quiet. There would be days and days in which he'd be able to talk to Kate. Alone with her, sometimes, when Gabriele was at the hospital.

Even so, there were an awful lot of names to try to commit to his annoyingly reluctant memory. Neighbours and relatives who'd turned up to help, or simply because a wedding tomorrow was irresistible, simply to mill around and drink coffee and have opinions. Nice, though, how fond of his sister everyone appeared to be, how glad for her that he'd come. And splendid the way Kate was so keen for him to like everyone he met and

everything he saw. She'd exaggerated when she said the place
was half-ruined, but it was dilapidated. Didn't look as if a
builder or a decorator had set foot here for generations. What
were they all laughing about in Italian now?

He asked his sister. She told him it was because he had
hay-coloured hair just the same as hers. The girls laying the
long tables, both of whom were in fits of giggles, had decided
that at the party no one would have to ask who the good-looking
stranger was.

'They say you've got my eyes too. Dear God, it's nice to talk
English again. Odd, but nice. And to go back to being just Kate.
Don't you ever call me anything but Kate, will you? Yes, Louisa
– she's the one pouting at you – says we've both got hay hair.
Not straw. Hay. And she reckons that, if others don't, she . . .
But I won't tell you the rest.'

Grinning awkwardly, Giles admired the high coffered ceilings
of the principal rooms on the first floor, the tall windows
looking onto the street or into the narrow courtyard, the
sepulchral fireplaces carved with mythological scenes. Two
flights of stairs higher, Caterina was excited because now she
was going to show him the apartment up under the roof where
Gabriele and she roosted. Where he was going to sleep in their
spare bedroom as the most honoured guest they'd ever had. And
where, best of all, her darling Lisa ought with any luck to be
waking up from her afternoon sleep.

This was the door. But then Giles must have said something
stupid – truly, he must concentrate on all these explanations and
names, he exhorted his embarrassed mind – because the others
were chuckling.

'No, no, Giles, Gabriele isn't a *Communist*,' Caterina said.
'He's a *Socialist*. These distinctions between one sort of admirer
of Karl Marx and another are terribly important in this country.
I hope you're going to sort out which is which. If in doubt, pipe
down. Or ask me, in a stage whisper.'

5

When Kate had crossed the Channel and then the Alps and had become Caterina to her new world and Kate Caterina to herself, she had effectively shed her past. Or at least, in Italy she appeared as a creature who had come to life fully grown. If she had been formed by heredity and environment, only she knew even a little about these forces, and what good or bad work they had done. Her father, who on his last leave from the Western Front had dandled her on his knee, and her schoolmistress mother whose determined dream it had been that the girl should go to Newnham College, were scarcely imagined by anybody; the last wisps of the ghosts faded into thin air.

Not that the good Tuscan burghers perceived this passage in her destiny like that. It quite simply never occurred to them that her husband might have settled in England. Heavens, it wasn't as if the fellow was some ragged Neapolitan rascal who would starve if he didn't emigrate to North or South America. Gabriele would inherit the family house. A career at the hospital had been lined up for him.

It would have been proper for the girl to convert, some of the Arezzo matrons sniffed. However, the whole city, Catholic and lay, those happy with the Fascist one-party state and those not, could congratulate itself on how fortunate the English young woman was – *l'inglesina*, as they all referred to her – to inherit ready-made the D'Alessandria position in society. When she first arrived, her family introduced her to precisely the right people, as those same right people were months later still remarking to each other. And her father-in-law the professor himself squired her around the chief glories of the city. He had been observed instructing her about Vasari's colonnade, using his walking-stick to point to its virtues. He had escorted her to the house where Petrarch was born. He had been observed holding open the door of San Francesco for her – and they were inside there looking at the frescoes for an hour, the proprietor of the Café dei Costanti opposite could testify to that.

Then, through Professor D'Alessandria *l'inglesina* had met other distinguished men. The art historian Gaetano Da Durante for instance.

It was true that Da Durante's comings and goings about the country were so incomprehensible as to arouse suspicions in minds favourable to orderliness in private as in public life. It was also true that there had been some mystery about his war. He had ended up by being atrociously wounded, no one disputed that. But earlier . . . Some discreditable episode hushed up, and a heroic action at about the same time not rewarded with the medal or the promotion which – well, something like that!

Anyhow, he lived in Venice, in a palace crammed with treasures, everyone said so. And it was enough to turn a girl's head, being introduced to intellectuals of national renown. What was more, through her sister-in-law, the Marchioness Cosima, she was invited into Roman drawing-rooms frequented by the glamorous and the powerful.

There was Grazia Damiani too, she was an offshoot of a noble family, they had estates near the Alban hills. It was true that, although still scarcely grown up, she was reputed to have already broken an impressive array of hearts, thanks to intelligent use of her red hair and of her mother's jewellery. And that minx didn't only flaunt some of the family's stupendous necklaces at parties, the salacious whispered. She'd even sold some of her mamma's jewels. Yes, honestly! To pay for her outrageous . . . And the dear, good lady still alive! Though naturally too terrified of the scandal to breathe a word. Still, to do Grazia credit, it was also reported that these conquests of hers had all been within the grandest Roman society. Beatrice Castiglia, on the other hand, since her husband's posting to Tripoli had *completely* forgotten that she was married to him.

As for how Caterina saw her Italian initiation . . . She had felt very young when she left one country, flung herself gaily into her marriage in another. So it had only been lately, growing up a bit more perhaps, or beginning to be at home in her Italian life, that she had started consciously to reach out for her psychological inheritance; to wonder, in some detail, what it consisted of.

She stood in a long tradition of Anglo-Italian friendship, and of English people of every conceivable type who'd come to live in Italy. So far, so good. All the books her father-in-law and her husband gave her, the way they made her feel welcome – everything confirmed that. The stories she read, the stories they told her – of Byron and Shelley in Italy, for instance. Funny stories, sad stories. Teases about how when the English got south of the Alps they tended to cheer up and start to misbehave.

No, that wasn't it! What happened was, you were taken along by Cambridge friends to some talk or other at the Italian embassy, where they were diabolical enough to introduce you to Gabriele D'Alessandria, who that minute as it happened was leaning against a pilaster and looking around mildly for an ashtray for his cigarette. So he shoved away the white and gold fluted pilaster with his shoulder – and that man could charm the birds down out of the trees, or maybe he couldn't, maybe it was just you, at any rate from that first minute he had you fluttering and singing for him all right. Well, if carnal romanticism couldn't raise its beautiful, lascivious, innocent head when it wanted to . . . So then in those London summer weeks it turned out that Italy, which before had never been much more than a lovely word, began to chime with a glory that you longed to be possessed by; and it turned out there was a palace in Tuscany, heavens above! So dizzy dreaming and dizzy desire did the rest, dizziness undid you. And it seemed this was your fate; certainly it was irresistibly exciting, and you were abandoning yourself to it; only fate was plainly just another word for chance.

How had it occurred? You came away from the embassy in the warm twilight, you came dreaming along the street under the plane trees already feeling guilty about Giles, already telling yourself that guilt was a despicably suburban emotion which henceforth was going to be far beneath your dignity. You came away from all your meetings with Gabriele in those sultry, luminous weeks with your notions as skitter-scatter as ever, only these days they were palpitating before one idea that doubtless was just as haphazard as all else but was tyrannous in a way that was new and you liked. You fished your latch-key out of your bag on the Canonbury Square front steps, thinking: Tuscany, and a passionate love. Thinking: a new awakening.

Golden swathes of light across olive groves, and an old grey
tower . . . Or would it not be like that at all?

But then . . . Now that she was here. Now that this child of the
North Sea civilisation was wedded to the Mediterranean one . . .
The richness of it could make Caterina's imagination feel faint
and at the same time exalted – something for which it had a great
aptitude. She'd been like that at university, she remembered
perfectly well. Not for her, the sensible way Giles in London
slogged along getting himself a useful qualification. Kate had
changed faculties – and even then she'd always been off wasting
time at lectures in yet other faculties, reading books that weren't
on any syllabus. And now Kate Caterina or who-have-you was
just as bad, always trying to make her mind centripetal, finding
it was as triumphantly centrifugal as ever.

So it was cheerfullest to go back to teasing Gabriele about
how, just because Julius Caesar had invaded Britain, by his own
account quite briskly and efficiently, that didn't mean she was
going to take any imperial lord-and-master nonsense from him.
The Romans had strutted about in their new colony. They'd
killed people and profiteered and given themselves airs for –
what? – four hundred years or so. But then they hadn't been
able to keep it up. They'd scuttled back across the straits with
their tails between their legs.

To which Gabriele would spiritedly reply that he thought
it was very decent of his fellow-countrymen to try to civilise
the British a bit, and if the attempt had been only modestly
successful that was still better than nothing.

At which point they would generally what they called come to
blows, which meant coming to giggles and caresses and making
sure the door was shut. And Caterina would be left, afterward,
wondering what it was like for the first Roman sailors making
their way up the tidal Thames between the marshes and the
woods. What it had been like for the British who stood among
their trees and watched the ships come. And for the British
who stood on stone quays, after four hundred years of being
a colony, and watched the last legionaries sail away.

6

The person who had been sitting within earshot of Lisa's cot while she slept was Luigi D'Alessandria, who had now outlived her other grandfather by twenty-one years.

In the amenable Catholic fashion, there had been nothing you could really call a separation between Luigi and Sonya. Indeed, so generous were the margins of liberty they had for years allowed one another that on occasions such as the weddings of daughters they performed in perfectly adequate harmony. Even so, the old gentleman had been happy to retreat upstairs away from the bustle of hymenial preparations.

A small man, spare-framed, elegantly suited, his white hair impeccably clipped and brushed, he had sat in Gabriele's and Caterina's living-room, in their rocking-chair. His neat head was so wizened and had such great hollows at the temples that it seemed a death's head, though with sad eyes which were watchfully alive.

Twice he had gone next door to lean over the sleeping child, lay the back of one bony finger against her cheek to see if her cotton coverlet had made her too hot in the summer afternoon up under the beams and the tortoise-tiles. Twice he had returned to the rocking-chair, which creaked. The shutters were closed, but silent in the dimness he had listened to the swifts' shrill cries as they swept over the roofs of the quarter. He had pressed his finger-tips together, and the slight rocking of his chair had died out, and he had gone back to fretting over whether he should make a last-ditch attempt to penetrate through all Esmeralda's mockery and her joking, all her effervescence and – and nonsense.

His white, neat eyebrows twitched. His last attempt had been a horrible failure. She had laughed in his face. She had fobbed him off with a lot of rubbish about those intelligent families who had made a point of having one son or son-in-law a member of parliament, a second in industry, a third a cardinal, a fourth a banker. So why shouldn't she bring a Fascist politician into the family, they might yet all come to thank her for it, Esmeralda had proclaimed, tossing her head as she went curvetting out of the room with that idiotic theatricality they'd all been longing for her to grow out of ever since she'd been about thirteen.

Or perhaps it would be better to ask Caterina to tackle one last time the not altogether unexpectedly problematic bride? But to what end? He didn't even know whether he wanted Esmeralda to chuck her fiancé at the last minute. There was nothing he was clear about!

A fiasco tomorrow would bring scandal on the family. Luigi D'Alessandria trusted that even at his age he would still be liberal enough of outlook to make nothing of this. Yes, yes – but even so. And the expenses already incurred! While although a social success tomorrow might bring money and political clout into the family, which heaven knew could do with such assets, it might also introduce a deadly danger. If only one knew whether these revolting Fascists were going to come to grief, and if so when, and how harmless or how bad was this going to be for the ladies of their élite. And as for whether marriage to Carlo Manzari was going to make Esmeralda happy or not . . . In his agitation making his chair rock again, her father wondered if she had ever posed herself the question with any seriousness.

How complicated life was! Yes . . . But time was, the complications had fascinated rather than always disheartening him.

Irritated with himself as he so regularly was by this last reflection, Luigi heard Caterina's happy voice ring from the stair. Making his liking for her overcome his regret that his solitude was being interrupted, he stood up to shake hands with Giles.

—〰—

7

When Gabriele was still in London, he had told his fiancée about his parents' estrangement, without going in for much explanation.

It was disappointing, to an orphan, that the acquisition of a family turned out to mean the acquisition of a crucially damaged one. However, Caterina had resolved right away to try to be impartial when it came to Luigi's and Sonya's differences. But it had been infinitely easier to begin to love her mother-in-law. For a start, Professor D'Alessandria's last appointment had been at Urbino university, on the other side of the Appenine chain, and even after he'd retired he still spent more than half his time there, in a tumbledown farmhouse with a few hilly unprofitable acres.

Whereas Sonya . . .! Caterina's impulsive heart failed utterly to moderate her praise for how that lady had, from the start, seemed determined not to be all the ghastly things for which mothers-in-law were well-known.

Of course, in her day she also had been a North European bride brought into this very house. Then Caterina discovered that her forerunner had been christened Hildegard Sonya, and only when she left Germany had Sonya adopted the latter, because even if in fact it wasn't an Italian name it sounded as if it might be. So just like herself, Sonya had changed her name, had discovered how a fresh identity could feel like new possibilities opening up.

So much, they had in common! Quite soon they were having long conversations about all manner of things. Even about religion. Despite Caterina having declared she did not believe in God – giving, as her ground, that she thought a world without a God was more free, more miraculous, gave greater delight. To which Sonya, already getting to know her a little, had replied that, yes indeed, the girl's intellectual and spiritual life was of such ebullience that you'd have to be quite an optimist to imagine it ever developing the coherence of religion.

Whereas with Gabriele's father . . . Old soldier, old patriot, and with a dour pride in past Italian achievements in government, in the arts, in philosophy, in the sciences. Nevertheless Caterina had often been shocked by how caustic about his country Luigi could be.

However, today her father-in-law was in a genial mood, she noticed with relief, bending over Lisa's cot.

Ever since she had known for sure that her brother was finally coming, Caterina's whole being had been suffused with the necessity of his welcome being a success, of his loving – no, instant love was too much to expect – of his liking her Italian family, the house, their way of life, her friends. By the time she had met him at the railway station, her chaotic consciousness had been like – like she didn't know what. But . . . Oh, she'd wanted somehow to transfer all her last three years into his head in one miraculous moment. Like grabbing up the feathers from a torn eiderdown, and flinging handfuls of them into his face, and crying: This is me, and this, and this too! While at the same time watching his eyes anxiously, for he must like the feathers.

Writing letters was all right in its way. But the real thing! So now as she picked up her daughter she had tears in her eyes, which was silly. But somehow, with Mummy dead, and she could barely remember Daddy, and Giles had been born posthumously, so now . . . It was a small victory, or at any rate it was bliss of a hurting sort, to have his niece to offer him. 'Well, she's *just* awake. Very drowsy, my love, aren't you? Up you come. This is your uncle Giles, whom I'm always chattering about.' And even though Giles was gloriously young – long, long might he remain unmarried! – surely he knew that most women were desperately proud of their babies, though of course you pretended not to be.

The dress-maker had come, was in Esmeralda's room for a last fitting of the wedding finery. Caterina knew she ought to go down to lend moral support or aesthetic acumen. But it was important to her, this gathering of her family where the day sky through the shutters' slats lit up the scene of her recent life, and where Giles was being shown the small printing press on which Gabriele type-set his against-the-government pamphlets. This mansard with its comfortable old bits and pieces of furniture, where day and night Gabriele and she lived, and made love. Lisa was retrieving her toy donkey from under the oak table, and her mother smiled to recall some splendid love made on the edge of that table earlier in the day.

Caterina opened a shutter on the shady side of the house, looked out at the westering sun's golden glow on the Santissima Annunziata. The others all knew they had to chat friendlily away, so that was what they were doing. Which meant that now for a minute she could stand a little detached, with her happy mind higgledy-piggledy with all the things she was going to tell Giles as soon as she got a chance.

All her discoveries! All the revealing things – like how it was Sonya who most indefatigably helped Gabriele at his press, because she insisted on being one of those who, in however old-lady-like a fashion, stood up a little against the barbarism. How funny and sweet they were, working elbow to elbow at the cramped desk with the cabinets of type and the hand-press. Sonya saying she was quite sure that prayer and kindness were of more avail than socialism and Baskerville 10 point and ink. Gabriele saying, Yes, Mother. Kindness certainly, and prayer if you wish, but pamphlets too. In a land where the editors of the newspapers are telephoned most days by members of the government, and sometimes by the Duce himself, to be instructed as to what news to publish and what slant to give it . . . Pamphlets too.

However, the thought of what might happen to Gabriele if his political activities were ever betrayed was a fear that never entirely left Caterina, and tomorrow the lower storeys of the house were going to be clogged with Fascist wedding guests making merry, so now her mind made an automatic, nervy, blind jump to how she'd discovered that old Luigi wasn't all acerbity – not by a long chalk.

In the garden here, they'd been, under the medlar tree. It had been his love of poetry that had decoyed him into university lecturing, and she'd asked him which Italians she should read, because honestly she might as well get to grips with her new language in that way as in another. Leopardi, he'd said. He'd fetched a copy of the *Canti*, offered to read to her. Quite soon, she'd noticed there were tears in his eyes.

The second time Caterina had surprised Luigi in the grip of a strong emotion had been when Lisa was born.

Of course, he'd shown his daughter-in-law great consideration before that. Something to do, possibly, with his having brought a German bride home to this house not all that many years before her country and his went to war against each other. A generation later, now Gabriele had brought an English bride home, and these days Italy was in a German alliance. The D'Alessandria family, the old professor would chuckle, just didn't seem able to get it right. Always marrying the wrong people.

But then, when the baby came . . . Doubtless the grandfather's anxiety and devotion were all muddled up with his own difficult fatherhood. Yes, children born to dual nationality in times of near-war and then war . . . And when Luigi should have been getting to know his little Cosima and Gabriele, he'd been in dug-outs in the Carnic Alps for the best part of three years as an artillery captain, apart from a few short home leaves, and a spell in a military hospital with diphtheria that nearly killed him. Children born to multiple identities, born to the cosmopolitan, which could mean freedom but could mean danger too. Then by the time peace of a lawless sort had come, and Esmeralda wasn't just a swaddled-up, whimpering, sucking could-have-been-anyone in a cot, and then Edoardo was born and he too started becoming who he was . . . Not many years after that, it must have been, Luigi's marriage had become pretty much a formality.

No, that too was all wrong for telling to Giles. But all her discoveries about what it was like being a wife, and what it was like being a mother – only maybe he wouldn't be as enthralled as all that. Then, the fascinating complications of being a daughter-in-law and being a sister-in-law. Baffling as all hell, often, but essentially happy. All the sorts of things you couldn't really talk about in letters, but which were all-pervasive, they became you yourself. How absorbing it had been, after years of life being just Giles and her knocking around in Canonbury Square, this suddenly being part of a family with its slowly evolving rituals, with its multiple loyalties, its sense of continuity. How uncomfortable it often made her feel, that she was going to have the Palazzo D'Alessandria for the rest of her days, not Cosima or Esmeralda or Edoardo who'd been children here. Yes, naturally she knew that this falling in love and getting married and having a baby were as old as mankind and womankind . . . But when you set about living it yourself it was always new and it was always strange.

No, come to think of it, with Giles she wouldn't make a terrific noise about that. She could tell him about the other side of the coin, though. Tell him about how paradisaically free, in retrospect, she had been in London and Cambridge, at nineteen, at twenty, at twenty-one. How when you got married a whole lot of things clicked into place and then were impossible to budge.

8

Left with Giles for a few minutes, when all the others had more promptly started bathing and changing for the Manzari dinner party, Caterina opened a shutter on the other side of the apartment. In the coming days they would meander the streets of the old city together. But at least now she would show him her view of the cathedral on the crest of the hill.

Then there was so much she wanted to hear, and so much she wanted to say, that she didn't know where to begin. Lisa kept clambering onto a chair, and thence onto the table, from which she could easily fall. Her mother lifted her down for the third time. She looked around for something harmless for the child to play with. She pulled open a drawer of scarves, which Lisa could unpack, and trail around, and drape on herself, and with any luck be distracted by.

Giles flopped into a chair. He grinned at his sister. He said, 'Tell me about Esmeralda.' Adding that she needn't remind him that her sister-in-law looked like a cross between Marlene Dietrich and some Mediterranen ravisher, because he remembered that from the London wedding. What was more, Kate wasn't to worry, he was already bracing himself not to be befuddled by this vision of carnal loveliness.

Caterina said she was glad to hear that, because it was ridiculous the way at parties Esmeralda always had a clump of smitten oafs standing round her. Yes, she was jealous of her looks. More than flesh and blood could do not to be.

She said that. And she thought: Yes, Esmeralda, why not? One has to start somewhere. News I'm longing for, news of London friends, can wait. Above all, the thing that is too horrifying to think of, the possibility of war which is so horrifying I think of it all the time, war perhaps between England and Italy, can wait.

So she smiled bravely back at Giles, smiled at him straight through the looming war and out the other side with no self-betraying quiver of her lips or wincing of her eyes. She began to talk, touching on this, touching on that. She told Giles how volatile Esmeralda could be, and that when she was listless she could say unkind things. But then the lights in her eyes would be switched back on, or something. Yes, that was it. Honestly it was as if she had a battery in her head that was disconnected sometimes. So she had two reputations at least, in Arezzo, Esmeralda.

Caterina stood before her brother, where she could keep an eye on Lisa. She told him how, when she'd first arrived in Italy, Esmeralda had swept her up in a razzledazzle social whirl. That fancy dress ball at the Rossini palace, when the two of them had gone as the Archduchess of Transylvania and the Archduchess of Somewhere Else, Illyria was it? But, yes . . . She reckoned Esmeralda's boredom with herself had lain behind her departure from Tuscany, her valkyrie raid on Roman society, her swift return with a fiancé, her trophy, this government politician no one here knew.

Gabriele stuck his head through the door, already bathed, already at the stage of cufflinks, and indecision as to ties. They might consider *beginning* to get ready, he suggested, or they'd never be there by eight o'clock.

Yes, Caterina said. She knew. Right. But she went on talking about how she'd missed Esmeralda when she vanished to Rome, using Cosima's house near the Pantheon as a sort of bridgehead from which to launch her incursions. Because with Giles here after three years, and with she being – oh she didn't know, but it had been building up and building up – she being who she was, where she was, when she was, so that . . . Well, anyway, she had an obscure but desperate sense of urgency in her heart, and she went on explaining about how terrifically happy she had been up at the top of this old house with her husband and her baby. Had been. Was.

Caterina knew she was talking, but she was no longer always sure which of her thoughts were getting out in words Giles could hear and which were staying in her head silent. It was all about how the unexpected gift, the additional grace, had been Esmeralda's friendship. Because sisters-in-law . . . Well, my God, imagine having to live in the same building as highfalutin Cosima! But Esmeralda and she had decided they were sisters with no law about them, and that was why, after tomorrow, with one of them tethered in Rome and the other tethered in Arezzo . . . No, no. Almost beyond doubt, it was nothing to do with Esmeralda. Though marrying a Fascist bigwig in times of . . . But she herself had a burden in her head, and a despairing urgency that – had she said this before? She didn't want to repeat herself. A burden that would bring her head to the floor. Only it was more like a welter. He'd heard the news about the Nazi-Soviet Pact, hadn't he? Of course, he must have done, how silly of her. At all events, if Giles wanted to imagine her life, he should imagine nights when Esmeralda came up here, and they sat on that sofa and talked. Late at night, often, after Gabriele had gone to bed if he had to be at the hospital early next day. Giles must imagine the night outside, and Esmeralda's and her two heads there.

Caterina stretched her arms forward toward the tatty old sofa, with her fingers extended, as if she were arranging two female heads in a mental composition she was making. She went on trying to find words to make clear to Giles even a little of the essence of who she'd become since she'd left him and flitted off to Antibes on honeymoon.

Something solid. Well, ever since the early twenties, Luigi had been writing a book. That was solid enough. Giles ought to see the heaps of notebooks the old boy had filled on his desk in the house near Urbino – he didn't work on it here. A book with the most appalling title. *The Degradation of Italy* – could Giles imagine? She meant, could he imagine an Englishman toiling away at *The Degradation of Great Britain*? Might be a damned good idea, mind you, but she couldn't see it happening.

Anyhow, these notebooks were all about the breakdown of law and order after the war, when Socialist militias and Fascist militias were terrorising the towns and villages. Beatings, shootings, extortion, protection rackets, you name it. There were pages and pages about the Liberals who hadn't got the nous to govern, and the Communists who were fanatics, and the Popular Party who'd do anything the Pope said, and – she couldn't remember *all* the parties. Anyhow then you got to the failure of Italian democracy, and the Fascist dictatorship and how most people were in favour of that, and the invasion of

Abyssinia and how most people were all for that too, dogged old Luigi year after year just noting things down, and it was so full of depressing information that it'd never be published, so that was all right.

No, no, that wasn't what she'd wanted to say. The point was, it was just like Gabriele with his pamphlets, they both wanted to set the record straight. Naturally enough they disagreed about practically everything. The son thought that the logic of history meant that socialist progress was inevitable. The father said that there was no such thing as the logic of history, and in the last century it'd been the industrialists who'd believed in progress, and these days it was the Marxists, and no doubt in time it'd be the capitalists again, or some other lot, so what the hell. But they were both dead set on leaving a trace of what they thought was the truth. Whereas Esmeralda and she, late at night . . .

Then it wasn't just people setting out what they reckoned was right, and not listening to other people. No, on a good night, in talk, in silence, in talk again, it seemed their two minds were free to play over all the ideas in the world, deciding nothing, stopping nowhere. Did Giles at all . . . ? The cathedral up there on the hill against the night sky, and here under this roof their two minds become marvellously free . . .

Oh, she didn't know. But feathers she'd wanted to fling into his face, joyously – he'd understood hadn't he? 'It must be abstract, it must change, and it must give pleasure.' Where had she read that? Well, it must be intangible, it must change and keep on changing, to be alive enough for her. It.

'Kate, you've stopped,' Giles said. Who didn't think she was aware of the tears in her eyes, and could no longer bear to have her looking at him without seeing him. 'You were rattling along, and now for seconds and seconds you haven't said a word.'

9

—⊷—

'My dear Gabriele, good evening. Now you absolutely must give me your thoughts on this Non-Aggression Pact between Russia and Germany.'

Carlo Manzari was forty-odd, and handsome in a comfortably fleshed and high-coloured style, with his arrogant Roman nose and sensualist's mouth and strong white teeth, with his brown hair beginning to recede. However, the real reasons for his repeated seductions of fashionable young ladies, as he knew, were his high salary and his political power. Now he was shaking hands with the man who tomorrow would be his brother-in-law, speaking to him with a smiling gaze and an openness that showed he assumed they were already becoming friends, or showed he wished to give this impression.

In the plushy drawing-room of the hotel, where the prodigiously tall gilded mirrors were meant to signify grandeur and the ridiculously large sofas were meant to signify comfort, the Manzari were mingling with the D'Alessandria. Very few of them had met even once before, and more than one on each side had already resolved that they were not going to meet frequently in future. These factors introduced a strained note into the conviviality that they all knew they had to assume.

'Of course,' Carlo Manzari went on genially, 'we've hardly had time to work out all the implications – but they *have* pulled a fast one on the English and the French, haven't they? I must admit, I never thought Ribbentrop was that intelligent. The brain behind the deal is Molotov, wouldn't you say? But, now – from your standpoint . . . ?'

Hesitating beside the two men, Sonya D'Alessandria's spirits sank. Politics already!

Gabriele D'Alessandria gave Carlo Manzari his most quizzical smile. 'Well, you must remember that I'm only a provincial doctor,' he began, and wondered whether that was being sly too obviously. However, he enjoyed the game of political sparring, in which the underlying realities of power and interest were never alluded to and the discussion never caused anyone to alter his opinion, but endless manoeuvres were executed, rhetorical points were scored, above all egos were soothed or seared, so he pitched in cheerfully. 'But if you want my opinion . . . Looked at from any standpoint, the thing has its comic aspects, wouldn't you say? Hard to guess whether Hitler or Stalin must loathe the agreement they've signed more. Naturally they're both playing for time . . .'

It was horrifying to the mother of the bride, but at the same time fascinating, how these two men instantly started fighting with words. At once! Fighting with words about 'the strategic advantage for the Axis of the new Russian agreement', about 'the unholy alliance of Communists and Nazis'. Apparently without imagining for a second that they might not, that gentler attitudes might be possible. She admired her elder son. But part of her was aghast at what she had given birth to.

'Yes, yes, my dear fellow,' Manzari was saying, 'but you're being so even-handed one has no inkling of what you really think. All this *realpolitik*, this worldliness!' With a laugh of perplexed admiration, Manzari turned to Sonya. She steeled her smile. 'Signora D'Alessandria, your son would make an indefatigable diplomat. One asks the most innocuous question, and look what one gets! Oh, by the way, Gabriele, yesterday England declared a formal treaty with Poland, and all leave in the British Services has been cancelled – had you heard? But we're such an international bunch here this evening that I'd better not . . . Your wife is English, isn't she? Though you'd scarcely guess from the beautiful Italian she speaks. But as I was saying – and for pity's sake stop me if I'm being tactless. From the point of view of someone who, unless I'm much mistaken – how shall I put it? – who probably has more sympathy for the Soviets than for the Nazis, or indeed for the modest outfit I have the honour to serve in . . .'

Sonya listened in nervous admiration as her son side-stepped again – or was he going too far? And Carlo's brown smiling eyes were attractive. She must remember to call him Carlo. Oh how she prayed Esmeralda would be happy! Let these two honestly be in love! Yes, yes . . . But was her prospective son-in-law being less duplicitous than her son, or equally so, or – well, more so would be impossible.

Now she was being buttonholed by an uncle of the bridegroom's, who lectured her on the necessity of Italy obtaining Malta, and Gibraltar, and possibly Crete – he found it difficult to decide about Crete. Then she was introduced to a bevy of Manzari cousins, whose names she never caught because at that moment some musicians she had not noticed began to play. But whomever she was talking to, it seemed to Sonya D'Alessandria that conversations about politics and war were flaring up like bush fires all over the room.

Somebody assured her that, before hostilities commenced against France, it would be necessary to relocate to the south of the peninsula the industries now operating in Genoa, Milan and Turin, where they were within range of Allied air attack. Somebody else pummelled her with explanations of how war could only be averted if 'the Danzig issue' were resolved.

Worst of all, Gabriele's and Carlo's voices went on ringing in Sonya's mind, appalling her. They'd only met a couple of times, but already they hated each other beyond any chance of kindness. A hundred years ago, they'd have drummed up some idiotic excuse or other for fighting a duel, or for having each other set upon by paid thugs. Well, thank God these days there was less harm they could do. Or was that not true? And what would become of Esmeralda, caught between these two fires?

Yes, what was going to happen to her gloriously flamboyant, her devilish, her forever irresistible Esmeralda? Women could be vile in all manner of ways, Sonya knew, but surely they didn't have men's natural genius for enmity! 'Expediency the only measure . . .' 'Naturally, Poland is going to be hacked to bits . . .' 'Reasons of state . . .'

All the Manzari clan had clearly been informed that she was German, and thus the bride was half-German. That must be why every single one of them felt it incumbent upon him to make flattering remarks about Hitler to her. Had none of them imagined how, during the last war, she and her children had had 'Germans!' shouted at them in otherwise pleasant streets? Sonya began to feel hot and flustered. She kept reminding herself that, however distasteful the Nazi-Fascist alliance might be, all this Italo-German friendliness was a lot more convenient for her daughters and her than its opposite had been. She moved through the party as if through a foul dream, in which what was frightening was that you never knew the truth about others' sincerity or guile, and what was defeating was that others would never know the truth about you, and soon you would forget what it had been.

Sonya thought: If I don't manage to wake up, I'm going to die of old age without ever having done anything more except stand politely beneath hotel chandeliers, while women trill to me and men boom to me about the marvellous friendship between Nazi Germany and Fascist Italy. She wondered: What would happen if, on the eve of her daughter's wedding, an old woman clambered onto a table, and announced that her chief function these days, aside from praying rather desperately, was to be an unpaid assistant printer of subversive pamphlets? I'd probably stagger and tumble and smash a whole lot of china – that's all I'd achieve.

She must get a grip on her straggling wits. She spied Luigi on the other side of the room, talking to that nice tousle-headed brother of Caterina's. But when she reached them, there was little alleviation to be had. Her husband was discoursing about empires, in his dismissive voice.

Everywhere she turned there was hardness! Suddenly on the verge of tears, Sonya *saw* Luigi as if for the first time for years, as if waking from an illusion. That head which she had cradled in her arms a thousand times when they were young and in love, in that lost innocence before all the wars.

She'd never hold him like that again. Or was a resurrection of their old, deep love possible even this late in the day? Out of this estrangement, could they . . . ? She imagined it as a stepping toward one another. That would be a miracle, a grace! So often, for so many years, she had prayed for it. However, when she approached him just now he had barely registered her presence. Spellbound, remembering, she watched the mouth she had kissed so passionately. The thin lips kept moving. Dry words kept coming out.

'Idiotic thing is, we Italians had only just finished chucking out the last of the foreign bully-boys who'd been bossing us around in our own cabbage patches, when off we went to be colonists ourselves. One scarcely expects a sense of history, or of justice – but no sense of irony either! After the centuries when Spaniards misruled in Palermo and Naples.' Sick with despair, Sonya heard in his destroying voice the pleasure he could always seem to take in human weakness. 'After the countless Austrians and French who have tyrannised over Milan, Venice, Florence, Bologna. Had we lost our wits? Off we trooped, the latest bonny imperialist swaggerers, to Tripolitania and Cyrenaica, to Somalia and Eritrea. Then from the Turks we picked up some islands in the Aegean, and . . . Why, only last spring they were pealing the church bells all over Italy to celebrate our invasion of Albania. Yes, my wife here's crony the bishop of this city had every bell ringing. Oh splendid, we're going in to dinner. No good listening to me if you want to be cheered up.'

Standing beside her husband as the party began to move toward the dining-room, Sonya summoned her courage. With the resumption of a trivial intimacy occasioned by the wedding, she would venture on a note more personal than was any longer usual with them.

'Luigi, this is all . . .' With her eyes indicating the whole festivity, the whole affair. 'All this has a terrible unreality to it.'

He shot her a sardonic look, and in reply gave a curt nod.

10

As the only person at the party who could speak no Italian, Giles Fenn had been happy to be befriended by Luigi D'Alessandria in what seemed to him the very handsome hotel drawing-room. As for the old gentleman's mockery of imperialist brutality and swagger, in which Sonya heard the voice of disbelief in human goodness that appalled her . . . Giles was a Labour Party supporter of a mild sort, and he liked Luigi's glittering, mocking eyes when he told stories about the bishop blessing a regiment off to fight with General Franco in Spain, and crowds lining the streets to cheer the men marching away.

The saving grace of empires was that they ended up by falling, Luigi said. But while they lasted . . . And he told Giles how in 1911 the Libyans had been fed up with being hanged and shot and deported, so at a place called Sciara Sciat a rebellion broke out, and the Arab resistance joined in, and the Italians had to do even more hanging and shooting and deporting before their civilisation could be restored. He told Giles about the more recent pacification of Abyssinia, where there had been the necessity of bombing defenceless villages and gassing villages. He added: 'Mind you, young man, you English have been pretty barbarous here and there too.' Giles had concurred readily, and gone into the dining-room with an excellent appetite.

An hour before, he had only understood about half of Kate's stampede of disconnected sentences. 'A burden that would bring her head to the ground.' It had been terrible to discover there were miseries in her life of which he'd had no idea. Terrible to find her at the mercy of nervous tensions or, or – something. And if it was anything that anyone here was doing to her! Then, that stuff about 'abstract', and 'pleasure', and . . . Didn't sound quite, quite wholesome, somehow. Of course, at university she'd had her strange moods, and had gone in for ideas that didn't convince you they were worth making head or tail of. Yes, maybe that was all it was. Just the same old weakness of hers for notions that were a bit nebulous for his taste.

Relieved to be able to put aside his anxieties, now Giles was hunting for his place at the dining-table. He found that he was opposite Esmeralda.

This occasioned him only a little trepidation and quite a lot of cheerful expectation. After all, not only was she the indisputable star of the occasion, she was also clearly by far Kate's best friend here. His sister had mentioned enough about Esmeralda's having found Tuscan life tiresome, and to amuse herself having conducted some quite vigorous social and romantic campaigning, for Giles to be intrigued. Amorous campaigning too, he heard his mind suggest, as he vaguely recollected assuring Kate that he would not be intoxicated by Esmeralda's beauty, and reminded himself to pay her only the most cursory attention, but then decided headlong that all the same there *was* something wildly sensuous about her lips and her eyes. But the party were only tasting the third of the seven courses that the chef had prepared, when Giles was longing for dinner to be over.

For a start, the long table was fractionally too wide, and was opulently encumbered with crystal bowls, silver candelbra and porcelain épergnes, and there was a shindy of conversation punctuated by uproars of laughter and even by merry shouts, so that being seated opposite somebody did not mean it was easy to talk to her. Esmeralda and he exchanged, with raised voices, a few sentences of a cheerful vacuity they were both happy to overlook. But she had her fiancé on one side, and his father on the other, so naturally she talked chiefly to them.

The other trouble was that Giles had the Marchioness Cosima on his right and her eight-year-old daughter on his left. Cosima addressed him graciously on the subject of her husband's and her friendship with Lord Perth, recently the British ambassador, whose daughter had married into the Roman aristocracy. They were also on affectionate terms, it appeared, with Sir D'Arcy Osborne, who was His Britannic Majesty's minister to the Holy See. But after that, Cosima effused – with courtesy, but resolutely – as to her intimacies in German diplomatic circles, till even innocent Giles became aware that he was being instructed in British unimportance.

He was of an optimistic temperament, and though he knew

he might find himself in uniform before long, he still reckoned self-interest would very likely keep Italy out of a war against France and England. Even so, he made polite efforts to deflect the conversation onto the landscape and history of the Dodecanese islands, where, he presumed to ask Cosima, perhaps sometimes she accompanied her husband on his tours of duty? But apparently it was intolerable to the lady to be banished from Rome, which was the one city in Europe where an intelligent person might find amusement. Mainly because, Giles, listening discouraged, began to grasp, in Rome one might frequent the delightful German cultural attaché, and the brilliant German chargé d'affaires, and the German military attaché who was the most . . .

He turned to his left. But little Carolina was so immaculately doll-like, and so scant in her replies to his cheerful enquiries about her summer holidays in the Dolomites, that he began to feel it was unkind to make her use her schoolroom English. Also, she didn't seem to approve of his exclamations about what a feast was being dished up. He turned back to her mother. And every time Giles turned to left or right, or even if he merely raised his eyes from his plate, he saw Esmeralda only five or six feet before him, and it began to make him uncomfortable.

Of course, she didn't really look like Dietrich – though she did a bit. But he would have hated to think people suspected him of trying to get more than his fair, paltry share of her attention. Was it his fault that her lovely face was just *there*, haloed by candelabra, straight before him, so he had to twist and turn to look away?

He resorted to his glass of wine. A waiter at once discreetly refilled it. Also, Giles began to think that Esmeralda was giggling rather too fulsomely. Outlying members of the Manzari and D'Alessandria families kept leaving their places to come to talk to her, and she was making an exhibition of herself, the way she clasped their hands (it was plain to Giles that often she scarcely knew who these relations were), the way she gazed with that ghastly, soulful happiness into their eyes. If she was Kate's best friend, why was she such an actress? Whiskery uncles; little girls with sashes; solid mothers, solidly bejewelled. No end of them. Clasp the hands. Kiss the cheeks. Gaze radiantly into the eyes.

Murmur a few breathless, probably almost ecstatic words. Then each time turn away with such a flourish of her head that . . . Giles again raised his glass. Oh well.

It was better after dinner, when the party broke up into convivial knots of people who really did want to talk to each other. Giles found himself contentedly ensconced between the D'Alessandria brothers, with the happy additions of a box of Turkish cigarettes and a bottle of some aromatic fire-water which they told him had been made time out of mind in a monastery somewhere in the Apennines – its name slid instantly from his mind. Anyhow they were cunning old monks, and the fire-water was commendably fiery.

Gabriele seemed a bit tense, or distracted by something, Giles thought. So he reminded him of their London confabulations on the subject of Garibaldi's landing at Marsala with his thousand men. Heroic tales of the fight for the heights of Calatafimi against formidable odds. The victory at Palermo against even steeper odds, with Queen Victoria's ships in the harbour lending tacit support to the fighters for freedom, because of the European powers England was the only one on Italy's side. Palermo stories like that of the storming of the Porta Termini under a cross-fire, when to give his men the courage to go forward a Genoese lad of seventeen called Francesco Something-Or-Other ran forward with a chair and sat down, holding up a tricolour, where the bullets were flying, to show how bad the Neapolitan shooting was.

Gabriele grinned, at once he seemed his old cheerful, forth-right self. Yes, he said, and the Risorgimento was still unfinished business, but that was going to be put right quite shortly now. He glanced around to check that the coast was clear, he sipped his monastery fire-water. It had been a mistake to instal those lousy Piedmontese kings, or maybe it had been a necessary short-term stratagem. At all events, they were going to have to be got rid of. But the big, the inspiring enterprise . . .

The snag was, Gabriele elucidated with merry pugnacity, that if you didn't complete the job of freeing the country, later you found yourselves back under a tyranny again. Mazzini had known the task needed doing thoroughly, and Garibaldi had known. You didn't free a people by putting a king over them.

And they'd been right. Look what happened, with the Royal Family politicking, and the Papacy politicking, and here we were, being ruled – in other words, being made fools of – by a buffoon and his Black Shirts.

'But this time . . .' Gabriele's blue, Heligoland Bight eyes lit up, he looked not thirty but twenty. 'We're going to get it right this time.'

11

—∿—

Behind the hills to the east of Arezzo, at twilight the moon had risen, ruddy-hued from the late summer dust in the atmosphere.

Eastward again reared the mountains, the backbone of Italy. Here it was that in the heroic days of 1849, after the loss of Rome, Garibaldi had led his last couple of thousand escaping fighters, riding all one day at the head of his column up the zigzagging track to a pass called Bocca Trabaria, with Anita riding beside him, and his white poncho blowing in the mountain wind. And here it was that in these inglorious days Luigi D'Alessandria, retired professor of poetry and reputed misanthrope, had the habit of escaping in his ancient car, grinding up the hairpin bends to the same pass. Because in the hills on the far side, near Urbino, in a ramshackle house called Ca' Santa Chiara, lay his less glamorous freedom.

Rising, the moon had paled to ochre over the hill cities, over the village graveyards with their clumps of cypresses, over high oak woodland, over lower slopes where in the vineyards the grapes were almost ready to be picked. Ancient cities, often still ringed by their walls, all over the heartland of that still troubled country. Urbino and Gubbio, Volterra and Todi, Spoleto and Cortona. Places from which people had set out that day to come to Esmeralda D'Alessandria's wedding, or would set out from at crack of dawn so as to be in the Santissima Annunziata in Arezzo by noon. Cities which, the bride's father had been known to opine, had been stagnant backwaters for the last three centuries. Their labouring classes kept in ignorance and superstition. Their bourgeoisie – with a few gallant exceptions, a scientist or a composer or a poet here and there – too flaccid to realise their own lack of distinction, content to take some credit for the high civilisation of the past.

Naturally, no right-thinking person had patience with the old cynic when he muttered these disgraceful lies. And anyhow, was he himself not a pillar of the Arezzo educated classes? What hypocrisy! Either that, or it was an unchristian self-hatred. Because one could live very agreeably in a noble old house, with a concert now and then, and duck-shooting on the marshes come winter, and either the consolations of religion or the *frisson* of a little free-thinking, and excellent dinners all year round. Well, that is, you could if you weren't one of the uneducated, dirt-poor peasants, of course. Nor had almost anyone, among the wedding guests debating which suit or which dress to wear in the Santissima Annunziata next day, foreseen the defeats and the hunger soon to be visited on the land. It was true that there were political prisoners, and they were maltreated; so that in some respects little progress had been made since the days, still less than a hundred years ago, of atrocities committed in the dungeons of the Papal States. But people averted their minds' eyes from that. And no one imagined the extent to which, in the next few years, torture would be used.

At Ca' Santa Chiara, the owner's friend Gaetano Da Durante, who was staying the night there on his journey across the country to the wedding, had by moonlight fumbled his arm into the twigs and foliage of a pomegranate tree, and found the key in its usual place. He had been welcomed by the dogs, and in the middle of this affectionate scene had been accosted by a dwarfish, crooked figure looming out of the shadows with a gun. But they had recognised each other at once. It was the neighbouring smallholder, stumpy crook-backed old Gervasio, who cared for the place and the dogs, and never stirred without his shot-gun.

Now the moon was high, and silver. Farther afield, on the Venetian Lido, that sandy littoral between the lagoon and the sea, at the Hotel des Bains a sumptuous suite had been made ready for the Manzaris' honeymoon. One of the nightwatchmen and one of the maids, meeting by appointment in that bridal chamber, opened the curtains to gaze at the luminous Adriatic, before they made vigorous love on the bed, afterward rearranging everything immaculately.

In Rome, Cosima's husband had attended an official banquet, where he had eaten and drunk too much. Then he had directed his driver to take him to the exclusive little brothel near Santa

Maria Maggiore that these days he favoured above his other
haunts. It was only patronised by the best aristocratic set, and
although the marquis had no objection to bumping into old
friends in whorehouses, he detested having to nod good-evening
to colonial service rivals or business rivals. (His wife had given
his labours in Rhodes as his reason for not coming to Arezzo,
because she had been unable to persuade him to attend so
unimportant an occasion. And though she did not know his
precise whereabouts, she knew what he generally did after
banquets.) The marquis was lying on his back, because that was
least exhausting, an enormous purple lamp casting glistenings
on his black-tufted thick torso, being ridden by a Serbian girl so
young she still had spots on her chin. He fondled her breasts, in
an absent-minded way. Then even that felt too exhausting, after
the chocolate gateaux, and the brandy, and the sweetmeats, and
the brandy. He lay, breathing hoarsely through his moustached
lips. After a while, the girl got off him, thinking a drink might
cheer him along. She crossed to the bottle of champagne, tipped
some into a glass for herself and swigged it, poured a glass for
him and brought it to the bed.

In the garden at Ca' Santa Chiara, the moonlight was softly
radiant on the oaks and elms, on the walnut trees and the
cherry trees. All the valley was silvery, with moon-shadows.
On the brow of the hill, a flock of sheep were white dots. At
Gervasio's farmstead, a hobbled horse made its obstinate way
to some different grass, awkwardly, painfully slowly, its hooves
making a slurring sound.

Indoors, Da Durante was reading. He was so fat, he looked
as if he was about to have a baby, and he had the innocent face of an ageing cherub. His round brow had only
a few wisps of hair left. He turned the pages, wheezing
steadily.

He looked up, to his old friend's familiar things. The bookcase
full of poets. The fishing-rods and guns in their cases. Barocci's
etching of the *Annunciation* – in which through the Virgin's
window the artist, loyal to his native city, had put the towers
of the ducal palace of Urbino, and in the foreground the Virgin's
cat, undisturbed by the Angel, slept on. His studio's woodcut
of *The Rest on the Flight into Egypt*. Luigi and he had bought

that together, one day, idling between the Milan antiquarians and print-dealers.

In the quietness of the country night, Da Durante heaved himself to his feet, waddled across to the desk. He had let one of the dogs in, for company, and it got up and followed him.

Old Luigi's bits and pieces that never changed. That enamelled box for pens. The favourite edition of Leopardi. Those notebooks, crammed with what had been done in Italy in these years. His enormous, simple grief for his native land. Da Durante gave a groan of laughter, of weariness, of liking for the man. And now, Esmeralda. He turned to look down at the dog. A pointer of sorts, liver-coloured. It wagged its tail. 'It's late,' he said. 'You'd better go out, and sleep in the dirt.'

12

In Arezzo, the D'Alessandria contingent had stepped out of the Manzaris' hotel into the warm night. There had been calls of, 'Till tomorrow!' and, 'Good night!' Esmeralda's laughing voice had pealed above the others: 'Oh, I don't expect I'll sleep a wink!'

As soon as they were away from the lamps at the hotel door, Gabriele D'Alessandria had kicked his legs as if to loosen stiff knees. He had stretched his arms till his shoulders cracked, had thrown his head back, laughed exasperatedly. 'I need some fresh air. Giles, Edoardo . . . Instead of going straight home, do you fancy walking as far as the square?'

Lies! The government of this tragic, goddamned country of ours is one lie after another! Gabriele D'Alessandria promised himself that one day he would brandish the truth in Carlo Manzari's face. The day would break when his side would come out speaking straight, he promised the magnificent colonnade where they were sauntering to and fro beneath the lanterns and the moths. They'd come out shooting straight too if need be, he promised the moon-drenched square sloping away.

Now Gabriele was making Giles laugh with his account of the invasion of Albania last Easter. Even tall Edoardo who had inherited his mother's blue eyes and golden hair was smiling as he strolled; though he had never yet in his life worked up the slightest interest in politics, and his glimmer of contented amusement came from his wondering how revealing of Grazia Damiani's delectable figure the dress she would be wearing tomorrow might be. And as for the black lines her stockings drew up the backs of her calves!

Of course, the Cabinet always trebled the figures for the number of divisions in fighting order, Gabriele confidently explained to Giles, tucking two finger-tips of his left hand into the minuscule pocket of his waistcoat, and with the slim fingers of his right making gestures of restrained, fluttering elegance to illustrate his points. They trebled the number of aircraft, trebled anything they could think of. They hadn't got around to building any aircraft carriers, so they announced that aircraft carriers were never going to be an important instrument of war.

Government by cretinous lies, that was what it was, and it made life well-nigh impossible for the generals and admirals, not that many of them had the brains for the job even if they *had* been well-equipped. So it wasn't till the nation went to war that the truth emerged, about the lack of just about everything from field kitchens to guns to radios, not to mention the total lack of coordination between the three Services, and the lack of training. Even going to war against a defenceless little nowhere like Albania . . .

Gabriele talked – and all the time his mind was moving deftly among his preoccupations. He was glad he'd got Italian citizenship for Caterina. Soon after they were married, he'd suggested it might be a good idea, and she hadn't seemed to mind renouncing her old passport. For that matter, quite recently, when the ruling party here had been going in for even more thuggery and skulduggery than usual, he'd said: Look, we can go to live in England if you'd rather. It's just a question of making sure I can work when we get there. But Caterina had said, No. This is the ground we've chosen, you and I. Let's make our stand here.

Gabriele D'Alessandria told his stories well, for the simple reason that his mental life was all one composition of the true, left-wing story of Italy in those years, which one day would be written and read, one day would be known. After the necessary revolution. After the wars that were unnecessary, but might be used to advantage. A truth he would tell, or, if he was killed, others who survived would tell. A socialist history, a weapon in the fight for freedom and justice.

'People setting out what they reckoned was right', Caterina had called it, blurting out the beginnings of some of her hurt to her brother. Caterina who knew the pleasure it gave Gabriele when he could *feel* his positive mind analysing and rearranging, feel it deciding about the true nature of this and the best tactical use of that. (It was very similar to the pleasure afforded him by his silver cigarette-holder, and his fashionably cut suits, and his immaculate cuffs and bow-ties.) Who if she had been a midnight ghost shadowing him, listening as she flitted from column to column along the arcade, would have smiled, tautly. Because her love for her husband was very great, at the same time as her despair at all Italy's embattled truths was very great.

So Gabriele was amusing about how the commanders of the invasion, who knew how inefficient they'd been, largely because the government had only given them a few days to prepare the whole operation, were all terrified of being court-martialled. But they were not court-martialled. Because the Fascists needed a tale of their own peerless military efficiency, so they invented one. The inept commanders, much relieved, found themselves declared national heroes, and had even more shiny medals pinned on their chests than they'd had before. Only the effect was slightly spoiled, because the propagandists were uncoordinated too, and while some of them were proclaiming a victory achieved against desperate resistance, others were announcing that the overjoyed Albanians had hailed the Italians as liberators.

In the D'Alessandria house, Sonya had withdrawn to her room. She had knelt down by her bed to pray.

In the drawing-room, Luigi stood with his back to the empty summer fireplace, a small, dapper figure beneath the high, decoratively painted beams and cornices. Gabriele's asthma would probably prevent him being called up as an army doctor, his father was thinking. Though if things blew up in this country, and the lad had to go into hiding, he might end up as a rebels' doctor. But his younger boy, Edoardo . . .

His own war had been a European civil war, Luigi had always said so. The Old World tearing itself limb from limb. Russians, Poles, English, Germans, Hungarians, Austrians, French, Italians, Serbs, Turks, all related, all at each others' throats. The most internecine thing. The old world-dominators unable to control themselves. And now if it was going to happen again . . . Only with Italy having switched allegiance, which for the old soldiers of his time, his war, would be an abomination.

Oh, take a turn about the room, light a cheroot, his mind said. But he could not. He stood, rigid with the cold horror of it, till he could feel the muscles in his shoulders ache. The Devil only knew what courses the European self-destruction would take this time. But if in the mayhem, with Scots and Slovaks shooting each other, and Bulgarians and Greeks blowing each other up, and . . . Edoardo, he thought. And that nice Giles. On opposite sides. But when the old man managed to shake himself out of his fixity, he had a different name on his lips. Stiffly he moved about the room, with glistening eyes. 'My poor girl,' he murmured. 'Oh, Caterina. What's going to happen to you?'

Up under the eaves, Caterina leaned out of the window. 'Here they come!' she called gaily, having seen three young men approaching the street door. 'Oh Esmeralda, look at the moon, look what a magical night it is! Not a breath of wind. Stars, and bats, and – is that a planet do you suppose? Darling, this time tomorrow night I'm going to be in floods of tears, I just know I am. Right from when I first came here, when I didn't know anybody, you threw yourself into loving me and giving me a wonderful time. I must have seemed terribly awkward and ignorant, this creature that Gabriele for some reason had decided he wanted to have, and as for my Italian! But you didn't tease me *too* much. And I'd only been here about a week when you took me to the opera.' Caterina giggled. 'Do you remember? The first thing you had to do was buy me a dress I could be seen in, and after that you were brilliant at pretending not to notice that I hardly knew what an opera was. So that now I . . . Oh I'm so silly. But Esmeralda you'll remember – oh – this – us – won't you? No, don't answer, I know. Listen, I tell you what . . . Let's get out some music, and dance. Quietly, so as not to wake Lisa.'

13

Like her brother Gabriele, coming away from the dinner party Esmeralda D'Alessandria had seemed to take off her mask. Sauntering homeward, she had slipped her arm around Caterina's waist, had laid her head on her shoulder, had said nothing.

Now she was hunting through the family's dance music. It was true that her figure was beautiful, in a willowy style, as she stooped to pick up each record, straightened her back to hold it to the light. It was true, that with her high cheekbones, and her nose which was pert if you liked it or too short if you didn't, and her brown hair expensively fussed into soft perfection at her nape and her temples, she had almost movie-starrish looks. But she would have made a disastrous actress, because of the irritation and irresolution that would keep staring out from beneath her finely arched and finely plucked eyebrows, and an obdurate hopelessness that would take possession of her mouth. This drew attention to the banality of her magazine-cover face. However, now she was animated, looking for something to her taste to dance to.

'Do you know what Papa has just been saying to me?' she asked, succeeding in making her exasperation sound amused, turning around with some Strauss in her hand.

'No.' Caterina came away reluctantly from her moon-shimmery sky, started rolling back the Turkey rug so they could dance. 'Tell me.'

'Well, I went to look for him, to say goodnight. I found him in the drawing-room, all on his own. Just standing there. In front of the fireplace, as if it were winter and he was warming himself. In almost pitch darkness. Not even smoking one of his cheroots. So slight, and straight, and . . .' Esmeralda gave a little laugh, jaggedly, but tenderly. 'Like a small stick, planted there. So I went up to him, and I said "Good-night, Papa" as merrily as I knew how, and I kissed him, and he was . . . So stiff! And cold, his cheek felt cold. On a sweltering night like this! How could he be cold? Standing by an empty fireplace like that. So I kissed his other cheek, and I hugged him, and I said he'd looked like a ghost standing there, I'd almost been frightened of him. Just talking, you know, in the silly way I do. And he said: "You don't have to do it, Esmeralda".'

On her knees rolling the rug, Caterina looked up. 'Oh my God, haven't you decided *yet*? And there was I, thinking we truly were going to be shot of you at last! Well, I guess if we all put our minds to it we can smuggle you out of town between now and midday tomorrow, and stick you on a ship to . . . With a one-way ticket to somewhere exotic enough to keep you amused for a bit, and stop you pretending to marry anyone for a bit. What about Samoa? Any good?'

'That's just it, that's what I told him!' Esmeralda's laughter sounded more like real merriment this time. 'I said, Papa, if I change my mind about marrying Carlo *once* more I shall go just as mad as I've driven all the rest of you. Quite apart from having left it so disgracefully late, that I'd scarcely have time to change my mind *again*, so as to be at the church at twelve.

'Look, is boring old Strauss all right? I just don't seem able to find . . . Yes, yes, don't fret, we won't wake your baby. Did I remember to tell you that I don't feel at all urgent about tying myself down with a baby? Though, of course, with Carlo's income, when the time comes there'll be no difficulty about affording a nanny, who can spend her days chattering to the cook and the scullery maid and all the other maids. An English nanny, naturally. Though, perhaps, not English, these days.'

'That's all right, then.' Caterina stood up, smiling to hear the usual Esmeralda posturing babble with which she'd hold at bay unpleasant decisions or uncomfortable thoughts. To what extent the vapidity and the bitchiness were assumed out of contempt for herself, or were innate and occasionally in sheer despair were let out, Caterina had often puzzled over – but she wasn't going to wonder about that now. 'Splendid, so I *can* flounce around in my new dress tomorrow after all. Even so, you see how much your father loves you.'

'I *suppose* he does! Depressing me with talk about how I don't *need* to get married, we're all fine as we are. Well of course I don't *need* to bother to get out of bed in the morning

– but does he realise how young Carlo is to have got as high as he is? Poor Papa, he even tried to make a joke! About how it was quite exalting enough having Cosima's husband in government circles, and to have *two* sons-in-law in with the régime might be a risky case of putting all your eggs in one basket. So if I even had the tiniest doubts about my . . . What did he call it? "My heart's inclinations". Darling Papa. It was all right to duck out, he told me. Perfectly all right to do a runner, even at the last minute. He'd stand by me. I wasn't to be afraid.

'So, of course, I replied that I had a giddy heart, just as I was supposed to have, and a fashionably dizzy eve-of-wedding head, and so I . . . *Now* look, *three* handsome men to dance the night away with.' Opening the door to her brothers and Giles, back from the square. Curtseying to them with terrific flourish, and giggling. 'Not to mention a fourth, who earns more than these three put together ever will, and who I trust is lying awake in his hotel, thinking of me. Lord now, which shall I . . . ? Giles!' she exclaimed, and made them all laugh by the way she swept him away in her arms to waltz. 'I *know* I've ignored you all evening, but now I'm going to make up for it with a vengeance. Caterina, why is your brother blushing like this?'

Esmeralda swung around the room with Giles, and then she twirled on her high heels and was suddenly waltzing with one of her brothers, and then a minute later with the other one. Caterina joined in, and soon they were all flushed, and all laughing with their attempts to dance almost silently to almost inaudible music so as not to wake the baby next door, and laughing because Esmeralda kept promising, 'All right, yes, I'll whisper!' But then either she'd speak in such a whisper that they couldn't hear her, and she'd pretend she was saying the most scandalous things about them – and maybe she was. Or she'd raise her voice, and they'd make themselves laugh all over again by whispering in unison, 'Sshh!'

'Dance with your wife for a minute, Gabriele. Yes, you absolutely must console the poor girl, because – *don't* pretend you hadn't guessed – she is ever so faintly envious of my partyings in Rome, or envious of my landing a catch like Carlo, or . . . Don't deny it, Caterina darling, I know you inside out. All right, I promise! Giles, your sister wants me to say my most outrageous things in Italian so you won't understand. She thought I was great fun to be with, when she first pitched up in Italy – and, indeed, by provincial standards I'm not bad. Now we're going to have to find her something, or someone . . . Because, you know, just going out on sunny afternoons with the pram, as far as the cathedral gardens . . . Where was I? Time to change partners again I think, and then a glass of – of anything that'll *do* something.'

Her voice aflutter with amusement. Her elegant body, and also her mind, twisting and turning. Her mind attacking in its own defence; effervescent with mockeries, half-truths, red-herrings.

'As I was . . . Oh yes! So I said, Papa, Caterina is a year younger than me and she's been married for three. But I'm twenty-six and I'm bored, and I don't know whether I'm dangerous or not but occasionally I try to be. Anyhow, if it isn't a flaming success, Carlo and I can lead fairly separate lives – like you're always trying to inch as far out on a limb away from Mamma as you can. And what is wrong with marriage? Highly efficacious against fornication, not so good when it comes to eliminating adultery. No, all right, I confess, I didn't say *all* those things. Or perhaps I did.'

When the three men had gone to their bedrooms, Esmeralda danced around the room once more with an imagined partner in her arms. Then she came to rest on the sofa. She sat perfectly still, and gave Caterina a slow glance of absolute candour, and then laughed under her breath. 'Just a minute darling, and then I'll let you snuggle down beside Gabriele, I promise I will. I just . . . Oh, I scarcely know what it is. But I think I want to say sorry to you. You forgive me all my hellishness, don't you?'

Her heart brimming with love and compassion, Caterina sat down beside her. 'There's no need. No need.'

'Oh I think perhaps there is,' Esmeralda replied with complete simplicity. 'It's something about me, I seem to have to keep singing my jingles and dancing my jigs in order to exist at all, and even then half the time I'm so utterly hollow that I could weep for the deathliness of it. But you know that, don't you?'

'Oh yes, Esmeralda. I know.'

'And now I feel, I feel sort of called away, or something.

Though Gabriele and you will come and see me in Rome, and I'll often be back here, I keep telling myself that. But you, Caterina, did you feel called away? You certainly came a fair distance. No, no, you were in . . . You were in deeper, sweeter love, I know that.'

Caterina let the quietness fall. Then she smiled. 'You know what you're doing a lot better than I did. Though now, sometimes I see my way a little more clearly. Shall I tell you something I've never told you before? May I? I want to give you something to take away with you, Esmeralda. Give you my secret name, give you who I am to myself, which only Gabriele knows.' She listened to her voice making her confession, making her offering. It sounded very naked, she thought. 'I who used to be Kate and am Caterina now. To myself, I'm Kate Caterina. Do you . . . ?'

'Kate Caterina. Both, neither.' Spoken softly. Her grey-green eyes still utterly candid, playing no games at all. 'Yes, it's perfect.' Esmeralda leaned, she hugged one arm around her neck, she kissed her. 'Kate Caterina . . . Now I have you.' She was smiling, but her voice had tears in it. 'No one will ever guess that I know who you truly are. I'll be as loyal as the grave.'

Again, the quietness fell. Then Esmeralda rose, she wavered. 'Right, I must be off. I must be on my way. Oh heavens – women the night before their weddings!' She reached out a hand, brushed her friend's cheek gently. 'Thank you.'

14

—ᴍ—

When the door had closed, Caterina's thoughts were too alive to let her think of sleep.

There was what Esmeralda had said in her flaunting way about her talk with her father, and what Caterina knew about the sadness of his love for his sons and daughters. How it had been the war. Coming back to strange children, and a wife who'd got dreadfully religious. For Luigi it had not been possible any longer to speak of divinity in the same breath as you spoke of mercy, or justice, or loving-kindness. It had been a matter, he had confessed to his English daughter-in-law, of certain sights and certain sounds you could not forget, nor find in yourself much aptitude for speaking of to your wife or your children.

There was Giles. Rolling out the rug again, putting her living-room to rights, Caterina regretted her outburst to him before dinner, which now struck her as an act of disloyalty to Gabriele.

For three years she had missed her brother. For three years she'd been ordering herself most severely not to idealise their love for one another, not to idealise their times together. But – how should she *not* have loved him with a passionate protectiveness? When Mummy died, he'd been a schoolboy.

Then despite all her resolutions to be calm and cheerful today, she'd got wrought-up with joy at seeing him, and wrought-up with ten thousand things to tell him and show him, and then stupidly she'd let some of the bad things come out. Because there were – what? – atmospheric disturbances, weathers in her that Giles wouldn't understand, wouldn't know how to get to grips with. And the stab of her disappointment in him had hurt her, when after her idiotic tirade she'd focussed on his baffled, kindly eyes.

Why couldn't he understand? No, no – it would have been more loving to remember him more accurately, not as some ideal listener to her hazy apprehensions, which were probably all wrong. And what was more, she thought with her night mind, with the lucid freedom of her mansard eyrie and two in the morning. (She heard the bell-towers chime.) Though there were possibilities that horrified her, there was also . . .

Drawn back to the blackly effulgent sky, Caterina propped her elbows on the window sill. There were, equally, all the funny, charming things in her life these days, all the innocent things, and all these she had wanted to offer Giles.

Some of the horrifying possibilities were very close. At lunch, Luigi and Gabriele had been going at it hammer and tongs, about whether the Fascists' worship of authority, dinned into the nation's heads year after year, would have really sapped people's ability to think independently and act bravely. So if Mussolini, out of sheer territorial greed, did sooner or later plump for war . . . A war it was hard to believe most people in the country wanted, and which the hard-headed could see was unlikely to be profitable let alone glorious. Would there be mass acquiescence? Or would people decide they'd had enough of this régime?

Gabriele and his father often discussed Italian history and politics at the dining-table, and Caterina had learned a lot from them. It amused her that the older man would invariably conclude that the old inborn weaknesses would re-emerge in new guises whatever you did, that any action taken would at best be consolatory for those taking it, while the younger man invariably knew what steps would lead to a happier future. A general strike, a mutiny, massive demonstrations in the squares – Gabriele had it all worked out.

Tonight, having Giles so wonderfully present brought home to Caterina how absent he soon might be. If England went to war, whatever Italy did . . . How irrevocably cut off from each other they'd be! Would they even be able to write letters? Perhaps through the Red Cross in Geneva, she vaguely imagined, and realised how ignorant she was about war time.

Next summer, he'd take his engineering degree. Perhaps even before that, the Army or the Navy or the Air Force would have snapped him up. And she hadn't even asked him which Service he fancied! Night after night, she'd stand at this window, she'd wait uselessly here and be afraid for him and not know. For years, maybe. How many? The last war had lasted for four. Yes, but that didn't mean a thing either way.

Caterina's mind was not overcast by any shadow of solitude. With her new family, above all with her husband and with her daughter, she knew how rich in love she was, and she rejoiced in that, quietly, humbly. Rejoicing too in a bat as it swept by on its haywire flight, and the etched shadows of the chimneys shed by the moon on the rippling tiles.

But not to be able to see Giles if she wanted to! Not to be able to shove a few things in a bag and hop on the train, with Gabriele if he could take a holiday and if not just with Lisa, and a couple of days later be boarding a ferry. So often, Gabriele and she had planned an expedition back to England, but then there'd always been some terribly good reason for putting it off. But the possibility had been there. The prospect of a ferry escorted by gulls – herring gulls, black-backed gulls – across the narrow, grey sea. Then the white cliffs, and the shipping in the port, and dour Dover castle which, when sailing away three years before toward her honeymoon and her new life, she had not been able to see without imagining poor blinded Gloucester trying to hurl himself down the scarp. King Lear, too, standing with Cordelia dead in his arms. The rope bitten horribly into her soft throat, its end trailing down.

Caterina gave herself a shake; but she remained gazing out at the starry sky, and the idea of writing to Giles began to shape itself in her mind.

He was still here, asleep in her spare bedroom. Europe was still at peace. But very soon he might be gone, and war come between them. She would write to him, and tell him more than it was possible to say in the jokey scribbles they'd always exchanged, and if the war became impassable she'd go on writing, and she'd get it all to him somehow or other in the end. She'd buy a whole bundle of school exercise books if need be, so that however long they were cut off for she could tell him her story, tell him all her stories. And so that if anything happened to her, he'd know he hadn't been forgotten. That irritating sister of his had been loving him, talking to him in her mind.

Caterina was not like Gabriele who could direct his awareness where he wished, shut this thought out, focus on that, be clear about what he wanted to be clear about, first this, then that, then on to the next thing. The harbour of her brainpan seemed to be connected to all the waters of the world, from the obscurest bights and sounds to the greatest oceans. She was stirred by ebbings and flowings infinitely wider, deeper, more powerful than she was. Dark moods and light moods suffused her consciousness according to laws, and expressive of forces, far beyond her rational comprehension, and often beyond her control. So now, the fact that she thought quite calmly of her brother reading her musings after her death, and did not distress herself by imagining what it would be like if she survived but he was killed, was because the tide flowing through her for that hour was serene, was flowing also through the August night that was all peace, and flowing through the peacefulness of Lisa's sleep.

On later peace-time nights and war-time nights, she wrote for other imagined readers. For Gabriele, or for Sonya, or Esmeralda. And later on, when neither Giles nor any of the others was the spirit she had need of, she found she was addressing herself to Lisa as she should be when all this was over, Lisa when she was grown up.

But the night before Esmeralda's wedding, she wrote for Giles. Because the preparations for these nuptials had brought back Canonbury Square three summers before, when she'd been finishing university and he'd been starting it. When the last act – the last gallant, comic, but also desperately sad act – of their anarchic freedom together in that grubby house had been their organising of her wedding. So that on the Dover train next morning, she had distressed Gabriele by bursting into tears at the thought of Giles abandoned, alone, in the house bestrewn with party débris and haunted by her, with aunts coming round to help tidy up. Because his coming to find her here had brought back her own first steps on her Italian stage. Her surprises, adaptations, discoveries, compromises. The few disappointments and the many delights.

Above all, it was the innocence and the happiness she had discovered here that she wanted to set down for Giles. It was Gabriele and Esmeralda that first summer taking her to the waterfall and the pool with its dragonflies where the three of them had swum, and then sat on the grass under the poplars and eaten the picnic they'd brought, and she had known that with these two her heart was calm and filled with joy. It had come mixed up with the brilliant kingfisher flashing by and the smell of fresh-water and sedge under a hot sun, mixed up with the bread and cheese and olives she was munching, and she wanted Giles to know about the peace and love she had found, she wanted him to be a part of this one day. That they should not be forgotten, the laughing at funny stories and the falling quiet again, the packing up the picnic basket and walking homeward through the cypress shadows. That he should know. Now, above all, with nations festering in their hatreds and their fears. Now when, in the country where she found herself, scarcely a day went by without sinister premonitions being borne in upon her.

Some new iniquity of the Fascist trades unions. A too independent-minded journalist found lying on his office floor, with bones broken, unable to see for the blood run into his eyes. Some new farce about the Fascist intrusion into everybody's so-called free time – because the Party had to control cultural associations, sports clubs, every damned thing. So a man could hardly go after work to drink a glass of wine and play a game of snooker without having to take out membership of a Fascist Billiards Club. Or you'd be peacefully doing your shopping in the market, and suddenly there'd be a Black Shirt parade going by, with their flags and their tramping jack-boots and that horrifying salute of theirs. With their shouted orders, their singing, all their disgusting togetherness and sameness.

Oh, another night! Right now, she must begin with first things. 'My darling Giles . . .' And then? Her first discoveries – from her relief at finding that the D'Alessandria were just as given to outspokenness and teasing as the Fenns had always been. Her new lease of life in Italy – from her first visit to Gaetano Da Durante's palatial but dusty apartment in Venice, where the reek of cats' piss had wafted in from the tiny garden of bay trees and pomegranate trees below, and where she had been astounded by his dozens of paintings by old masters she'd never heard of. Paintings with ornate, heavy, gilded frames, hung in his noble rooms, hung in dim corridors, stacked three deep against walls. How it had been all right to ask courageously, 'What does mannerist mean?' because he had told her, simply, without impatience or superiority.

Action! She walked over to her and Gabriele's desk, sat down, switched on the lamp. She took a sheet of paper, a pen. One true sentence, for Giles, to begin with. She wrote: 'My dearest darlingest Giles – if this war between my two countries comes, I just wanted you to know that, however bad things get, deep down you and I aren't divided, we can't be.'

She put down her pen. She read what she had written. Her horrors and her loves brimming equally, she tried to think of all the things such apparently simple, perhaps empty words might come to mean.

15

—✺—

Thinking she had heard her daughter whimper, Caterina softly went next door. Perhaps Lisa had murmured, had turned over – but she was sleeping now. Looking down at her, Caterina thought that Giles might like to know that she sang the child to sleep with English lullabies and nursery rhymes. He might like to imagine that.

So much to tell him! Especially if his visit was cut short by war breaking out, and there weren't going to be other visits till no one knew when. So back at her desk she wrote that she often spoke English to Lisa when it was just the two of them, and Gabriele and she both spoke English to her at bedtime, and she was trying to teach her 'Baa baa black sheep', and 'Humpty Dumpty', though it was early days yet. She lulled her to sleep with 'My bonny lies over the ocean', with 'The foggy foggy dew', with any old ditty that came into her head. Gabriele and she were determined that she should have English story books as well as Italian ones, and Sonya had joined in the spirit of the thing and sang to her granddaughter in German, so Lisa was going to be a right little cosmopolitan.

So Caterina wrote, that night and on many nights over the next years. Jotting down things that had been in her head to say, or quite different things which unexpectedly came to her. Or, often, sitting down to write, but writing nothing. Listening to the air which was teeming with ideas that withered or flourished, that changed and went on changing.

Nursery rhymes. 'Oranges and lemons, say the bells of Saint Clement's'. So that led her on to how honestly, these days, half the time she felt half Italian. And it was odd how sometimes for days and days she could bring to mind as many memories of her girlhood in a far-away country as she liked, but those places and those times had lost their colour, design, meaning. Only then it would be old songs or snatches of poetry that brought back her past life and her past selves. It could be quite involuntary. Whoever she seemed to be one fine day would suddenly have to rub shoulders with some of her old selves; all at once she'd be being jostled by them right here in Arezzo, in her new life. Because, perhaps, of the bells of Saint Clement's. Or because of Cordelia being hanged in Dover castle. Because of Poor Tom skulking on rainy farms, and Lear mad in the fields, and the doctor with his music. So she would obscurely but headlong know how Shakespeare had got those British Isles in that tragedy all right, got them to the marrow – in that play, above all. She would know it. Because of a few lines, or only a phrase or two, which would visit her and bring all the rest, bring that great, love-sick, opaque knowledge cascading into her mind. It would be, 'And my poor fool is hang'd'. Or, 'rank fumiter and furrow-weeds'. Or, 'cuckoo-flowers'.

Concentrate, Kate Caterina! she admonished herself. Here she was, at her first attempt to write things down for Giles, already going off among ghostly visitations that couldn't possibly interest him.

Concentrate on . . . All day tomorrow, lurking beneath the conventional jollity, there was going to be that sickening sense of not knowing anything about a lot of the wedding guests. Not knowing who knew what and whom you could trust how far.

In this house, of all places! Where you'd never needed to be politic, because nobody ever took offence. If someone felt you'd scored a hit, he just said something equally barbed straight back at you and then burst out laughing.

Yes, in some respects it was lucky Giles didn't speak Italian, because it'd seal him off from certain conversational risks. Nice for him, though, to be in the Santissima Annunziata for an hour. Even Fascists and Communists and wars couldn't stop the old churches having dignity. And the flowers! Sonya and she had spent *hours* putting flowers in vases, and she was proud of their handiwork.

Frowning at her thoughts' meanders, Caterina gazed around, pen in hand, at the cream-coloured bookcase which had long ago been painted with blue and gold and red diamond-shaped patterns, at the sofa which if it had been a horse you'd have said was spavined and wrung-withered and ready for the knacker. Tonight, had Giles begun to understand Esmeralda a little? That bravado with which, when she'd been wishing her brothers and him goodnight, she'd pretended to appeal to them all for permission to get married in the morning. How Esmeralda had appealed to their sense of the romantic and, when that hadn't worked, to their sense of occasion, and then, in mock desperation, to their mere sense of humour. Did they not think it would be *funnier* to get married than not? What did Giles think? She would be grateful to him for an opinion, which should be, please, dreadfully male, and hopelessly English, and deliciously unmarried.

Caterina had watched the amusement in her brother's eyes, seen the beginning of respect, of liking – she was almost sure she had. But had he understood about how Esmeralda had to dramatise her volatility? How she must forever be acting in order to see and hear herself act, know fleetingly who she had fleetingly been? There was, Caterina had come to consider, at the core of Esmeralda's self-performance a self-dismissal that had modesty, irony, goodness.

Then, would Giles have understood how the trouble with Esmeralda was not that she didn't know whether to marry this man or not. That was only superficial, a mere detail. The real trouble was that, if your consciousness was composed of endless recessions like Esmeralda's was . . . Yes, honestly! One mirror behind another, going away and away. So naturally she was always backing away from everything, and seeing disablingly widely and variously, so she could never decide about any matter, or only by being wildly arbitrary.

Caterina wrote all that, the words coming helter-skelter so she hardly lifted her right hand from the paper. Quite forgetting that Giles could not conceivably, in one superficial evening, have intuited any of her misty intimations about her friend, and anyhow would be faintly repelled by them.

Esmeralda who'd tease you till you crimsoned, and who was seven times quicker-witted than she was, but who always – well, nearly always – kept her sharpest mockery for herself. Esmeralda who sometimes would play-act till neither you nor she any longer knew whether she was amusing or deceiving others or herself. But who then might stop dead in her tracks, and give you a glorious wink, or just shrug and turn away.

Heavens! you'd think I was half in love with her, Caterina

thought. But, then – what the hell. Life would be lustreless without her.

So she wrote on, about how in Italy she'd come to be haunted – happily, fascinatedly haunted – by all the decisions she hadn't taken. Just think, if she'd stayed in London; or if she'd said Yes when that Indian Army captain asked her to marry him; or if . . . One of her old Cambridge flames was helping to administer the Virgin Islands these days. Or if she'd concentrated her fissile mind a bit more effectively and got a First, then she might have . . . All the possible lives one might perfectly well have been living but happened not to be. Often Esmeralda and she brought them to mind, wondering, smiling. Then, they were haunted too by all the paths that they might take in the future, and the others – but which ones? – that would go on looking like sure bets right up to the last split second. To live in possibility! The richness of that, and the freedom! Not to mention how aware it made you of the precariousness of the life you really did appear to be living, its arbitrariness and lack of substance.

Cramp. Caterina dropped her pen, with her left hand started to rub her right hand back into suppleness. She'd have to throw that last couple of pages away.

Yes, she mused with abrupt grimness: but when I've finished with all my wanderings through memories and half-awarenesses, what then? When all this which seems so real has altered irrevocably (she tried to imagine such furious mortality, such obliteration); when half of us are dead, half the houses are being lived in by new people, the old tables and chairs and the old passions and ideas have been dispersed. When I'm through with what appears to me this so terrifically important passage from the past in one country to the present in another, and this passing from peace to war probably, this passing from a modicum of coherence of soul to everlasting dividedness. The *end* of all my nights' searching through the dross of my days for what might for a moment transcend, for what might redeem, might win back. Good heavens, is that what I think of everything and everybody? Edoardo's football matches and his girlfriends; Esmeralda marrying into the smart set in Rome; even darling Gabriele forever setting the world to rights in theory . . . Dross, eh?

Well, maybe, she thought indifferently. Sitting motionless at her desk now, her head slightly cocked in the quietness as if she were listening. But – in mere consciousness's twisting about among its images like convolvulus winding through a hedge . . . Some shadow of grace possible in that?

Yes, just conceivably, she decided, plumping for what seemed sheer, hopelessly unreasonable chance, and smiling.

16

—⚘—

Telling herself that she must get at least three or four hours' sleep before the jamboree tomorrow, Caterina undressed in their dark bedroom. She slid under the sheet without waking Gabriele. She was conscious of the cool linen lying on her, and the warmth of his body beside her, and the window with its square of stars. She'd forgotten to close the curtains. Never mind, it would be nice to be woken early by the light. And then she must have slept intermittently, because the connections between the dreamings or wakefulnesses she was aware of were not at all clear.

It was winter sunshine, and she was tramping through the countryside with Gabriele, near Ca' Santa Chiara it must have been. Buzzards wheeled out from the oaks on the crest of a hill. Down in the valley, a brook rustled. They walked, and the hazels had catkins already, and the branches of the elms held up their sprays with tiny pink buds, and in her heart the confused sweetness of change, of becoming, took possession of her brain and her limbs, so she woke hot, damp, tangled in the sheet, gasping.

Caterina fell asleep again at once. But tonight it seemed there was an upsurge of delight that would not abandon her, that toyed with her in dream after dream.

She woke, coming to the surface from a night off the Sardinian coast when Gabriele and she had been out in a fishing-boat laying nets, and between nets they had stretched out on the deck and made love, with the hull stirring beneath them and the mast-head inching against the stars. She had the smell of summer sea in her nostrils, the taste of salty skin on her lips. She woke to dawn radiance over the Arezzo roofs, and a swishing sound.

Her mind felt free and happy. She got up, washed, dressed. Before long, Lisa would wake Gabriele. They'd be fine together, for an hour they wouldn't need her.

There was so much that she seemed to have comprehended during the night, dreaming at her window, dreaming at her desk, dreaming in her bed. And now, on an early morning of

great lucency like this, so you felt still and clear of mind . . .
It was the street-sweepers with their besoms, that was the
rhythmic, swishing noise down below. And that flicker was a
lizard scuttling past the window on the tiles. She saw it stop,
cock its greeny-grey, alert head.

Suddenly recalling her mother-in-law's anxieties about the
wedding and her graver fears for the marriage, Caterina decided
she would go to the first mass of the day with her. She never had
before. But Sonya always went, early each morning.

Glancing at her watch, Caterina stole out of the apartment,
pitter-pattered down the stairs. In the hall, moving with the
exuberance imparted by her new idea, she overtook the church-
goer, who was picking up her hand-bag from the oak chest with
the calm of everyday acts.

'I'm coming with you,' she announced, giving her a good-
morning kiss. 'You don't mind, do you?'

'My darling, of course not. But I'm a little surprised.'

'Oh, I haven't fallen off my horse on the road to Damascus
and bumped my head, or anything exciting like that. I just . . .'
Giving her a shrewd, sidelong smile as they stepped out into the
street. 'We're in for quite a day.'

Sonya assented, silently. Then, with grimness around her
mouth, she said: 'Oh, if I thought our troubles would be over
by tonight!'

Caterina took her elbow, squeezed it. They walked down the
short slope to the church door.

The priest was moving about by his altar. The congregation
gathered in the front pews, dressed almost wholly in black.
It was cool in the church. Caterina sat down beside Sonya,
but it was impossible to whisper courage to her because she
immediately knelt down to pray, and when she rose from her
knees the mass began.

Caterina thought how hurt she must often have been by
Luigi's quips about the existence of religions proving the non-
existence of God if nothing else did. She recollected Sonya once
responding mildly that, so far as she was concerned, to know
nothing at all about what was infinitely beyond her, but to place
her trust in God and His goodness, and hope to strengthen the
weak spirit with ritual and prayer, seemed natural and as such

acceptable. So now the younger woman ached with awareness
of Sonya beside her turning toward a fount of strength and love
greater by far than any mere daughter-in-law.

But then quickly she forgot her. Lulled by the murmurous
Latin, Caterina remembered her own joyous discovery that the
emptiness of the concept of God was one of the blessings of this
world, which thus was freed from authority. Was a richer world,
with no shadow of doctrines, less calculable, more ambiguous.
Her mind leapt gaily forward into her unbeliever's paradisaical
freedom (which came as naturally to her as God came to Sonya),
where all was mutabilities, intermittences, self-generations.

What was it she'd just understood, during that strangely
possessed night? Oh yes, about how when Esmeralda and
she were talking, sometimes, what they were really trying to
do was to struggle a little bit free of their circumstances and
their old selves, in order to be able to look back, imagine them
clearly. And that emergence from but at the same time into
oneself, that being still a bit entangled in one's old conditions
but also beginning to get to grips with one's new liberties, was
exactly like Michelangelo's *Captives* they'd gone together to
see in Florence. Those massive prisoners sculpted in the act of
struggling free of their bonds, wrenching free of the stone they
were made of. How simple it all was, really.

So she was going to write that down, one night. Lots of her
stories, she'd tell. Stories she wasn't living, stories she was –
some more apparent, some less. Discoveries of deep-sea fishing
on summer nights, of elm trees in mid-winter sunshine beginning
to bud pink, of stone captives trying to break free and become
themselves. Discoveries of how paintings and books and music
could be good, because briefly they freed you from your pokey
self. Because story wasn't just one damned thing after another.
Story was immeasurable things happening all at once and
leap-frogging over each other and then falling behind and then
reappearing ahead. You often didn't know in what sense these
things were real, but that didn't matter. Shades of more abstract
and less, she thought triumphantly. The potential it offered the
mind! Story was—

Sonya was murmuring something. No, it was the whole congregation saying one of the responses. Caterina paid attention.

Only a minute or two had passed, they were still right at the beginning of the service. How distracted she got!

For the rest of the mass, she made herself think of Sonya's fears for Esmeralda, and how she herself could best be loyal to them both. It was humiliating, how she thought she'd come here with kindness in her heart, but had at once gone off into musings of her own.

After church, the two women walked home to breakfast, side by side, each in the cell of herself.

17

On the morning of her wedding, Esmeralda D'Alessandria appeared more calmly radiant than anybody had expected, with only faint tremors of excitement rippling through her happiness. Which, all the female bridal experts agreed, was precisely as it ought to be; and all the male connoisseurs of young womanhood found obscurely satisfactory. She even succeeded in seeming to wish not to be relentlessly the centre of attention, and took a flattering interest in the dresses of the other women getting ready in the house. Though Sonya, when her daughter generously but perhaps too fulsomely praised her hat, said evenly: 'Dearest, you can't fool *me*.'

When the hairdresser required Esmeralda to sit still for a whole hour she complied with uncharacteristic docility, and chattered about that lady's daughter's troubles with her perfidious young man, and the virtues and hazards of protracted engagements, without alluding to Carlo Manzari's eagerness to marry her in August, having only clapped eyes on her for the first time in May. Then the dressmaker arrived, in case a few last stitches were needed. They *were* needed, and there was much tweaking here and readjusting there. Esmeralda stood still with angelic patience – admittedly, in front of a long looking-glass, so she could keep ascertaining how satisfactory was the combination of the most beautiful girl in town with the most silkenly glorious white peacock of a dress that had gone in through the portals of the Santissima Annunziata for many a long year.

At eleven o'clock, with only an hour to go, her eighteen-year-old cousin Rosalba turned up. Delightful and dangerous, as Caterina had warned her brother. Dangerous from the flutters of her lashes to the heave of her lace-ruched bosom whenever she sighed or exclaimed, both of which she did frequently, and to the manner in which, having been introduced to Giles, to begin with she completely ignored him. Esmeralda was still in the hands of her adorners, having her veil firmly secured to her head by artful but invisible devices.

As a woman who ten years before had sallied forth from that house to that church, to marry not a politician on the make but a marquis with an inherited fortune, Cosima was taking a benign but detached interest in her younger sister's finest hour. Carolina, who might only be eight but was already adept at telling people that Papa was in Rhodes whenever Mamma instructed her to, was however still innocent enough to be knocked breathless by the apparition of shimmery loveliness that Esmeralda had been magicked into. She stood, a small, black-eyed, speechless doll, and she gazed at – oh, at the Sugar Plum Fairy – or the Princess of Heaven – or – Carolina didn't know what. But she precipitately resolved that she was going to be married one day (a matter that had never occupied her thoughts before), and she was going to look *exactly* like that.

In the kitchen, the scullery maid, borrowed for the occasion from a neighbouring family, was winching buckets up from the well, and decanting half of them into crocks where vegetables were being rinsed, and the other half into cauldrons. The cook, Signora Immacolata, who had been a mainstay of the D'Alessandria household for long enough to remember Gaetano Da Durante when he was thin, was positioning some of these cauldrons on the black iron range and hanging others from chains over the hearth. The fires in both had been lit, and at regular intervals an armful of billets for the former, and another log or two for the latter, had to be fetched from the wood-pile in the courtyard.

Louisa and Emilia needed a sharp eye keeping on them, Signora Immacolata fretted, what with all the chopping up of this and stirring of that and seasoning of the other that she'd told them to get cracking with. A hundred and more people to lunch, so she'd had to accept Signora Sonya's offer to bring in a couple of girls from the quarter. But Louisa's fingernails were a disgrace, not to mention her language. As for that Emilia she was, well, it was unchristian to think ill of souls, but she was a slut, that was what she was. And they were both being paid more than their getting under her feet was worth.

Immacolata snorted. She mopped her forehead. She mopped her thick, red neck. Though honestly, what was the point, when the only thing that would have done the trick would have been to strip off her clothes and sluice one of those buckets of water all down her. Just fancy, if she *did* that, and the professor came in! Now . . . She tipped red wine from a flask into a tumbler, swallowed it, smacked her lips. Ah, that was better. The *penne strascicate* had to be parboiled, and then at the last minute she'd toss them in a pan with her famous *ragu* and bring them to perfection. That was skilled work, she'd have to do that herself. Now – the roasting joints to see to. Those giggling little tarts!

Signora Immacolata's neck had not always been thick and red. Gaetano Da Durante, when he had been discharged from that military hospital in 1917, had been distressingly thin. He had come to convalesce in this house. Luigi D'Alessandria, writing to his wife from the Front, had insisted.

Gaetano had sat in the walled garden all that summer: pale, thirty-something, pitifully weak. Immacolata had brought him out beef tea, on a tin tray gaily painted with svelte blondes and top-hatted dandies. She'd been married for ten years, but was still in her twenties, and must have been comely enough, she supposed – remembering, smiling. They must have fed the invalid on solid food too in all those months; but it was the beef tea always served in the family's most exquisite Florentine porcelain that she remembered, and his cigarettes, and his quietness, and the line of shadow his Panama hat drew across his face which was naturally chubby but had been made gaunt. She remembered his chestnut hair that had been so curly she'd longed to rub her fingers through it, and his brown eyes that watched her coming toward him across the garden.

Then one day, in the shade under the medlar tree, in the siesta-time heat when everyone else was in their bedrooms, she had set down his cup on the round wicker table, and their eyes had met again. She had said: 'Show me your scars. Show me your chest. I want to see.' He had stood up, slowly. He had unbuttoned his shirt. She had lowered her eyes from his. She had run her finger-tips very, very softly over those horrifying tracks the surgeons had sewn together, over the ragged patches they had done their best with. Tenderly, she had touched his slim waist, where something had gone in, and through, and out. Then Gaetano had said: 'You take your shirt off too.'

It had been good, it had tasted very sweet indeed, going at it with sudden hunger, sudden recklessness, in the medlar shade, in the dog-day silence and heat. One of those war-time things. Immacolata brought it back, fetching a basket of loaves from the larder. And ever since . . . When Gaetano came to visit, often they'd caught a twinkle in one another's eyes. It would be so today.

The person who was failing lamentably to delight in the wedding morning was Luigi D'Alessandria. After his talk with Esmeralda by the empty fireplace in the drawing-room, he had been too depressed to drag himself to bed. He had sat slumped in an armchair, smoking cheroot after cheroot, castigating himself for his failures. As a soldier, as a husband, as a literary scholar, as a father. Brought under bitter review, his life presented only a succession of attempts to break out of his mediocrity, followed by invariable fallings back into his innate inadequacies. Yes, even as a soldier. He'd always been dreaming of brilliant exploits, but in the end he'd just done his bit like everyone else.

A man who had served his country honourably, he was known as. Well, he was now. Though immediately after the Armistice, the Socialist gangs had had the pretty habit of beating up any man they found wearing uniform, guilty of having helped keep the enemy out of Italian towns and villages.

Honourable . . . But Luigi remembered. That time the Austrian attack overran their trench, the fight going now this way and now that, and he'd lain in the mud and faked dead. Those Austrians had gone on, and then two of them came along the trench bayoneting anyone they weren't sure of, and there was a lot of screaming. They got to about twenty paces from him, and a young fellow scrambled to his knees and shrieked at them to have mercy on him. He clasped his hands, he blubbered at them.

But those Austrians had been having a bad time, and they were scared too. Luigi could still shiver at the lad's Friulan voice howling for pity, and then his animal screams when they started killing him, and how long it could take to finish a man. The Austrians grunting and cursing. The Friulan boy thrashing about in the mud, even after one of them got his foot on his neck. How his screaming altered as blood began clogging his lungs.

Luigi could not forget how while this was going on, with infinite caution he'd got hold of the pistol he'd been lying on. Lucky, for him, how long they'd taken, with their bayonets. Been told not to waste bullets on that kind of job, maybe. He'd shot one of them in the back, the other whipped round, but he got him too, though it had taken more shots to kill the two helpless men. Hours later, the Italian counter-attack reached him.

Today, Luigi D'Alessandria had gone out into the town early, knowing how redundant he was in his own house, hoping that the summer morning would cheer him up. These days, he spent so much time at Ca' Santa Chiara on his own that it should have been possible to enjoy the salutations of his Arezzo neighbours, and the ritual of buying his newspaper on a sunny corner, and strolling to the Café dei Costanti for a cup of coffee and a brioche. The trouble was, everyone he bumped into congratulated him on his daughter's wedding. And then at the café no one seemed to suspect that he could be anything but proud of one daughter who lived in aristocratic pomp in a Roman palace, and now the other who'd collared this rising star among the Duce's parliamentarians.

Luigi's brioche was unaccountably sticky; he scowled as he wiped his fingers on his handkerchief. His newspaper consisted of nothing but sycophancy and lies. He folded it. Going through the motions of being the head of a loving family, of being the proud father of a blissful bride. All day, there'd be the mockery of it. Going through the motions of a religious rite and a social rite; going through the motions of a celebration of innocent love, of hope for the future . . . Sitting at his table by the café window, Professor D'Alessandria carefully unclenched his small, white fists.

Why was Manzari doing it? Mere lust could be, and would be, sated outside marriage. To cement an alliance with Cosima's disgusting oaf of a husband? That, now, was quite probable. And concupiscence of a more refined sort. Esmeralda might bring no money, but she *looked* superb, and she had the Devil's own chic, and even within matrimony a beautiful woman could be an obsessing pleasure, for a while. (The proprietor of the Costanti had never seen the professor stare around with such unseeing, black looks. And on such a happy day! All Arezzo was in festive mood in Esmeralda's honour.) Yes, the money necessary to a man like Manzari, the money over and above his very handsome salary as a member of parliament, would be secured, doubtless was already being secured, from elsewhere. From commissions discreetly paid on government contracts – wheels always needing to be oiled. From investments that he'd make shrewdly, being tipped off by less than scrupulous cronies at the Treasury as to probable, indeed arranged, movements of the money market.

Well, at least there'd be some old friends to chat with at lunch, Luigi D'Alessandria told himself, resolutely looking for consolations. Gaetano, for instance. Excellent!

He stepped out of the café to go home – he who knew about Gaetano Da Durante's encounters with Immacolata under the medlar tree twenty-two years ago. He knew another secret, too, about that summer when most of the men had been away at the war. He knew that what his friend had done with the maid he had not done with the mistress of the house. Yet their passion had reduced them both to despair, as each in their ways had confessed to him in the autumn when he was back on leave.

Sonya who, in her war-time isolation in this city, practically incarcerated in the house with her three children (Edoardo had not yet been born) whom half the people here called half-enemy, had found in half-killed Gaetano Da Durante a sympathy, a kinship of spirit that rapidly . . . Well, soon she could only with great difficulty control her perturbation when he entered the room. When he came in, that shabbily dressed wraith from the Alpine trench war, taking off his hat and holding it. That kindred, wounded wraith in whose haggard face she could still see the handsome apple-cheeked lad of before the war. Sometimes she could hardly breathe for longing; and an anguish of tenderness; and guilt; and the knowledge that what she was renouncing would have been a truer life.

Gaetano who in those years had been homeless and prac-tically penniless. Who had been horrified to use like this the hospitality his friend had offered, and who had sworn that he had never touched Sonya. Who had offered to go away, at once, and never see either of them again. And who had been told, by the husband of the object of his passion – told with a shaking voice, with all the courage and love he was capable of – not to be a fool, to sit down again, finish his glass of vermouth.

What a summer! What an autumn! Luigi's lips twisted as he walked back to get on with his long day's acting. Well, at least they'd been *alive*, all of them. Immacolata, too. She might not have known much for sure, but presumably she'd intuited a fair amount, and quite likely had imagined more than was true. *Alive*. Even he.

18

—⚇—

Through those late August days when, after twenty years of bad dreams and pretences and lies, the Old World was slithering back into war, in the capital cities the embassies and the ministries were buzzing like summer hives. (In Rome the Foreign Minister, Count Galeazzo Ciano, was conferring with the British envoy Sir Percy Loraine – though without his most doughty political henchman, Carlo Manzari, who was usually at his master's side during all the most taxing negotiations, but who today was in Arezzo to marry Esmeralda D'Alessandria.) Filled with gloomy apprehension as he knotted his tie and chose himself a button-hole, Luigi D'Alessandria fancied he could hear all that far-off deceitful wordiness, though what was actually ringing in his ears was Edoardo's merry shout 'No, I can't find it anywhere!' and a door slamming and rapid footfalls going away.

In every bedroom in the house, people were decanting pitchers of water into the enamel basins so they could wash; they were struggling into their best clothes; they were brushing their hair before the old liver-spotted looking-glasses with their chipped gilt frames. Scowling with his effort to delight in all these last-minute festive preparations, Luigi tweaked and then crossly yanked his tie until he realised he had crumpled the thing irretrievably. He tore it off and went to his chest-of-drawers for a replacement.

The sinking of ships all over the seas was going to begin, he thought sarcastically, while here we . . . Oh, we messed about. Years of the bombardment of armies in the field and the bombing of civilians in towns were about to begin. An inconceivable number of deaths by shooting were about to begin, deaths by hanging, by burning, by drowning, by bayoneting, by being hacked at, by starvation and disease . . . And all this on a civilisation-wide scale, right across the old heartlands of Christianity, of the gospel of mercy and love. Then, the rape of women and girls all over the countries at war – not to make too much of the soldiers of a different stamp who'd bugger a lot of young men and boys. Emprisonment and forced labour, woundings and mutilations and tortures. Conduct that right-thinking people would naturally continue in the face of all the evidence to consider contrary to mankind's deepest nature. While here we imbeciles . . . While here and now I with my hair still to brush, with a lot of my smiling and my lying still to do . . .

Savagely supposing that this strip of silvery-grey silk would be unobjectionable, in his braces and his still unbuttoned waistcoat Luigi crossed back to the looking-glass. Now, a competent knot for pity's sake, and no peacockish twitching at the bloody thing. People would start arriving outside the church door at any minute, he ought already to be downstairs. Yes, but if the catastrophe was truly about to break at last . . . And honestly, it no longer looked possible that the invasion of Poland could be prevented. Were we mad or sane – going on shrugging on our suit jackets, walking our daughters up aisles and stopping in front of altars, throwing celebratory lunch parties? Yes, and how many souls here today would be listening to the far-off buzzing in the ministries? How many of them had got the nous or the magnanimity to wonder what reverberations all that statesmanly insect flitter-flutter might be going to have, in this unimportant but likeable city, in the lives of an Italo-German bride and her English sister-in-law?

Wedding guests were starting to assemble beneath the lime trees between the house and the church. Sometimes Caterina stooped so Lisa could hold onto her finger, sometimes she lifted her up in her arms.

High in the brilliant air, the church bell rang. Ah, there was Sonya, Caterina's eyes picked her out. Talking to Gaetano. To wonderful Gaetano who really had taken her under his wing lately, till she'd felt she was getting to know him at last. Who had again invited Gabriele and her to stay in Venice with him, only this time Gabriele hadn't been able to get away from the hospital. But Sonya had said Lisa would be fine with her, Caterina absolutely must go, Venice with Gaetano was an opportunity never to be missed. So with some misgivings she had gone. And he had introduced her to scholars and to sculptors, to diplomats and to duchesses – well, they'd seemed enormously impressive to her; and he'd taken her to discover churches and paintings nobody else seemed to know were there.

Feeling reinforced now that this staunch D'Alessandria ally had arrived, Caterina waved. With the fingers of her left hand, she blew him a kiss. Gaetano Da Durante's eyes lit up. He took off his hat. Fatly, he gave a small bow.

After being seduced by dreamy abstractions the previous night, now Caterina was in a worldly frame of mind. She was proud of the elegant throng of her family's guests, and proud to move through it as the young married lady of the palace that reared over their heads. She was looking forward to seeing her handsome, successful husband and his beautiful sister the bride appear in the archway, and for the moment she was delighted to find herself standing next to the bridegroom.

Carlo Manzari and she had met two or three times during the engagement and she had fallen under his spell right away. It transpired that not only was Carlo one of Galeazzo Ciano's closest aides, the two men were also friends. As all the world and his wife knew and tended to comment on unfavourably, the Foreign Minister was the Duce's son-in-law. Esmeralda had already begun to meet this innermost clique, and she had insisted that, even if Gabriele was going to be ridiculously superior, Caterina absolutely *must* start by letting her give a Roman dinner party in her honour.

For all of fifteen seconds Caterina had been aghast, and indignant in advance at the prospect of mingling with the Fascist élite, who might expect her to behave deferentially toward them, and might say things about the land of her birth that would make her furious.

But courteous Carlo Manzari, without ever being so gauche as to plod these understandings out in words, had brilliantly established that, despite a whole lot of divergences between them which it would be futile and tedious to discuss, for his part he looked forward to being not a dull, unavoidable relative but, he hoped, her friend. It had been established that he knew Gabriele was on the Left so he imagined she might have similar sympathies. That he himself had joined the Fascist

Party because he reckoned it was the best instrument for Italy's advancement and his own, and that these were unexceptionable ambitions. That whatever happened between Italy and Britain, one's private affections were not going to be soured.

So many things had been silently clarified straight away! Clarified, and made nothing of. Caterina had found it admirable, so she had joined in the spirit of this new camaraderie with relief and delight. So civilised. And as for swanning around among the people who counted not only in Venice, but also in Rome where as Esmeralda's best friend she would have an elevated status, the prospect was thoroughly alluring.

'What do you think, Caterina?' Carlo now asked her smilingly, as they stood waiting for his bride to emerge from the house. 'Was Esmeralda truly put out when at the last minute Galeazzo and his wife couldn't be here to see us married? Heavens above, it's not exactly as if there isn't a good reason!' And he added, with the clear intention of giving her hope: 'They're still negotiating, you know.'

'Oh, sometimes it amuses her to pass herself off as unbelievably superficial,' Caterina answered, liking his man of the world's confidence, and liking the flicker of concupiscence she always seemed to catch in his eyes, and wondering about him as Esmeralda's lover. 'Like when she was so delighted when she could tell our nice parish priest here that the bishop had agreed to marry her – or she pretended to be delighted. But I bet you anything you like she's late now. By the way, what's happened to Edoardo? I can't see him anywhere.'

19

The bishop did not emerge from the Santissima Annunziata to mingle with his gathering flock, though he was looking forward to being one of the most distinguished guests at lunch. He was a tall man, with something of an imperial eagle about his beaky countenance and his commanding glances. So despite a rather tussocky wart on his cheek he looked the part, in his sumptuous vestments, with his mitre on his head and his crozier in his hand. Up at the altar, this overseer of the spiritual life of the citizens of Arezzo had a brace of lesser clerics to give quiet directions to and condescend amiably to as he waited with dignity for his congregation. He entertained no doubts as to the D'Alessandria being, with the honourable exception of the Signora Sonya, a sorry bunch of heathens. But now, with the second daughter marrying power just like the first one had . . . He shifted his gentle grasp on his crozier. It was indeed to be regretted that the Foreign Minister and his wife had been unable to be here today. Still, it would be interesting, at lunch, to get to know the bridegroom a little.

The last cars and the last horse-drawn carriages had rolled up with the final wedding guests, who were looking at their watches and exclaiming that it was a relief not to be late after all. The beautiful old house and the beautiful old church looked down on the men who greeted one another with the Roman salute as the government had decreed everybody ought to; on the startled face of Giles Fenn, who had not fully grasped that from the Baltic to the Tyrrhenian and from the Rhine to the Elbe people really were going around jabbing their right arms up in the air and shouting whatever it was; on irredeemable old Luigi D'Alessandria, who shook hands with his guests as they arrived, which was all wrong. In the garden, irrepressible Edoardo had uncorked a couple of bottles of the wine that was meant to be drunk *after* the church service. Half a dozen of his flamboyant friends and he were making outrageously merry, fortunately concealed by the garden wall from the respectable black and grey hats and pale parasols milling about soberly outside the church door.

Everyone was waiting for Esmeralda, who was still in the hands of her preeners, gossipers, bedeckers, fussers, gigglers. The Marchioness Cosima and her mother and father had been greeting their guests for what felt like half an hour at least, and when all the bells of the city rang twelve they exchanged glances of humorous despair.

Luigi D'Alessandria had been playing the host and the father of the bride with such determined aplomb that for minutes together he quite convinced himself of his own contentment. The only hitch was, that his mind *would* keep reverting to his suspicion that, despite all the family's efforts to delude themselves, this marriage of Esmeralda's *was* going to prove a hideous mistake, and then painful lines would furrow his forehead and his mouth would set bitterly. Even welcoming his guests alongside his elder daughter had caused him twinges of gloom, because for this task Cosima and he dredged up a merry complicity that merely reminded him of the friendship that might have existed between them but for which it had long been too late.

However, right now he had bullied his mind into cheerfulness by making it recognise that one's children grew up, they pushed off on their adventures and misadventures. What else could a man expect? And it was agreeable to have so many old friends brought together.

In his double-breasted suit made for him not long after the Armistice and wearing a white rose in his button-hole, Luigi shook hands here, he chatted there, moving almost jovially about the throng, over which the pollarded lime trees and the faint, hot breeze cast a freckling and speckling canopy.

'Only sixty you know! Not dead yet!' he rejoined to a fellow who these days was a prosperous doctor in Bologna, but whom he'd first met during a bombardment on the Isonzo when they'd both flung themselves into the same dug-out. 'Yes, the bride's a bit slow off the mark. Knowing Esmeralda, it's probably deliberate.'

He moved courteously on, because he must give his chief hospitable attention to the Manzari relatives and friends. Most of the people he'd looked forward to seeing appeared to have got here. Good, good! The Della Quercia, with whom they went sailing and fishing in Sardinia in the summers. All his life he'd been a keen trimmer of sails to wind-shifts and layer of nets for sea bass. The Damiani, who had that small ruined city down in the marshes south of Rome, where they'd made the mediaeval hall habitable. Last time he'd stayed there, they'd set him to work helping them plant specimens of rare trees, because the ruined city walls made a splendid enclosure for an arboretum and that stream ran with water all year long. Old friends to puff a cheroot with after lunch – excellent! Then . . . Oh, the absolute cream of the Arezzo families, naturally – or, looked at another way – what was it Caterina had said? *The butcher, the baker, the candlestick-maker.* She'd been crooning her English incantations to Lisa, and he'd overheard odds and ends. There she was now, with Gaetano and Sonya and the bridegroom.

Twenty-two years ago, it had not only been Da Durante who had offered to go away. D'Alessandria had said he was sorry he'd been married in a Catholic church, so he couldn't offer to get divorced. But if Gaetano and Sonya loved each other, he would stand aside. It had been she who had said: No, I'm married to Luigi, and I love him. Had said, truthfully or not: This is just a summer fever. So after the war they'd tried to start their marriage afresh, and it hadn't worked too badly, and Edoardo had been born, but it hadn't worked quite well enough. For a while, they had seen rather less of Gaetano. After which . . . It was a tribute to the man that he'd remained equally good friends with both of them.

Of recent years, Gaetano Da Durante had become almost famous. He was forever being invited to come and decide how much of a Palma Vecchio was by the master and how much by his studio. And not only in Italy. He was always dashing off to Paris – and it was he who'd been called in when that lost Andrea del Sarto, if that was what it really was, cropped up in Yorkshire.

Almost famous . . . Dining with Croce in Naples, staying with Berenson in his villa near Florence. Berenson and he used to bicker amicably about when a Titian was a Titian and when it wasn't, or how much of a canvas was by one of the master's assistants and if so by which one. They'd tease each other about how much money they'd been raking in for authenticating this canvas or that. So now those of the Tuscan upper bourgeoisie who hoped for an echo of the great philosopher's or the great connoisseur's table talk made a point of coming up to shake his podgy paw. He smiled at them all, equally, with his round, innocent face. But when his host came up, they hugged one another warmly.

'Esmeralda has been putting on weight Luigi, is that it?' His eyes twinkled. 'Can't get into her dress as easily as she could last time she was married in it, I suppose. I'll just run upstairs, shall I? – well, not run – and give her a hand. I'll squeeze her into her bodice, we'll be down together in a flash.' He chuckled. 'Just look at me! I'd frighten any girl into her dress. Now – what's all this about your not putting me next to Caterina at lunch? You know I always have to sit next to my girlfriend.'

'Haven't we?' Luigi met his old friend's laughing eyes, impulsively convinced that a wedding in sunny weather was the acme of civilised living, with a hundred excellent people in a handsome church (suddenly he was sure they were all excellent people, including the ones he was meeting this morning for the first time), and then all sitting down in harmony to a good old-fashioned Tuscan feast. 'Well, you'll just have to shift the name-cards around, as you usually do.'

Gaetano Da Durante turned to Caterina who was standing on his other side with Lisa in her arms, and the merriment died out of his brown eyes. He gave her elbow a squeeze, and looked at her with anxious liking. 'You know, dear girl,' he muttered so only she could hear him, 'you don't have to spend any more time in Rome with them than you want to. But come to stay with me in Venice as often as you like.'

His words were drowned, as Edoardo and his troupe of disgracefuls issued out of the garden calling, 'She's coming!' 'The bride, the bride!' 'Here she is!' 'Oh, where's she got to?'

Carlo Manzari laughed. He caught Caterina's eye, and she thought how handsome he looked on his wedding morning, and how it was probably all rubbish what people said about him being one of the most ruthlessly ambitious men in Ciano's faction. In what she thought was the nicest, calmest, jokiest

way, he said: 'I reckon she sent them ahead to do that, what
do you think?'

'Could easily have done!' Caterina exclaimed gaily, giving
him smile for smile, and already forgetting what Gaetano had
said, though later she often remembered it.

I hope Giles is loving this, she was thinking. The blue sky
and the green trees and the golden light, everyone in their best
suits and their best dresses, the happy expectancy. I hope he
loves the church. And the lunch afterward! He won't be able
to believe how many courses there are, and how many hours
it'll all go on for, and how delicious everything is. I hope –
I hope a lot of muddled things. Because what we've come
together for today *must* be innocent, it *must* be good, her
heart prayed. Because Esmeralda is vital, this twist in her
fate is . . .

'Oh, look, Lisa darling!' she cried, and hitched the child up to
her shoulder, and pointed. 'Here comes Esmeralda, with Papa
and Rosalba.'

With her brother on one side and her cousin on the other,
the bride came slowly forward between the lime trees. The
wedding guests all turned to gaze at her, and exclaimed at
how beautiful she was and how beautiful her dress was. A
grey gelding between the shafts of a smart new chaise neighed,
and a passing terrier cocked its leg against one of the wheels.

Esmeralda was slender and her white dress was not volu-
minous. She looked simplified, refined, Caterina thought. Yes,
with her veil down . . . She looked a lot simpler than she
was, she must have wanted that. Reduced to her elements,
somehow.

'Well, I did my best!' Gabriele's voice was laughing as he
joined them. 'Pins, stitches. And she kept saying she wanted
practically *no* make-up, but practically no make-up seems to
take a particularly long time. Then, just as I thought we were
off, she decided she was going to smoke a cigarette. Morning,
Gaetano, nice to see you. Carlo, I *am* sorry – but here she is.
So, darling, how's our beautiful daughter? Enjoying her social
baptism of fire?' He leaned to kiss Lisa's cheek. 'She's glorious
in that little bonnet.' And he pulled his sleeves down his wrists
so his gold cufflinks showed.

Now that the bride had arrived, the congregation moved into the church. Esmeralda slipped her hand into the crook of her father's arm. She stood, holding her bouquet. She seemed detached, muted, behind her white veil.

20

'Well, so now the D'Alessandria have got themselves another son-in-law in the régime. Who'd have imagined it? Still, I hope Gabriele is as clever as everyone says he is.'

'I always said she'd make the most ravishing bride. Just you wait till she puts up her veil and turns round so we can see her face. Who's that incredibly fat man?'

'The art historian? What's his name . . . Wheeler and dealer, more likely.'

'Just think of all the men she must have refused! He's a lucky fellow, I wouldn't mind taking her to Venice for a month. Though in some respects Caterina, you know, *l'inglesina*, is more my type.'

'Honestly, how can you be so vulgar? I bet she can feel her heart thumping, poor lamb. Say what you like, it's a day in a girl's life which . . . Oh look, there's the Prefect.'

'They say Manzari is making an awful lot of money, that's why she's marrying him.'

'Seed pearls on the buckles of her shoes? How do you expect me to see her feet from here? I'd have to crawl through everyone's legs, like a dog. So Terrani wanted to marry her, did he? Not surprised she turned *him* down.'

'Well, after her parents, and her sister . . . Let's hope she makes a better job of marriage than they have.'

The service began and all the conversations among the congregation died away, apart from the occasional whisper to a restless child.

Shut away from the city's trampling crowds, from its hundreds of clattering cart wheels and its fewer whirring car wheels, its thousands of hithering and thithering voices, and shut away from the sky's heat and brilliance, in the church the candles by the high altar kept up their pale, silvery golden blurs of the luminous in the colourless daylight. And at once the grey stone columns and pilasters with their Corinthian capitals, the mottled sheens of the polished marble, the ancient Madonna flanked by silver angels, the flowers, the familiar Latin of the familiar and solemn rite, the faint scent of incense, began all in combination to have their ways a little with the members of the congregation, according to each person's susceptibility. So that some looked gravely preoccupied, and others were so moved that they discreetly dabbed away tears from the corners of their eyes, and others smiled to recollect things that had been amusing or still were dear to them.

The hub of that half-hour was the bride and groom, and the bishop who was marrying them. Yet none of the hundred people directing their attention at that trio had a scrap of interest in what the bishop might think or feel. And for the time being Esmeralda and Carlo were wholly inscrutable, performing as their ritual required, speaking fore-ordained words. Encased in their ceremony, encased in the enormous change they were causing, although not yet enmeshed in its effects and liberated into its effects, they stood side by side before the noble-looking man with his mitre and his crozier – beyond all asking and all telling.

There had been tides: of hope, passion, calculation, desire, dread. This woman and this man had been washed up there, together, on the altar steps, where what they wanted done to them was being done. They were utterly mysterious as they stood there, she all white, he all black, secluded in their confusing selves.

To the Manzari clan, Carlo these days was such a meteor that their overriding instinct was to be grateful for him, and proud of him, and to bask in his amiability. So now they had little doubt that to marry this Arezzo beauty must be the right move for him, simply because it was his decision, his pleasure, to do so. Some of them hoped, slightly severely, that she knew how fortunate she was. Among the D'Alessandria and their connections, there was a feeling of relief that, after all the whirligig moods, and the enervating days and nights when it appeared that any decision come to on the swings was immediately reversed on the roundabouts, now the die finally did seem to be cast. On both sides, there was the customary tender concern for one of the pair, and a cooler anxiety that the other should prove satisfactory.

In that congregation of celebrants each left to his attention's meanderings, a few of the more alert were aware of stray ideas and emotions fluttering among them. Memories of weddings and hopes for weddings. Reflections on marriages happy and unhappy; on affairs of the heart; on wise or unwise alliances.

In the air of the church, among the pews at the front of the nave and the pews in the transepts, there was an aliveness together of some people's thoughts for whom the significance of the whole thing was sacramental, and of others' for whom the combination of the religious and the erotic would always hold an irresistible fascination. There were the dreams of those who sighed for the sheer romance they saw incarnate in Esmeralda, all mixed up among the ruminations of others who were already looking forward to lunch.

A few of those present were aware, also, of how here in the splendour of the Santissima Annunziata all might be order and ritual and peace among men. All might possibly be touched by the grace of an omniscient, conceivably a benign God. But even so, possibly it might have been luckier to live in less interesting times, marry into a less ominously clouded future.

Half a dozen in the congregation, or maybe a few more, remotely sensed the inevitable mechanisms and the evitable chances that had brought these governments to power in these European countries, with these freedoms of action and these lacks of it. During the service, they sensed how crucial the buzzings in the embassies might prove to be, when it came to the fate of all the marriages being embarked upon in the same days. They knew that even in the time it took to perform a church service, the fate of a nation could be decided, and they resolved not to forget to turn on a radio at some stage before nightfall. Far off, they were conscious of the German and French armies facing each other across one frontier, the German and Polish armies facing each other across another. They wondered which way Italy would jump – for peace? for war? They wondered whether the British fleet was going to be mobilised.

But not even Luigi D'Alessandria (who appeared impassive throughout his daughter's wedding), with his lucid mind for mankind's crimes and follies, had in his blackest fore-dawn wakenings imagined that Italy would send an ill-equipped army to take part in an invasion of Russia, and would declare war on the United States of America. He would have been as astounded as the most simple-hearted of his guests that day, by the notion that it might be sane, let alone in the national interest, to do either of these things. Nor had he imagined that his native land was going to be invaded, twice – once by their own allies and once by the other side that they were trying to switch to being the allies of. Nor that a civil war would be fought here. Nor that train-loads of Italian Jews would be deported to extermination camps.

No . . . But although D'Alessandria could not foretell the specific stupidities and calamities, he was aware of such propaganda-fed ignorance and obedience in the streets, and aware of such greed, duplicity, arrogance and bellicosity in the ruling class, that he feared the worst. So he stood, like a graven image, with his wizened head looking more than ever like a parchment-skinned skull. His eyes never left Esmeralda. The blood quivered in the hollows of his temples. His heart ached for her, with a dumb, unknowing, helpless ache.

21

—⁓—

Beatrice Castiglia was so enjoying her husband's absence in Tripoli, where he was making commendable quantities of money and knocking the natives into shape that, when the wedding service reminded her of him briefly, her thoughts were positively affectionate. Really, this year she had felt quite a rush of her old girlish high spirits – and it was gratifying to be able to compare unfavourably Esmeralda's white dress with the one *she* had been married in. And anyhow, weddings ought to be in the evening, she'd always said so.

Signora Immacolata had with some misgivings temporarily abandoned the kitchen to her underlings. She had bathed, had put on her best dress, had tidied her hair. Her husband Orazio and she had reached the church just as the service was beginning.

They stood at the back of the congregation, and Immacolata shifted until she could make out Gaetano, right up at the front because he was a sort of honorary member of the family. Orazio had never known anything about that fling, and the marriage had gone on being a contented one, and children had gone on cropping up. Indeed, she'd often suspected Nicoletta might be a medlar tree child, with that sweet round-cheeked smile of hers, and being born toward the end of the last winter of the war. Nicoletta was married now, with two little ones.

Immacolata mused contentedly on her growing brood of grandchildren, and her mind flickered back and forth between this rite in church (she was a devout Catholic), and the rites of the kitchen and the dining-room, which were just as important. Her *fagioli all'ucelletto* with all that rosemary and garlic and oil, and a sausage swimming in the middle of each dish spreading its goodness and savour – no, she needn't fret about her *fagioli*, they were always a success. The *arista*, the joints of pork, were in the ovens, roasting. Still, leaving her kitchen in those girls' charge . . . ! Yes, there was old Gaetano. He'd eat a second helping of her *fagioli all'ucelletto*, if he didn't eat a third.

Signora Sonya and he hadn't been able to fool her about how desperate for each other they were – and good luck to them, she remembered thinking at the time. After all, she'd got what *she* wanted: good, passionate, illicit love-making a few times; and, undisturbed, undamaged, her good marriage too. Though she'd never made out if those two had had the nous to enjoy the passing hours that the Almighty . . . Holy Mary, forgive her. And the professor, he'd have had his war-time girls. They couldn't fool her about that, either. Men and women, that was what it was. War time, that was what it was. Life. And yet . . . Dogged, the way these twenty years Gaetano had kept turning up out of the blue every few months. Kept coming to sit with Sonya in the garden in summer, by the fire in winter. There was devotion for you, all right.

Several of the wedding guests were there because the family had felt it impossible *not* to invite them. The Podestà and the Prefect were two of these. Umberto Terrani was another. It was true that Gabriele and he had been at school together, and then in Marxist-Leninist cliques together, where the interminable ideological braying had just about extinguished any possibility of principled action. But subsequently Umberto had either fallen most poetically in love with Esmeralda, or had made a comically maladroit attempt to seduce her. Opinion varied, as to that – though not as to Esmeralda's having laughed in his face. There'd been squabbles between Communists and Socialists, too, with the old school-friends ending up on different sides of the fence.

However, a degree of liking had endured. And Caterina, introducing Umberto Terrani to Giles outside the church door, had whispered afterward to him how funny it was that Umberto had been born into a family of staunch monarchists, who had named him after the Crown Prince. So this House of Savoy label had got stuck onto a baby who, when he grew up, couldn't bump into you in the street without launching into an explanation of the merits of the coming dictatorship of the proletariat. Yes, a pious boyhood in the Church of Christ, Caterina had said, laughing. Then re-baptism, by total immersion, in the Church of Marx, Lenin and Stalin. She couldn't herself see the point of stultifying your mind once, let alone twice, but each to his own taste.

Umberto was a handsome bastard, though, Giles conceded cheerfully. Lean, bony, with something attractively wild about his black hair and his black eyes, about his air of recklessness, as if he was about to burst into some flamboyant activity. Fancied himself as a lady-killer, Kate had said. Well, Giles could half-sympathise. Because she'd also told him he was going to meet *lots* of beautiful young women, and that had certainly proved true.

He was still getting their names muddled up sometimes. But the general impression of vivacious and flirtatious loveliness was bewitching. There were Beatrice and Grazia and Rosalba and . . . Giles's grammar school Latin was not up to following the service. At first he had fallen back on noticing a few dissimilarities from a Protestant wedding. But now he realised that a wedding was an excellent opportunity for admiring pretty girls. Who was *she*? with the chestnut hair, who once again had glanced in his direction.

Lisa was naturally the star of the pew that held the bride's family. In her diminutive pink and white frock, her white shoes and her white bonnet, she had reposed placidly in her mother's arms and gazed about her for the first two minutes of the service. But then she started to say what she thought, using her modest repertoire of Italian or English phrases, which in other circumstances the family were delighted to hear her try out. Several people smiled to watch Caterina D'Alessandria jiggle the child, and whisper to her, and point to what the bishop was doing so she could get absorbed in those magical ministrations.

When the congregation was sitting down, the little girl could scramble harmlessly along the row of laps. (The only time that her grandfather's expression softened was when Lisa decided she would be happy to be held by him briefly.) But then everyone rose to their feet, and she insisted on being put down, and the next second she was stumping forward to join Esmeralda. Blushing, Caterina swooped to recapture her, glancing guiltily at the bishop, who neither frowned nor smiled.

Sonya D'Alessandria was close to tears. She crossed herself often, and her lips moved continuously in prayers of her own.

That both Lisa's grandfather and her father took their turns holding her during the service was commented upon, by some present, as an instance of extraordinary modernity: it still being axiomatic in most of Italian society that male pride required complete aloofness, at least in public, from nursery preoccupations.

Gabriele could feel the life in his veins. He was proud of his beautiful wife beside him. The memories of their own wedding that arose, and the brightness in Caterina's eyes when their smiles met, were a strong pleasure to him. And when it came to the future, to the dangers . . . With his enviable ability to think what he wished to, Gabriele D'Alessandria rejoiced that he did not live in uninteresting times. The worse things got under the Fascists, the better. Let them display their true colours. At which point: action! Oh, and this new marriage . . . No, Esmeralda wasn't in love. She was just having the time of her life. And when it came to the politics – these were risky games his sister and he were playing, yes indeed. But Gabriele was as optimistic about his own shrewdness as he was about everything else, and he had little doubt that Esmeralda and he would know how to handle things.

As for Caterina, half the time she was glad she had Lisa to cuddle and to murmur to, because it stopped her brooding on what she knew of Luigi's and Sonya's fears. The other half of the time, her atheist's soul was enraptured by the momentousness of the rite being enacted. Yes, her blood was up – knowing what a shrine the Santissima Annunziata was even to the unbelievers among the D'Alessandria, and suddenly conscious of how it had become a shrine for her too. Because Gabriele and Esmeralda had run about in here when they were little, as Lisa did now; or because . . .

Caterina didn't know. But she knew she loved the place, from its grey and white paving-stones up to its dome. She liked the terracotta San Rocco pointing to the wound in his leg and San Francesco showing off his stigmata, the former having a good shock of wavy hair and the latter such a tonsure that to all intents he was bald. She loved how valiant the silver angels were, holding up their candles. She loved the bluey-green marble, and the pink marble pilasters that had blue lustres in them too, and the lovely mediaeval Madonna with her crown,

and . . . Her blood was up all right, thinking of her marriage
and of Esmeralda's in a heady tangle of tenderness, and the
spirit's love, and the passionate.

Now the bride and groom were about to exchange rings.
This was the moment. Caterina lowered her eyes from the
Madonna, whose weeping it had been, during a thunder-storm
in fourteen-hundred-and-something, which had caused the old
humble oratory to be rebuilt as this glorious church. She gazed
at Esmeralda in her white silk a few feet before her. Well done
my darling! her spirit called out. Courage, that's what it takes.
Oh look, there's a midge or a fly or something in your veil.
What dreadful thing does it mean? Well, you don't seem to
have noticed. So – courage! As marriages go, it's a risky one,
but dare-devilry was always one of your few virtues. Go for it,
girl. There! I'm proud of you.

Her cheeks blanched, although her heart was juddering with
these profane exhortations, Caterina's dark amber eyes had a
tearless, exultant glitter.

22

—◊◊—

When the service was over, everybody came milling out into the sunshine. A batch of children sprinted off in a race to the front door of the house. There they checked, suddenly stricken with the near-certainty that such hollering and galloping might offend some adult sensibilities.

A boy of about nine, in knicker-bockers and pleated jacket and tie, whose hair had been plastered to his scalp with a wet hairbrush but was resuming its curliness, sniffed the air like a hound. The other children all turned to him. Because he was one of the oldest, or he was a natural showman, or they wanted a leader to make them forget their indecorous bolt away from the church.

'Cooking! Lunch!' he announced – although the kitchen was too far from the hall for any aromas of roasting to have reached them. But he was a spirited boy, and he knew his way around the Palazzo D'Alessandria. So sniffing, and pretending to lose the scent, and pretending to cast about and then pick up the delectable trace again, he led his pack, all in their best jackets and their party frocks, and all immediately beginning to imitate their leader's antics, across the courtyard, past the wood-stack, through the archway into the scullery.

At the kitchen door, he crouched, ready to spring. 'Found it!' he yelled, and hurled himself forward – slap bang into Louisa, who shrieked, but luckily was not carrying anything. She recovered herself instantly, and started cheerfully wrestling with her small attacker, gasping, and laughing, and breaking away to push her hair off her warm forehead, and spluttering 'Lord what a little beast you are! Now, are you going to let me get on with dishing up lunch?'

Outside the Santissima Annunziata, the bride and groom were having their picture taken. The photographer had set up his camera on its tripod, and now he kept fussily shoving his head beneath his machine's black cloth. ('It's wearing a black veil!' were almost Esmeralda's first words as a married woman.) Then he would emerge again to make self-important pronouncements about the subtleties of focus, or how essential it was to have the most modern type of lens, such as he had. Then Carlo's and Esmeralda's immediate families had to stand beside them, and more photographs had to be taken.

'Come on, Gabriele!' the bridegroom called merrily. His face was slightly flushed, his eyes sparkled. He looked very young and debonair, everybody agreed, and not at all the astute tactician who sat on all those government committees. And then, as his brother-in-law came, smiling, to stand beside him: 'No ducking out of this, you know.' He clapped Gabriele boisterously on the shoulder. 'Terribly compromising for both of us, I shouldn't be surprised.'

A number of those present had died violent deaths before there was next a D'Alessandria wedding in Arezzo. But today, it was a satisfaction to many people to be in a position to congratulate a bridegroom who was one of the youngest members recently appointed to the Lower Chamber of Parliament (the empty ceremony of voting had been dispensed with, in the new Italy), and who might well expect junior governmental responsibilities before long. Kissing this particular bride, especially for the men, could only be a most pleasant act.

As soon as she was out of the church, Sonya D'Alessandria went back to hoping nervously that everyone would just enjoy the wedding in a normal, agreeable fashion, and then praise God they'd all go home, go away. Making herself not focus on how horribly it was going to hurt to hug Esmeralda goodbye. Making herself not think, either, of the joy it would have brought her to see the girl married with a different order of love to a man you honestly felt desired only her happiness.

Heavens, what was that she was hearing? Sonya winced. Oh, it was that Manzari uncle, droning on again about how the Mediterranean was going to have to become an Italian lake.

Acquire Corsica, acquire Dalmatia. Gibraltar, Djibuti . . . A port in the Balearic islands . . . The words bumped against each other ponderously in the man's mouth. Malta, Nice, Biserta . . . They knocked alarmingly in Sonya's head. Did none of these people have sons of military age? Or imagine that, if Italy started attacking here there and everywhere, she then might in her turn be attacked? Did they ever think what their talk *meant*? And the younger men sounded just as bellicose as their fathers. Surely they could work out that it wouldn't be possible to fiddle cushy diplomatic postings for *all* of them.

Her anxious gaze found Edoardo's fair head. Oh Lord, he was smiling as that little devil Grazia chattered away to him, no doubt wonderfully beguilingly. His mother prayed that he had some worldly shrewdness.

Additional tables had been laid in the dining-room, and in the drawing-room which had been converted for the occasion. The massive double doors between these two chambers stood open, and at first there was much eddying of guests searching for their places. Then almost at once Louisa and Emilia started coming and going, who with their black dresses and white aprons and smiling faces made charming waitresses, everyone said. Signora Immacolata directed operations, and was very stately on this important occasion, and tried to make sure her giggling assistants kept their most daring comments *sotto voce*.

All the family's finest silver and china was on the white-linen-covered tables, and a lot more had been borrowed from cousins to make up the necessary numbers, and extra tureens and platters had been borrowed too. There were vases of flowers on all the tables. The Venetian chandeliers had been lit in both rooms, and even in the summer daylight they shed their pale, spangling effulgence over the feasters. The high stone mantelpieces were also decorated with flowers, and candles in silver candlesticks.

Glancing around as she took her place at the principal table, beside the bridegroom's father, Sonya D'Alessandria could not help being pleased with what she saw. Only of course minor confusion at *once* broke out, because here was incorrigible Gaetano calmly changing the seating arrangements right before her eyes, so he had her on one side and Caterina on the other. And the children's table already promised to be amply uproarious. It had been Sonya's idea to sit all those under about twelve together. (Though not Lisa, who was too little, and sat on her mother's lap, and was already being tempted with titbits by Gaetano.) The children had found their places, and had settled down expectantly, looking very sweet, Sonya thought, with Carolina presiding most decorously at the head of their table. Only the high-spirited boy with plastered-down curls at *once* started to hold what was plainly going to be riotous assembly at the foot. Because now the first steaming dishes of *penne strascicate* were being borne into the room, and the first fragrant tureens of *ribollita* with the oil glistening on its surface, and the children all broke out in bubbling voices of delight. Then immediately there arose a chorus of groans and wails, both theatrical and sincere, when Louisa and Emilia quite properly brought the first helping to the bride's table.

Indeed, the lady of the house could not help considering, it did seem a shame to keep hungry boys and girls waiting, just so that Esmeralda, who was far too highly-strung to eat sensibly at the best of times, let alone this day of all days, could toy with a silver fork in her right hand, and whisper something in Carlo's ear, and cast admiring eyes at her left hand where for an hour her engagement sapphire had been joined by her wedding ring. And so that Gaetano, who by rights should have been starved for at least a month, could tuck his napkin into his collar so he looked quite ridiculously like a vast baby in a bib, and rub his hands, and say jovially: 'Good idea, to corral the little monkeys up in one pen. Keep them waiting, that's what I say, while their betters begin lunch. Ah, *ribollita*! Excellent! And plenty of *cavolo nero* in it too, just how I like it. Trust Immacolata to treat us decently. More, Emilia, please. Don't skimp. I've got a decent-sized frame to maintain. Now, what was all that nonsense I heard about some deluded fellow wanting to marry you?'

Most of the company had little real interest in either the bride or the groom, and were content that they had been the cause of this admirable entertainment, and should continue to play their appointed parts and remain inscrutable, while they themselves took thought only for their own enjoyment. As platter after platter was brought to the tables, and the decanters of white Vernaccia were emptied and refilled, there was a lot of enthusiastic discussion of Tuscan cuisine. Those in the know indulged in accounts of local recipes, and Signora Immacolata was repeatedly consulted and profusely congratulated, until she felt quite reassured about her decision to serve a hot *ribollita*, because there was also *panzanella* for those who preferred a cold summer dish. She was particularly proud of her *panzanella*, its chopped up tomatoes and red onions and basil sheeny with the very finest oil. Visitors from farther afield offered accounts of how such-and-such a dish was prepared in *their* province. Everyone was sociably united in their readiness to grant that other regions had first-rate cooking, while remaining secretly convinced that their own was best.

Several of the Arezzo gentlemen present had professional dealings with one another, and during the course of the wedding lunch, which went on throughout the afternoon, two prominent landowners came to an understanding profitable to both. The sportsmen chatted about their shot-guns and their woodlands, their fishing-rods and their streams, their skis and their mountains. The mothers rated their daughters' prospects, and bemoaned the trying responsibilities that fell upon those obliged to employ domestic staff.

Whenever Louisa or Emilia came near him, Gaetano Da Durante teased them about their romances, and invented outrageous complications and scandalous outcomes, just as everyone expected him to. They squealed, they blushed and dimpled, they appealed to the Virgin Mary to bear witness to their chastity. They teased him back about how he'd got so gross he was the despair of womankind, and they pretended to refuse to serve him any more food, just as they were expected to.

Several flirtations were usefully advanced. The tall windows were open to the blazing air, and the white curtains stirred fitfully in the sultry eddies.

At one moment, a bread roll, thrown with extraordinary skill or luck, sailed across the drawing-room and hit Immacolata on her behind, just as she was replenishing a decanter which, being within reach of Da Durante's arm, tended to become empty rather often. She, at least, appeared in no doubt as to who the culprit was. She marched cheerfully over to Edoardo and tickled him stalwartly until, choking on his tears of laughter, he begged for mercy.

23

—❦—

Unseen and unheard in the merriment, cat's-paws of anger and fear and hate troubled a mind here and a mind there.

Caterina had taken her daughter into old Luigi's study next door, and made a nest for her among the cushions on the chaise-longue. Flushed and exhausted from the excitements of the day, and as full of delicious things as she could possibly be, Lisa was practically asleep already. Her mother was perched beside her, murmuring 'Bye baby bunting' and watching her eyes close.

Caterina stopped repeating that nursery jingle. She waved a fly off the drowsing child. She went straight on into singing 'Rockabye baby on the tree top', because Lisa liked her familiar rhymes – and, it suddenly occurred to her, old songs could have a strengthening influence on the shaken adult mind too.

Innocent, familiar words, however simple. 'When the wind blows the cradle will rock' . . . Yes, but if the country didn't shrug off the Fascists soon – shrug them off as a degrading uniform is at length shrugged off, as an insult is shrugged off as beneath reply. If the Fascists joined the war on the Nazi side, and practically everyone up and down the land went along with that, because – oh, well, because . . . Some of these nice young men eating and drinking with Giles might be trying to kill him before long.

Cat's-paws. 'When the bough breaks the cradle will fall', Caterina went on doggedly, knowing that not all those old ditties were composed only to comfort. Feeling an icy wind blow dark ruffles across the sinister waters of her mind. Keeping her voice soft, happy, full of love. 'Down will come cradle, baby and all'. And back to the beginning again, because Lisa's eyelashes had stirred. Back to 'Rockabye baby' again – because whatever skies fell, children still needed to be sung to sleep, or anyhow their mothers needed to stay sane. 'In the tree top' . . . Stay sane, and at family weddings behave suitably.

Gabriele D'Alessandria had reacted to the sight of Carlo

Manzari finally there, lording it in *his* family house, about to carry off *his* sister Esmeralda, with a furious desire to grab his new brother-in-law by the throat and shout at him. About the finishing-off of an admittedly always feeble democracy, the subversion of the judicial system, the suppression of rights and liberties of all kinds, the beatings to death by government thugs.

Gabriele kept up the charade of feasting contentedly at Esmeralda's wedding. He had Carlo's sisters on either side of him. But angry recollections of bloodshed had sparked in him an intense desire to shed blood. The muscles of his jaw twitched. He kept seeing visions of how, after a most enjoyable brisk fight, he'd pitch the bridegroom headlong out of the window. Then he'd lean out, to see him lying on the street below, with a few of his smashed ribs stuck into his lungs, and maybe with his back broken for good measure, so he'd be dying all right. It would just be a question of returning to one's lunch, while Manzari got on with it, down there on the stones, among the flies.

To imagine this was so pleasing that Gabriele cheered up quite naturally. After all, these vulgar little Fascist ranters were going to come to no good. If anything, one should be sorry for Manzari. So he merrily asked the bridegroom's sisters where they had taken the children on holiday, and reminisced about his own boyhood summers on the coast of Sardinia.

Not much of Luigi D'Alessandria's buoyancy had survived the church service, and the last of it was draining out of him now. Yes, all the debasements of the country he loved, the defeat of the values he'd believed in, were summed up in this sham celebration, he thought with the last flickerings of his proud indignation as it died away into inert bitterness. Lunch was interminable. The air was stifling. The drone of self-satisfied voices was intolerable. He prodded his fork listlessly at his *penne*. All this eating without appetite one was obliged to go in for. And now there'd be the pork.

Well, at least we taught her to read and write. He had thought that, in his limp despair, at the end of his daughter's wedding ceremony. Because although since the turn of the century more people in the country could read and write a bit than couldn't, even now there were still godforsaken regions and godforsaken social classes where an embarrassing number of brides couldn't so much as sign their own damned marriage certificates, let alone go in for any more fancy literacy. And now, stolidly making polite conversation with Signora Manzari, he was alarmed that if the party went on much longer, which it would, and he went on losing control of his mocking mind, which was all too probable, he might start saying things which would convince her that he was mad, or drunk, or deliberately being offensive. Things about the uses of literacy and the uses of ignorance. For that matter, far worse truths about the uses of brides. Truths which, in a society which prided itself on its belief in modern progress, it would always be improper to allude to – and certainly would dismay Signora Manzari now, who seemed a nice woman, but whom he'd never get to know well, or like particularly.

He must get a grip on himself, go through with this farce dutifully. He must above all not burst out into passionate speech about how in fact it wasn't just that his beautiful Esmeralda could sign her own death warrant in a pretty hand. It was that in his opinion she was uncommonly intelligent, though of course she'd never done anything much with that agile mind of hers. If anything, a professor for a father and a childhood in a house full of books seemed to have put her off brain-work of any sort. And come to think of it, her decision to marry this fellow didn't demonstrate tremendous perspicacity.

Concentrate! He must listen pleasantly to talk about his new son-in-law's flat in Rome, which was fashionably close to the Spanish Steps apparently – and which was going to be Esmeralda's home forever after, not this house of his here any more. He must enquire in more detail, in much more detail, about the new furnishings that the groom's mother had ordered as her present to the young couple.

Yes, because – dear Christ, *could* this be true? Because for the last few minutes he quite simply had not had the guts to turn to his daughter on his other side. Didn't think he could face her with the sort of proud, loving, sad, happy, jokey chat a girl might expect from her father at her wedding feast.

He hadn't got the guts, either, to cry out to her – to cry even in a whisper only she would hear – Don't you see the horror of your sham love affair, your sham marriage to come? As he ought to have cried out to her last night, if he'd been man enough to break through to her. That vacuous service in the church, this inane feasting.

Luigi's head ached with his longing to get away. As an excuse for not speaking either to his right or to his left, he went to take a sudden interest in the carving of the *arista*, which his two sons had been coping with perfectly adequately. There was the change to decanters of red wine, to his favourite Vino nobile di Montepulciano, to make a discreet fuss about too.

Well, at least toward the end of lunch people would change places, seek out their friends. He'd be able to light a cheroot, go and chat to Gofredo Damiani about his rare trees down at Ninfa, chat to Michele Della Quercia about his Sardinian fishing trips. And as to the future . . . He'd fritter away the last few years of his life in this friend's plantation and on that friend's sailing boat – and at Ca' Santa Chiara, in his own humble refuge at the end of a muddy lane. Well . . . good riddance. And preferable, just conceivably, as a way of evading harsh truths, to Carlo Manzari's showing up docilely to vote in a parliament where they'd often stationed armed Fascist militiamen in the lobbies and the corridors.

The trouble was, all the pork had now been carved, all the potatoes roasted with rosemary had been dished up. The bride's father assumed a jolly expression and went to sit down beside her again.

All the mutedness and isolation that Caterina had divined in Esmeralda with her veil down had vanished as soon as she was married and her veil was up. Her greeny-grey eyes had resumed their habitual devilry. Her beautiful face and her switch-backing moods and her fearless voice had resumed their devilry too. She had made a point of enchanting several of the better-looking men at the party. In the bishop's hearing, she had made a flippant remark about her bridegroom's and her vows of constancy. She had neglected to detain in conversation, even for a mere thirty seconds each, a number of the duller guests, who consequently were feeling disgruntled.

Now she turned to her father, with wickedness in her smile. 'Trust you, Papa, to sink into your usual gloom on my wedding day. Now, tell me the absolute truth. Are you going to have the decency to stay on here for a week or two, or will you bolt for Ca' Santa Chiara first thing tomorrow morning?'

24

At the table where Edoardo and Giles, Beatrice and Grazia and Rosalba were gathered together, the teasing and the laughing and the flirting had been prodigious. The young Englishman had eaten and drunk with gusto, had decided that Italy was a splendid country and that having one's sister live here was an admirable good fortune. Certainly, there was this little matter of an impending European war. But with a bit of luck it wouldn't amount to much. And in the meantime . . . Why, you never knew – one fine day, one of these beautiful coquettes might be his.

Not Beatrice, she was married, he must remember that. Or, most probably Beatrice, *because* she was married? Well, any-how, right now there was this important choice between what was apparently called *mascarpone* and some other marvel called *panna cotta*, between coffee ice cream and whatever that other pudding might be. There was Edoardo's cheerful invitation to taste all four. There were all these draughts of robust red wine – and apparently there was going to be a dessert wine too, called Vin santo, and special biscuits you ate with it. So that what with Grazia's coppery ringlets, and Rosalba's swelling breasts in that satin, and Beatrice's exceedingly eloquent eyes, the world seemed suddenly rich in vague, exciting possibilities. With nothing else to do all the live-long day, so far as he could make out, except eat pudding and drink wine and be flirted with. Though it was true, a breath of fresh air *would* be nice. So he accepted Edoardo's suggestion that they step out onto the balcony for a minute.

Some of the primmer matrons had sniffed that Beatrice Castiglia might be a married woman of a sort, but if that frisky creature was Sonya D'Alessandria's idea of a chaperone at that table . . . ! But even the stuffiest ladies smiled indulgently when they saw the two fair-headed young men standing by the balustrade in the luminous late afternoon.

No anger, or fear, or hate, shadowed their sunniness. Edoardo gave Giles a grin. He said: 'I just wanted to say something. Look, if this damned war does break out. Of course, if you get either of my brothers-in-law in your . . . Oh God, how do you say it in English. In your aim?'

He made the gesture of raising a gun, squinting along the barrel.

Giles was grinning too. 'If I get either of them in the sights of my rifle?'

'That's right! In your sights.' Edoardo chuckled. 'Then for heaven's sake take steady aim and squeeze the trigger. But if it's me . . . Shoot to miss. I will, if it's you.'

'I don't suppose it'll turn out *quite* that straightforward. And imagining my probable military prowess, you'll be safest if I aim to hit you. But – yes, of course.'

They raised their glasses to drink to this proposal, eyeing each other over the glinting rims.

'Shoot to miss.'

'Shoot to miss.'

II

—⁓—

THE DÉBÂCLE

1

—m—

Gabriele D'Alessandria's arrest by the Military Police as he walked out of his hospital on the third day of the German invasion of Poland, the day of France's and Britain's declarations of war, coming so hard on the heels of his sister Esmeralda's wedding that her husband and she were still in Venice, gave Arezzo plenty to talk about. And ripples of consternation spread rapidly all over the country, to all the places where the wedding guests had returned home. To apartments in Rome, to villas outside Florence. To the hill cities and the country estates.

Not only ripples of consternation. A number of those who in the Santissima Annunziata had indulged in agreeably pious or agreeably sentimental feelings, now let their compassion be tinged with righteous moralising and pleasure in others' misfortunes.

The Prefect, who had been so happy to accept an invitation to the Honourable Carlo Manzari's wedding, remarked to the Chief of Police the very next morning, without waiting for this latest miscreant to be brought to trial, that to be quite honest he was not sorry that subversive schemer had got his come-uppance at last, and it was no bad thing when at least once in a while justice was done. The bishop let it be believed that the D'Alessandria were in his prayers. But he did not resume his habit of occasionally visiting them.

The two landowners, who during the hymenial lunch had come to such a satisfactory understanding about gaining control of the local Fascist wheat marketing agency, met again to conclude an agreement about sharing a government subsidy for the draining of marsh-land. They concurred that Luigi D'Alessandria's marrying his two daughters highish into diplomacy and politics was a strategy that appeared to have misfired. Though of course it was early days yet, and the old boy might be able to prevail upon his sons-in-law to have his son's sentence commuted.

They then forgot about Gabriele entirely, and fell into debate about whether they should use the subsidy for the purpose for which it was intended. Or invest it on the Stock Exchange. Or spend the money to buy land that didn't need draining. Or send it across that admirably porous northern frontier to a Swiss bank, which was what a lot of rich Italians were doing with their spoils in these uncertain times. One of them had a brother who was a financier, and the other had a judge among his first cousins, so whatever they decided to do shouldn't be too difficult to arrange.

In the months to come, Luigi D'Alessandria was mostly in Rome, where toward Christmas his elder son was tried by one of the Special Tribunals for political offenders, and sent to the prison on the island of Ustica to begin to serve his seven years.

The year before, the government hadn't only passed the law kicking Jews out of the civil service, out of the armed forces, out of teaching, and saying they couldn't marry people who weren't Jews, and kicking Jewish children out of Italian state schools. There had also been a law ordering Italians not to address one another with the formal *lei* or the informal *tu*, but invariably as *voi*.

At Esmeralda D'Alessandria's wedding, a number of the guests had noticed the presence of several Jewish friends of her family. It had been these same conformist-minded citizens who had remarked that the bride's father had with wilful disrespect for authority gone around addressing those he knew well as *tu* and those he knew less well as *lei*, just as he always had. What was worse, when others gathered under the pollarded lime trees had thrust their right arms forward and upward with their palms flat, and had uttered the correct Fascist salutation, on the old professor's dry lips a smile of amused contempt was thought to have been observed. For which mockery of established triumphancy only the constraints of wedding etiquette had saved the old man from being savagely set upon with any weapons that came to hand.

Luigi knew he had so-called friends who were now discovering that they were not so surprised as all that to see the D'Alessandria family find itself on the wrong side of the law. He could imagine too the pleasure being taken in some quarters at the figure he himself was cutting. The member of the declining upper classes with his son and heir suddenly in irons as an enemy of the state, or some such bombastic nonsense. The white-headed intellectual, who'd always been so reserved, reduced to traipsing around public offices, and borrowing money from his sons-in-law to pay expensive lawyers, and trying to bring undue pressure to bear.

If you liked the old man, the thing had different aspects to it.

If you were the aristocrat Gofredo Damiani, whose red-tressed niece Grazia was wreaking such havoc among susceptible young gentlemen, and causing their mammas to think ungenerous thoughts, their papas to dream predatory, lascivious dreams. Damiani whose cardinal passion in life was the creation of an absolute Garden of Eden within the ruined city walls of Ninfa in the wet-lands below the Alban hills.

If you were Michele Della Quercia, whose passion was something to do with sea winds and sea horizons. The loneliness of that, the freedom of that.

If you were Gaetano Da Durante, whose passion was for Renaissance painting – if it wasn't, as Esmeralda would ringingly proclaim, for food and drink. And, she might whisper to a young female confidante, for sex. For which, she had it on excellent authority, he was prepared to pay really quite lavishly. Gaetano who knew that Luigi's right arm quite simply wouldn't go up in that cretinous salute, because his own wouldn't either.

If you were Damiani, or Della Quercia, or Da Durante, there was something admirable about how Luigi D'Alessandria set his small jaw, and that first autumn of the new war dourly got on with his unequal struggle against pettifogging bureaucrats and barbarous laws. Got on with being obstructed and deceived, being treated without respect and spoken of without kindness.

When the Fascists had introduced the oath of loyalty to their régime that university professors were required to take, on pain of dismissal, D'Alessandria had sworn it like practically everyone else. Not because he put any value on his profession. Because he had a family to support. For this acquiescence he had subsequently despised himself, in an intermittent, feeble sort of way.

At the earliest opportunity, he had retired on a small pension, and had felt relieved to turn his back on at least one of his defeats in life. He had gone on feeling hopelessly out of step with the course his society was taking. He'd gone on taking notes for his *The Degradation of Italy*, and planning how the chapters might take shape. Vaguely he hoped that, if he ever managed to complete it, the book might be discovered after his death, and possibly be published if the country he loved had by then freed itself from its latest indignities.

Sitting doggedly in the Roman lawyers' grandiose offices, Luigi D'Alessandria listened to all the excuses they came up with for not getting known as defenders of enemies of the people or whatever the rant was. He listened to how, when you were up against the Special Tribunals, and the prisoner *was* a member of a banned political party, and he *had* written the pamphlets that had been traced back to him, there was mighty little to be done, for this reason and for that reason. Unless, naturally, you had a cousin in the Department of Justice, in which case . . . Oh, use your head. *Justice*, in *these* courts?

Luigi would get distracted. He'd forget Gabriele, and what might be being done to him and what might befall him in the future. He'd find himself longing for an innocent old age in which with a friend or two you went offshore fishing in summer, and in winter you went to earth with your wood-shed well stacked with logs and your house well furnished with books. Or he might find himself recollecting how strangely magical it had been that January when it had snowed and snowed, and he'd been stuck at Ca' Santa Chiara with blizzards some days and dazzling sun on snow-drifts on other days – stuck there with Benedetta at the height of their love affair. A good fifteen years ago, it must have been.

It would not be the memory of Benedetta Farsetti that would make the dignified gentleman taking the best legal advice uncomfortable – on the contrary. It would be the consciousness that his hope of briskly doing anything he could for Gabriele was tinged with his yearning to get back to his country house for the winter, when the *last* thing he should have been thinking of was to abandon Sonya and Caterina.

Yes, and then the spring would come, Luigi would remember

guiltily, unstoppably. Blackthorn in the copses suddenly showing white sprays, and the almond trees looking like brides,
and . . . *Brides*! That wasn't a happy thought. Well, naturally
this lawyer fellow was no bloody use. But this evening he was
dining with Cosima and her husband, and Esmeralda and *her*
husband, to see if at the Court of Appeal, eventually . . . Not
that he knew if either of those two sons-in-law of his were doing
more than going through the motions of trying to help. Or to
see if, because of Gabriele's asthma . . .

When cold winds tattered the petals, the first green on
the blackthorns would start showing through the white. To
be there! In his modest liberty. Then his apricot trees would
blossom pale pink, after which there'd be a lull before the cherry
trees and the pear trees.

Disagreeable, though, the sort of consultations you got
bogged down in. Not to mention the chicanery you found you
were prepared to stoop to, when it came to your son. Yes – but
the spring birdsong from dawn on, and the elder budding green
but not the walnut trees yet, and the chill luminous days.

At the same time, uprising through Luigi D'Alessandria's
desire to be away from floundering ignominiously in a mire of
actions in which it was impossible for him to take any effective
action, there came a sharper and sharper conviction that it might
not be good enough to go and rot self-indulgently in pleasant
circumstances. It might not indefinitely be good enough, either,
merely to take notes about the degradation of your country.

2

Luigi D'Alessandria got the country spring he'd longed for. He got the violets in his garden's rough grass and on all the hillsides around, the pollen blowing off the firs in pale clouds. He got the plum trees in blossom and then the apple trees.

He left the Roman lawyers' offices, where they'd made him realise how useless his dogged parleying was. He left his house in Arezzo, where for years his presence had been useless, and where he'd never felt more redundant than in the days after Esmeralda's mockery of a wedding. With the vast, invisible cataclysm of northern Europe going to war with itself, though not southern Europe thank heavens, or anyway not yet, and his own sour recognition that war in Poland meant mighty little the week your son was chucked into gaol. With the small, immediate scurry to get Giles away to the French border in double quick time. With the local newspapers coming out with the most outrageous articles about Gabriele, about the D'Alessandria family's 'disgrace', even its 'downfall' according to one journalist. With that unbreakable or that irredeemable spirit Esmeralda on the telephone from her Venetian honeymoon as blithe as a lark, rattling away not about her incarcerated brother but about the generals and the film stars and the foreign and domestic princelings who were also having an idyllic time at the Hotel des Bains. She had discovered water-skiing, and Carlo and she had gone riding along the beaches where Byron had exercised his horses, and . . . Oh yes, Count Borromeo was in the suite next door to Carlo's and hers, with his third wife who was nineteen like his daughter and *much* more beautiful. Esmeralda had twittered on . . . About the dear count's first marriage, which the Pope had very decently annulled, despite its having produced children and albeit at ruinous expense. About his second wife, who had so considerately died.

Luigi D'Alessandria remembered – and frowned, driving up the hairpin bends to the mountain pass called Bocca Trabaria which for him meant escape, meant liberty. It was early in the new year, the heights were still shrouded in snow; but lower down it had been thawing, and the road over the ridge had been cleared. Grinding along slowly with chains on the car's wheels, trying not to skid on the icy slush, Luigi's heart lifted as it always did at the thought of Garibaldi and his force crossing that Apennine ridge in the summer of 1849. Yes, even in the darkest times of the struggle for a free Italy, even after Rome had been lost, the hero had found a couple of thousand ragged men to fight that escape by his side.

Those had been the days! Italy had undergone her years of shame, then as now – but by God she'd had her moments of glory too. Luigi steered cautiously between two pot-holes, and his proud love for his country flared up invincibly, despite his decades of disillusionment. Even when the cause must truly have appeared hopeless, a few indomitable souls had always been found. Though that guerrilla army had dwindled away dreadfully quickly, and in the end . . . At the end of that escape, there'd been three of them left, and hundreds of enemy soldiers combing the Comacchio dunes and marshes and lagoons, closing in for the kill. Garibaldi had waded ashore that last time with one wounded friend limping beside him, and carrying the dying Anita in his arms – and still he got away.

With the low, late-winter sun at its midday height, the mountain wind was cascading its cold brilliance through the leafless beech hangers and over the slanting meadows where white cattle grazed. Luigi D'Alessandria had never been a slap-dash driver, and he took his descent from the pass even more prudently than he'd negotiated the climb, peering through his windscreen into the dazzling sheens and the black shadows, bumping over the slithery ruts in second gear. But his old heart rejoiced that he was away at last, and he smiled to think how surprised Gabriele would be, who had long ago resigned himself to his father's political disbeliefs and despairs, by the romantic love of his beautiful land which could still stir him. Even the thought that he was leaving the lad in prison while he made his escape could not depress Luigi today.

Here was a fountain, where from time immemorial the pure, icy mountain-side water had splashed into a stone trough.

Proudly recalling the defiant way Gabriele had answered the Special Prosecutor at that ludicrous trial, the prisoner's father stopped his car, got out to cup his hands and drink. Heavens it was good to be back here, where the mule-teams brought wood down the paths to the charcoal burners' huts. Where after the thaw the air smelled of wet loam, and you heard the cow-bells tinkling from the pasture.

Inspired by his own freedom in the soughing forest and the blowing light, he didn't believe Gabriele would serve all those seven years. Maybe scarcely half of them. One way and another ... On grounds of ill-health. Or there'd be a change in the political wind, and the régime would want to curry favour in this camp or that, or the propagandists would require a few acts of magnanimity. Why, Luigi thought with his today's boisterousness, you never knew – the whole pompous dictatorship might come tumbling down from one month to the next!

The political prisoners were turning some of the gaols into the best universities in Italy, people said. Organising courses, giving lectures. Doing the vital job of teaching intellectual freedom which unfortunately the real universities weren't often up to. Look at that magnificent creature soaring up there! That wasn't a buzzard. An eagle of some sort. Or would the gallant enemies of the state, when they were locked up, just continue with their endless ideological feuding? Yes, quite probably they'd be brow-beating honest thieves and murderers into attending their classes, where the poor wretches could be bored silly with this or that sect's brand of Marxist-Leninist purity.

In one of the first hamlets at the head of the Metauro valley, Luigi stopped for bread and cheese and a glass of wine. He immediately decided that all three tasted wonderful, after weeks of rich living in the capital, and the friendly courtesy of the woman who served him this modest lunch made him long to believe that life out here might still have cleanliness and dignity.

Well, anyhow, the sham didn't seem to have infected the air of this particular parish quite yet. Listen to the stream chuckling beneath that little stone bridge – melted snow, that was. Primroses in the way-side grass, and over there the men already out in a vineyard with their pruning knives and their hanks of twine. And just look at those pollarded willows, with their new sappy wands that golden pink so bright that each spring you were startled by it.

Yes, thank you. He smiled at his hostess. Yes, most certainly he would try a slice of her apple tart, and drink a second glass of her husband's wine to wash it down.

Of course, there was nothing to prevent a prettily splashing stream and the sham in human conduct coexisting. But Luigi was so happy to be away from the air he'd had to breathe in Arezzo and in Rome, that he let himself shrug that aside, driving on down the valley he loved through the foothills he loved, cheerfully recognising here an old belfrey of particular charm, there an oak of such splendour that he'd been admiring it for years.

There was no equivalence between being uneducated and being a decent person either, he knew that too. You only had to take a boundary dispute between two peasant farmers. The most infamous politicians in Rome wouldn't have anything to teach them when it came to dogged, pitiless guile. Yes, yes; but even so . . . With the sky scoured cloudless, so when you looked up you couldn't see the gale raging through it, there was just that sapphire emptiness shining so lucently it hurt your eyes. With the sun on the blossoming almond trees in the fields where the young corn was coming up brilliant green . . . Naturally, that the region looked like Arcadia didn't mean a thing. Why did he keep forgetting? For the matter of that, Rome *looked* pretty fine – its problem wasn't its looks.

Luigi D'Alessandria turned off the valley road, up his homeward lane into the hills, his sanguine mood suddenly slashed through by an old anguish and slashed about by sharp new longings too. For months, he'd gone through the motions. Esmeralda's getting engaged, her wedding. Gabriele's trial. He had done what he could, for his daughter and for his son, futilely. He'd pretended to be who he could. The proud father of the bride. The man who could take a lawyer seriously. But now, a respite. To be free at Ca' Santa Chiara for a while . . .

The longing to be away, the desire to be himself however fleetingly, brought foolish tears prickling at the back of his eyes. However uninspiring to others what remained of his real self might be, and however uninspiring he was to himself, at least that modest aliveness wasn't sham.

Old Gervasio's farmstead on its hillside hadn't changed a bit since last summer. Good! Oh, except that, as every year, the cattle needing forage all winter meant that the upright poles, around which at harvest the conical stacks had been built, now stood very gaunt, wearing only tatters of hay. Well, next June would put that right.

A daughter's choice of a Fascist politician for a husband; a son's choice of revolutionary socialism by way of politics . . . Oh, forget them. Yes, but when he'd been Gabriele's age, he'd got fired up by those ideals. *Liberté, égalité, fraternité.* They sounded all right.

Jolting around the last corner of the track that led down to his own house, Luigi saw its brown roof through the bare acacias and oaks. He must be prepared to find the damp had got in here and there. Light a fire, that would be the first thing he'd do.

3

Ca' Santa Chiara was a brick farmhouse of no great distinction, although to its owner some of its arches had charm. He drew up in the yard, which was muddy now, and when the warm weather came would be tussocky. Even baled up in his greatcoat, with boots and scarf, with gloves and cap, the end-of-winter day's drive had chilled him to the bone. Getting out, he stamped his feet, he thudded his arms around his sides to start the blood moving.

The dogs came bounding up to him. There was a nondescript, bob-tailed terrier, who had one bad leg, which had given him the habit of trotting obliquely with his hind-paws following slightly to the left of his fore-paws. There was the liver-coloured pointer, who unknown to Luigi had on the eve of Esmeralda's wedding been a party to Gaetano Da Durante's meditations. And there was Luigi's favourite, the shaggy white *maremmano* sheepdog Furia who nearly floored him with the warmth of her welcome.

He thumped her shoulders, he pulled her ears. In her joy at this reunion she broke away and galloped in a mad circle, so that momentarily her master could fondle the heads of the terrier and the pointer. Then Furia launched herself at him again, plumy tail flailing, fore-legs reared up to pound at his chest. He shoved her down once more, looked around cheerfully at his unkempt property.

There was the well with its winch and bucket, and the wood-shed stacked chock-a-block with sere logs. The plum tree by the gate was in full blossom, being buffeted by the last of the short day's blowing sunlight. The old place looked splendid in its modest fashion, Luigi decided with uncharacteristic ebullience – and Ca' Santa Chiara was a dog's paradise, he'd always said so. They had their baskets in the barn, and when he wasn't here they had Gervasio or his wife Maria to feed them. The three of them were the masters of the whole desmesne, so that no mere rabbit or cat or rat dared set paw in the yard, and in the meadow and the orchard and in the spinnies the most furious hunts and killings were regular occurrences.

'It's all right for you, isn't it?' Luigi was trying to pat three heads at once with his two hands, only each time he stooped for the terrier, the bigger dogs tried to lick his face. But he was grinning more impulsively than he had for months. 'It's all right for important people like dogs. Down, Furia, down!'

The door of the small, rickety barn had needed repairing for at least a couple of years, he really must get that seen to. As for cleaning the dead leaves out of the house's gutters, tomorrow morning he'd fetch the ladder and do that himself. Sixty wasn't that old! Hell, he'd feel new life flickering up in him if he wasn't careful. No, sixty-one these days – he kept forgetting. Well, he might make old bones, or he might already be into his last year, he didn't care. He'd got clear away, the spring was coming once more . . . That amazing way that all nature knew what to do – and did it, in concert. The ash tree, the chaffinch . . . Extraordinary!

Ca' Santa Chiara was a typical farmhouse of the central Italian hills, with its living quarters on the first floor. Downstairs were the stables (empty in this case), the store-rooms, the wash-house.

Night would fall quickly, he had a lot to do. Luigi reached his hand into the pomegranate tree for the key, trudged briskly over to the outside staircase, climbed it, let himself in. How bleak the place looked! Just a few grey bars of light from the shutters' slats. And cold! Not a fire lit here all winter. Out in the yard, it was balmy by comparison. What was that crate on the table? Ah, a case of wine left by Gaetano in friendly homage. But you could smell the damp in the rooms.

He bustled about, opening shutters in the kitchen and the living-room and one bedroom. He went out to the shed for a bundle of kindling, and soon he had a blaze crackling up in the big stone fireplace and was going back for more wood so he could light the black iron range in the kitchen too. With the shutters wide, he could see how dusty the place was. Signora Maria must be feeling her age. Perhaps she'd had pleurisy again this winter. It was his fault, too, for vanishing for half a year. She must find it discouraging, to keep stumping down the track every once in a while to air and dust a house no one ever returned to.

Professor D'Alessandria's relationship with Signor Gervasio and Signora Maria was a web of exchanges and loyalties. No money ever passed either way, but they worked his smallholding alongside their more numerous acres, they coppiced his small wood, they kept an eye on his house.

Luigi was delighted that they should reap and cart the hay from his one meadow, and delighted to see their sheep grazing his aftermath. When he was away, he rejoiced to know they were tilling his vegetable garden and selling the surplus produce, just as when he was at Ca' Santa Chiara it was a vague but solid satisfaction to know that he would never want for provender. It amused him to know that all the district reckoned his neighbours got somewhat the better of the deal. It also amused him that Gervasio and Maria would not quickly live down the disgrace if he were ever observed being reduced to *buying* a haunch of veal or a sack of potatoes.

As for peccadilloes like Gervasio being scrupulous about feeding the dogs, but never brushing them, despite repeated requests to do so occasionally . . . Well, he never brushed his own dogs, either. And when it came to more important matters . . .

It was good to know that as soon as the firewood in your shed became depleted, Gervasio would notice, and would have a word with his silent, brawny son Bruno, and soon more logs would have been cut and stacked. It was good that Gervasio had the shooting all over the parish, because with that hunch-backed old ghoul prowling around with his gun in all weathers you weren't going to get outliers taking an interest in the place. Not that at Ca' Santa Chiara there was much to steal – except a few early editions of poets, and a few engravings and etchings, which the local malefactors probably wouldn't recognise as having any value. Oh, and a couple of shot-guns and some fishing-rods, they might steal those.

Knowing that his arrival would have been noticed, and wondering whether the first visit would be paid him tonight or tomorrow morning, Luigi went down to his store-room for oil so he could refill his lamps. Coming back up the stone staircase to the porch (the house had no internal staircase), he shivered in the nightfall wind. The glory of that plum tree's creamy pink regalia in the sunshine so short a time ago! Now it was a pallid ghost being shaken in the dusk.

In the living-room he lit his lamps, he stuck candles into sticks and lit them. The fire was guttering already. Kneeling by the hearth, he blew on the embers. He laid on more kindling, building a sort of wigwam for the flames to spread through.

In due course he must eat something. He put his head into the larder. There'd be no fresh food of course, but the staples were always there. Flour, rice, olive oil. And festoons of last summer's onions and garlic still hanging where he'd hooked them up, and a cured ham of Gervasio's. He ferreted among the spices. Yes, he had saffron. A *risotto alla milanese* he'd make.

The dogs padded after him wherever he went; his home-coming was going to have to be declared some kind of festival, they could be indoors dogs for one evening. Now, the bedding would have got damp in those cupboards. He must bring some sheets and blankets through to this room to be aired for a few hours. A homecoming . . . Was that what it was?

'An excellent house for your second marriage, Luigi,' Gaetano had once said of this place, and chuckled. 'Or rather, a perfectly suitable haunt for an old satyr and a young concubine.' Gaetano who had known all about Benedetta Farsetti and what a temptation she had been, when she was his most brilliant student, or perhaps she was just effortlessly the most beautiful, anyway she was the one he had the love affair of his life with. Benedetta with her laughing black eyes and her bobbed black hair. Benedetta with her inner quietness you could always hear, like hearing the sea far off, so he'd always sensed that this passion must merely be an interlude for her, soon her silence and her solitude would come flooding back again. Bloody old Gaetano, always understanding everything. Insufferable! Understanding what a temptation the idea of a new inspiration, a fresh chance had been . . .

Luigi decided he was warm enough to risk taking off his greatcoat – which he wasn't, really, but it distracted him from memories of Benedetta. Busily he put larger billets on the fire, he took the Sardinian fisherman's knife from his desk and used it to cut open the case of wine on the table. Of course, there was plenty of local wine in the *cantina* downstairs, but if Gaetano had brought something special . . .

He took out a bottle, looked at the label, took out another. A Barolo, a Nebbiolo . . . Half a dozen different Piedmontese reds. One of these might do the trick, with a bit of luck. Typical, the way he'd been feeling happier than he had for months, and then from one minute to the next a melancholy would begin to shadow him which – which he was going to ignore, he was going to shrug off.

What had Gaetano been up to in Piedmont last summer? Chasing some canvas by a half-forgotten Old Master, or chasing some *demi-mondaine.*

Luigi poured himself a glass of one of the rich, strong reds, and sipped it. He stood the bottle by the fire to warm up a bit. Big-hearted stuff, those Piedmontese wine-masters knew how to make – that was better! And to be back here, a free man of a humble sort, amidst your own few odds and ends. Your own skis and trout-rods propped up in that corner between two bookcases. A pair of twelve-bores which had been your father's before they were yours, glinting dully in the gun-rack. But why whenever you came back to a house were half the pictures always hanging crooked?

It had been bad, though, in Rome. Dinner party after dinner party with those two ruthless, rich men who'd possessed themselves of his daughters, who now treated him with impeccable correctness and gave nothing away. Esmeralda's husband was infinitely the more sophisticated of the two. But Luigi had his doubts whether he was actually any more sympathetic than the coarse marquis.

However, that train of thought would lead him fatally to his usual twinges of disappointment in his daughters. This in its turn would lead to him wishing Gabriele would do his own political thinking for a change and not absorb all his doctrines from dogmatic books. Or into wishing Edoardo wasn't so damned merry to be forever trotting around from football matches to dances, before equally thoughtlessly enlisting for some criminal folly tarted up as national glory.

Yes, and what he'd seen of Caterina in Rome had disappointed him too, it had been as bad as seeing Edoardo in his brand-new infantry lieutenant's uniform. Or Caterina had touched him with dread, and pity. Or – what was it that she had done?

Luigi made himself start straightening crooked pictures about the room, and at once he felt better. Barocci's *Rest on the Flight into Egypt*, his *Annunciation* . . .

Caterina's tirelessly brave chat with Cosima and Esmeralda and their husbands. Her hectic eyes as she sallied forth with them to the opera to see *Aida* – because you never could tell, these people *might* be on her side, and anyhow they had her destiny in their power, so she was going to play her part with all the debonair style she could command. Sallying forth to a Foreign Ministry lunch with Count Ciano, whom Esmeralda and Carlo absolutely insisted she must get to know. To a party where none of the suave ladies and gentlemen would do anything so maladroit as to allude to the fact that she was British, or she had been, or she was whatever luckless mess she was, and that her husband was a political prisoner. Where they would all see right through her, through her valiant acting; and she would see nothing clearly, but she'd have to go on performing like the doomed wretch she was.

It could also be bad to have Caterina before your eyes in Arezzo. She nearly always kept up her happy, jokey way of talking to her daughter, as if nothing had happened. She kept up her chatter about Gabriele too. What Papa likes, what Papa would think. That sort of stuff. Only sometimes Lisa would ask, 'Papa?' and look around for him. Then you might see Caterina tighten her suddenly unsteady mouth. And she had a way of hunching up one shoulder, swiftly ducking her glistening eyes down onto her upper sleeve.

Luigi gave himself a shake. With a small, veined hand, he brushed the wretchedness off his forehead.

He straightened Tiepolo's *Death Holding Audience* and, standing motionless to contemplate it, he forgot Rome and Arezzo, he forgot Caterina. There was skeletal Death sitting on the ground with his great book, and a few poor people standing around. They leaned forward with sad curiosity to know – were they inscribed there? What fate was written for them? When? And for those they loved?

The frame was filthy dusty. Concentrating wholly on the image before him, Luigi wiped it with his handkerchief and then wiped his fingers, not with the fussy gesture he had used in the Café dei Costanti on the morning of Esmeralda's wedding, but simply, thoughtlessly, because it was the natural thing to do.

4

~~~

Early the next morning, Signora Maria and her daughter-in-law Giuliana, a girl still scarcely out of adolescence, descended upon Ca' Santa Chiara to give the place a tremendous spring-cleaning. With buckets and mops they sluiced and scrubbed. They opened every door and window in the house, so the breeze that blew in set everything swinging and banging. On the walls the pictures that had been straightened swung crooked again, and a small Guido Reni etching, a *Madonna and Child*, was blown down but luckily the glass didn't break.

Both stocky, rubicund Maria and lissom Giuliana sang as they toiled, though not always the same song at the same time. They attacked all the swags of cobwebs with feather dusters. They dragged the rugs outside to beat them. The weather had changed, it was a mild, dove-coloured day, with the air so dense with clinging moisture you could hardly say whether it was raining or not. The dust from the beaten rugs blew away, dully and wetly spangling, over the yard toward the fruit trees.

Back in the house, the spring-cleaners washed every dusty pot and pan in the kitchen, and piled them up on the stone draining board in glistening heaps to dry. They took down every curtain in the house and bore them away to the wash-house where there was the indoor well. They primed the pump, they cranked away at its clanking handle, they filled several tubs with water and curtains and suds.

Feeling inadequate when faced with all this effective action, Luigi D'Alessandria went into the larder. Signora Maria had come carrying her regular largesse, and he thought he could at least put things away. But he found the eggs had already been neatly set out in their carved wooden tray, looking like a game of draughts all ready to be played. There were a couple of loaves in the bread-bin, and a jam tart. Signora Maria baked once a week, and she baked on a heroic scale. He opened the meat-safe. A packet of freshly made sausages. Gervasio and Bruno must have slaughtered a pig in the last few days. Another packet, which still oozed smears of blood and turned out to contain offal. Giblets, chitterlings, he wasn't sure what all these lumps were. This was where the dogs would come to his assistance.

Maria had also brought a terracotta pot with three hyacinths in it, which she had set in the middle of the dining table. The hyacinths were just coming into pale mauve, curlicued flower, and at once started to scent the unlived-in air.

Luigi went out into the yard to see the sacks of grain in the meal-bins in his barn, and the maize that had wintered in its drying racks with their narrow pitched roofs. This good husbandry, all this sensibly ordered abundance, gave him exactly the sense of satisfaction with life which he had half-consciously gone in search of. Still possessed by an indolent desire to do something useful, he went to the shed where tools were kept. He took a whetstone, started to sharpen his scythe.

It was peaceful, standing in the outhouse doorway where he could watch a flock of goldfinches flitting about the yard and the elder trees and the walnut trees. A blackbird was singing. His whetstone on the steel blade made a steady rasp, rasp, rasp.

Luigi hung the scythe back on its peg, took down a sickle to sharpen. Across the valley, on the other side of the brook making its murmurous music, and beyond the tall poplars whose uppermost boughs level with his gaze were budding reddish green, the smallholder on the opposite slope had made a fire. Idly, Luigi watched the man moving about among his trees. At that distance, he looked about the size of a thumb nail. The breeze was dying, and the air was a steadily descending water-logged mist, it was turning into a soft rain even as he watched.

In a dry season, no one would risk lighting a fire for fear the hillsides caught. But this was good bonfire weather, all the land wet. Luigi decided that when his blades had a good sharp edge on them, he'd rake together some of the dead leaves and the pruners' lop and top, he'd have a bonfire in his garden too.

Luigi D'Alessandria had never been so aware of time as he became that spring. He was not like Caterina who found that sometimes a few lines of poetry or a snatch of an old song would bring back her far-away girlhood to her. No, it was present time which began to bewitch the old fellow, that spring when Mussolini was reaching his decision to enter the war, and the press was whipping up more and more anti-French and anti-British hysteria in preparation for this magnificent event, so in Rome some foreigners were beaten up, and then similar attacks occurred in other cities. It was present time, and it first felt as if it were turning and building up like a tide far out at sea, it first made him long to feel it come surging into his mind in long, slow waves, that morning while he was tending his bonfire.

Orchard prunings, some broom that had been cut back, a dead rosemary. Luigi built a big fire, going contentedly to and fro with his dogs at his heels, pitchforking boughs and brushwood onto his crackling blaze.

A pair of hoopoes were flying about the hillside. That was a sign of the spring migrations. Distractedly he hoped they'd build their nest in a safe place where the magpies and jays didn't find them, he hoped they'd rear their young. Then he remembered he hadn't yet told Gervasio and Maria about Gabriele being in prison. Come to think of it, what were their politics? Apart from the age-old peasant politics of taciturnity, that is. Well, anti-clerical at any rate. Off and on Gervasio had growled enough contempt to place him fair and square in the high old Italian tradition of priest-hating. You never knew, his grandfather might have fought with Garibaldi.

Luigi leaned on his pitchfork. The blackbird was still fluting. He could hear the sheep-bells. Myriad flecks of grey ash towered up and drifted in the grey drizzle.

He was caught by the happiness of standing there on the dun hillside, breathing the tangy wood-smoke that smelled like the only incense his spirit would ever require. In the jaunty goldfinch flock there was an aliveness that he'd never known so acutely before. There was a gaiety in the glamorous hoopoes with their cockades on their heads. There was an ancient, cruel nobility in the pair of buzzards wheeling high in the murk, kept up there by hunger. At his age, to sense these things with this sharpness! It seemed a touch of grace. Perhaps life might yet hold for him some new challenge, some part he could usefully play, who could tell, maybe an old man's last nebulous inspiration . . . Almost certainly not. But the possibility was good.

And then he felt it – that grey-headed man leaning on a pitchfork, looking into his bonfire's flames' waverings. He felt time quick with that burning life, as quick as the goldfinches darting in the rainy mist. But it was also time slow, time immeasurably slow; time a deep tide flowing into his head from forever, and bringing him everything; time which would go on flooding, so he brimmed more and more full of awareness – and still that tendril of smoke had not uncurled.

Luigi D'Alessandria never deliberately chose not to return to Arezzo. But as that spring passed, so when he gazed across the valley it was no longer the blackthorn wearing white on his neighbour's hillside but the hawthorn that caught the eye, it became unthinkable to renounce his inoffensive liberty, unthinkable not to live the time that was burgeoning with all its gifts and all its promise in his consciousness.

There was friendly if infrequent correspondence between the D'Alessandria house in Arezzo and Ca' Santa Chiara in the back of beyond not far from Urbino. But Sonya and he each stayed where they were, with the mountains between them.

5

—∽∽—

The only real friend Luigi D'Alessandria had in the region was Gregorio Farsetti, whose young cousin Benedetta had been the lighthearted heroine of that intoxicating winter interlude.

Farsetti lived in the hill village of Sant'Ambrogio, in a large, handsome house with its own church and a crypt. He too had quit the university as early as he could. Luigi liked Gregorio for that, and he liked him for his marriage which had been successful unlike his own, and for the profusion of life the man surrounded himself with, or seemed to generate quite spontaneously and naturally.

Gregorio Farsetti was six feet tall, so he towered over D'Alessandria. With his gaunt head and his indomitable bearing, he made you think of an Old Testament prophet, though there was no trace of mysticism in this active, kind old man. He was still undauntedly vigorous when it came to working alongside the farm-hand who'd come to scythe his orchard grass, or the bricklayer rebuilding one of his terrace walls. His noble old house always seemed to be full of people, who were always cheerful, at least while they were there. It made a heartening contrast to Ca' Santa Chiara, where for months nobody except the occasional neighbour came by.

Sons and daughters, sons-in-law and daughters-in-law, small grandsons and granddaughters, and all their friends . . . Gregorio was quite a patriarch in his religionless style, and whenever Luigi went over there a feast for a company at least twenty strong seemed to be in the final stages of preparation, and he was invariably beguiled into staying for dinner. The party would be merry till late into the night. Someone would play a fiddle or a guitar, and songs would be sung.

It wasn't only people who appeared to proliferate and prosper at Sant'Ambrogio, it was life in all its variety. Gregorio Farsetti had geese and ducks, turkeys and hens, peacocks and doves, all of which reproduced their kind more successfully than in less happy desmesnes. He had horses, mules, donkeys, he had dogs, cats, rabbits, and each of his grandchildren on its fourth birthday was presented with a tortoise, which joined the other armoured lumberers in the courtyard rose-beds.

Farsetti and D'Alessandria were each many things that the other was not, and they liked one another for this. But the chief thing Luigi kindled to in Gregorio was the vein of melancholia in his nature, though it was nowhere near as pronounced as his own, and the man had a marvellous ability never to let his despondencies embitter what he said or cast a shadow over the merriment of his household. Luigi admired this whole-heartedly and tried to learn from it. So now on these spring evenings it was good to stroll while talking together to his friend's vegetable patches, where it being Sant'Ambrogio all crops unhesitatingly flourished, and then to saunter on to the hives where the bees were like none others in all Italy for industry and productivity or, indeed, for savagery. There had also sprung up the ritual by which once or twice a year Luigi might casually ask how Benedetta and her Venetian husband were getting on in that watery city of theirs, and Gregorio's eyes would give him a flash of wry amusement, he'd respond that so far as he knew his cousin was fine. No children, unfortunately, even after ten years of marriage – but fine.

German troops in Vienna one year, and in Prague and Warsaw the next. This year German troops in Copenhagen and now in Oslo too, though what sounded like some exceedingly tough Norwegians were still fighting in those forested mountains of theirs. It wasn't going to stop here either, the two old friends agreed. Or Luigi might ask, had Gregorio noticed how Europe's psychoses, or the Old World's bouts of self-mutilation, or whatever they were, were recurring at shorter and shorter intervals? There'd been the Napoleonic wars, and then the next convulsion of the so-very-civilised West had been the Franco-Prussian war half a century later. Then after less than fifty years there'd been the Great War, their war; and now, after scarcely a generation, the Powers were at it again.

On half a dozen evenings that spring, at Sant'Ambrogio where there were always voices or footsteps in the background, where jobs about the house were always being done, where there invariably seemed to be a grandchild and a puppy tumbling on the lawn, or the whole household would have been solemnly summoned to attend while two six-year-olds attempted to race their tortoises along the terrace, Luigi found he could talk to Gregorio about some of the dreads that haunted him. About how Sonya's war last time looked like being re-echoed in Caterina's now. About how it was becoming embarrassingly plain that, just as in Germany there might be opposition to the dictator and his warring, but if so it was dismally ineffectual, so too here in Italy there might be opposition, but if so where the Devil was it?

A few thousand political hotheads like Gabriele – fine, fine. But a general dissatisfaction, an opposition you could count in hundreds of thousands? A rebellion big enough to make the nation change its mind about the Axis and its war? Say, one or two men in every village and in every city street who simply refused to be conscripted. That would be the sort of mass defiance Luigi reckoned the government wouldn't have a chance in hell of overriding.

What was needed was a whole lot of cussed disobedience, for pity's sake, like that fellow Gandhi was getting into hot water for organising in India. It was high time for a bit of standing up and being counted – what did Gregorio think? And anyhow, weren't we Italians supposed to be brilliant at not doing what we were told?

Sitting on one of his garden benches in the evening sun, watching a peahen and her chicks, Gregorio Farsetti might reply with his indomitable equanimity that Luigi was dead right, twenty years of this pinchbeck dictatorship did seem to have filleted the backbone out of a lot of people. Centuries of being sodomised by religion didn't help, either. Yes, when it came to totalitarian power structures, the Catholic Church gave the Fascist Party and the Communist Party a run for their money all right. Certainly Luigi was going to stay for dinner, he was having no nonsense about that. Beef stew, should be good. Now, another thing. He wasn't to get so depressed all the time. Italy was going to know how to wake up, Italy was going to surprise a lot of moaners before too long. Well, anyway, the wretched country wasn't going to get itself saved by a brace of old gaffers like them. Time for an aperitif, didn't Luigi think? A neighbour had brought him a tub of first-rate olives, and they went very well with a glass of wine.

Even after German troops had captured Amsterdam and Brussels, and were closing in on Paris for the third time in seventy years, and the Italian press was all squeals of joy, Gregorio Farsetti was still surveying his property and its inhabitants with patriarchal satisfaction, and doing his best to keep his old friend's spirits up.

Early summer came, with its orchids in the meadows, its mowers in the hay fields, its fireflies in the night gardens and nightingales singing. Luigi D'Alessandria was still haunted to desperation by how nine people out of ten appeared to have convinced themselves that Fascism had somehow just happened, like a plague or an earthquake, and it would be the same if the country now entered the war. But tyrannies at home and wars of aggression abroad did not just happen. They required half a nation who desired them and who caused them, and the other half who went along with them.

However, even when Luigi didn't drive over to Sant'Ambrogio, the mere thought of staunch old Gregorio ten kilometres away cheered him up. Doubtless dotted about all over the land there were a few stubborn souls who went on thinking matters through each in his own manner, and didn't just wait for State or Church or Party to come up with a gang attitude.

When, with German armoured divisions having already fought their way to the Channel, Italy finally declared war against France and Britain, there were no protests, the government ran no risk of being toppled. Not a single politician resigned, though a few years later many of them were pronouncing that they'd been against the Italo-German military alliance all along.

Luigi had been out on his sultry hillside with a sickle, cutting the undergrowth back from around some young trees he had planted a couple of winters before. Afterward he had driven down to the Metauro valley to the village shop, to buy things like coffee and razor blades. The place doubled as the parish café, and it had electricity, unlike Ca' Santa Chiara, and a radio. Several of his neighbours were gathered, listening to it. Outside the window, on the near side of the willow grove, swallows hunting for gnats were swooping low along the stream.

It had been coming for so long, that as he listened to the blood-thirsty rant and the martial music his first thoughts were not of Edoardo who'd joined the colours, or of Caterina whose civil war was going to be fought to the kill now, nor even of the shame of Italy attacking her old ally France when she was already beaten.

At Sant'Ambrogio they'd be listening to the same news. Every duckling and every peachick in the place would need to have it drummed into their empty, happy little heads that as of the last ten minutes they were in a state of belligerence, and must expect the vengeance of the French and British empires – though that might take a while coming, unless they could get out of the habit of losing battles as close to Paris as the river Somme and as close to London as Calais. In the North Sea, too. The day before yesterday, the aircraft carrier *Glorious* had been sunk, the destroyers *Ardent* and *Acasta* had been sunk. Yes, come to think of it the Farsetti goslings might be safe for a bit.

While all around, the hill fields of ripening corn were stained red with commemorative poppies, for those who had eyes to see.

6

─🐚─

The beginning of Caterina D'Alessandria's journey into her dividedness and her solitude had come that evening the previous September when Lisa was splashing in the bath-tub. Outside the open window were the tops of the lime trees and the hurtling swifts, and Caterina was kneeling by the tub, thinking: It's happened, England has gone to war. She had one hand in the tepid water, pushing Lisa's cork boat toward her. She was thinking: Giles, Giles – achingly, uncomprehendingly.

There was a tap on the door, and Sonya's voice asked, 'May I come in?'

Caterina turned her head; she said, 'Of course,' because Lisa's grandmother often attended her bath-time; and as soon as she saw Sonya's face she thought there'd been something strange about her voice.

Sonya said as calmly as she could: 'My darling, I'm afraid it's happened at last. Gabriele has been arrested. They've just telephoned from the hospital. Luigi has gone to the police station to find out what he can.'

Caterina juddered as if her guardian fiend had seized her by the scruff of the neck and was shaking the wits out of her. Her hand in the water bumped and splashed. She latched it onto the rim of the tub beside her other hand and all ten knuckles went white. She screamed something Sonya couldn't understand, and of course the baby began to wail. Then Caterina was on her feet and she wasn't screaming anything, the sound being torn out of her gaping jaws was an animal shriek that went on and on. She gulped more air. She gasped furiously, 'Don't let her drown!' and tore out of the room.

When Luigi hurried back to the house, he found his daughter-in-law striding across and across the stony hall.

'I hate this place!' she howled at him with her fists clenched at her sides, her jaw jutted, her head jerking so her hair flapped across her wet eyes. 'I despise it all, I loathe it all I tell you! Oh God, I'm sorry.'

Caterina went down on her knees on the flag-stones, she hunched over like a beaten animal, she sobbed.

Luigi knelt stiffly down beside her. He hugged her quivering shoulders. 'Oh my poor Caterina, I know, I know. But he'll be all right. We'll get him back, truly we will. Listen, my dear girl. At the police station they wouldn't let me see him, I'm afraid. In fact they told me he'd already been sent down to Rome, which I didn't believe, though very likely he will be in the next day or two.'

Sonya came down the staircase with Lisa, comforted, dried, and in her night-dress.

Caterina lifted her head, she sat back on her heels. She mopped her eyes. 'I'm sorry. It's just all a bit . . . Sorry, sorry.' She sniffed. 'No stiff British upper lips around here, anyway, that's for sure.'

That was how Caterina lost her old, charming, normal world in which you could generally overlook the lack of even decent parodies of justice or liberty, because merry occasions like sister-in-laws' weddings and brothers' visits had gone on happening, hadn't they? – so everything must be going to work out more or less all right. That was the start of her years and years that had the queasy feeling of a dream which she couldn't wake up from but which never quite convinced her either – because for a long time life went on seeming pretty civilised. Caught in the toils of an ancient civility she was, in that family palace of hers, in that equable town, and it made her head feel sick and unreal.

In Caterina D'Alessandria's section of society in that one provincial city, they had long since given up remarking on the insufficient ripple of her hair. As for speculation about when she might produce a son, this now gave way to arch remarks about how it didn't look as if she'd be producing children of either sex for a while, if ever again.

The tender-hearted sighed for how lonely she must be, and sighed for Lisa who would not have her father when she was little, let alone have brothers and sisters. The righteous hoped that Gabriele D'Alessandria might be learning how little good ever came of getting mixed up with Bolsheviks and plotting to overturn the established order of society. The prim trusted that his wife had not been infected by his hare-brained egalitarian notions. They got ready to be philosophical about the effects upon a marriage that a seven-year separation might have. They trusted that *l'inglesina* would let no breath of scandal come near her, and got ready for remorseless prying.

Caterina knew all about that, doing her shopping in stores where they treated her as friendlily as ever, beginning to avoid others where they were colder now and broke into discussion of her as she went out. She was getting to know a lot of new things, pushing Lisa in her pram up to the cathedral and the holm oaks and the ruined citadel, every afternoon, come rain, come shine. At other times suddenly charging out of the house with the startled child in her arms, because it was more than she could endure to be pent up in those protective stone walls any longer. Striding up the hill with her mind screaming: Seven years! Oh my darling, who will you be when they let us be together again? Who will I be, in seven years? Lisa will be nearly nine! And then with her mind abruptly turning rather cool: So this is how it happens! You brace yourself for the catastrophe as best you can, but then it turns out to be worse than you'd expected, because not only does war between Britain and Germany break out and bring a portcullis crashing down across what used to be your small liberty, but right then the bloody Fascists here arrest Gabriele so another portcullis crashes down across your marriage. Well, she supposed that while the world was at it, was occupying itself with her insignificant case, the Fates or who-have-you might as well show they qualified for the job. So you never had time to say a proper goodbye to your brother, what with all the rumours about which frontiers were being closed, what with the scramble to get his bag packed when his washed shirts were still hanging up soaking wet, and the other scramble at the station when Rosalba came dashing through the crowd and stole a kiss. You never said goodbye to the man you were married to at all. Hadn't clapped eyes on him since he'd bicycled to work that morning and ended up in a police van, with hand-cuffs on apparently. All you knew already with terrible clarity was that these utter breakings off, all these impossibilities of picking up the threads and being more sensible next time and loving better next time . . . They were already doing their damaging work, they must be, the pitiless breakings off, the comings of dead silences.

Well, she'd be off up to the cathedral come light rain, not in a downpour. From that September when one of her two countries went to war till the following May when the other one did, so she hadn't only got her husband in gaol and her brother on active service though she hadn't a clue where, she'd then got her husband's brother on active service too, only unfortunately on the other side. But in spattering showers she'd set off as usual, in boots, mackintosh, hat. Haunted by that dot called Ustica off the coast of Sicily where Gabriele was in some foul barracks, in an arid desolation over the glittering sea, with maybe a few carob trees – and she knew the dust would give him asthma, or the dread of the next attack might itself bring it on.

Caterina could *feel* Gabriele fighting to be calm, trying to be calm without the nervous fighting. She saw him during an attack, as she so often had, when she'd held his hands and felt how cold they'd gone. She saw him stand up and grip the back of a chair in that way he had when it was very bad. Stand there fighting to breathe in and, even worse he'd said, fighting to breathe out. Her heart reached blindly toward him, with the love that might make his fight easier, or at least be comfort of some poor kind.

There he was! In a cell with a barred window, standing with his fists clenched on a chair-back, his chest heaving. She touched his weakened pulse, trying not to know about the severe attacks when the spasms came without intermission and if they went on too long might be fatal. She reached out her finger-tips, touched his cold, clammy face. Trying not to know that he might not have enough adrenaline for the injections he'd need, the last lot she'd sent might have been lost or stolen like the parcel before, and as for the prison's so-called hospital! That gasping, that coughing till he was sick. That terrible rasping in his chest which went on and on, till you could *see* the strength going out of him. His eyes. That fighting in his eyes.

From the holm oaks by Arezzo cathedral, Caterina would look away to the far hillsides' vineyards and olive groves, with a handsome villa here and there. Again and again, in her tired, jumpy mind, she'd reckon up who had actually come out on Gabriele's and her side and who had not.

These days she was always alone, with her child, in the public gardens. Alone not because all her neighbours had taken to avoiding her, although some of them had. Alone because often she avoided them – she made herself realise that. And because the young mothers who'd turn out to have been at school with Esmeralda, and the elderly gentlemen walking their spaniels who'd turn out to have been at school with Luigi, would be put off by her restless straying back and forth under the trees day after day, put off by her manifest imprisonment in her own thoughts.

Rosalba D'Alessandria might be nineteen and voluptuous, but she appeared to be made of more principled stuff than some of the dowagers who sniffed at her for being a coquette. When her cousin Gabriele had been arrested, Rosalba had come hurrying round to the house that very day. Heaving bosom, pouting lips, fluttering eyelashes and all, she had launched herself into Caterina's arms. She had fired off questions that nobody could possibly answer. And as autumn became winter, and winter became spring, she had kept coming back to hug Caterina again.

Yes, Caterina would think, Rosalba was all right. But what had happened to all the other lousy friends she'd made? All those girls who'd come to the Rossini ball, when Esmeralda and she went as two devil-may-care young Austro-Hungarian archduchesses. That night when Grazia Damiani refused point-blank to dance with Eduardo, because she'd believed that rumour about Elisabetta Rossini and him – not that one blamed her, every whisper of it was true. Beatrice Castiglia was in Rome, and she never wrote, and she never rang up. Esmeralda's latest letter told of how Beatrice and she had been to a dinner party Cosima gave in honour of the Austrian minister to the Holy See, and they'd been to a reception at Court too, they seemed to be living it up undauntedly.

Right, to hell with Beatrice. Anyone else? Caterina would swerve off her gravel path, because she'd recognised the chatterers sauntering toward her. She'd go striding off nowhere across the grass. She'd swing round and come striding back, because Lisa was drenching her new little shoes in that puddle.

Any true friends? People who might feel there was something not *entirely* right when your husband was locked up for seven years because he'd written some pamphlets advocating the restoration of free speech, the restoration of democracy, airy-fairy fiddle-faddle like that?

Well, Gabriele had been a prisoner for less than a couple of days when she made herself walk down the street to buy bread. She had ordered herself in through the bakery door, but she had not managed to walk very far into the shop, because the three customers already there had fallen quiet on the instant, and had turned to stare at her. She had parted her lips, to say something. 'Good morning', perhaps. But no sound had come out.

The baker's wife had tried to say what she felt, but had failed. She had started several sentences, and had fumbled her simple wrapping of the loaf in her hands, and had flushed, and crossed herself. She had ended by just standing there at her floury counter, gazing with welling eyes at Caterina, who stood before her with a white, haggard face.

The blacksmith, too. He had not been at the Rossinis' fancy dress ball any more than the baker's wife had. But when Sonya and Caterina had gone along to order the new fastenings for the shutters, he had greeted them at the gate of his smithy with: 'I'm sorry to hear about Signor Gabriele, ladies. He's a fine man.' Straight out, just like that. Wiping his grimy hands on his leather apron. 'We need more fellows like him. Men who aren't afraid to think for themselves, and stand up for the rest of us a bit too. Yes, I'll come and take the measurements. New bolts for the doors, the Professor thinks you ought to have as well, does he? Well, I won't say he's not right. Let me show you the sort of things I suggest.'

He had led them back beneath his smoke-blackened arches, into the gloom encumbered with half-made bedsteads and railings and drain-pipes. The forge cast a hot, ruddy glimmer, and you could just make out how the walls were festooned with lanterns and buckets, with scythe-blades and axe-heads, with shapes you couldn't make sense of. In pride of place on a low altar stood the anvil, like a short, squat, horned god.

'Yes, things look peaceful enough now,' the blacksmith had gone on in his tranquil rumble, 'but it only takes a scuffle or two. Then before you've had time to kiss your wife, you've got a nice little riot going on. Then if the Black Brigades or the Carabinieri show up it gets worse. Either way, it's looting soon enough. Now, is this the kind of thing you had in mind? I make the locks and keys myself, too. Here, see.'

7

—∞—

Caterina would twist and turn beneath the holm oaks. She watched the wind blowing regions of sun-brightness and regions of cloud-shadow over the land, for upward of three war years, while the Rome-Berlin Axis held.

Who else was on her side? Count La Marecchia! How could she have forgotten him? La Marecchia who had been born so long ago that he recalled having his childish curls patted by the great Garibaldi himself, a laying on of hands that had caused his parents great joy. La Marecchia who knew her other country and loved it almost as much as he loved his own, and like her was a haunter of the cathedral. She'd meet him climbing laboriously up the wide, handsome steps to the door, leaning on his two silver-headed malacca canes. La Marecchia who understood how often she longed desperately for the Thames estuary and the marshes and the barges' sails. The Essex coast, the Kent coast. Must be those girlhood weekends, with Mummy and Giles – that was why the shipping came back to her, and the sea-light over the tideway. The gammy-legged old count who understood her despair at this Italian police state because he shared it. Surveillance, censorship! she'd rage to him under her breath in the dim cathedral. Spying. People ratting on each other. People fabricating evidence to settle old scores. Christ what a country! Yes, yes, she knew it was the most marvellous country in the world, but it was going through a bad patch.

It would have been good to be able to tell Gabriele about what a fine friend to her Count La Marecchia was being, with his suits that had been the last word in fashion in the days when Queen Victoria in Buckingham Palace and King Umberto and Queen Margherita in the Quirinale had presided over the friendship between their countries. The tapping of the ferrules of those two absurdly elegant sticks of his could be the most inspiriting sound she'd ever heard. Could Gabriele imagine? Well, not as exciting as the Canonbury Square door-bell ringing that mad month when I fell in love with you, my darling. My darling.

My darling. You *will* remember to come back to me, won't you? To your silly Kate Caterina who's all divided in two and all unhappy. Who's worse than that, who's broken into dozens of ugly little pieces and scattered all over the floor, but who loves you with one of the few whole feelings left in her heart. Come back to your Kate Caterina.

In her mind she would tell Gabriele about how one day, sitting beside her in a pew in the cathedral, her ancient friend had recalled putting on a tail-coat and going in excited trepidation to the carnival ball at the Quirinale in – oh, in around 1885. How the honour of accepting a royal invitation had paled into its rightful insignificance when he danced with an English young lady, the Honourable Hermione Double-Barrelled-Something, who was of a loveliness that . . .

Well, he'd quite lost his head, and had spent the rest of the spring planning his summer on the Isle of Wight, because Hermione Something-Terribly-Grand had let fall that Papa always raced his schooner at Cowes Week. La Marecchia's tales of Anglo-Italian sympathy were generally told with resolutely cheering-up intentions, and this one finished with the then youthful Tuscan aristocrat's multiple infatuations at Cowes that long ago summer. His command of the language had been just about adequate when it came to dining out – but for yachting! His stay-sails were all mizzens and his tacks were all gybes, but he was blissfully beguiled by one English rose after another, and had just resolved to pass the rest of his life in a house overlooking the Solent when his money ran out.

Caterina longed to tell Gabriele about that hideous afternoon when she heard the Duce on the radio proclaiming thunderously how necessary it was that, after the lapse of two thousand years, perfidious Albion should once more feel how hard the iron Roman heel could be.

Her head in a sick whirl of panic, with one beseeching glance of her wild eyes she had thrust Lisa into Sonya's arms and had rushed out of the house. Away! Physical exertion, solitude!

Without thinking where she was going, she went striding uphill, blind to the heads that turned to stare at her. Oh my darling, her mind cried, do you remember our jokes about the Romans in Britain and how decent of them it was to civilise the

simple folk there a little, as well as murdering a fair number of
them? But this! An Axis attack across the Channel! Next thing
we'll have Mussolini parading down Whitehall with a guard of
Bersaglieri, that seems to be the plan now.

The cathedral was a sanctuary. Caterina's stride was so rapid
and her thoughts were so disordered that she did not notice the
other figure on the wide steps.

But he recognised her, and leaning on his silver-mounted
canes he called: 'Signora Caterina! My dear young lady, is this
the way you treat an old friend? Particularly, I shall make so
bold as to add, at a time when the likes of you and I should
be making a point of being nice to one another.'

Caterina came toward him, making herself tread calmly. 'Oh,
I'm so sorry, Count. Yes, you and I . . .' Suddenly, tears were in
her eyes.

Wearing a creamy white suit with a gold watch-chain and
a minute but pavonian bow-tie, La Marecchia straightened
himself as far as his stoop would allow. He gave her agitation a
smile of grandfatherly affection, even of approval. He resumed
his halting ascent.

'You and I, and a few other contemptibles,' he echoed her
with urbane equanimity. 'Yes, I think we may be fairly certain
that if Mazzini and Garibaldi could see their country this
summer they would be ashamed. But all is not lost. The first
thing to remember is that when our public life stinks, our private
life may not – though the two are connected. Unfortunately, the
second thing to remember is that the calamity is our fault as well
as that of those we despise. Now, my young friend, when I have
heaved my carcass as far as the side door, let us go and sit down
in a pew together.'

Caterina could tell Gabriele stories like that, in her mind. She
could cry out her fears to him too. If the Nazi-Fascists win this
war, what then? When there are German and Austrian and
Italian satraps and their local flunkeys calling the shots from
Cairo to Copenhagen and from Kiev to Cardiff. No free England
for us to escape to. And I know you, my brave Gabriele, you'll
never give in. You'll die in one of their concentration camps and
I'll die in another, that's what we've got to look forward to.

That sort of howl was simplicity itself. When it came to

wailing to him that she was no earthly good without him, too – that was heartfelt enough, and it was a form of self-contempt that she could face up to. Sitting in the cathedral, she would weep that he was so confident and clear-headed, she'd been all right when she had his strength at her side, but she wasn't all right now.

What Caterina was hopeless at was whispering to her husband the truth about Esmeralda, who was just a chic Fascist consort these days, that was all there was to say about *her*.

When Esmeralda had declined to cut short her honeymoon merely because her brother had been arrested, her father's mouth had hardened in recognition of some truth he had already known, and her mother had gone down to the Santissima Annunziata with a shuttered look in her eyes to pray. As for Caterina, at first she'd been too distraught to comprehend that Esmeralda did not intend to rally round the family until it would not inconvenience her to do so; she had held the telephone to her ear and listened to the hedonistic twitter in a daze of wretchedness. Oh, when they were all in Rome once more, dear Galeazzo Ciano would advise them as to what line to take. In the meanwhile, Caterina was to keep her spirits up, she was to play this very coolly indeed . . .

But when she'd visited the flat by the Spanish Steps for a week, and the next year when she was there over Easter and again in the summer, Caterina tortured herself with dread that the deep, real Esmeralda had never existed or had died. Those nights in her first years in Tuscany when they'd sat up late, the musing in harmony and the smiling over things – had she invented them? And even that night before Esmeralda's wedding . . . 'I think I ought to say sorry to you. You forgive me my hellishness, don't you?' No, she hadn't imagined that! 'I seem to have to keep singing my jingles and dancing my jigs in order to exist at all, and even then half the time I'm so utterly hollow I could weep for the deathliness of it.' That was the true Esmeralda; that was her voice. 'Kate Caterina. Both, neither . . . I'll be as loyal as the grave . . .' But far worse was when she faced up to how well Esmeralda and she got on together when they were merely, ceaselessly, jazzily play-acting; when they were two fairly despicable butterflies. Sallying gaily forth to the opera. Sallying forth to a reception at the Department of Justice because it might be possible to interest Under Secretary This or Under Secretary That in Gabriele's case.

Back in Arezzo, Caterina would sit miserably in the cathedral, marvelling at her old London life which would only ever be memory, marvelling at her new Rome life which was recurrently present but which she contrived to believe was unreal, was not essentially her at all. What was it Gaetano had said? 'You don't have to spend any more time in Rome with them than you want to . . .' A priest might go to his confessional in the tenebrous aisle where only a lamp on a shrine glimmered, or a man and wife might rise from their knees and cross themselves and go out. Lisa would be exploring this way or that among the chairs and the tombs, or sitting beside her mother swinging her legs and wanting to be told a story. And icy tremors would course up Caterina's nape into her brain.

So this was what it came down to. A well-shaken martini; a new dress paid for by Esmeralda, in other words by Carlo; a deferential chauffeur who drove you to an ambassadorial gala where they paid you compliments. Afterward, you denied that scene, you reduced it to a charade. That wasn't the real you. The deep-down you was brooding here now. She was who must be judged, you insisted, such was your hypocrisy.

Yes, but: 'Kate Caterina . . . Now I have you.' Though since Esmeralda had been married she'd never spoken like that, never given you that candid gaze. Or was it that you'd never made that voice and that gaze possible for her?

Seeing her hands writhing in her lap, Caterina would clench them into a double fist. She'd clamp her knees together as hard as she could, she'd bow her head.

8

In those years when Gabriele was a prisoner on Ustica, those three summers and three winters when Caterina's two countries were at war against each other, all day she would long for her night solitude upstairs. She would long for it and dread it at the same time. So often, her days were given over to habit, that deadening second nature, which had second-order contentments that had to be good enough to be getting along with, things such as playing silly games with Lisa. But those attic nights, Caterina was in amongst the cruelties and enchantments of her first nature.

She would tuck Lisa up in her cot, being careful not to think too vividly about the happy evenings when Gabriele had been there at his daughter's bedtime. She'd sing to her. Old sailors' songs, often, because her mother had come of a Merchant Navy family, so Caterina had sea shanties in her blood, 'Spanish Ladies' and 'Shenandoah'. Or she might sing 'Donkey Riding', because Lisa went through months when she always wanted to hear that one.

> Were you ever in Quebec
> Stowing timber on the deck?
> Where there's a King with a golden crown
> Riding on a donkey.
> Hey! ho! away we go
> Donkey riding, donkey riding.
> Hey! ho! away we go,
> Riding on a donkey.

Lancashire ships, Mummy had said, trading to the Americas. And the great thing about songs with a refrain was that Lisa didn't mind how often you sang her the same words.

> Were you ever off the Horn
> Where it's always fine and warm,

> And seen the lion and the unicorn
> Riding on a donkey?
> Hey! ho! away we go . . .

That ditty was nonsensical enough already, but some nights
Caterina mixed in so much rhythmical craziness of her own
that she found she'd invented whole new verses and only the
original tune remained.

When Lisa was practically asleep, her mother went through
into her sitting-room, still lingering, listening in case she cried.
But usually Lisa did not cry. And then there was nothing else for
it but to face up to her thinking. She could tidy things away for
a few minutes. She could pick up a book, knowing she'd only
manage to read a couple of pages. But then there'd be nothing
else for it.

The first time Caterina attempted to write Gabriele a letter,
she tried and tried to convey even a shadow of all that was in her
heart, and after twenty minutes she had scrumpled up several
sheets of paper and was in tears. In the end she wrote him a
very short letter, giving him the family's news. It was mainly
about an ivory bracelet of Sonya's to which Lisa had become
inordinately attached, and how she toted it everywhere with
her, and was always playing with it, and became distraught
whenever it was mislaid, which it frequently was. Yesterday,
they'd finally found it in the watering-can.

She signed her letter, 'With love from Kate Caterina', in
the simplest way. It was not quite the 'I am all right, I
hope you are all right too' of children's missives, but it
wasn't far off it. Gabriele's letters home were as steadfastly
lighthearted as his wife's and his mother's to him. Yes, the
winter clothes had arrived. Thank you! Wonderful! What was
more, a friendly guard had got them some apples to supplement
their ghastly rations. Could Caterina imagine? One whole apple,
he'd devoured! After months of no fresh fruit, no fresh anything.
The exquisite, painful pleasure to his taste-buds, honestly he'd
thought his mouth was going mad.

Then the urge to make something *grow*, make something
flourish, had been irresistible. So he'd got hold of a discarded
tin and he'd filled it with earth and he'd planted his apple

pips – after first eating the core, you bet! What was more, he had another apple, which with great strength of mind he was saving to eat tomorrow, and one way and another, after the first months which hadn't been a lot of fun, now it looked like becoming possible to get a little fresh food sometimes.

The following summer, Gabriele wrote that his apple tree was all of three centimetres high now, and one day he was going to plant it in the garden at home.

In all his letters, he never wrote about the hardships, the injustices, the squalor – not even in the bland terms which the censors would have passed. He never wrote either about the Communists setting up their iron Party discipline, complete with expulsions, even in captivity. Not that his Socialists were guiltless, though they weren't quite so blinkered. Not a line about the ideological rule imposed on men whom you'd think might have lost enough freedom for the time being.

News of the family, please, that was what he wanted, and news of the neighbours too. Life, he wanted – real, outside, free life. How was old Orazio's sciatica? Good about Immacolata's cat having kittens, and their keeping the prettiest, the little tortoise-shell one, for Lisa.

So Caterina wrote back to him about Edoardo, who these days was with the occupation forces in south-eastern France, and judging by his letters was having a decidedly merry war, in which the excellence of the Provencal wines and the ups and downs of his battalion's football team featured prominently – as did Susanne, and Monique, and Delphine, and Juliette. Naturally, he only recounted half this nonsense in order to shock his mother. But couldn't Gabriele just *see* that disgraceful young brother of his lounging around the Nice quays and cafés in his beautifully cut uniform, chatting up any pretty girl who'd listen to his execrable French?

Some of what Caterina could not put in her letters found its way into the night writings she'd begun on the eve of Esmeralda's wedding.

She could write to Gabriele about Rosalba, whose charms and flirtatiousness were quite unimpaired by the war he would be pleased to hear, and who was being wonderfully loyal to her. Coming round to the house week after week. Accompanying her

shopping sometimes, or on her walks with Lisa – when her pres-
ence could give an exceedingly welcome sense of protectedness.
Yes, even to have the frail defence of curvacious, giggling
Rosalba walking at your side.

Caterina went that far, but no further. She never wrote to
Gabriele that the trouble about going for a stroll with Lisa
was that the child was utterly fearless, and would trot up to
anybody to say hello, and to discover if they felt like playing
with her or talking to her. And Caterina never knew if the
people her daughter set about making friends with were going
to be pleasant in return or not.

It was impossible for her to tell her husband about the time
when in the Far East the Japanese were being victorious in battle
after battle, and in the market-place here a man had rounded on
her, had shouted in her face that the British didn't always have
it their own way, and spat at her feet. Caterina had turned tail.
Her heart juddering and tears in her eyes, she'd gone stumbling
away through the stalls, dragging Lisa along, who had started to
whimper naturally enough, and then at the end of her mother's
arm had begun a shrieking, clawing fight to break free. Caterina
had been aware of growling voices, and faces that stared, and
a shouted argument that seemed to be breaking out behind her
but she wasn't going to hang around to hear who thought
what.

She couldn't write to Gabriele about the draper, either. Even
without the censorship, these were moments she could never
have described to him, so as not to give his imagination vile
scenes to work on. So these episodes ended up in her notebooks.
When he was free again, he could know everything.

These days, she was trying to school herself to be brave.
Making herself go back to the market the following Saturday,
instead of letting it be Sonya's turn. Things like that. So despite
her having become pretty certain the draper was such a believer
in the government of his country that he loathed and despised
her, she forced herself to go into his shop to ask about the new
kitchen curtains, though on this occasion she allowed herself to
leave her little daughter at home.

A couple of nights previously, British torpedo bombers,
flying from the aircraft carrier *Illustrious* in the Ionian, had

made a successful strike against the Italian fleet in Taranto harbour.

Whether the sinking of one battleship and the bad damaging of two others as well as of two cruisers came into it or not, the instant the draper saw Caterina come in through his door, he broke off whatever he'd been saying to his apprentice. He spluttered something obscene. He drew himself up to his full height, and roaring the Fascist greeting with all the force of his lungs he stabbed his right hand up and forward. Taken aback, but swiftly compliant, his apprentice did the same.

Caterina went white and began to tremble, but she knew what she had to do. Wobblingly she raised her right arm to return the salute. Her open palm wavered up till her fingers were prodding the air in the direction of the crucifix that the draper had hanging beside his calendar. Gasping slightly, she opened and closed her lips several times, like a fish.

When the master of the situation considered his triumph complete, he lowered his arm. Curtly he informed *l'inglesina* that she was no longer welcome in his shop.

9

—◆◆◆—

Often at night Caterina didn't write a line. Other times she went at it hell-for-leather, a page, three pages, five, sometimes tearing them out afterward and sometimes not. She'd smile to think that she was just as bad as Luigi with his heaps of God-awful depressing notes. Just as bad as Gabriele too, whose mind was always putting the record straight, putting events in just the right light.

Or perhaps she was a bit different from them, Caterina liked to think, because hers wasn't a setting of anything straight. Hers was more a setting down of unstraightened crookednesses. She tried to keep it like that, out of dogged love for Esmeralda. In honour of their nocturnal talks when no mere conclusion had ever been arrived at thank heavens, but their minds had adventured gaily, spiritedly – or so it had seemed at the time. And of course into her notebooks went all her romantic visions of Giles, who to her was eternally the figure of blithe innocence, and Gabriele who was her heroic fighter for justice. Her idealisations of those two straightforward, vanished men ensured that her imagination could go on adoring them inordinately.

Any of Caterina's inspirations might set her off, and then she'd be away, glancing up at her shabby furniture in that attic, bowing her head in the lamplight once more and scrawling pell-mell about her discovery of Leopardi's poetry and what an unschoolmasterish guide Luigi had turned out to be. Only then she'd veer off at a tangent, all about how if the people of Shakespeare and the people of Leopardi were really going to continue murdering each other in great quantities it would be more than she cared to get mixed up in. She'd take Lisa and she'd bolt – far, far away. To New Zealand, to Chile . . . Must be possible to get a job of some sort. Yes, she'd start by contriving to escape to Spain, which so far had had the wit to stay at peace, and then – from one of the Atlantic ports . . . Far enough away to get the sight of European civil butchery out of her eyes. Yes, Lisa could wait for her father by the

Pacific perfectly well. The map of South America showed its west coast enticingly peppered with islands. Mountains draped with clouds, azure gulfs – what was it she'd read? Old Spanish towns with cupolas, with miradors. Orange groves . . . Maybe it wasn't like that at all. But it might be.

Or it would be her discoveries in Venice, and what an irresistible companion Gaetano Da Durante was. Yes, she'd been back there with him, seeking out Tiepolo canvases and Tiepolo ceilings – only they'd had to be forever sitting down to feasts of fish and wine, which she'd found splendid the first couple of times, but on a regular basis a little debilitating. Because it transpired that just around the corner from every Tiepolo painting in town there was invariably a secluded eating-house where Gaetano happened to be an old friend of the proprietor, and where the squid stew and polenta were incomparable, or they had a manner of baking a big bass which Caterina absolutely must try.

She wrote about the day when Gaetano had escorted her for what felt like miles, on foot, to Sant'Alvise. An unglamorous, mediaeval church. No marble to speak of. They had gone in. A few lamps gave enough glimmer to show how shabby the place was, without being much help when it came to making out the pictures.

Caterina had stood beside him in the gloom, listening to him wheeze as he told her that Tiepolo hadn't only been the most brilliant painter of light and colour of his age and with a genius for composition. He'd also been an incisive portrayer of imperial dominion. Now, if this torch would oblige them by working; and if she'd come a yard or two this way, taking care not to trip over the broken step . . .

A canvas with all the pomp and brutality of the Romans running that colony of theirs in the Near East a couple of millennia ago. With a sunlit sky and ragged trees. With Christ fallen under the weight of the cross He was carrying.

Look at the eagle and the trumpet, Gaetano had said, wielding his flashlight. All the panoply. Look at that flag with SPQR, Caterina, and that poor devil of a local mystic they're going publicly to torture to death. Look at the muscular, dominant men who will do nothing good, and those muscular, unaware horses, and the pensive, weak men who won't do any good either. Look at the thieves they're going to torture to death at the same time. Well, I dare say their administration had a lot of trouble from thieves.

From Caterina's night scribblings at her desk at her attic window, in those first years of the new war, you got quite a full picture of Gaetano Da Durante, though it was just as fragmented as all her other portraits. Broken up with accounts of Sonya's and her endless struggles to find more or less safe homes for children evacuated from industrial cities after the British bombing raids – children who were already orphans, some of them. Those two women were doing a lot of work for the Red Cross. Broken up by her own wails of anxiety because she didn't know if the house in Canonbury Square was a heap of rubble now. Didn't know in which of the British armies in which continent Giles was fighting, if he was still alive.

You got dozens of images of Sonya, too. Sonya in the empty church of the Santissima Annunziata where Caterina would find her, kneeling before the beautiful mediaeval Mother of God. Kneeling before the valiant silver angels and the phoenix rising up on its golden wings. Sonya in the drawing-room with a tin of yellow bees' wax, polishing the north German desk that had come from her old family home. That desk still had her father's penknife in one of its pigeon-holes. Even his spectacles, which somehow she had been unable to throw away. Sonya talking softly about how when she was still a girl she had fallen in love with the church music of the great German and Italian composers. Yes, they were the sung masses that had first brought her to Italy, lay behind her meeting the man she married. Then to embrace the Church of Rome had been the most natural thing in the world, part and parcel of her happy embracing of Italy. Simply part of her growing up, too. In her twenties, comprehending better her mind's readiness to find metaphysics rational and holiness natural.

Right from the start of the new war, Caterina and Sonya had resolved that, whatever horrors the two countries of their births perpetrated, they were going to be at war against each other in the most loyal and loving way two women had ever achieved. It was not straightforward though, sitting together at the kitchen table that summer of 1940 listening to reports of the fighting in the Dunkirk perimeter. Later that summer, listening to reports of the Battle of Britain.

Caterina wrote about Sonya's light blue eyes which would look back into hers with a brave, intolerable anguish there was nothing you could do about. Her eyes that knew about the German Army preparations for an assault across the Channel. Her eyes that said: Your people, and mine. This, again.

Caterina wrote about hearing Churchill declare that, if an invasion came, that island was going to be defended, whatever the cost. They would fight on the beaches, they would fight on the landing grounds, they would fight in the fields and in the streets, they would fight in the hills, they would never surrender. She wrote flashes of her sudden desperate longing to be there, however ineffective her help in the defence might be. How she sensed her kinship with all the British people that the war had caught dotted about the world, who now like her must be haunted by the Straits and the English coast, and must be consumed like her by this stubborn, unreasoning knowledge that they ought to be there. Tribal, it must be, she supposed.

Her handwriting was never sedate and when she was passionate it went haywire. She scribbled about Dover castle, about Gabriele and she sailing away on honeymoon, and her written words looked as if they were playing leap-frog with one another and turning somersaults. Why had she never made the opportunity to go back? And now . . . The grey castle, the cliffs. The jackdaws and gulls. How did it go? 'This chalky bourne', yes that was right. Then, 'the shrill-gorged lark' and 'the murmuring surge'.

How stupid she was in her emotions! Happy enough in her marriage – till they threw her husband into gaol and on the instant he became nebulous, a skein of wisps in her head. Happy enough to leave England and live in Italy – till a hostile and victorious army reached the Pas de Calais. Shakespeare must have meant rock samphire, in that line about the fellow halfway down the cliff gathering the stuff. Not the samphire that grew on mud shoals and needed to be covered and uncovered by the tide at nice regular intervals. There you were – those childhood weekends on the Thames estuary marshes had taught her something.

'We shall fight on the beaches.' She was getting muddled. Yes, but there were a few things she knew as clear as all hell. About invasions, for example. Only they too made mincemeat of her mental coherence.

'The fishermen that walk upon the beach . . .' She could see them! The little harbour town, the ships, the dinghies. WHERE WHERE WHERE was Giles?

All that, Caterina could write. All those incoherent outbursts – Gabriele would understand them all right. Because when he was free, she was going to say to him – say in her most offhand voice, of course, because it wouldn't matter a bit: Darling, if you want to know the type of nonsense I've been thinking. If you want to know the nonsense woman I've become . . .

What was less easy was to record all her partying with Gabriele's enemies while he was in prison. Still, at long last she was making herself write it down. How she had continued going to Rome sometimes, to stay in the flat near the Spanish Steps. What an end-of-empire style of life Esmeralda and Carlo were conducting, and how she had begun to delight in it too when she became the other flashy young woman whom the Honourable Manzari occasionally escorted about the capital from this reception to that. How she had come to admire his tact and his worldly shrewdness more and more, she'd warmed to what often seemed his real kindness to her, though of course she hadn't a clue how sincere he was, whether he really liked her or was merely behaving courteously.

Never in her life had honesty been so painful, but she forced herself to write these things down, keeping at the back of her mind that she might tear these pages out before Gabriele came home. She wrote how sinisterly easy it was, to get to like men who were your other country's enemies and your husband's enemies. What a relief it was, that they let you live between theatres and dinner parties. What a blessing they were, these men and women who knew how to make you live at this level of jokes and flattery, of anecdotes and flirtatiousness. Sinisterly easy, too, to realise there was no earthly point in kicking up a fuss. Why, if she ever *did* stop playing the game, ever did speak up for herself, speak honestly . . . She could imagine the smiles of pity for her inability to behave adroitly. Yes, it was easy to decide your duty was to perform any antics that might ensure your daughter's safety. Easy to enjoy the fashionable society, laugh at the witty remarks, sip the champagne. It wasn't as if any of her new acquaintances ever said anything disagreeable to her, after all. She didn't appear to be worthy of anyone's enmity.

But the funny thing was – could Gabriele imagine? The ridiculous thing was, that in this collision of the Axis and the Allies, Caterina honestly didn't think Esmeralda gave much of a damn about which empires ended up by falling and which remained totteringly on their feet. It was all fine by her, so long as she was allowed to go on living the moment with this terrific zest of hers. She always showed up in Tuscany with a spring in her step and vivacious eyes, and then a party invariably burst into life. Yes, Gabriele would be able to imagine the readiness of the city's upper classes to return to being habitués of the Palazzo D'Alessandria the moment the powerful Carlo Manzari and his glamorous consort set foot in the place.

Caterina made herself go on. What was so extraordinarily exciting, she wrote, was the freedom with which she'd glide through parties in Rome or in Tuscany at which all the guests politely pretended to believe she was just as much one of themselves as everyone else was. It was like attending a masked ball, in wonderful wicked old Venice in Tiepolo's time. Yes, these parties were masquerades! She heard snatches of pompous talk about 'Italy's moment' and 'the destiny of the nation', but she drifted through the throngs as if wearing a mask that made her real soul enchantedly secret. No – it was more that the convention was that everyone pretended their masks hid them.

'Going into the Sudan . . .' 'Going into Tunisia . . .' 'Our protectorates in the Balkans . . .' But what could they do to her, who had Carlo Manzari as her relative, as her friend? They couldn't touch her. She wore an invisible mask which made a delicious mockery of who she was, gave her the liberty of that, gave her the licence of that.

Had she remembered to write down for Gabriele that Carlo

and Esmeralda were not in love, precisely? That phrase gave far too wholesome an impression. But since their struck-by-lightning engagement when they'd still been complete strangers to one another, and since that wedding with its atmosphere of effortlessly triumphant hypocrisies and their snobbish month at the Hotel des Bains, there'd been ignited between those two born sybarites a – she didn't know what – a sensual complicity, or . . . Well, they were rejoicing in the carnal all right, those two. No, she hadn't yet worked out whether either or both of them occasionally went after fresh game.

One night Caterina imagined she was dead and Gabriele came home at last. She had become a spirit and she stood up from the desk where she had been writing. So vividly, his approach was alive to her! She withdrew to one side, because that was Gabriele's tread on the stair, coming up calmly. Now he was opening the door.

Breathless, unable to cry out to him, unable to move her ghostly limbs or make him see her, Caterina watched Gabriele come into the attic flat where once he had lived with his young wife. He was thin and pale; he wore the suit he had been arrested in, which was shapeless and stained now. He looked around, wonderingly, in the night stillness and quiet. His gaze went through the ghost and past her, she wasn't there, she wasn't alive.

She saw him cross over to the desk that they had always shared, see the bundle of her war writings lying there. She saw him touch it meditatively with his finger-tips. He drew up the chair, he sat down to read in the lamplight.

Caterina stood in her death, in her agony of love for him, tears streaming down her cheeks.

He looked up from the written pages, musingly.

10

—⚏—

One of the advantages of everybody blacking out their windows, one of the positive merits of war time, Caterina reckoned, was that in cities you got practically as brilliant a panoply of heavenly bodies as you got in the countryside. For her nocturnal meditations, often she did not black out her attic windows as the regulations said you ought to, but she did not switch on her lamp either. With her shutters wide, with her curtains drawn back, with the sky more or less radiant depending on the moon, she would kick off her shoes and sit on the sofa, knees up, arms hugging them. In the dim effulgence, where the pieces of furniture were familiar dusky shapes and the windows were silvery squares.

Naturally, like this she couldn't write anything. In those war vigils, nine-tenths of her night mind's swooping and darting thoughts left no traces. But she was most free at these times.

The propitious nights were when Caterina's imagination never doubted that her early, happy times in Italy were the true life, and the war was just an inane aberration that must soon be overcome. The gaiety and the brilliance she'd discovered – how they came back to her! They were everybody's true heritage and they were hers as well.

There'd been that month when she was with Gabriele at Ca' Santa Chiara. Just the two of them – and she'd been pregnant, though only they two knew that then. Heavens, how they'd gloried in the heat of those summer days! They got up early each morning, because the dewy freshness and the crystalline light were good. They put on their flimsiest clothes, they took their coffee out into the garden where the white fluff was drifting off the thistles.

Later in the morning there was just the paradisaical country basking stupefied beneath that magnificent sun. On the opposite hillside, in the pasture the white cattle drowsed in the shade of the oak trees. Gabriele and she had lazed in the garden practically naked, keeping a vague eye open lest Signor Gervasio

or Signora Maria took it into their heads to come down the track
for some reason. They raided Luigi's bookcases for poets. They
spread a rug in the shade of a lime tree, which was in flower
and smelled headily sweet.

That sensuality and that lightheartedness – they'd been worth
living, all right. And now for a minute she had seemed to possess
them again, as if there'd been an outburst of generosity in the
spirit of the world, or a beneficent trigger in her brain, or . . . !
She didn't know. And of course the past was worth no more
than the present, she'd been as moribund with habit and as
mired in the phenomenal then as now. Or had she not *always*
been? And if in time past or in time to come for a blessed
moment of freedom her imagination brought her a truth beyond
time, a truth and beauty that were momentary and endless . . .
Was that possible? That was what she'd live and die for if she
could. But were real hints of that vouchsafed her, or was it just
another consolatory fantasy the mind came up with?

Alas it was incontrovertible that there were these grotesque
apparitions now, the jumped-up bureaucrats and the shouting
militiamen. But Caterina banished them from her mind by
summoning back a dinner party in Cosima's palace near the
Pantheon. She'd only been married a few months, and with
the excuse of attempting to lighten her English darkness a bit
Gaetano Da Durante had wanted to see if he could get her
to remember whether it was the invading war-lord Alaric, or
perhaps it had been Odovocar, or possibly Attila, that Pope Leo
the Great had gone out to face at the gates. Well, she was *almost*
certain it had been the heroic Leo, and that Gregory the Great
had been great in some other way. At any rate, then Gaetano
made them all laugh with his accounts of Popes who'd been
statesmen and patrons of the arts and fornicators; other Popes
who'd been peculators and murderers and fornicators; a third
lot of Popes who'd been place-men, such nonentities that no
one had ever noticed whether they'd been much in the way of
peculators and fornicators or not.

Of course, he hadn't said it exactly like that, but he'd made
it pretty clear all the same. Cosima had primly ordered him to
stop – which he hadn't. Or he'd only stopped for five seconds
while he smiled at her and blinked at her with his round face

of an ageing, insubordinate cherub, and the chandelier-shimmer gleamed on his bald frontal bone behind which his archive of art historical lore was packed, and all you could hear when his chuckle and her reprimand died away was his chest wheezing.

Those had been the evenings! Her new family to discover, and her new civilisation to discover, and getting hopelessly muddled up between the Saracen invasions and the Magyar ones. Gaetano had decided boisterously that she was *never* going to recall with any precision the Norman army that had sacked Rome in ten-eighty-something, or the German and Spanish army that had done so in fifteen-twenty-something, with horrifying atrocities on both occasions. But there'd been some pretty dashing Roman women who might be to Caterina's taste, he reckoned – though of course they'd often had to act through men, make intelligent use of their men.

So Gaetano had launched into the story of Marozia, who'd been the daughter of a noble family ten centuries ago. She'd been the mistress of one Pope, and then the mother of another, and one of her other sons had been made Prince of Rome, and in due course she'd snaffled the Papacy yet again, for a grandson of hers this time. Didn't Caterina think the Lady Marozia would have been worth watching while she played her cards? Yes, Gaetano, oh yes! she'd wanted to cry out. Only she'd had Cosima interrupting with severe piety on her other side.

The blessing of imagination meant that Caterina could lose herself in stories from all over the war. So when the British empire in the Far East was falling, she passionately imagined young women much like herself kissing their husbands goodbye. Trying to get away with their children from Shanghai or from Sarawak or from wherever the defeats had loomed. Trying to get south down the Malay States on a truck, get on the last ships out of Singapore. It still haunted her, how tenuous were the chances that had her living the life she *was* living and not another. It haunted her, not to know all those individual far-flung fates, and not to know whether here in Tuscany she was going to be luckier or less lucky.

Then a letter from Giles in Cairo wound its way to her, thanks to the Red Cross in Geneva. Caterina started to cry while she was still reading it, from the shock of her joy that he was still alive and her fears for him fighting in Africa. Her confused sadness for her brother and for herself, and her proud love for him, made her weep so tempestuously that when Sonya found her she was still sitting on the oak chest in the hall where the postman always left the mail, and she still hadn't realised that the letter had taken more than a year to reach her.

Several sentences had been blacked out by British military censors. Conceivably they had alluded to the possibility of the recipient (and her whole country) being liberated by the writer (and his whole army) one fine day, if only matters in Africa could first be satisfactorily concluded. At all events, plenty of lighthearted chat for 'my darling old Kate' remained. There was a bit toward the end about: 'Give all the family my love, especially the irresistible Rosalba please'. There was: 'Tell Edoardo to remember to duck'. After that, whenever you saw Caterina with anxiety in her eyes, but at the same time with a defenceless half-smile of absolute love on her lips, you could be pretty sure her spirit was with Giles in North Africa, and she was waiting for him to show up and rescue her.

Unfortunately, nights came when the curse of imagination meant that she could hover over others' spirits, but she could make nothing of herself.

She seemed to be too many different and self-contradictory people with no connections between them, that was the problem. Or she was too many insubstantial figments, none of whom convinced her as being a real person. She was the Kate Caterina who had spent the first twenty-two years of her life in a far-away land, and often felt she'd stepped out of her girlhood as simply as she stepped out of a dress, only then 'Oranges and Lemons' would bring the stupid tears prickling behind her eyes. She was the Kate Caterina who was usually contented enough when she was playing with Lisa, or trying to teach her things – until all her imaginings of the whole war being fought made her feel cut off from the child with her limited comprehensions, the child whose innocence she tried to protect from a lot of horrible imaginings. She was the Kate Caterina whose husband the Fascists had gaoled, but who with apparently quite instinctive amorality when she was in Rome led a fashionable life among Fascist grandees.

She would stray downstairs and wander about the deserted rooms of the Palazzo D'Alessandria like a cooped-up ghost, turning on a lamp here, turning one off there, seeing herself as she passed one of the tall, ornate looking-glasses. Her head would start to ache. She would drop into one of the gilded and tasselled chairs, with her finger-tips pressed to her temples. The terrible half-truth that desire is vain because it is satisfied, that was what she couldn't get past. Her girlhood with Giles, her falling in love with Gabriele, her discovery of Italy, her friendship with Esmeralda: it was all idolatry; they were all graven images she'd been distracted by and which still stopped her in her tracks. Oh, naturally, in her mind she could map this wilderness of her experience as minutely and as bitterly as she fancied, she'd tell herself. She could appease her intellectual conceit like that if she wanted to. But as for redeeming all her delusory time, the whole parade of her heart's flutterings and her brain's murky glimpses . . . No doubt that was impossible, that was only ever self-satisfying fraudulence, she'd think in despair.

Nights came when Caterina was shut into that Arezzo eyrie, with Lisa asleep, and it seemed to her in the long silence that evil, or truth, was waiting all around her consciousness, waiting in the darkness just outside her small lit mind, just as she was waiting nervously for whatever might be going to happen to her daughter and her in that particular town, and wasn't likely to be good. Waiting, and listening to the endless rumours from Rome, which were always about a possible coup d'état and were always only rumours.

The war was bigger than Europe now, there wasn't an ocean you couldn't be torpedoed in. The war was a machine as big as the globe, with its cogs that were crimes and its levers that were hopes and its pistons that were delusions, and everywhere the machine was clanking out its tortures and griefs.

She could lean on the window sill, and it would be out there in the night air, in all things under the stars. It. Everywhere. It was all around her consciousness, waiting to come in.

One thing the war with its many voices had already whispered to Caterina was that the truth – the loathsome truth, that she'd reckoned to go on hiding from herself – would in the end be wrung out of her by some small, cruel, unmerited catastrophe, or merely a mistake, or the flip of a coin. Maybe something springing from what had appeared an insignificant enough failing, like having no head for heights or always being sea-sick. Or something like having been born where and when you were, or having married the person you'd married.

Caterina could order herself to think what she called sensibly. All the same, often after five minutes she was staring at nothingness with wide, dark amber eyes under her fair eyebrows and lashes. Because with life lapsing from her second after second, the nothingness of people and times was what she saw. The nothingness of the man she'd married, above all . . . Till the more she brought him to mind, the more chimerical he seemed and the more chimerical their ever having been in love seemed. They were hopelessly ill-suited to one another; it had been a bush fire of sensuality and nothing more; being in love had been an *ignis fatuus* that she'd imagined and that had led her astray, had beguiled her this far and then had vanished . . . In panic, she'd convince herself of all that.

She would not despair. Doggedly she'd set to work to bring Gabriele back to their real life with her words, redeem him out of this shadowiness he'd fallen into. Her words were going to have to be a charm. She'd charm him back to her.

My darling, do you remember our bedroom at Ninfa those hot nights, with the windows wide, with only the mosquito netting between us and the scents of the garden, how we made love with the river splashing below? The difference from Sardinian nights offshore, because when you've been swimming in a river your skin feels and tastes and smells quite different from when you've been swimming in the sea. Yes, the noise of the waterfall such that we couldn't hear the night birds, and the love-making good, and the moonlight good, and the lying afterward drifting in and out of sleep, and the waking with the river's voice still there.

Caterina could bring the past back, but often these nights it didn't come back freely and transport her, because what she also brought back was the knowledge of how evanescent it had been. The wretched thing was that now she lived those moments with more intense clarity than she had then, when she'd been happy-go-lucky and thoughtless. And it was all artificial now, the intensity. She regained, but she lost too. She was made to know how lost her lit-up times were, and how lost she was, left with just her images.

Late one war night, she forgot battles in North Africa between the British and the Italians, she forgot prisons on Tyrrhenian islands. Seconds passed, a minute. Perhaps two, or three. Caterina sat still, wrapped in her old expectancy, the world coming to life in her with its ancient innocent becoming.

Experience couldn't ever be limited and it couldn't ever be complete. She knew that now, with great humbleness and utmost simplicity. In the chamber of her consciousness she seemed to see hanging tall swags of the most gossamery curtains there'd ever been, or maybe mosquito netting was what they were, and these trembling veils of gauze caught even the ghostliest notions the world wafted her way.

She waited, with her face softened, all anxiety smoothed away, her eyes alert. Stories came, and images. A Pacific seaboard of forested mountains, with islands, trading schooners. An old Spanish port, all miradors and palm trees. Churches in orange groves . . .

Caterina was yanked back to Gabriele's and her attic, aghast at how happily she fell to imagining a life without him.

11

—m—

Caterina had long ago agreed with Sonya that she could no more rejoice in this tragic Italy's defeats than she could in its victories. But by the summer of the Axis surrender in Tunisia, there were so many things wrong in her that even the victories of the British Eighth Army, the army she believed Giles was serving in if he was still alive, only afforded her the bitterest pleasure.

Caterina had changed. These days there was a hard anger and despair in her eyes as often as not – in her eyes that before had charmed people with their soft hesitancy. The bold curves of her chin and mouth looked aggressive most of the time, and certainly didn't look beautiful. Because whatever she was busy with, there'd be that same war time beating in her head, drubbing the same thoughts she was sick to death of thinking. War truths about how there might be people in every parish from the Alps to Sicily who no longer felt at home in their own country, internal exiles like the blacksmith, like Count La Marrechia, like Sonya and herself; but in all these years of the Fascists and their war there'd been no uprising, and she knew in her bones there'd be no uprising now. Political stabbings in the back, now that the African colonies had been lost – Lord yes. Politic rats scuttling off the foundering ship of the Imperial State – oh, all that. But no rebellion. For Christ's sake, the few thousand men of spirit who might have led a fight for freedom, men like Gabriele, were all either in exile or in prison, she would reflect with bitter pride, hating herself for her cold arrogant contempt, but going on feeling it, and feeling it poisoning her.

'None will break ranks, though nations trek from progress.' She couldn't recall which of the poets of the last war had written that line, but it kept echoing back to her and it horrified her.

War time would beat and beat in her tired brain till her head ached. 'None will break ranks . . .' Dear God – *none*? Well, no, it seemed not. There'd be her endless telling herself not to become embittered, and her endless telling herself that anger was right. There'd be the same hating herself for gadding off to parties in

Rome with Cosima's husband and with Esmeralda's husband, so who was she to talk, she was in this shit up to her neck. The hating herself for doing any courting of pashas and nabobs that might get Gabriele's sentence reduced though somehow it never seemed to, doing any courting that might shore up Lisa's and her frail defences, bring them through this war free, not in a concentration camp. There had lately been renewed talk of getting Gabriele released on grounds of ill-health, so she had been particularly assiduous in her trotting around Rome with Carlo Manzari, and at dinner parties paying his influential friends flattering attention.

Now to this tyranny of eternally thinking the same thoughts was added her determination not to give way to optimism. The great northward Allied drive for the European heartlands would not come through Italy, it would be an assault on Greece and then up the Balkans, Caterina had told herself again and again. No, it would be an invasion of southern France. On and on it went, the rigmarole in her mind. Even if Sicily *were* attacked, that would simply be a feint . . .

War truths. Well, maybe one day there would be some different, peace truths to refresh one's mind with. You never knew. It was possible. But in the meanwhile, one of the worst of the things which had gone wrong in Caterina was her relationship with Sonya.

For three years, the Palazzo D'Alessandria had gone back to being a house of women, as it had often been during the last war. The only novelty this time was that Sonya and Caterina had persuaded Signora Immacolata to accept their help in dishing up, and then to eat with them in the dining-room. As month by month everybody's meals got more and more frugal, they might as well all sit down to their nothing much to eat together. So it was that, in one household in the land at least, a régime that vaunted the authoritarian and the hierarchical effected the introduction of more democratic manners.

Sometimes Rosalba came to lunch and sometimes she didn't, but it was merriest when she came. Their saddest war-time meals were when Immacolata went back to her own house in the evenings, and Rosalba didn't come, so Sonya and Caterina sat down to dinner on their own, and the big house all around them could feel very empty of life. Even Lisa, who was five now, put to bed up in her attic room, could seem a spark of usually joyful vivacity insufficiently strong to combat all those dead rooms. Only some evenings, if she could not sleep and felt lonely in her bed, the child would pitter-patter down the flights of stairs in her nightdress, and then the two women at the dining-table would smile to hear her footfalls approaching across the next room. Of course it was all wrong that the small wraith should be wandering about the gloomy mansion instead of sleeping. All the same it would be good to see her white face in the huge marble doorway, and good to cuddle her and make a fuss of her for a few minutes before taking her back upstairs.

Being walled up alone with her mother-in-law for war year after war year was never going to have been easy for either of them, Caterina would sternly remind herself. Even so, it was wearying that these days Sonya found mirth of any kind practically impossible to generate and on a bad day difficult to tolerate in others. It was depressing to dine night after night with this woman whose second world war had aged her by ten years. She had a primness about her mouth that was new, and her hair had lost its last glints of gold and was a dull ash colour. Her eyes had that shuttered look almost all the time, outside her spirit which was withering away. She fingered her rosary for minute after minute.

Gone were the times when their happy talk had ranged far and wide, even touching on philosophy, and whether religion or the lack of it made you more free. Now at dinner Sonya would worry aloud endlessly about Edoardo who was certain to be killed in the great battles for Europe, and anyhow right now was probably getting into debt, or into some other disgrace, perhaps catching some frightful disease. Every evening she would harp on about her fears for Gabriele, living on a prison diet that was sure to have already ruined his constitution.

Even worse, at dinner Sonya had a tendency to talk on and on about the stories of mass executions of Norwegians and Dutch, of Poles and Russians and French, of Yugoslavs, Czechs, Greeks – what could seem like most of the peoples of the Old World. By a cruel dispensation, it was her Christian need to find moral answers that made some phantasmal sense which inflicted the gravest damage on what had been her lively, peaceful soul.

Caterina had her own horror at what was being done in Nazi-Fascist Europe; she had her own despair at how most people asked nothing better than not to comprehend and not to feel, so they didn't comprehend and they didn't feel. But however much she admired Sonya's spiritual courage, there were nights when she thought the conversation was going to make her scream.

Latterly it had been about the slaughter vans, in which according to one rumour thousands and thousands of victims were being locked and gassed. Sonya had become obsessed by these vans, appeared capable of talking only about this new inhumanity and the moral questions it raised. When Caterina tried to imagine what it would be like when she and Lisa were shut into a van with a crush of other people and then the gas was turned on, her stomach clenched and her cold brain swam. And all the while, in the dim lustre of the dining-room that by rights should have enclosed a large, exuberant family eating and drinking abundantly and all talking at once, her mother-in-law's reedy voice agonised on and on.

'Evil on this scale . . . Last-ditch stand against spiritual death . . . Free will . . . What do you think, Caterina?' (Caterina bit her lip. Her fingers in her lap squirmed.) 'Sophistry . . . Justification . . . Our Lord . . . Atonement . . . Bliss hereafter . . .'

When Caterina could not stand it in the house and the city an hour longer, she was dogged about biking out of town to labour in Signor Orazio's smallholding. Often, when she despaired of Italy's refusal to acknowledge the errors and crimes and acknowledge defeat, so it was a torment to her to go on living in a world where all simplicity and goodness and truth had been contaminated and forced to hide. When she couldn't understand why soldiers and civilians together couldn't stand up and betray the bloody Nazis and get rid of the bloody Fascists, preferably by shooting most of the top dogs out of hand, yes she knew that would include Carlo Manzari and that was fine. When she was sick with angry despair at the Allies pontificating about 'unconditional surrender', which made it practically impossible for an Italian government to negotiate a separate peace. When

Sonya had been talking and talking about her theology until words meant nothing at all. When she could feel her own twenties petering out miserably and all her youthfulness was gone for good. When Gabriele was so shadowy he didn't exist, and as for love . . . Yes, and as for her brain forever yammering that either the Italians or the Germans had probably killed Giles long ago, it was no good hoping – either that or he'd been sent to the East and the Japanese had killed him. When it was more than she could bear, to go on remembering the Blackwater estuary, go on remembering him as a boy with rolled-up trousers and muddy feet rowing Mummy and her up a creek through the marsh. More than she could bear, all her eternal wondering why, her wondering to what conceivable good end . . .

Caterina always propped her bike against the bole of the same Spanish chestnut. She'd walk over to the shed, which Signor Orazio had cobbled together years ago from retrieved planks, hurdles, palings, sheets of corrugated iron. The door had once been a stable door and it had a horse's name, Arlecchino, written in curly script and weathered almost away.

She'd heave the door open, scowling on account of her soured mind that kept telling her things she didn't want to listen to. Oh, she'd had a cushy time of it so far. Sure, she had. Apart from the total falsity of the life they made you lead. Apart from never being able to say what you thought. Having to give these distinguished, these cultured ladies and gentlemen the satisfaction of observing how cravenly you danced to their tune. 'Good evening, Your Excellency. My brother-in-law has just been telling me about the extremely interesting despatch which came today from the governor of Zagreb. It appears probable that . . . In your view? Progress . . .' Now, among these shadowy pitchforks and scythes, among the seed boxes and the coils of cord. Must be the spade here somewhere. No, that was the shovel. 'Our man in Dubrovnik . . . Sterling job of work . . . Yes, Esmeralda and I are going to the recital. So your wife and you, Excellency? Delighted . . .' Oh yes, a cushy time of it, so far. Not to mention the other self-hatred she couldn't write about for Gabriele when he was free. Couldn't exactly talk to his mother about at dinner, either. This new loathing and new gratification. Because naturally the inevitable had occurred. After a few of Caterina's worldly Roman evenings, she'd ended up in strange rooms with men she hardly knew, making longed-for, cold, frivolous love.

Of course, the minute the democracies were nice enough to smash the totalitarian governments to hell, half the Axis population would burst out cheering, Caterina would think savagely, swinging the spade over her shoulder. More than half, quite probably, human nature being what it was. But until then . . . No, don't think that! Anyhow, it could look like the Red Army was going to do the lion's share of the smashing. Yes, but she hadn't exactly filched a pistol and plugged a bullet into Manzari, had she? On the contrary – she found him delightful company, and she thought the way he'd invariably treated her was very civilised, under the circumstances. No, no, come to think of it, if she was going to get herself hanged as a murderess, better assassinate Ciano. Keep your counsel, and keep your nerve, and then surprise them all. Kill the Foreign Minister, just fancy! Might get a footnote in the history books. Only . . . What sorts of things might they do to her before they hanged her? And Charlotte Corday didn't have a little daughter, did she? Oh, you'll always find an excuse.

Digging beside Signor Orazio for hours, sometimes the verminous thoughts scampering round and round Caterina's brainpan trap would get tired, they'd stop, give her some peace. After she'd discovered that, she never complained about the pains in her back, or about the un-young-ladylike calluses that appeared on her palms.

What with the rationing and what with the evacuated children, the household needed to bulk out its rations as best it might. So there was the reassuring certainty that all this stupefying digging was useful. It was good too that Orazio was a quiet man. Better still, often he'd go off to tend his hens or his rabbits, or he'd go to do some pruning, and leave her working alone. Then all she'd hear would be her own panting breaths, and the sound her spade made jabbing into the ground, and the sound the heaved lumps of earth made when they fell.

Caterina still had her ghostly consonance with all her countrywomen – all her countrywomen of her other country – scattered about the world at war. For that matter, there must be others here who'd been born British or American or French – she just seemed to be the only one in her particular neck of the Tuscan woods. And as for all those farther away . . .

She might be hoeing between Orazio's rows of beans. But her imagination would fly to young women much like herself, perhaps with little girls much like Lisa, who were in Cairo and had husbands at sea in Admiral Somerville's fleet, or were in Calcutta and had husbands in General Slim's army in Assam. That conjuring mind of Caterina's wove and rewove her stories, putting flesh on her ghosts' bones, even after the conjuring mind had become embittered, ungenerous. Yes, and then on to her true sisters. Not those conducting a fashionable colonial existence, with maybe a bit of Embassy work thrown in. Those like her caught behind enemy lines, those silenced like her, in Europe, in the East. Then – those in prison camps, which so far she'd avoided.

Voices! Unheard. But Caterina heard them with her mind's ear, she would stop work and lean on her hoe. For a few moments her peaceful sky would ring with far voices, there was a tolling of stories like bells. Then she'd grin at her foolishness, bend once more to her winter mud or her summer dust.

Only, it was strange . . . Before, she'd never particularly liked or disliked how chancy her apparently real life could feel. But now, as the war years had grown more horrifying, and as her imaginings had grown better informed and more labyrinthine, in her loneliness Caterina began to rejoice in how tenuous the life she happened to be living felt to her. That matters might easily have turned out quite different . . . This caused a promise of delicious freedom to bubble up in her mind.

If she'd blundered in some of those other directions, instead of come blundering this way. If she'd dreamed other dreams, deluded herself with other misapprehensions and hopes. If she hadn't bumped into Gabriele at that lecture in London, and ended up by chucking over her whole way of life and dancing off here with him. If you could tweak a thread of the tissue of this oh-so-convincing reality, and the whole fabric would start to ravel before your eyes . . . All right, then! There were suggestions in this which she kindled to. In her bitterness, she looked at this meaninglessness of events and saw that it was good. Above all, there was an insubstantiality in her very self that she decided she rather liked.

At the same time, on Caterina's overwrought nerves, everyday occurrences began to sound deep chords out of all proportion to their unimportant and completely natural horror.

One July evening at the smallholding, Orazio shot a snake. It was a grass-snake, not a viper. Caterina heard Gabriele's voice telling her years ago that the peasants always killed snakes when they could, even the ones they knew perfectly well were harmless. It seemed to be part of their culture, he'd said. It was stupid, but there was nothing you could do about it. So she knew all about that, and it was nice to remember being with Gabriele and his telling her those sorts of things. But when she stood over the broken snake she started to tremble, and when the dog came moseying to get at the carrion she screamed at it, and threw stones to drive it off, and had tears in her eyes.

A few golden and grey and pink twilights later, she was digging up Orazio's harvest of onions, as he had asked her to. She crouched over the rows, rootling with the trowel in her right hand, lifting the bulbs clear with her left. The night that would shroud the American and British armada as it approached the coast of Sicily was falling, but Caterina was concerned to finish lifting the scores and scores of onions while she could still see what she was up to. Then tomorrow the crop would be laid in the sun all day and give off a pungent odour. After that, Orazio and she would slice off their roots, and twist them together by their wispy topknots into bunches so they could be hung up in the storehouse.

Cackling came from where Orazio was penning his poultry for the night. Then the hens and the quails stopped flustering. But there arose another sound, there was a crying in the air, and Caterina stood straight with her scalp shivering.

She gazed up, beyond the olive trees. Aloft in the sultry dusk, a buzzard was flying with a creature in its talons: a kitten maybe, or a leveret, or a stoat.

Her heart pounded, she rammed her nails into her palms. The prey's high, rhythmic shrieks being borne across the sky died away slowly.

—◊—

12

'They've landed, they've landed,' Rosalba chanted gaily to herself, carrying a tureen into the empty dining-room of her cousins' house. She set the steaming soup down on a lace mat on the walnut table with a flourish and sketched a curtsey before it.

The tall white curtains along the south side of the room kept out the heat and dazzle of the summer lunch-time sun, but transmitted the pale, shimmery, mote-dancing presence of the brilliant light striking against their outward sides.

These days Rosalba worked as a nurse at the hospital where once Gabriele had been one of the promising young specialists, and she could not recall when she had last bought a new dress. But she wore her old dresses with the innocent self-assurance she'd always had, and even when there was nobody in a room she would enter it as if the vacant air must naturally be seduced by her lilting walk and her shining black eyes.

'The British have taken Syracuse,' she sang, surveying the five places laid on the polished walnut. 'Vegetable soup for lunch today, and the British have . . .' She sang it as if it were an old ditty she'd picked up in the market-place, but broke off to concentrate as she poured water from a Venetian carafe into the five glasses. 'Vegetable soup yesterday, vegetable soup today . . .'

At Lisa's chair, Rosalba plumped up the cushions that would raise the child so she could get a proper purchase on her spoon. When had it been – oh, ages ago! – that she'd suggested trying to get Caterina a job as a nurse too? Caterina had wanted that very badly, but Aunt Sonya had put her foot down. Lisa had lost one parent for the time being, she had better see as much as possible of the other one – that was what Aunt Sonya had said. The household would have to get by as best it could on the half of Uncle Luigi's pension which he had the bank pay to his wife. But things were going to get a lot more satisfactory quite briskly now. On the slenderest evidence, Rosalba D'Alessandria had no doubts at all about that. So she sang, with her black curls framing her face of a pretty, debonair sylph, by the parade of fifteen-foot creamy veils between her and the sunshine. 'They've landed, they've landed. Vegetable soup tomorrow . . .'

The others all came in for their lunch. Sonya paused, erect and immobile with her hands on the back of her chair at the head of the table, and everyone else stood with suitably downcast gaze while she said grace. Only today Rosalba was in such a blithe humour that she could only just refrain from crooning 'They've landed' or 'Vegetable soup' under her breath. So to compensate herself she winked at Lisa, which made the child open her eyes enormously wide and gasp with delight, so Rosalba had suddenly to look very demure indeed.

Dressed in one of her old-fashioned black silk dresses, with a small gold crucifix studded with garnets on a delicate gold chain around her neck (she had given up wearing even her soberest dark greens and dark blues), Sonya came to the end of her ritual Latin words. She had noticed Rosalba's merrily anarchic wink and it distressed her.

Yes indeed, today all over Nazi-Fascist Europe the alienated and the silenced were rejoicing because yesterday at dawn an army had landed on the southern Sicilian beaches, this might conceivably be the beginning of the end. Yes, already Syracuse had fallen, the first city had been wrested free. For years, Sonya's almost annihilated love for her two countries had done nothing but clog her throat with tears, but now her heart too had been touched by hope. Even so, could Rosalba not for a few seconds give thanks to Almighty God? Had she not thought how many lives must still be lost, even if the liberating Allies were blessed with an unprecedented series of victories, which was practically impossible? Honestly, the way this flirtatious chit had come dancing into the house today! (Through a change of which she was utterly unaware, Sonya D'Alessandria had come to disapprove of all youthful romanticism and high spirits.) What was more, had she no qualms about celebrating her country's invasion? Probably the little minx was already dreaming about the tank commander from Surrey or Mississippi or somewhere, who was going to carry her off and conceivably even marry her.

Rosalba pulled back her chair with a loud scrape and sat down hungrily. 'Surprise surprise, vegetable soup!' she exclaimed. 'Do you suppose the British and the Americans have got their tanks stuffed with good things to eat? Roast chickens, marvellous puddings . . .'

'I'm sure they would be very happy to be luxuriously provisioned,' Sonya interjected severely.

'Did the radio say how many hundreds of tanks?' Rosalba cocked her head to one side, and set herself to kindle a flicker in the eyes of Caterina opposite her. 'Well, anyhow, by my brilliant calculations that makes about one million roast chickens, five million sausages, ten million bars of chocolate . . .'

'Can we have roast chicken?' piped up Lisa.

'My love, you know my husband sometimes kills one of his hens,' Signora Immacolata said placidly. 'There's a lot of folk less fortunate than we are.'

'Yes, but they're such scrawny old boiling fowls,' complained Rosalba cheerfully. 'Good for making stock, and that's about it. But a young, plump, tender bird . . .'

A spoon clinked against a bowl. On the dish of apricots on the massive oak sideboard, several flies crawled. A warm puff of breeze made the curtains tremble.

Sonya was thinking about all the invasions, right back to the ancient Greeks landing in Sicily, and then the Arabs, and later the Normans. She thought about Caterina's people and her own people, fighting out their rivalry down there now. Then, what was going to happen here in Tuscany? The old Grand Duchy might long ago have been one of the cradles of European civilisation, but now the place was just waiting to be fought over yet again.

She glanced around at the pilasters, the pediments over the doorways, the carved coats-of-arms. How many regiments of how many different armies had Arezzo seen, over the centuries? And now, this time . . . Heavens, the city might be fought for street by street! Was this old house of hers going to be shelled? Set on fire? Would soldiers of one side or the other crash in here, ransacking or shooting? Caterina and Rosalba would be all right if these warring gentlemen were of impeccable gallantry. But otherwise . . . The blacksmith had come again the other day, he was forever fitting sturdier bolts everywhere and never wanting to be paid. Sonya frowned to think how unavailing this good man's help would be against soldiers and their weapons.

Unconscious of the matronly disapproval that only loosened its hold on her downy old lips when she parted them to insert brownish green soup quivering in a polished silver spoon, Sonya reflected wearily on all the times Tuscany had been bandied about from this sovereignty to that. Habsburg-Lorraine grand dukes. A Bourbon prince who for some reason called himself King of Etruria, didn't he? Then Napoleon's sister as grand duchess, so the place was maladministered from Paris like any other colony. After which . . . Oh, more musical chairs.

'Just think, Caterina, the next landing may be a lot further north!' Rosalba was chattering brightly away, breaking off fragments of bread and dropping them into her soup, raising her napkin to her lips as if to get them ready for a kiss of the utmost strategic importance. 'Perhaps even as far north as Tuscany. They could come ashore on our nice sandy beaches perfectly well, couldn't they? Imagine! I might be going for a swim at Castiglioncello, and Giles and his merry men will come wading ashore to liberate me, and I'll sweep him off at once for the most sumptuous fish dinner he's ever eaten in his life. Clams, baby octopus, sea bass – you name it. What else will I do? Apart from helping him to another sole and choosing him the ripest peach in the bowl. Well, I'll gaze at him with adoring admiration of course, and I'll listen to his stories as if I believed every heroic detail. I'll pour jugs of wine down his throat, and . . . Only come to think of it – unless the war packs it in, I won't get to the other side of Tuscany to go swimming ever again. When did you and I last bathe in the sea, Caterina? Well at any rate, if that handsome brother of yours insists on liberating you before he turns his attention to liberating me, I shan't change out of my swimsuit at *all* passionately, so don't you go giving him hopes.'

'Rosalba! *How* can you have forgotten that a year and a half has passed since Caterina had her wonderful letter from Giles?' Sonya's pain rasped in the strictness of her voice. The girl winced and for a few moments looked contrite. 'We have no notion where Giles may be by now, or – or what may have happened to him.'

Sonya did not need to turn to Caterina to know that tears of dread for her brother, of passionate hope and of love would have sprung to her eyes. When she did turn to her, the tears were there: luminous, unshed. But so was a quiver of gaiety about her mouth.

Rosalba muttered petulantly: 'I've been doing my best to be boringly sensible for three years. I think I'll give up.'

'It's all right, Sonya darling.' Caterina laid her hand on her mother-in-law's wrist, gazed at her with those tear-eyes that were also bold. 'I mean, they *have* captured Syracuse, and so far as we know haven't lost it to a counter-attack – so it's nice to be a tiny bit optimistic just for five minutes, don't you think? I believe . . . I believe that if I go on never allowing myself to hope even a little, I shall wither away bitterly inside, or I'll suddenly crack like a dropped plate, or . . . Well, even if one day everything does go better than it's been going, it'll be too late for me, I won't have any gaiety left for anybody to revive. Not real gaiety, that comes bubbling up – just the assumed sort.'

Caterina turned to Rosalba. She smiled, not at all tremulously now. 'Oh yes, *let's* imagine impossible things! My God, when I . . . Swimming in the bay at Castiglioncello and then strolling back to the village for feasts of fish. You never know – that old way of life may even come true again! It may even come true for you and me and for Gabriele and Giles. But tell me . . .' She dimpled, as she had not done for a long time. 'Rosalba darling, I know you've always been terrifically good at being enchanted by every dashing man you meet, in the most admirably even-handed fashion, and yet not really ever being enchanted by anybody. But . . . You'd quite like it, if my brother happened to walk into the room right now, wouldn't you?'

The night before Caterina had scarcely slept, for all the hopes pelting through her mind and her struggle not to give way to hoping. Looking haggard, she had gone out about the town in the early morning. Sitting at a table in the Café dei Costanti she had glanced through three newspapers to see what justificatory verbiage the government was authorising. She had overheard the proprietor contemptuously discussing the rumours that some of the Sicilian regiments were melting away before battle was joined. Caterina had jumped up, with a fretful stride she had gone out again. She had roamed the streets without knowing whether she expected people to shout curses at her or to throw their hats in the air and cheer – but nobody had done either of these things.

Now when lunch was over, all afternoon she repeatedly tuned in to Rome radio and London radio and switched them off, and in the cool of the evening her restlessness overpowered her again. The city's trees in their summer leaf were statuesque mounds of dapple-green. High in the blue and golden sunshine, towering swifts were skirling. Caterina wavered in the arched doorway of the Palazzo D'Alessandria. She flitted away down the shady street, once more she took to haunting the familiar squares and thoroughfares with her thoughts cascading. Was she imagining it, or was there a strange lack of fury against the invaders and an equally strange lack of rebellious rejoicing at the chance of freedom? Perhaps the streets would ring truer than the papers or the radio, would tell her more. So . . . No question of the whole nation uniting in arms, in the way that Greece and Russia, say, when they were attacked had fought furiously in self-defence; but no question yet of a national upris- ing to unite with the invaders either. Regiments that deserted, but did not go over to fight on the other side . . . Did this mean there really *was* something rotten in the Italian state, or was this weary fatalism the quintessence of wisdom? How could one answer such a question? Were these the wrong questions to ask?

Completely unable to make up her mind about anything, and swinging left or right at the corners without the faintest reflection, Caterina was companioned everywhere by Giles who had been in North Africa and might conceivably be with the invading Eighth Army, by Gabriele who if soon the prisons were opened would immediately try to get into the fight in one way or another. But tangled up in her fears for those two was a mocking spirit of defiance, and she walked quickly, lightly, glancing this way and that with bright, bitter eyes. She had a devil-may-care joy that the battle for Europe had begun, that Italy was going to be fought for now and not later. Right, let's have whatever is coming to us, her soul prayed. Oh look, there's La Marrechia's housekeeper, taking delivery of a cartload of firewood and haggling over the price by the sound of things. How fat she's grown, when all the rest of us are getting thinner! 'Good evening, Signora! No, I can't stop I'm afraid.' Now, what was I . . . ? The bombing so far has been nothing compared to what we're going to get crashing down on our heads, there doesn't appear to be much doubt about that. Oh, what the hell! Anyhow, it's true what I said at lunch. It *is* possible that we may live into our happy times again. Conceivable, far off . . . like the atonement Sonya prays so despairingly for. Yes, even Giles and Gabriele, even Rosalba and I. Feasts of fish under stripey green and white awnings, bottles of wine, everyone talking at once and laughing. And Esmeralda – oh my darling, yes, you too!

Caterina stopped dead in her tracks in front of the green-grocer's trestles and crates. He was beginning to close his heavy shutters for the night, but seeing Caterina D'Alessandria suddenly at a stand-still as if she'd just that second remembered the aubergines, he asked courteously: 'I'm about to go home, but if there's something you need?'

'No, no, thank you,' Caterina replied with a distracted smile, a shadow of distaste crossing her face at the realisation of how silly and conceited it was to think it mattered what happened to one. Death, she thought. Daddy bought the house in Canonbury Square to live there with his wife and children, but a war between the German empire and the British empire came, statesmen and generals took various decisions and they extinguished him without a thought. He never saw Giles, and I hardly remember him. Certainly I have no idea who he really was, what his consciousness was like to him. Neither Giles nor I have ever visited his grave somewhere in Flanders, if they truly are his bones under the stone with his name on, and now his house in London may easily have been reduced to rubble by the next war. At Giles's death if he's still alive and at my death it will truly be almost as if Daddy never lived – and that doesn't matter either, not deep down. So now, faced with the job of freeing Europe from some of its loathsomeness, it's ridiculous to make a fuss about one brother and sister. The task is colossal but I expect the pick of the men are up to it and the pick of the women too. I trust this one woman is up to making herself modestly useful. Certainly it looks as if the likes of Sonya and

I are going to have more Red Cross work to do around here rather than less. If an Allied shell or an Axis machine-gun or something else finishes me off, I hope Lisa is spared, I can't help hoping that. But then she will grow up in circumstances in Italy or in England or somewhere else which would have been almost incomprehensible to me, just as these dreams and passions of mine will have died with me and be imaginable to her only hazily and inaccurately.

Feeling liberated by these ideas and perfectly calm, Caterina regarded the handsome old houses and the bustling street, she tried to envisage all this life going on after the activity in her grey matter had ceased and she was just unconscious bones and muscle and offal mouldering in a pit. Death, she thought for the second time. Death: not being here. How quickly this city will forget me, forget that I used to be a familiar figure in these streets, some people liked me well enough and others didn't. How sensible the world is to forget so much, disburden itself of so much! Unaware that passers-by were staring at her with amusement, she shook her head, she smiled. Look, that boy running somewhere with his cap in his hand, and the warm summer daylight dying under the arcade – and, just imagine, no me!

Should she go home now? No, a thousand times no – this aliveness and this freedom were too seductive. So she drifted on through the evening crowds, at peace, watching, listening.

13

—∞—

The eventual collapse of a brutal system founded on people lying to others and lying to themselves may have been inevitable sooner or later, even if only thanks to the laws of impermanence. But this did not mean that the débâcle was widely predicted, or that it did not take several years to be accomplished.

At the highest pinnacles of society, where they were at the furthest remove from the calamities endured by the vast majority in the country, and where there was the irresistible temptation to give some credence to their own habitual talk of their own importance, ladies lavishly festooned with jewels and gentlemen with glittering orders pinned to their chests continued for a long time to discuss Italy's imperial grandeur on the world stage. Even after the defeats in Africa and Russia, the Marchioness Cosima went on imperturbably holding dazzling receptions, at which Count Galeazzo Ciano and his wife who was Mussolini's daughter were often to be seen. So was the marchioness's sister Esmeralda Manzari, who was widely chattered about as the most beautiful and flamboyant of the smart young women in Ciano's set.

The Roman drawing-rooms went on vying with each other in elegance, and vying to show off the powerful and the fashionable. Magnificent celebrations were planned for the twentieth anniversary of the Fascist revolution.

All the same, up and down the country there were men and women in less exalted positions (people such as the Marchioness Cosima's father, who had quite dropped out of society and was rather an embarrassment to her) who had long had presentiments that the dictatorship and the war-mongering might be going to produce exceedingly unpleasant consequences. And not only for far-away foreigners, either. Here at home in Italy, where savageries would have a different complexion altogether, and where the Allied air-raids which went on and on could seem the shadow of destruction to come.

Luigi D'Alessandria had gone on taking notes for his *The*

Degradation of Italy. In his old professor's methodical way, he'd sit down most winter mornings at his desk at Ca' Santa Chiara, in the living-room with its trout-rods and its shot-guns, its bookcases, its Renaissance prints that Gaetano Da Durante had helped him to buy. Each spring when the warm weather came he shifted his notebooks and his files, his copies of economic reports, of diplomatic and military reports, out to the loggia, where he had wicker chairs and a rickety table.

Reliable information was infuriatingly difficult to come by. Still, every day D'Alessandria shoved a notebook in his pocket and trudged the mile down the winding track to the village store, where the Metauro ran through its willows and poplars. There he and a few other locals would sit in the shabby room with its damp-warped shelves, its crucifix and its football calendar. They listened to Rome radio to find out what the official bluster was. They listened to the BBC and to the Swiss radio, and he made himself useful by interpreting for his neighbours. It was illegal to listen to the foreign stations, so they kept an eye on the road in case of policemen. Well, not their local sergeant. He often sat down to listen with them. Better still, not only Gregorio Farsetti but a handful of D'Alessandria's other one-time colleagues also secretly shared some of his disgust; they sympathised with his attempt to write his book, they helped when they could. Luigi became aware of a skein of the alienated and the sceptical, a ghostly Italy of people who were cautious about making their real selves known to one another, but who then would exchange their messages.

An industrialist here and a civil service chief there; a scattering of judges, ambassadors, admirals; some of the aristocracy (not Cosima's crowd) . . . Putting out feelers through the universities and through a few old friends like Count Gofredo Damiani down in Rome, Luigi was encouraged by how high in the state disaffection could be found. Looked at another way, it was amusing to watch the privileged classes positioning themselves to make sure *they* continued to enjoy power and wealth in whatever the post-war dispensation turned out to be.

Just as for years D'Alessandria had been one of the few to make a record of the concentration camps and the killings in the African colonies, so now practically nobody else in the

homeland, though plenty of witnesses on the other side of the
Adriatic, compiled such a detailed indictment of Italy's policies
for the territories annexed in the Balkans. Amused and certain
though the old piler-up of facts was that, even if he and one
or two others like him did go to the trouble to write their
books, it wouldn't take long for the nation to forget half the
abominations of these times and forgive itself the other half.

'When the ethnic groups do not correspond to the geographi-
cal borders, they must be made to coincide by the transfer of
populations.'

Not easy to hold your head up very proudly, as a citizen of
a state whose Head of Government issued such directives. Still,
those were the orders from Rome, and the military commanders
went at it hammer and tongs, and Luigi D'Alessandria kept his
pride in working order by going at his destruction of their
reputations hammer and tongs too, in his terse sentences, letting
the facts speak for themselves.

In Montenegro, they were systematically burning villages and
gunning down the inhabitants. In Slovenia, after the massacres,
General Robotti had ordered 'total deportation' of the survi-
vors, in order that the state might be peopled by Italians, so
now his troops were setting about that duty too and the concentration camps were filling up. Then, the justice. D'Alessandria
compiled lists for each occupied town, month after month. In
this manner, a friend visiting Ca' Santa Chiara could look up
the city of Split, for instance, in one of his notebooks and
discover that twenty resisters had just been hanged; and you
could read on, to other tribunals and other days of judgement.
Or you could look up Ljubljiana and find a hundred hostages
had recently been shot there, but glancing back up the record
you could see that not all months were that bad.

As for Croatia, the road signs were all in Italian now, and
Italian was being shoved down the schoolchildren's throats,
and Croatians were meant to Italianise their names. An Italian
kingdom of Croatia had been founded and a Savoy princeling
enthroned – not that he ever bothered to visit the wretched place
and sit on his throne. Still, Pope Pius XII hastened to bestow
Vatican recognition on the new puppet state, so that was all
right. Order was being imposed on the unappreciative natives

by the occupying forces and by local Catholic militia bands. It had been necessary to murder over three hundred thousand Orthodox Serbs there, to facilitate the solution of ethnic and religious difficulties.

Naturally, D'Alessandria's war writings never got anything like as higgledy-piggledy as his daughter-in-law's. But toward the end, all his subjects were getting jumbled up, which they never had before.

On a single page, you might get typically professorial ruminations about how what he trusted would prove to be the final years of Fascist misrule resembled the last years of the Bourbon kingdom in the South, or for that matter the last years of the Papal States. A ruling caste of sycophantic courtiers and cardinals, barons and police chiefs and informers. Bribery for quite simply everything. Even the same prohibition of foreign newspapers.

Then the next paragraph might record, with no superfluous commentary, that near Zadar on the Dalmatian coast, local partisans had blown up some electricity pylons, in retaliation for which the Prefect there, General Barbera, had ordered sixty-five hostages to be shot.

Hard on the heels of that, you might be regaled with the excellent news that Gervasio's and Maria's son Bruno had, on the grounds of his being the only son of a crippled father, eventually been released from his regiment in Macedonia and had come back to take over the farm on which the family's livelihood depended, much to the relief of all the hamlets around. A celebration had at once been organised, with an accordion player. D'Alessandria wrote about the barn-yard feast that the housewives served up on trestle-tables spread with white cloths, and the great jugs of wine, and the singing that broke out as soon as everyone had begun to satisfy their hunger. He described the crescent moon coming up behind the hay ricks in the dusk, and how straightforward it was to make merry if you were not right that moment either being sinned against or sinning. He described the bonfire which cast its tawny light on the outhouses and the oak trees, on the couples dancing on the threshing-floor, on the children and dogs skirmishing about, and how that night they seemed to be back in a vanished, happier time, in an innocence that had been lost. He himself, who had filled in all Bruno's forms applying for exoneration and had taken them to be stamped in all the right offices, was one of the most honoured guests. He danced the first waltz with the returned hero's wife Giuliana, who still looked too girlish to have been let marry any man. Everybody clapped and everybody smiled, and the grinning musician went straight back to the beginning of his tune in order to make that dance last double its time.

Every time D'Alessandria visited Rome, or a friend from the capital who happened to be in his province came to visit him, he got news of the Opposition's tireless clandestine plotting. They were a rag-bag of Republicans and Monarchists, of Liberals and Communists and every conceivable splinter group, and Luigi admired the courage a lot of these unarmed men and women displayed. The trouble was, they were united only by their passion for talk and for disagreement, and by their inability ever to achieve anything. But he reckoned a lost war would bring the whole Fascist edifice crashing down quick enough; and when it seemed to him that the war was so plainly and irretrievably lost that even the King and his Privy Counsellors and his Ministers must have noticed, he found it hard to keep his hope under control.

His own snatches of stories, where there had never been any committed to paper before. Reminders that he jotted down for himself – such as that he must ask Gaetano if down in Naples his philosophising friend Croce still considered that history was rational and the victory of evil impossible. His veering moods, which began to come thick and fast . . . Reading his notebooks after the war was over, that was one of the ways you could trace the quickenings of new life in him, which seemed to beat at a wilder tempo as the crisis of his country's war was reached.

D'Alessandria wasn't just taking notes; he'd started to write his *Degradation* at last. His head swirled with dreams about how the civilisation he loved was going to reawaken, how he might live to see the land of his birth free and dignified once more. Yes, and if this nightmarish interlude was really going to be banished, the recent past must be analysed, a great truth-telling must come.

The old man felt more useful than he had ever been in his life before. He dreamed that he might see his book published; he even dreamed that he might be called back to speak at universities again a few times at the beginning of the new peace, in a last flicker of professional success. (The truth was, he had never been at all eminent as a professor and his only notable work, a monograph on Leopardi published twenty years ago, had gone out of print almost immediately.) Lots of fellows made it to three score years and ten, why shouldn't he? And if the war was soon going to be over, he must work fast.

Perhaps here and there about the barbarous continent others were writing a *Degradation of Austria,* and *of Germany,* and *of Hungary,* and *of Slovakia.* His heart swelling with pride, he imagined how he might live to find himself one of a small élite who had not endured these years in vain, who had kept records, had written the truth.

Now that he'd got cracking, Luigi D'Alessandria worked doggedly, roughing out an essay on the Fascist subversion of what had been a perfectly creditable legal system, and another about the intervention in the Spanish civil war on General Franco's side. He had been amassing notes for so long, that it was really just a matter of ordering the material he already had to hand. These first two pieces he quickly polished till they were clear and concise enough for publication.

Feeling encouraged, he started an essay on the relations between the Fascist and Catholic hierarchies. He had found out through diplomatic contacts how reliably informed the Vatican was when it came to policies and actions in the Third Reich. Pius XII had never excommunicated Hitler; he had never spoken out against either the Nazis or the Fascists; he had never denounced the anti-Jewish legislation in Germany and Italy. However, it was possible that he still might, so Luigi broke off work on that theme, intending to take it up again when he had a fuller picture.

On the blazing July day when in his family house the other side of the Apennines his niece Rosalba curtseyed to the soup tureen, Luigi D'Alessandria was tackling the vexed subject of the manner in which for years the government had churned out propaganda about how the African colonies were a land of opportunity for enterprising citizens to open up and make profitable – but he was so excited by the landings in Sicily that his concentration had gone haywire. Still, sitting in his shady loggia he kept at his work as best he could. The core of this essay was to be his account of how thousands of poor families had believed the propaganda, had left their miserable conditions in the home peninsula and sailed south to do the opening up and the profiting. Only by the late '30s the colonies were still neither peaceful nor profitable, so the propaganda about the new horizons was quietly let drop. The next thing was, the emigrants were stranded in territories where the war was being fought and lost.

That year as usual the elegant hoopoes with their cockades on their heads had nested in one of the thickety copses at Ca' Santa Chiara, and this morning one of them was forever flying about in front of the loggia.

Luigi frowned, trying to marshal his wits and his sentences; but he kept smiling too at the thought that a Fascist downfall couldn't be far off, and must surely mean that the political prisoners would be released. Then, that beautiful, distracting hoopoe again, and the murmur of the bees in the lavender, and the heatwave, so one way and another this morning . . . For minutes at a stretch, he sat with his pen poised over the page. By God though, had Syracuse *really* fallen? A government and an army that couldn't perform their one absolutely sacred duty, the defence of the frontiers! How was bloody old Mussolini going to answer this?

Another distraction was that D'Alessandria's mind was working simultaneously on a further essay he intended to write, about his suspicion that Italy already had more to fear from her German friends than from her Anglo-Saxon enemies. It was a bad habit Rome had slithered into, that of asking Berlin to help them out of their disasters. This had been the case after the shameful assault on Greece. It had been the case after the defeats suffered against smaller British armies in Africa. And the sinister thing about the Germans forever bringing more helpful military top brass onto Italian soil, and more helpful brigades too, was that if . . .

That was a golden oriole. Motionless so as not to alarm it,

Luigi watched the bird check its swoop on a branch of the walnut tree before his gaze. Honestly, today he was hopeless! Trying to write one essay while mulling over another – whatever next? He was tempted to toss a few odds and ends in a bag, set off in the car over the mountains so he'd be in Arezzo to welcome Gabriele when he came home.

The golden oriole glanced this way and that with swift turns of its lustrous head. Then its mate swept banking around the corner of the house and the pair were away through the sunshiny trees.

14

As for the July night of the palace coup d'état when Mussolini's own Fascist Grand Council voted to dump him. The following day, everyone reacted to this spasm of the moribund body politic as their natures compelled them, with little reference to the advantages or disadvantages of replacing a discredited dictator with a more doddery one. (Marshal Badoglio was seventy-two and was no longer, if he ever had been, renowned for his intellect.)

Almost everybody hoped that, although Crown and Government had to proclaim that no treachery was planned, negotiations to make a separate peace would now be swift and successful.

The innocent (as in all times and all places, this was how the unimaginative designated themselves) did not see why, after waging an aggressive war for three years, when it now transpired that maiming and killing all those thousands of people in different lands had not brought the glories and profits you had hoped for, you should not be allowed safely to chuck it in, go home and start holding forth about the virtues of peace. The more reflective worried that to negotiate your way out of a catastrophic war would require formidable cunning and timing, if Marshal Badoglio and his ministers and diplomats and generals were not to destroy the country in the process.

Still wearing her day-time clothes and carrying a dented kerosene lamp, Caterina had wandered fretfully about the house all night. Everybody had been assuring her that the political prisoners must be going to be released now. Instead of suffusing her with joy, this had plunged her deeper into her panic that she hadn't a clue who Gabriele was going to be when he came home. She didn't even know who he'd ever been. She didn't know whether her love for him was simply a vapour her brain had exhaled or a dream her senses had dreamed. She didn't know anything worth knowing.

Air, she must have air! And light too. Good, natural light.

It must be day soon. Back in the pitchy drawing-room for the tenth time that night, she opened the two halves of one of the tall windows, she shoved the ponderous shutters outward on their squeaky hinges. The daybreak was grey with tints of yellow and mauve. From the pollarded lime trees, the dawn chorus was fifing and fluting.

Standing framed over the gulf of the street, Caterina took deep, slow breaths. She sent her mind out to all the lost dominions, to Tripoli and Addis Ababa, Asmara and Mogadiscio, not to mention all the scrappier outposts, wondering about the lives the colonials had lived, wondering what was going on there now. The Americans had captured Palermo, the frontier wasn't in Africa these days. She listened in the daybreak stillness, because it seemed to her imagination almost as if she ought to have been able to hear – oh, she didn't know! – but perhaps hear mutters and growls of rainless thunder high overhead, hear some cataclysm in the dawn sky. But all she heard was a mule slowly dragging a waggon over potholes, bumps, loose stones, and then two cats screeching.

Caterina laid her palms on the cool stone of the sill. Two more carts were rumbling by on the unkempt paving stones below. None of the streets had been repaired for years, not since before the war. She raised her eyes beyond dewy terracotta roofs to a solitary cypress etched against the sky and hoped that Gabriele was not going to abandon medicine for a career in politics. Though he would, she was nearly certain he would.

Even in those centres of civilisation where radios disseminated news of the change of régime almost instantaneously, Caterina was far from being the only person who could not be relied upon to take the correct sort of interest in it.

Gaetano Da Durante's annoyance at the outbreak of war had been principally because it cut him off from Paris and London. Still, he had continued his flittings about his own country. He stayed in collectors' villas, when they required his advice about valuations and authenticities. He took English tea in their palaces with widows who might wish to sell the family Bellini, if it was one.

Today Da Durante was in Ravenna, and he was in a state of high excitement because he thought he was onto the traces of one of the only eleven pictures Guercino had executed on copper, a painting of which the whereabouts had for some years been unknown. He had just entertained his informant, a Jewish connoisseur who had escaped from Budapest and these days led a shadowy but fairly safe existence in Italy, to a sumptuous lunch, by way of reassuring him that his own intentions were moderately honourable, and he was waddling back through the streets toward his hotel when he saw a gang of young men shying bricks through the windows of the Prefect's house.

'Eh? What's this?' Da Durante was wearing a baggy suit and a panama hat, and he was sweating, for the day was hot and he was in haste to get to a telephone and speak to his banker. However, for a moment he focussed on the scene, blinking and wheezing.

A policeman appeared at the end of the street, saw what was happening and immediately retreated back around the corner. More bricks and stones flew, glass tinkled. By shouting obscenities, the throwers gave each other courage. Nobody appeared at the door or the windows of the violated house.

'About bloody time too,' Gaetano snorted; and he went straight back to fretting about how if he bought this radiant, glimmering composition, the hitch would be that he'd long to keep it for himself. Well, you never knew, he might find a way of doing so. Funny, too, how that Hungarian fellow had appeared quite indifferent about the offered second tray of oysters. Worse still, he hadn't seemed particularly impressed by that exquisite dish of *polenta* with octopus – when there was scarcely another restaurant on the whole Adriatic littoral where they made it that well. Gaetano couldn't be doing with aesthetes who were above octopus stew. That young waitress was a charmer, too, and she knew it. Lucia, that was her name.

He puffed on down the street, rehearsing how he would warn his banker to be ready for profitable action. The trouble was, he *always* bought pictures with the declared intention of selling them shortly at a handsome profit, and at several financial institutions pernickety bores in pinstripe suits had become alert to this.

With placid good humour, Gaetano Da Durante plodded through a tumult of people shouting loudly and waving flags.

What the hell, didn't he usually pay the interest on the loans these clerkish nonentities puffed up into company directors advanced him? And after twenty-odd years of astute buying and a minimum of reluctant selling, his collection must be worth about, oh, roughly . . . Brilliantly inspired buying, once or twice, though he said it himself. The way he'd ferreted out that Correggio, when no one else had known that was what it was. Honestly, though – a wispy little character who throughout a long lunch sipped two thimbles of that vintage Bollinger (Gaetano himself had drunk a couple of bottles of the stuff). Still, those poor devils of Jews, these days . . . Or was it Bucharest he'd escaped from, in Romania, not Budapest in Hungary? Oh Lord! Yes, but the vital point at issue was: did the fellow *really* have the handling of that Guercino?

Belching, Gaetano stumped up his hotel staircase. He'd return to that restaurant, on his own, this evening. Have something light. Oh, simply a platter of mullet, probably. With lots of asparagus, of course. He'd see if that Lucia might have her susceptibilities.

In remote backwoods of the kingdom, the news of the shuffling of failed war leaders as Head of Government sometimes took twenty-four hours, or occasionally even longer, to arrive.

Countess Flavia Damiani, in her palace on the Corso in Rome, had enough statesmen of the realm in her drawing-room on the night of the coup d'état to be several jumps ahead of any news that the official radio was yet likely to dish out to the populace. But her husband was away at his idyllic estate below the Alban hills, in his ruined mediaeval Ninfa with its icy stream and its summer-long sunshine, tending his tangerine groves, and the next day he didn't come back, nor the day after.

This was far from uncommon. There was always some story about a crisis in the greenhouses or an emergency in the arboretum. Countess Flavia knew how contented her husband could be for days and nights at a stretch, living in the fourteenth century hall he'd restored, talking only to his gardeners and his cook – and surely even in that Arcadia of ruins and woods and farms *someone* would have heard of the change of government and mentioned it. Even so, she drove out to Ninfa to find him.

Countess Flavia strolled beneath her husband's towering
cedars and japonicas and maples, through his clumps of Chinese
bamboo and Japanese bamboo, past his beds of recherché
roses. There he was, kneeling with his face in the undergrowth and his backside in the air, grappling with something
or other.

'Wretched irrigation runnels, forever getting blocked,' Count
Gofredo muttered as he stood up, wiping his dirty hands on his
trousers so that he might more acceptably embrace her. 'Oh
yes, so I heard. So it's Badoglio, is it? Thought he preferred
playing bridge to playing politics. I say darling, did you come
through the walled garden? I've never *seen* the lemon trees as
magnificent as they are this year!'

At the same time, from the rocky Sardinian coast Michele
Della Quercia's sail was spied in the offing. All the blue afternoon, his wife watched that white, lateen triangle creep inshore
on the fading zephyr. When she reckoned he'd be in their bay
in twenty minutes, she started to walk down from the house
on the headland, and she was standing on the small dock,
carrying her parasol over her head, when his vessel came
nudging alongside, and the boy leapt ashore with a warp to
loop over the bollard.

'The Duce's been ditched!' she called gaily. 'He's scuppered,
he's finished! They say they'll go on with the war, but they must
be going to try to make peace.'

Her husband and his skipper were already lowering away
the two halyards and dropping the long gaff in steady jerks
toward the deck, so they were beginning to get enfurled in
canvas.

Old weather-beaten Michele shoved a descending billow
away from his head and stared at her. 'Done for, sweetheart,
honestly? By God, when I think of all the . . . ! You're not
joking? Slung out, the filthy fraud?'

He whipped the calico hat off his head; he waved it in jubilant
arcs across the sun-drenched evening calm, where the barren
hills watched and the sea lapped peacefully.

'Just imagine, when Luigi hears this! Or will he have heard it
days ago? I get so – at sea – you know what I'm like, my love.
Hey, do you hear that?' He clapped his wizened skipper on the

shoulder, and the gaff took another downward lurch. 'Hurrah! Hurrah!'

Michele swung his vigorous arm, his hat spun away and settling on the glassy bay began to be waterlogged.

15

—◊—

Upward of two hundred miles to the south-east across the Tyrrhenian Sea from where Della Quercia's calico hat was gradually sinking, on an Ustica quay his godson Gabriele D'Alessandria was bargaining blithely but forcefully with the captain of the fishing-smack *Stefania*.

The poverty-stricken harbour town was really just a village of squat shabby houses, where hollering children in patched clothes scampered about on sturdy legs and dirty feet. In front of the island's dumpy church with peeling plaster, a wall-eyed goat was tearing at some refuse that even the mangy dogs slinking about wouldn't touch. In the lengthening shadows, women in black had carried kitchen chairs out of their front doors. Most of them were knitting or shelling beans or gutting fish. One was carding a lump of yellowish wool, teasing it out first with a big iron comb and then with a wire brush. Outside another humble door (it was so humble that it resembled a broken shed door skewed off one of its hinges) a rickety spinning wheel was being turned by a graceful woman still in her twenties, already dressed in black from neck to ankles like her elders, who kept pushing a stray lock of hair back from her face. Earlier there had been a thunderstorm. Now on the earth and stones of the waterfront, shimmering puddles ran together the mud colour they lay on with the luminous pale blue of the evening sky which after the storm seemed to arch inconceivably high above the sad, infertile, lonely island.

The scruffy quay had fish crates heaped about, rusty stanchions on which nets had been swagged to dry, bollards with mooring lines. The anchored vessels and the quay were as exclusively given over to men as the waterfront before the houses was the women's domain, though there were no men of military age. Two old seamen were repairing a long net, sitting cross-legged with their reels of tarred cord and their hanks of twine. They spliced and knotted methodically, picking up their bone-handled knives and laying them down. A butterfly came flitting over the glassy anchorage between the masts and rigging of the fishing-smacks.

After nearly four years of malnutrition, Gabriele was a scarecrow with a pasty, puffy face. But his mind was hosannahing his freedom so jubilantly that he had dizzy moments when it cost him some effort to concentrate on the wily sailor standing before him. The old idiot seemed to have no comprehension of how glorious it was that the years of oppression were over. Indeed he had already grunted that Mussolini was the finest man who'd ever led this country, and he seemed unsure whether it might not be better if these wild fellows, the political offenders, were shoved back behind bars as soon as possible. Just to be on the safe side, Gabriele planted his feet slightly apart, he set his hands on his hips and let a tone of merry pugnacity harden his voice.

There was absolutely no sense in a man like himself jumping aboard the next ship for Palermo and getting stuck the useless side of the Front Line – surely the captain could see that? For pity's sake, the nation's destiny hung in the balance, Gabriele exploded, far too elated to be ashamed of the cliché. There was vital political work to be done. There was very possibly going to be hard fighting to be done too, he was happy to say, so if – what was his name? Ah, Captain Sergio. Right. He himself was Gabriele. Delighted to meet you. So if Captain Sergio honestly believed that now they'd got themselves out of that hell-hole prison up there, he and his friends were likely to let cretinous quibbling stand between them and where they wanted to get to ... For God's sake, they'd commandeer him and his miserable boat if he wasn't careful, Gabriele threatened nonchalantly – seeing the alteration in Captain Sergio's shrewd old eyes as he grasped that these curmudgeonly politicos really did have cash, and would pay their passage to the islands eastward, probably be simple enough to pay too much.

Gabriele rounded off amicably now he knew that his argument was won. Captain Sergio haled from the Aeolian Islands, did he, so he would simply be sailing for home, perhaps a little ahead of schedule? Excellent! Gabriele himself was Tuscan. (However friendly this scion of a long-established family and heir to its palace might now be attempting to sound, he was unable to prevent a hint of pride ringing in his voice as he made this statement.) He was Tuscan, and his wife and baby were in Tuscany. No, he must remember, she wasn't a baby any longer. At all events, his wife was in Tuscany, so surely Captain Sergio would understand that he didn't want Yankee generals and Brit generals and all their tanks and all their merry men getting between him and her.

Gabriele's head swam with excitement. He was incapable of sensing whether this suddenly matey talk about wanting to get home to a young wife, which was completely alien to his nature, was ringing true or false to the dour mariner standing there in the salt-smelling evening, with his brown-stained twist of cigarette and his expressionless eyes. Tonight they were going to sleep on that deck! His enchanted gaze battened on *Stefania*'s tarry planks. Tomorrow at daybreak they'd hoist that tattered-looking sail, or see if that rusty donkey-engine could be cranked into thudding life. This miserable outcrop of a prison island was behind him. They would sail to islands that were not prisons. It was as simple and as marvellous as that. Just look at those white-flecked martins soaring high over his head, hurtling down over the anchorage! He swung his exultant glances around, where the sunset glowed on the poverty and meanness of the land, glowed on the rich promise of the sea.

It came so naturally to Gabriele to think issues through faster and more decisively than others, and came so naturally to him to take command of any situation, that he had hardly noticed how he had regularly put himself forward to parley with the prison governor on his friends' behalf. Their last interview, a couple of hours ago, had been the most satisfactory of all. Gabriele had wound it up by announcing that if His Excellency didn't stop shilly-shallying, if he didn't at least *pretend* that orders had been telegraphed from Rome about what to do with his political prisoners, or maybe pretend he was capable of taking the initiative . . . Why, Gabriele had pointed out with a smile, they could both of them see that some of the guards were about to make themselves scarce. He and his comrades would simply slip away with them. And come to think of it, with the Allies advancing steadily in Sicily, and the German defenders by all accounts fighting back a lot more determinedly

than the Italians . . . Hadn't the governor better come clean
and admit that he was thinking of running away too? Oh,
naturally not yet. It would be prudent to wait and see which
way the fighting went, would it not? But His Excellency was
surely not going to claim he could not imagine circumstances in
which a discreet disappearance into private life might suddenly
have overwhelming attractions.

The self-freed men had stridden down to the harbour, slapping one another on the back and every now and then yodelling
from sheer delight. Gabriele had already made his own mind
up with utter clarity, so he took the lead in finding out who
wanted to scuttle to Palermo and who was game for a long
escape ahead of the battles. Sorting out the men from the boys,
he had declared cheerfully to his three companions as soon as
they were hived off from the rest.

Then on his own he had gone about the fishing-smacks, tackling this seaman and that. Now, having reached his agreement
with Captain Sergio, he stooped to pick up his bundle and gazed
around for his friends. Here they came, in the dark blue washes
and smouldering red embers of the sea dusk, carrying several
unfamiliar bags which with any luck contained provisions.

Freedom! Gabriele thought with surefire confidence, clenching
his fists and clenching his jaw, feeling the exultant blood
clamouring in his head, telling him that some violent action
soon would begin to satisfy his long pent-up hatred. Freedom
at last, and the true battle for Italy just beginning, and an escape
across this darkling sea.

Yes, but . . . A successful escape? Gabriele was so inspired by
his own working-out of his audacious plan (it already appeared
to his innocent imagination as the rank of exploit that even in
these measly times ought to merit the writing of newspaper
articles and the award of medals) that he kept overlooking the
sheer unlikelihood of success. A hundred and fifty miles of open
sea to cross, at the very least – and they might meet warships,
of either side. This fishing captain, or others they sailed with
further ahead, might turn nasty. Oh well, then they themselves
would simply have to turn nastier. Now, he must remember
that nearer the Italian coast there might be mine fields. What
if it proved impossible to get aboard vessels of any kind, what

if they were stranded on some island or other? And if when they got to the mainland they found the Fascists were back in power, what then?

Well, it would be an adventure. Gabriele leaped victoriously down from the quay onto Captain Sergio's deck.

With the passionate but limiting clarity that was his nature, Gabriele wasted no time grieving over how low his country had fallen, now when the so-called freeing of cities like Syracuse and Palermo meant nothing more or less than their being conquered by foreign troops and removed from the control of their own citizens. Munching unleavened bread and dried cod in Ustica harbour, his lithe mind was already working out how the Allied advance might best be exploited to ensure exactly the desirable form of liberation for the whole peninsula. In other words, ensure the Socialist Party's preferred political settlement when the war was over.

The cod tasted horrible. Worse, there was pitifully little of it for the voyage. Never mind, at sea tomorrow they would catch fresh fish in abundance, Gabriele assured his companions. All four of them were landlubbers as it chanced, and their anxieties while *Stefania* was still moored snugly to the quay made it even more pleasant to be the one who knew a thing or two about the sea.

Gabriele had taken off his battered, cobbled-together shoes so he could feel the deck under his bare feet. Now in his grubby cotton trousers and grubby cotton shirt he unpacked his bundle. This was an exceedingly woebegone army greatcoat, which had kept him more or less warm day and night last winter. Into it, today he had wrapped his other few garments, Caterina's letters, his asthma inhaler, a small apple tree growing in a tin, and that was all. He now took out the apple tree, stood it by the gunwale where tomorrow it would get plenty of sunlight.

'I'm going to plant that in the garden at home, as soon as I get there,' he said happily.

He neatly wrapped up his other possessions again and knotted the arms of the greatcoat so the bundle stayed a bundle. Lying back luxuriously on the planking, he settled it under his head, gazed up at the constellations. There was Vega, and . . . He yawned. Yes, Cassiopeia.

Gabriele kept his eyes alert in hope of seeing a shooting star. That would be a sign, a good augury. Now, the first leg of this escape was going to be the eighty-odd miles to a brace of little islands called Alicudi and Filicudi. Not a lot of joy to be got out of them, probably. He must remember to ask Captain Sergio if they'd even got wells. Sleepily, blissfully, Gabriele focussed on practicalities. On Panarea, he'd been told, fresh water had to be brought in by freighter and almost nobody lived there. Under the present circumstances, that could mean that what little food and water they had they wouldn't want to part with. After that, on to Stromboli, the volcano island. Just imagine! A conical mountain sticking up out of the sea, with a red glow on its summit at night, and smoking – that'd be something worth steering for!

A new, terrible strength had been born in him during his prison years. Gabriele knew that so irrevocably that he scarcely brought it to consciousness to question it. From now on, by some miracle he was going to be fiendishly clever and utterly innocent at the same time. Yes, and in the campaigns to come he was going to fight with a savagery that would sate something unexamined in him, these were going to be battles that must be won at all costs. Gazing up at the summer stars, he envisaged with sharp pleasure the violence he'd yearned to inflict on certain of his gaolers. Then he started imagining how on the islands ahead very possibly, and in Naples certainly, there would be girls who for a handful of change would do this with him and that with him. None of these sickly sweet dreamings caused him to doubt that decent people would go on liking him for the excellent fellow he was.

Through hundreds of prison days and nights Gabriele had tormented himself with fear that Caterina in her loneliness and despair would have let herself be seduced; he had invented lurid passions, disgusting scenes, titillating scenes. At other times, he had known with deep-down trust that his wife and he would rediscover their pre-war selves undamaged; if anything, these ghastly years would have tempered their spirits; they would joyfully set to work to build their new love on the foundations of the old. With the same inconsistency, often he had brooded bitterly on the years Lisa and he had lost, and just as often he had blissfully imagined the expeditions he was going to take her on, the fun they would have, the friendship that would grow.

But tonight in the exhilaration of his freedom Gabriele rejoiced in the scent of the warm sea, in the hull that stirred beneath his back, in the tap of cordage against the mast. His eyes aglitter with the night panoply, he knew there were times when you had to sacrifice your private life. Terrible times, when you made your offering with tragic pride. Lying there, he dedicated his soul anew to his country and his cause, compared to which his marriage and his family hardly mattered at all.

16

—⚂—

Gabriele D'Alessandria had enjoyed those long ago summers, when the Della Quercia boat had come over from Sardinia to pick up his father and him from a cove on the coast of Tuscany, and now on this first morning of his freedom none of the things that at once began to go wrong discouraged him.

The mate of the *Stefania* was supposed to come aboard at dawn, but an hour later he had not appeared and Captain Sergio had refused to go and search for him. The old skipper was sitting on a hatch placidly smoking a cigarette, utterly insensible to the pressing need for a brisk get-away. He had even begun to dispute that the money agreed upon last night had been for their voyage as far as Panarea, and to say that for that sum he could take them no further than Alicudi, a speck of land so insignificant that they might rot there a long time before they could secure any sort of onward passage.

Gabriele was not dismayed. He was pleased with himself for having foreseen that fresh water might become a problem, and his companions and he had formed a relay, trudging with buckets from the standpipe on the wharf to the barrels on board. When these were full, they went off about the dead-alive village to rustle up old tubs and drums. People seemed to want a lot of cash before they would part with even the most valueless objects. Gabriele was horribly conscious of how finite was the money that his family had sent him periodically for the meagre comforts it had been possible to bribe his gaolers into acquiring and for his eventual journey home. Never mind, the great thing was to get this escape under way, he announced cheerfully, staggering along the quay with an iron jerrycan so rusty that the water in it already looked brown.

Not a breath of wind fluttered in the glassy morning, and with fuel in such short supply it would be prudent not to start using it up straight away. Courage, Gabriele said – what were these oars lying along the scuppers for if not for rowing with? Whistling at his work, he started checking that the thole-pins were all in place and each had its loop of rope. With two men standing up and pushing at their oars to starboard and two men to port, they'd be able to sweep the heavy vessel clear of the land, where they could pick up the first of the day's breeze.

The oars seemed unbearably cumbersome to the freed prisoners who had never rowed in their lives before. Nevertheless, to the amused disdain of the captain and mate, the unfit and soft-handed crew laboriously got the vessel shifting away from the wharf. Unwieldy oars bumping the thole-pins and splashing the water, yard after slow yard they made headway through the pellucid calm across the bay.

'Lucky they're not coming after us with one of those fast corvettes.' Gabriele gave a gasping laugh that was more like a grunt, and raised one arm to mop the sweat that was already coursing down his forehead into his eyes. 'Of course, they will be soon enough if the Fascists stage a come-back. Do you suppose the governor is on his terrace with a telescope, admiring our stylish disappearance?'

Half a mile off-shore, there was a shoal where lines could reach down for the fish that swam low over the sea-bed. From his barred window, day after day Gabriele had dreamed of being out there in one of the craft that looked as if they were annealed into the sparkling blue Tyrrhenian under the illimitable sun-blazing heaven. He had longed to be a free man lolling out there with a fishing-line in his fingers.

Well, now he *was* a free man. Even better, he might still be one tomorrow, he thought jubilantly. Had he not fallen asleep on the deck last night a free man – and woken up, bruised by the boards, wet with dew, still amazed and still at liberty? Was he not right now freeing himself farther, oar heave by oar heave?

'We're about over the shoal, aren't we?' he asked Captain Sergio, gazing around in the windless dazzle, and noticing that the old seaman was already getting out the lines with their sinkers and hooks.

There was no need to decide on a halt. The rowers could continue no longer. With aching shoulders and smarting palms, thankfully they shipped their oars.

They baited the hooks the first time with morsels of dried cod, but after the first small fish had been hauled up and dropped flapping on the deck they had fresh bait. Unshaven and sweaty, Gabriele sat on the gunwale and played his line with a slow, lazy bending and straightening of his elbow, making sure it didn't get tangled with Captain Sergio's line, and trying to engage him in friendly conversation. The old boy was taciturn and no mistake. Still, his heart was probably in the right place, Gabriele decidedly buoyantly, for no better reason than that to the enquiry, 'Is catching enough for a meal on this shoal always this slow?' the passably civil reply, 'Worse, often,' had been returned.

The stove on the stern deck looked more likely to set *Stefania* on fire than to cook the morning's catch so that it was palatable, but Gabriele didn't care, letting his gaze roam down into the aquamarine sun-shafted depths where his line slanted out of sight. It was true that the vessel's entire navigational equipment consisted of one chart of the Tyrrhenian and a compass that didn't look as if it had been corrected for decades, if ever. But Captain Sergio must know his way around this sea like his own back-yard. They'd steer by guess and by God, island landfall by landfall until . . . What about summer calms that went on and on, scorching doldrums when a boat hung immobile between sea and sky and the limp sails gave no shelter and the drinking-water turned foul?

Gabriele glanced up, dreamily. A patch of ruffled, darker blue glitter was blowing toward him. 'A wind!' he cried, jumping to his feet. 'A wind! We're away! Let's get that sail up.'

With rapid swings of both hands, he coiled his line. It came up taut, shaking off droplets that spangled in the sun. He had been in such an excited reverie that he'd hooked a fish without feeling it tug, but he could sense the slight weight now and he reeled in more steadily so as not to lose it. Up the twisting, jerking, silvery body came, hanging by its mouth. Gabriele dropped it at his feet, grabbed for it with one hand. The dying creature slithered from his grasp. Cursing merrily, he got a grip on it at the second attempt, gave the hook a backward yank to extract it from the gaping jaw.

Their meagre catch was heaped on the shady side of the hatchway. The mate took out a knife, started to slit open bellies, hoik innards out and toss them over the side. Then the carcasses had a sack chucked over them, and a bucket of sea water was sluiced over that to keep them cool.

The gaff was hoisted, the idly flapping sail was sheeted in. Slowly the ponderous hull gathered steerage way, and as she answered to the helm her captain swung her onto their course. Slowly, with the faintest chuckle at her stem, *Stefania* made headway toward the east.

Gabriele stood grinning delightedly at the catspaws which were coalescing now so that you could honestly say that as far as the eye could reach the whole sea was rippled by wind. He looked astern, to Ustica, which still bulked disappointingly huge. Still, no Military Police launch was coming after them. Perhaps it was true, his heart exulted, perhaps those lousy Fascists really were done for. 'My God,' he muttered through grating teeth, 'if they ever try to get me back on there . . . !'

Then he unclenched his fists, rammed his straw hat more firmly onto his convict's crop, and went aft lightheartedly determined to take his turn at the helm before long.

'I think the wind's freshening,' he burst out impetuously to Captain Sergio.

'Could be blowing hard by afternoon.'

When after a few hours the smudge that was the last of his prison island dropped below the western horizon, Gabriele wheeled his gaze in triumph around all points of the compass and saw only sea.

17

Gabriele was not like Caterina, who doggedly summoned her good times back to her mind and despaired at how artificial their intensity was. He was not of those who only long afterward know or imagine that their grey matter has ever flushed pink from sheer innocent joy, and ruefully recognise that a lot of what made for that happiness was their scarcely giving it a thought at the time.

During that voyage aboard *Stefania*, Gabriele's lucid mind immediately began to *know* that this was a blessed interlude. As he got accustomed to the patterns of weather, so that each supercession of wind by calm did not make him instantly bad tempered and soon after that miserable, but instead he waited with sanguine patience for the next breeze. As no ships came near them, and the only aeroplanes they saw flew on high and far. As he began to let himself half-believe that, though surely they must be the only madmen to venture to sea slap-bang in the middle of the first of the great campaigns to free Europe, they really might be going to slip secretly away between the Allied armies who with any luck were completing their conquest of Sicily just over the southern horizon, and the Axis armies who were presumably still in inviolate mastery of the mainland over the other horizon to the north. As his gamble seemed as if it truly might be going to come off, despite *Stefania* being far and away the slowest craft he'd ever sailed, because after a few days they were cruising through the Aeolian Islands still unmolested and sighting other harmless craft going about the sane business of life. Yes, and surely the invasion of the mainland, when it came – or could it already have come? – would be launched across the Straits of Messina fifty-plus miles to the south-east, so away here in this back of all the sea's beyonds no one would bother their heads about one fishing-smack among many. Times came when they were ploughing stolidly eastward, and Gabriele found he'd been holding his breath as he stared at the horizon's blue laid on blue till his eyes ached from the sea glare. Then he'd watch the wake rumpling astern. He'd shake his head, he'd smile, he'd laugh softly.

On Ustica, reliable facts about the fighting for Sicily had been hard enough to come by, and now at sea not even rumours reached them. Gabriele watched the stubble on his companions' jaws become the beginnings of beards, and when he ran his hand over his own head and face he could feel the difference. They ate frugal meals of dry bread and bits of scorched fish, but it was enough. They washed by diving into the sea, climbing out again up a rope ladder hung over the side. Gabriele felt his kinship with all the traders and fighters and vagabonds who had sailed these seas time out of mind. He remembered myths and histories he'd read at school, stories of the Phoenicians, of Levantine merchants, of Barbary corsairs. Voyaging through the azure days and starry nights beyond the reach of radio, the armies and navies they were trying to slip between could have been those of any century, the war they longed for news of could have been any of the Mediterranean's wars.

All the small hitches seemed to get themselves sorted out eventually. None of the big disasters occurred. Hours came when Gabriele was as carefree as the wind thrumming in the shrouds, as the white horses galloping on forever over the blue sea. Where would the Allies land next, in Sardinia? If only Marshal Badoglio's secret emissaries were negotiating the surrender skilfully, and plans were being hatched for Rome to be occupied in force before the Germans made a preemptive strike, then the next *coup de théâtre* might be – what? An attack even as far north as Livorno conceivably, that would change the face of the war by God. Yes, a landing in Tuscany! And he'd escaped, he was sailing for home! It was true that even if everything went smoothly they would land down in Calabria, and then he'd have to make his way north right up the peninsula. Oh, he'd make it somehow!

Gabriele's only previous travels through Calabria had been in the autumn of '39, under armed guard, in handcuffs, with a chain linking him left and right to the other felons in his batch being sent south. Day after day he had sat in chains in police station cells down the length of Italy. He had stood on station platforms chained, sat in railway carriages chained. But he was

in such victorious spirits now that even this did not sour his idea
of the South. He repeated the word as if it had mantric potency:
Calabria . . .

His most exultant times of all were when he was at the helm,
and he lost himself in dreams of action. With this doughty
old *Stefania* barging into the waves, and this sunshiny spray
with rainbow colours flying. With the heavy tiller in his grasp
juddering and tugging now this hot wind had got up. With that
great gliding bird following the boat – did even herring-gulls
come that big?

He sang under his breath and he narrowed his eyes to peer
into the salt-stinging dazzle of blue ahead. He hardly thought
of the past, except to recall sailing the Della Quercia boat off
Sardinia with Caterina and how sexy she was offshore with
almost no clothes on and then with no clothes on. Yes, when the
war was over, he must remember to take lots of sailing holidays.
Chuck in medicine and get himself voted into parliament at the
very first election – that went without saying. But plenty of
sailing too. Plenty of love-making also. (Images of Caterina in
provocative poses began to blur, not with penniless Neapolitan
girls this time, but with young beauties who might come the
way of a successful man in the post-war world.) Come to think
of it, how would Esmeralda be getting on in the smash-up of
Fascism? And that shit she'd married? Well, that shameful
dictatorship was beaten, the end couldn't be long coming now.
Though looking to the future . . . Splendid that the Russians, the
British and the Americans were coming to rescue the European
heartlands from their tyrannising and their mass-murdering. But
one hoped that these useful conquerors were going to be obliging
about packing up and going home afterward.

Trying to be a protective elder brother to Esmeralda had
never been an uncomplicated part to play, what with her going
straight from being a harum-scarum tomboy to being a society
belle with her self-destructiveness quite unimpaired and without
much of an interval for simply being friendly. Still, now Gabriele
let his dreams about getting home in time to be one of the Tuscan
guerrilla leaders get mixed up with equally delightful images
of how he might save his sister from the consequences of her
rash marriage. About her husband, he was undecided. In some

imaginings, he magnanimously intervened to spare Manzari's life. In others, he sternly allowed justice to take its course. Both these turns of events were so eminently satisfactory, that the steersman of the lumbering *Stefania* made no effort to choose between them.

He'd settle his back against the gunwale, wedge a foot against the eighteen-inch belaying-pin to which his mainsheet was cleated, brace himself against the shuddering helm. That island ahead was Lipari. They were making it, they were getting there! What had he been ...? And Gabriele would go back to his excited dreaming (which he thought of as the soberest calculation) of how, if an Allied air-borne force seized the Rome airfields ... And then of course it would be vital that the Brenner Pass was held ... Yes, yes – but this immaculate world through which you sailed with a steady wind on the quarter! All the wandering seafarers of the Mediterranean, back to the Carthaginians, back to the Greeks ... How old this experience was! What was that story – it came in Virgil, or somewhere, he remembered it from school – about a helmsman who drowsed, who fell overboard and drowned? He could imagine that, his mind lulled by the vessel's rocking motion, his mind aswim. A good death. Down, down, in the washing coolness and the silence. Blue, very blue.

At Lipari, Captain Sergio refused to be cajoled, bullied or bribed into taking them an island farther. Sun-burned and optimistic, Gabriele shrugged nonchalantly. He carefully wrapped his apple tree up in his jersey, folded everything into his greatcoat, tied the sleeves, slung the bundle over his shoulder, and set off about the harbour to see how one got to Panarea.

18

—⁂—

His hair and beard rimed with salt, Gabriele walked lightly along the quay, thinking his light, precise, confident thoughts half the time and in a joyful daze the other half, noticing all manner of things and approving of them all.

The sea-reflected sun shimmering on the moored craft pleased him. So did the cheerful whites, reds, blues and greens with which the hulls were painted. It was excellent how the warps slanted down from the gunwales to the surface of the bay, and then were refracted and appeared to descend at a different angle through the clear water where you could watch schools of minnows darting about.

Though Lipari might be the most important of the Aeolian Islands, it appeared, now he began to take in the signs of impoverishment and backwardness, that the twentieth century had so far given the place nearly as much of a miss as it had that God-hated Ustica. Still, Gabriele told himself, when elsewhere progress had often simply meant mechanised slaughter, maybe these people weren't as unlucky as all that.

Now, he must find out how the Sicilian campaign had been going, and . . . Just you wait, he exhorted the anchorage, the masts, the men reeving new halyards. Just wait till we've liberated ourselves from our liberators, so that the serious business of brushing aside the old conservative ruling class can be tackled and we can get new people putting new ideas into action. Then you'll see! he gaily promised a funereal old woman who was creeping along with a brace of terrified white doves tied by their legs hanging upside-down from her tight fist. He strolled on, his mind only half absorbing the crone's head that had scarcely reached to his chest, her wispy beard, her poor twisted limbs. Now, some fresh food to eat, and . . . Dear heaven, had he dreamed this apparition, or was this gorgeous girl really offering to sell him a bag of plums?

Gabriele had wandered as far as the corner of the little port where peasants brought their produce to sell. His mouth

abruptly longing for the touch of the ripe, fresh plums, longing
for the sharp act of crushing his teeth through the flesh of the
fruit and feeling the tart juice spurt onto his tongue and under
his tongue, he concentrated on the smiling face before him, his
hand already reaching into his pocket.

'Bread,' he said, suddenly in love with the word. Yes, she was
pretty. Either that, or he was in a trance. Anyhow, all was well.
'Not just plums. Fresh bread, too. Is that possible?'

Several of the market folk were clustering around the stranger
who had arrived on Sergio's boat and had this stumbling fervour
in his voice, quite apart from his speaking an Italian some of
them found hard to follow, not like their dialect at all. He
had a wild look, and his eyes shone with happiness as eyes
rarely shine.

'Don't rip me off,' Gabriele said simply, smiling around at
them. 'I was in gaol, on Ustica. One of the political prisoners,
I'm not a crook. And I've still got a long journey before I get
home. Just tell me what a fair price is, these days, for a bag of
plums, please, and a big hunk of bread.'

'Here, that bread will need something to wash it down,' a
short, gnarled farmer with bandy legs said. He filled a tumbler
with white wine from a wicker-clad flask. The flawed glass of
the old tumbler was thick and greenish, so that when the wine
was held out in the sunlight it had greeny golden flecks and
shadows and glinting whorls.

'Don't pay me,' the farmer said. 'Let's hope we all get out of
prison before long.'

'Dead right,' rejoined Gabriele, grinning at his new friend
and raising the verdant-looking wine. 'Won't you drink a glass
with me?'

Standing beneath an old sail rigged up to shade a few yards
of the waterfront, he ate a plum and then a mouthful of bread,
then another plum and then another mouthful of bread, until he
had finished them. Then he handed the emptied tumbler back
to its owner, thanked him and asked where the local barber's
shop was.

The barber's establishment overlooked the quay, and had
canvas curtains in the doorway. Inside, it proved to be a
dusty cubbyhole, with a foxed mirror, with enamel jugs and

basins. On the colourless wall were hanging a leather strop for sharpening razors, the Virgin Mary brightly painted on a tin oval, a crinkled photograph of a football team, and a cross made of plaited palm left from some long ago Easter-tide procession.

Gabriele had completely forgotten how his heart would have thudded if he could have brought a crowbar smashing down on the face of a prison guard, and how it would thud when some nameless girl was taking off her clothes for him. He had forgotten too about how insignificant individual happiness was when weighed against the stern duties of a patriot. The bread and plums and wine were translating themselves into dreams of his triumphant return to Arezzo. He sat in the barber's chair, which was a wooden café chair, and discovered to his satisfaction that in the glass before him, beyond his own face (he was surprised and faintly flattered to find what a pirate he looked) he could see between the hooked-back canvas swags to a section of the anchorage.

Would the barber please make his head look a bit more civilised, Gabriele asked, settling down to enjoy the entertainment offered in the looking-glass. Over there was a dinghy being sculled by what appeared to be rather a young boy smoking a pipe. On a slipway, a group of men were all heaving in unison as they careened a barge for caulking.

Must make myself more or less presentable for Caterina, he thought with a flicker of his old dandyism, and found that his reflection was smiling at the thought of smartening himself up for her. This foolish grinning in the glass would never do, so Gabriele reminded himself severely that he still had hundreds of miles to travel, and composed his features into a manly indifference. Only, the smile would keep coming back. As for exploiting poor girls, what *could* he have been thinking of? Squalid, too. Yes, better not bother about the back-street girls.

The island of Panarea, when he crossed there aboard the barber's cousin's boat, proved to be just as beautiful as Lipari in its arid loneliness, but even more poverty-stricken. Still nothing dimmed Gabriele's ardour. Was the place incapable of producing forage for any creatures except goats, or of growing anything much beyond prickly pears and for some reason an abundance of caper bushes? Well then, they would nourish themselves on goats' flesh flavoured with capers, he couldn't wait. And fish – there must be fish? He remembered a restaurant in Antibes where they had an excellent recipe for skate with capers. (This was a recollection which borrowed lustre from the fashionable Riviera and from a lot of honeymoon romantic sensuality. Indeed, the taste of skate and capers seemed to be quite inextricable from the sight and the feel of Caterina naked in a hotel bedroom.) Anyway, his present companions and he had been Mussolini's prisoners, they were the élite of the land, they'd eaten prickly pears and worse than prickly pears. Water was in desperately short supply? They would be happy to drink wine. There wasn't much wine and it was thin, sour stuff was it? Well, heavens, they'd pull through.

Gabriele kept reminding himself that when he reached the mainland this idyllic interlude would be over. With a lot of the ports and railway junctions bombed, then partially repaired, then bombed again, rumour had it that whole regions of the South were to all intents cut off. The new military dictator's instructions to his armed forces to keep law and order would naturally mean that most of the bourgeoisie were solidly behind him, despite the ghastly stories that were rife about towns where troops really had fired into protesting crowds. Gabriele heard too about cities where half the population were so frightened of the air raids which went on month after month after month, that they went out into the country to sleep rough in barns and sheds, returned each morning on foot, on bicycles, on the carts coming to market. Came back to queue for hours for their daily ration of bread, which had been reduced to one hundred and fifty grammes.

But in a minute Gabriele would resume his happy dreams about how the Socialist Party was going to place him high on its list of candidates for Tuscany as soon as democracy was restored. Or he would imagine his arrival in his own house, how his mother would weep for joy and dear fat old Immacolata would burst splendidly into tears as well.

Caterina and he were going to plunge straight back into loving one another as truly and as passionately as ever, more so if that were possible. These days, his ebullient heart never had any hesitation about telling him that, and he never imagined that she might perhaps have grown in directions alien to him, or that he might seem changed to her. Of course, he must be prepared for it to be upsetting when Lisa didn't recognise him. But Caterina and he would have their attic nights for catching up on all the love-making they'd missed, and catching up on all the jokes and the murmuring. Perhaps she would have another baby soon. He hoped so. He hoped it might be a boy.

As for when, despite half the nation's merchant fleet having been sunk or put out of action, a tramp steamer heading for Stromboli and then north to Naples most miraculously appeared ... Standing on that rusty deck, Gabriele gazed at the volcano in the middle of the sea as if that particular miracle had been exactly what was required to justify *his* vision of the truth of things.

Ten days later, when far behind him the Allies had finished their conquest of Sicily and were about to attack across the Straits of Messina, he was tramping into Arezzo, gazing left and right at the sights of his boyhood with a faint smile of triumph on his lips. There was the primary school yard where he'd scuffled, here was the garden where Esmeralda had sicked up all those éclairs. Then behind him he heard wild cries and running feet.

'Gabriele!'

'Gabriele!'

'Oh my God he's back!'

'He's back!'

Louisa and Emilia were on him, hugging and kissing, exclaiming. They stood back to admire him and check that it really was true. They flung themselves on him again, they tousled his hair, both talking at once and interrupting his replies.

'Four years! We've all been on tenterhooks these last weeks.'

'Run and tell Rosalba, run!'

'Run yourself! I'm not letting go of him. Oh, when your mother ... !'

'Honestly, you might have telephoned!'

'Yes, of course Caterina's all right! When she claps eyes on you she'll howl with tears, she'll go all to pieces, you wait. What bliss for her!'

'I don't suppose you've forgotten how to cheer a girl up, have you? Been practising on Sicilian gaolers' daughters, I shouldn't be surprised.'

Word that Gabriele D'Alessandria was home spread from street to street, it didn't seem necessary to run to tell anybody. People emerged from doorways and hugged him and kissed him. A small crowd of old friends and acquaintances and people he hardly recognised escorted him toward his family house. They thumped him on the back, they kept congratulating him. He grinned at all of them and began to feel bashful though he didn't understand why he should. He kept explaining that in the South these days only important people had access to telephones that really worked, not gaolbirds and vagabonds like him, but the message didn't seem to get through and still everyone kept on asking why he hadn't rung up. Then they all stopped at a hostelry. Amid a lot of confused exclaiming and recounting and explaining, glasses were filled with the good local red wine and the hero's health was drunk.

The blacksmith emerged from his smithy at the shindy of the triumphant procession. When he saw the cause of it, he made as if to stride through the throng to shake Gabriele's hand and welcome him. But then he was caught by a feeling too strong either to express or wholly subdue. He pressed his lips firmly together and shook his head slowly from side to side. He just stood there, with his fists on his hips, watching the return go by.

Rosalba came skittering down a stony alley and leaped into her cousin's arms, clinging around his neck and kicking her high heels up behind off the ground, her cries of joy strangled by her sobs. This caused the slowly progressing tumult to come to another of its standstills. Above their heads, unobserved at a palace window, an ancient gentleman leaning on two sticks looked down.

Gabriele set Rosalba back on her feet. 'Come on, cousin,' he said. 'The last couple of hundred yards seem to be the slowest of all. But let's get there if we can.'

19

As soon as it became known that the authorities were bowing to popular pressure for the release of most, anyway, of the political prisoners, Gaetano Da Durante had set off from Venice to wait for Gabriele. Knowing without thinking about it that this was the right thing to do, he had stopped overnight at Ca' Santa Chiara and then the two old friends had driven on together over the mountains to Arezzo. They had materialised in the stone hall of the D'Alessandria house: Gaetano wheezing heavily, carrying a portfolio under his arm, taking off his panama hat and mopping his bald dome with a blue and red checked handkerchief; Luigi standing still and quiet, apparently comfortably cool, glancing about him with watchful eyes.

For many years, Sonya had silently rejoiced that Gaetano's and her long ago passion had been transmuted into this congeries of loyalties and comprehensions, into his devotion to her whole family. For years he had shown up unannounced when anything important was afoot – for Lisa's birth, for Esmeralda's wedding despite having forgotten to answer the invitation, at times like that – so now Sonya had half-consciously been expecting him to appear. As for Luigi, she had long resigned herself to being pleased for him if he was less unhappy living independently from her, so she welcomed him home in this spirit, simply and without comment. It seemed eminently fitting to her that at this climacteric of their nation's and their own lives, she should have her two lost loves to flank her, like a pair of battered but friendly effigies.

The portfolio turned out to have a pair of Francesco Salviati drawings in it.

'A present for your little Lisa,' Gaetano informed Caterina gruffly. 'Well, I suppose it's a bit more seemly than if I gave them to you. And better than selling them to some damned museum. Tell her not to do that, or anyway not till after I'm dead. Oh, and . . . For God's sake – while I'm about it . . .'

Gaetano had cleared his throat loudly, as if in embarrassment.

With his round face of a cherub in its fifties nearly blushing and the gestures of his podgy hands getting more and more brusque, he pulled the other drawings out of the portfolio and spread them on the table. There were a *Design for a Pilaster* by Correggio; a *Head of the Good Thief* by Beccafumi; an *Angel Playing a Violoncello* by Gaudenzio Ferrari . . . Most awe-inspiring of all, there were two Fra Bartolomeo landscapes.

Caterina had never imagined such generosity. The trouble was that for the last two days and nearly sleepless nights she had driven herself to weeping distraction with her longing for Gabriele to come home at last, her determination not to believe in it till she had him in her arms, and her fear that their marriage might have become mere cloudy shapes and thin air. This meant that she was quite unable to focus appreciatively on the drawings, or even to say thank-you very coherently.

Gaetano muttered, 'No children of my own, you see. Well, none that I've ever acknowledged.' He peered morosely at a *Flight into Egypt* by Lelio Orsi. 'Suppose she might like the donkey. What do you think?'

By now looking thoroughly disgruntled, he listed the dozen or so subjects and artists on a sheet of paper, writing so badly that they were practically illegible. He scrawled that they were a present for Lisa D'Alessandria, signed it.

Tonight the massive front doors of the Palazzo D'Alessandria had been wide open for hours, because of all the visiting that Gabriele's homecoming had inspired. All through the war evenings, only two or three rooms had ever been lit at the same time, and it had been exceedingly rare for anybody to pay a visit. But tonight parts of the house that had not been dusted for months or even years had been flung open, and passers-by saw that nearly every window in the huge old building was glimmering behind its curtains, and nobody seemed to be bothering a bit about the black-out. Well, Arezzo had not yet been bombed, the neighbours in the dark street reminded one another cheerfully, and with any luck tonight would not be the night for the first raid. So they decided that they too would go in, to raise a glass to the young master of the house.

Enlightened opinion in society was still attempting to grapple with all the military catastrophes and the political turmoil.

The preferred method was a two-pronged reasoning. Firstly, you argued that the war was by no means so utterly lost as the appalling facts appeared to demonstrate; and secondly, that anyhow you yourself had never been anything like so at your ease with either imperial aggrandisement overseas or dictatorship at home as other people might tactlessly remember you as having been. Even so, a number of *bien-pensant* ladies and gentlemen, who four summers earlier had been honoured to attend Esmeralda D'Alessandria's wedding to the Honourable Carlo Manzari, now decided not to be seen among those celebrating her subversive brother's freedom. And certainly they would have been astounded to imagine that, only a couple of summers later, some of those poor wretches who had gone to prison for their anti-Fascist principles would have become the astute Resistance heroes quickly getting their hands on the political levers in the reborn nation, and as such would have to be lionised.

All the same, there was a terrific coming and going beneath the arches of the entrance hall, and up and down the staircase with its stone balustrade that for centuries had been cool to the touch of visiting hands even during the most torrid summers. The family's frugal celebratory dinner had been interrupted so repeatedly that no one could recall whether they had actually sat down and swallowed anything much or not. Now all the drawing-room windows were open to the sweltering mid-August night, though the curtains hung motionless except when Rosalba swished one to and fro to make a breath of cool wind. The chandelier was ashimmer as if to cast its glittering, indifferent blessing over a peace-time ball. The record-player had been carried down from the attic and several couples were dancing.

None of Gabriele D'Alessandria's friends from his student days in Padua was there to make merry over his return. (One was in a British prisoner-of-war camp near Tobruk. Another was dead, in the Ukraine.) But what seemed like *all* the Arezzo hospital doctors and nurses had appeared, some of them with wives or husbands in tow.

Count La Marrechia was there, in a white suit with a gold watch-chain looped across his waistcoat and a tiny yellow rose in his buttonhole, the tapping of his malacca canes quite inaudible in the hubbub. He had come, as he informed Gabriele, 'Not to talk to you, my dear boy. Good heavens no. Just so that I can die having seen the joy in your wife's eyes.'

Sonya was moving with delighted dignity through the party that had spontaneously combusted in her house, and was a lot noisier and less formal than any throng that had gathered there since peace time and Edoardo's heyday as a young host. She was greeting her guests with more warmth than she had displayed since the war began and she was enjoying making light of the whole glorious affair.

To all the people who fulsomely told her how wonderful it must be for her to have Gabriele home safe and sound, the old lady replied: 'Well, he wasn't going to stay away forever, was he?' To those who exclaimed upon how well he looked, all things considered, she amused herself by remarking tartly: 'It isn't curious at all! So far as one can make head or tail of his rambling story, it appears he's been on a long yachting holiday, with lots of fresh air and lots of fresh fish and rather too much wine.' Or, by way of variation: 'You should have seen him when he first arrived, before Caterina took him to the bathroom and scrubbed him for about an hour and a half, and got rid of that horrible beard, and brought him back dressed in clean clothes.'

Sonya found it particularly amusing to make light of the music of rejoicing in her heart, because her daughter-in-law by contrast was so overcome that she was making everyone smile, and causing some to dab their handkerchiefs to their eyes.

Several hours had passed since Caterina had hurtled down the last flight of steps and into Gabriele's arms, and now after nightfall she seemed if anything to be *more* prone to sudden cataclysms of tears and to wild utterances, which clearly bore tremendous significance for her but bewildered her listeners. It seemed that tonight all her warp and woof of tensions, all her Chinese boxes of solitudes within solitudes and alienations within alienations were taking their toll at last. It seemed that some crescendo was building up in her; that too many things meant too much, so that neither silence nor words were up to the job.

Most of the time she held tight to Gabriele's arm, making no attempt not to keep gazing at him with brilliant, possessive, victorious eyes, and apparently quite beyond noticing that there were other human beings in the room and they too were delighted to see him. But then she might cry out to Gabriele crazy-sounding things, about how 'it was like those carved prisoners trying to wrench themselves free of their stone'. Or, 'I had to dream it all back. I had to whisper you back to me. I needed a charm, or something. Oh for pity's *sake* Gabriele! *Can't* we have ourselves to ourselves for an hour? Do we *have* to be here?'

Luckily Gabriele seemed to understand quite a bit of what she meant, people noticed. Or at any rate he hugged her when she wept, and even in his eyes a glisten was once seen. She'd be fine after a good night's sleep, everybody agreed.

For the last ten minutes, Caterina D'Alessandria had recovered her poise, or at least she had seemed content to squeeze her husband's arm and to smile at people in a dazed fashion. But now abruptly she dragged him to sit beside her on the chaise-longue. She launched into a tirade, staring feverishly into his eyes. Her fractured sentences tumbled out, all about, 'You haven't yet read all my stupid scribblings, but you understand don't you? No, perhaps you'll never understand. That will be . . . You do still love me, don't you? Oh I could tell you of times in Rome when . . . That sister of yours!'

Their friends politely moved out of earshot. Happily there was always Lisa to make a fuss of. She had already had her first tantrum of jealousy of the father she did not really remember, and it was all that Sonya and Immacolata could do to stop the exhausted child becoming as overwrought as her mother.

Still, whenever the young mistress of the palace raised her voice, shards of what she was saying could be heard.

'I've had this idiotic conviction . . . If in the thick of this war between your people and mine . . . Just a bagatelle, constancy, in war time – do they say that, have they understood that? But if you and I could somehow . . . I think I may have become obsessed. Not good, eh? Funny how the worst isn't the living in a world where you don't often know who you can trust. There are the intimations, they're worse. Hazy notions about

Esmeralda, Carlo, other people. Hazy notions about myself . . .
Who's playing this game, who's playing that game? I tried to get
you out of prison, you believe that, don't you? Esmeralda and I
did everything we could. But nothing I . . . My darling, politics
aren't going to separate us again, are they? You must promise
me that. No, it's all right, don't worry. I'm not that stupid. Of
course we'll be separated again. I know the sort of thing this
war is going to do.'

A minute later, from the chaise-longue her voice rose again,
she was hammering her ideas into Gabriele's head as if these
were the last moments she'd ever have for making him understand. 'The split in me for God's damned sake, you know, the
two halves. No, that's wrong. All the divisions, Gabriele, all
the bloody awful cracks. No, it's not your fault. Nothing is.'
Then she lost her way; her voice became fearful, agitated. 'I got
a letter from Giles, I know I told you – but he wrote it years
and years ago. So you see, when it comes to having a chance
in hell of imagining his story right, imagining him as he is . . .
But you, in Naples the poor girls are all such . . . Mustn't use
bad words. Mustn't! And who am I to talk? Oh, sometimes
I'm cold as ice,' her voice suddenly clanged. 'I see how small
and meaningless we are – God yes! I think one's got to cast
a damned cold eye on life, don't you? That's what it deserves,
or that's how it's seen to best advantage or something. Did I
tell you how bitter I've become, how horrible with hatred and
despair? That's bad, that doesn't do any good, does it? So you
ought to know that, and . . . You're good, you don't hate. You
don't even hate your enemies, not really. Or are you bitter now,
have you changed too, has prison changed you? I've been locked
up too, don't you ever forget that. I'm still locked up, I can't get
out of this.' Her piteous voice rose, wailing, lost. 'Tell me! Why
won't you tell me what I ask? Yes, you have changed!'

Ever since Gabriele had walked joyfully in through the front
door, his family life had been the unquestioned centre of his
existence. Now he held Caterina's hands, he smiled into her
eyes. 'Sweetheart, we can talk about everything as much as we
want later. We've got all our lives, my darling! But now . . .'
He swung his smiling eyes around the merriment. 'Of course,
I know all this disreputable bunch deserve the most severe

ignoring by us. But – do you think we should very graciously be friendly to one or two of them?'

Caterina flared up. 'For God's sake, in our own house can't I . . . ? What are they all doing here? Oh no, I'm sorry my darling – but it hasn't been easy, *please* believe me.'

'Come and dance,' he replied, raising her to her feet. And with his lips close to her ear, 'Kate Caterina.'

Sonya D'Alessandria was delighted to see couples dancing in her drawing-room again, but she hardly heard the waltzes. Deep within herself, she was rapt by this new, thrilling music of thanksgiving, of the most sombre victory. She recognised tonight how chilly and joyless she had let herself become, and this seemed a simple, natural recognition, and it seemed a simple and natural matter now to resolve not to let her spirit become too crabbed. The war was a long way from being over yet, and the future might hold griefs worse than any she had yet known. Despite this, her soul must remember how to praise.

She listened to her heart's rich paean. Yes, it was so utterly right: that the brave and innocent man who was her son should be free, should come home. Better than this, what was there? So tonight she turned to Almighty God, not with anguished doubts about the problem of evil, but humbly and joyously giving thanks for His mercy, and praying that one day Edoardo would come home too.

Sonya smiled at herself, because of course she was absurd, the way that simply having her son return to her, having this husband and father restored to his wife and daughter, caused her at once to emerge serenely beyond all her wrestlings with metaphysical impossibilities. Yes, she was ridiculously human – and naturally another day she'd go back to tormenting herself with doubts. But tonight the miracle was that being ridiculously human struck her as a perfectly all right condition. So when Gaetano asked her to dance she accepted him with a smile, recalling with pleasure that despite being disgracefully overweight, on a dance floor he'd always been light on his feet. Caterina over there was being ridiculously human too. Good, good! All was well. As for Gaetano the words could have been invented for him, Sonya decided.

Luigi D'Alessandria, after his long absence from Arezzo, after his long abeyance from his previous roles, did not play the head of the family, or he only did so spectrally. But his sad eyes in his small, delicate, gaunt head shone as he moved through his family's guests, and there was plenitude in his heart.

Rejoicing in his handsome son who had been lost to them but had come home, rejoicing in the aura of victory the lad exuded, Luigi had utterly forgotten his habitual misgivings about doctrinaire admirers of Marx and Lenin. He had forgotten his twinges of guilt for not having grappled with the Roman lawyers for longer too. So long as there were men like his son Gabriele around, he thought buoyantly, the country would get to its feet. Naturally, in a few days he himself would vanish away to Ca' Santa Chiara once more. Ghosts must know how to be ghosts. But now it was a sharp happiness to him to feel he was scarcely visible, he was scarcely real, and to see his son command the stage.

Luigi watched Sonya and their old friend revolving staidly together, he chuckled to think that Gaetano was far too fat ever to be a ghost, and he went on happily feeling himself a spirit returned to haunt his old life, see how his world would be without him. How good to be a ghost! To glide back, to listen, to watch; not to count any more, not to matter to others, not to matter to yourself. The family would all be fine without him, naturally they would. Why, they already were! But he broke off from this train of thought because his own words had reminded him of his notebooks, of the task he had set himself. Yes, even a man already half-inexistent could have his uses. To listen, to watch, to write it true rather than false! He'd get back over the mountains, he'd get back to work in a few days. Perhaps La Marecchia too felt spectral sometimes. He must remember to ask him. Just think, when he was a little fellow in a sailor suit, having his head patted by Garibaldi – and look at the old boy now, tottering gaily about with those sticks!

The telephone in the study kept ringing, and it was always people wanting news of Gabriele and then wanting to talk to him. He rang up both his sisters in the capital: 'Just to let them know that, despite their two bloody husbands' most assiduous efforts to keep me corralled up, in fact I'm free.'

Tonight even Gabriele's ability to think straight was being

tested, what with everyone continually asking him questions about his escape so that he had no chance to begin asking all the far more vital things that *he* wanted to know, and what with all his best efforts to reply being interrupted by other questioners wanting to be told quite different things.

He was aware of the side of him that was a son of an old family of this city, whose head was buzzing with determination to take up a responsible position in this society and make some money. He had already noticed what bad repair the house was in, and mixed up with his dreams of after the war securing for his mother a decidedly more affluent old age, and his dreams of having a son, were quite detailed plans about what he would get the builders to start work on the minute the war was over, and hazier images of how later in a successful career he would buy other distinguished properties and leave the D'Alessandria better set up than he had found them. (No more than he had ever doubted his ideals of social justice had Gabriele ever doubted that one should inherit one's father's palace and then in one's turn have a son to leave it to.) Yes, he'd start by having the leaking gutters and the rotten window-frames replaced. Then, these principal rooms on the first floor all needed redecorating – and as for the bedrooms, it was better to forget how tatty they were.

Well, money would do the trick, given time, he concluded cheerfully. And now too he was aware of the side of him that was the passionate reformer. This other man's head was buzzing with the need to stop receiving all these neighbourly congratulations on his return, and go into a huddle with a couple of his socialist friends so he could catch up on the latest political intrigues, find out who was up and who was down, what winds were blowing, how he should best position himself.

Then, his mother appeared terribly altered, she looked stricken. Of course, tonight she was in tremendous fettle – but he could tell. He wanted a quiet talk with his father, too, about all the things he had discovered in prison and on his journey home. Things about himself, things about the war. Gabriele had an urgent feeling that his father and he might have a lot to discuss, they might have consonances to rejoice in, they might become better friends than they had ever been before. Yes, but Caterina seemed pretty unbalanced. Uneasily he made himself know that there were reasons for her frayed nerves, and that now he was going to help her get better, if the war let him. She will be healed, she will be whole, he promised his mind. But he was unable not to feel a throb of depression at the thought of her miseries he'd have to try to cope with, the scenes he'd have to face. And if it really turned out she had psychological weaknesses that hadn't been evident before? Oh Lord, marriage! he thought with an instant's gloomy irritation, hoping that she wasn't going to be a drag on his career.

To cheer himself up, Gabriele whirled around the floor with his wife, and then for a few breathless seconds he danced with Rosalba, and then he was almost sweeping Caterina off her feet again. All his guests smiled at the returned escaper who was changing his dancing partner at shorter and shorter intervals. Then they broke into laughter and clapping when Lisa suddenly overcame her jealousy and decided that Papa must waltz with her too.

Gabriele beamed, he swept his wife and his cousin around, and when it was his daughter's turn he stooped double and guided her through something like the right steps with infinite gentleness. Forget all the sides to yourself and forget the damage done to others, just for one night, he exhorted himself. He was the master of the house – he felt that, with an ache of sorrow for his father's multiple abdications and with a surge of satisfaction on his own account. He was home, he had several glasses of good Tuscan wine coursing in his veins, the Axis was going to lose this war though it might take a year or two yet.

If only Edoardo was all right! Tonight Gabriele felt amused condescension toward his married sisters. The élite of the country always knew how to float along on a political or military flood tide and then float the other way on the ebb and in due course come bobbing back on the next flood again, Cosima and Esmeralda would be fine. But for a minute he felt a protective pang for his younger brother. Subalterns on the losing sides in wars weren't any sort of élite. Just think, if Edoardo could get back here and they could talk things over, he'd soon show him that the Allies were Italy's best hope. Then they'd stand shoulder to shoulder, they'd be brothers as brothers should be.

Downstairs, the lit doorway was standing open hospitably. Gabriele liked the thought of that, and only just restrained himself from running downstairs to see if any more of his neighbours felt like coming in to join the party. Then he changed his mind and ran downstairs after all, without telling anybody what he was doing, because he'd been assailed by the ridiculous hope that Edoardo might come walking miraculously through the town, tonight he too might come home. In the doorway Gabriele stood smiling at his own foolishness and with tears in his eyes, looking along the empty street.

Then he made himself run quickly back up again to the drawing-room and throw himself into the party with renewed zest. Yes, this was the life! Friends dancing, friends clapping you on the shoulder. Caterina's supple waist under your hand, her glittering eyes. And those windy days sailing for home, with spray flying – they'd been worth being born for too.

It was a good democratic gathering, Gabriele saw with approval. Doctors, tradesmen – all sorts. Count La Marecchia. Gaetano Da Durante, who at thirty had still been a penniless lieutenant but must be worth a fortune these days. (Tonight Gabriele was attracted to the idea of men whom wars had kept poor but who then had become successful.) The blacksmith and his wife, the baker and his wife. This was the civilisation he believed in, this was everyone's true inheritance! Over there Louisa and Emilia were dancing with their fiancés. Those two girls had been more or less engaged to the same boyfriends for donkeys' years, repeatedly declaring them to be unsatisfactory but never ditching them. Why, even old Signor Orazio had been tempted indoors and upstairs wearing his Sunday best, that gave you an idea of the importance of the occasion. He was dancing with fat, ruddy Immacolata, it did your heart good to see them. And there was their married daughter Nicoletta, dancing with Gaetano. Over the years, lots of people had noticed how she resembled him. People had caught each others' glances, smiled, raised their eyebrows, as if to say: Well, yes! And isn't life amusing, and isn't life strange?

Lisa had still not really remembered her father, but she was shrilling merrily. He listened more attentively to the little girl jumping up and down before him. Oh, right.

Gabriele swung his daughter up in the air and sat her on his shoulders. 'She's an awful lot heavier than she used to be,' he gasped, grinning at his wife.

20

'My God that felt good,' Caterina said in the attic dimness. 'Let's do it again.'

Gabriele laughed softly. 'Give me a chance, darling.'

The first time they made love had been when she was washing him and they went down on the bathroom floor like two famished creatures, laughing, clawing at each other, babbling mad things, and Caterina had cried for the wildness of it, cried for how strange it was and how familiar it was. For a few minutes afterward, with the fine lassitude flooding through her limbs she had been perfectly happy and calm. But then as soon as they had to get dressed and emerge to do all the talking that had to be done, as soon as she could not be alone with Gabriele to rediscover who they had been and discover who they were going to be, she had fallen prey to a myriad unsettling thoughts which her mind could not find words for. Even worse, in the drawing-room Caterina had known there were tumults in her soul that her mind could not find thoughts for. But now, naked on their bed with moonlight bathing them, after making love for the second time she again felt simplified, replete, utterly at peace, and she was not bothered that this well-being would not last long.

'Go on telling me about your journey home,' she said, her voice light with happiness. 'So on Lipari a beautiful girl fed you plums and bread, and the barber had a cross made of palm hanging on his wall – have I got that right?'

Later, she would give him her four years of night writings to glance through if he felt like it. Tomorrow, or the next day, or – oh, some time! Later she would try to explain how unnerving it was that you could change into someone you hadn't been before, or into someone you hadn't known you were. In her case, you could do this merely by going down to Rome, discovering how naturally you took to swanning around in the Manzaris' fairly dissolute circus, discovering you even took a ghastly sort of pride in how immaculate you could make your superficiality, though of course the loathing and the self-loathing were mounting up all the time underneath. Oh, later! The meaningless infidelities too, and how after months and months and months of no sex you could . . . Would she ever tell Gabriele about those vacant, satisfying couplings, which she hadn't actually written about for pity's sake but which might not be all that difficult to deduce from what she *had* written? Oh yes, probably she'd tell him one day, she resolved serenely. Neither of them was a prude. But far more important, they'd find time for the happy making of plans. Would her darling Gabriele like another child if that turned out to be possible? she had already asked him. He'd been thinking of that too? Perhaps a son, sooner or later? Wonderful! A boy, a girl, either, both – she couldn't wait.

Gabriele would go back to working at the hospital. Soon the war would be over. Lying beside him on their cool bed, Caterina felt ocean ripples of indolent happiness lapping in her mind.

'Gabriele, you really *haven't* been doing this with horrible girls in Naples, have you?' she murmured lazily, for the pleasure of hearing him reassure her for the fifth time. 'No, no, it's all right,' she went on before he could bring his luxuriating mind back from the Aeolian Islands. 'You've told me about the . . . What were your words? They were frightfully cleverly chosen. Oh yes – the squalid sexual services, which the gaolers on Ustica offered to organise for you affluent prisoners, and which some of your friends fell for, but naturally you didn't, because the services would have been so awfully squalid wouldn't they? Then there was Naples, where in some streets it seemed to my darling Gabriele that every other man he bumped into was a pimp, but where luckily his nice doctor's brain was stuffed with facts and figures about venereal disease and this had a sobering effect. At least, I hope to God it did, and if you say so I believe you. But what I really want to know is . . .'

Blissfully aware that she truly didn't care whether Gabriele had in four long years had a girl or two, and if he had she forgave him outright because now they had one another to love for always, Caterina wriggled over, she started nuzzling his shoulder. Her words came out interrupted by kisses on his neck, on his ear.

'I understand about how miraculous that voyage was, and how everybody you met seemed to be innocent. I mean, you told me how old Captain Sergio would make his little speech about the Duce being the greatest leader Italy had ever had, and in the same breath he'd drive a hard bargain to help you anti-Fascists escape, but essentially he was a nice man. But when you got to the mainland, the magic must have worn off, didn't it? They say that down in the South there's real hunger, in Naples people are living in the caverns and cellars because of the raids. Did you still manage to decide that everyone you met was an angel in disguise?'

She lay so calmly beside him, that Gabriele had quite forgotten her incoherent outbursts earlier that evening. It was paradise to lie on the clean white sheet in the sultry air and feel her mouth move on his skin. His spirit was tranquil, filled with how brave she had been through these years.

'Oh yes,' he said, 'on the mainland we were back in a dictatorship all right. We were back in a lost war and often nobody I met seemed to be all that innocent. Living a lie day after day for years can have that effect. But of course, I forgot – you know that as well as I do, my beautiful darling. As for how thoroughly I managed to fool myself about people . . .' Gabriele chuckled. 'Well, what do you make of this? For part of the road north to Rome, I shared a . . .'

'Oh marvellous, a story!' Caterina rolled onto her back, she wedged a pillow under her head.

Gabriele propped himself up on one elbow, he gazed at her body in the faint moonlight. 'Kate Caterina,' he said slowly. He ran his finger-tips slowly and lightly over her hip, over her breast. 'Kate Caterina.' Still he could scarcely believe in his repossession of her, of his old home, of his own true life. Marvelling, he let his delight brim in his mind.

'Go on,' she urged him, arching under his hand to get the caress she wanted. 'I expect I shall start to purr in a minute. Trains that had been requisitioned for the Army, buses for which there might be going to be petrol tomorrow but then there wasn't – was that what it was like?'

'Yes, pretty much. But this time we'd got hold of an old rattletrap and its driver. He'd got a withered arm, poor man, but at least it had kept him out of the war. We'd got hold of a can of black-market petrol, we were travelling in style. Who were we? There was a sergeant. His right leg had been torn off by a shell, at El Alamein. He'd been in hospital for months, being patched up, and they'd given him a peg-leg. He could hobble along, with his crutches. There was a young woman too, very ragged and thin, with two children who whined all the time.

'So you see, we weren't a wonderfully presentable party, all squashed into that old car, and the heat was infernal. Still, we were cheerful enough. Or we would have been, if the woman hadn't kept moaning about her husband who hadn't come back from the Russian campaign. Where was the river Don? she kept asking me. Who had been fighting there? What for? Why were our lads there? So I tried to explain, but by thinking about it she'd work herself up and get more and more frantic.

'Her husband, her Marco, had been on that accursed river Don with the rest of our lads – or she thought he had, that was what somebody had told her. What had happened to Marco? What had happened to all the thousands of them? She was pretty distraught, she'd keep on asking things you couldn't possibly answer. There'd been a great battle, a nightmarish retreat through the snow toward somewhere. That was what she'd heard. Was she a widow? She wanted to know.

'Then in the middle of nowhere the driver stopped in some godforsaken village, and tried to raise the price we'd agreed on for the trip to the next town. I was the one who still had two legs, so I jumped out and . . .

'Well, sweetheart, I quite surprised myself. I whipped the jack out of the boot. He was cursing me and looking around for his rough friends who no doubt usually helped him on these occasions. But I . . . I hit him around his shoulders with that jack convincingly enough to get him back into the car, get him driving on again.

'Hadn't felt so pleased with myself and all the world since I'd taken the helm of that old tub *Stefania*. Using an iron jack to beat a fellow with a withered arm – imagine! And the funny thing was . . .

'Of course, to begin with I used language nearly as foul as that bastard of a driver's. When we were jolting along again I kept tapping the jack against the dashboard and telling him what I thought of his character and reminding him to keep driving. But after a bit . . . You know my love, it was extraordinary how we all made friends. That driver wasn't so bad as all that. Or he was fairly bad, but we sort of made friends all the same, after I'd promised to stop waving the jack around.

'At any rate, he and I and the sergeant with the wooden leg and the poor girl with her two snivelling brats . . . She wasn't more than a girl, honestly. We finished up that evening sharing our bread and cheese, and singing songs.

'Oh, and funnier still.' Gabriele laughed. 'With that driver being as friendly as all hell, naturally we settled about going on in his car the next day. And you know . . . He tried the same trick again. But this time, we laughed him out of it. Didn't have to use the jack at all.'

Hours later, Caterina drifted a little way out of her oblivion, or her dream notions began to mingle with waking notions, her wakefulness still had dreams in it. She thought she was conscious of lying on her back in the faint moonlight from the window, but then she forgot that. 'Live it through to the end,' one of her inner voices seemed to tell her. What was it that I . . . ? blurrily she asked her mind. 'Right to the end,' and then something about keeping faith – but being faithful to what? To an idea, a spirit? No, it was all about not knowing your own stories let alone other people's, never knowing who we are – that was it!

Gabriele is back, she thought, but still too asleep for this to move her. Gabriele is home, but I don't know who he is – yes, that's right. But what was it that I always wanted to understand about life, what was it that I was on the brink of knowing for the first time?

Gabriele is sensible, when you ask him what it was like he tells you a story, he gives you an impression. But I . . . That bit about him taking a jack to a cripple, what was all that about? That can't have been Gabriele. There you are, I *don't* understand, I said I didn't! This sheet that keeps getting snagged around my legs, that's the problem. 'Keep faith' and 'right to the end'. Yes, I heard that. But will I get to the end, or will I be broken long before? So perhaps it was never people I loved, not deep down. Perhaps it was just experience itself that beguiled me, it's just consciousness that's always led me astray. Well, I can't do anything about that.

Caterina's legs kicking at the tangled sheet woke her up completely, and at once her half-awake half-adream notions began to be forgotten. She sat up naked in the silvery dusk and tugged the sheet straight.

Surprised by bliss, she turned quickly over and in a passion of all-comprehending happiness and uncomprehending love started to kiss the man beside her on his chest, so that he stirred and half woke up. She checked, because she knew he was dead beat, she wanted him to sleep till morning, she was going to draw the curtain so he might sleep till noon. Then she lowered her face so the tips of her hair again brushed his skin and she went back to kissing his body, but so lightly that her own lips hardly knew when they touched him, and he lay still again.

21

It was early September. Caterina stared up from the sofa at her husband. 'Wh-what do you mean, you're going away? You're going to l-l-leave me?' She stumbled to her feet, her face white. 'Oh, of course I knew you might go to work at a hospital in another city, b-but . . . But it never occurred to me you wouldn't take Lisa and me with you, and now I . . . *What* did you say?'

Events in the country had been precipitated fast. The situation was still unclear and anyway was changing continuously. Gabriele had only had a few hectic hours to come to his decisions, to begin to work out even the foggiest plans and to prepare himself for this conversation; but already in his heart he had put his mother, wife and child to one side, his nation's war was his overriding passion. Now he tried to infuse all the love and all the steadiness of spirit he possessed into his eyes and his voice, but Caterina's irrelevant twitter about hospitals irritated him.

It was also a pity that he was standing with his back to their sunlit attic window, so his face was shadowed. She could not see his expression. In her distracted alarm, she drew no strength from his eyes. She did not even concentrate very successfully on what he was saying, or listen to his tone of voice and gain courage from that.

'Caterina my darling, please, do listen to me calmly. Hospitals don't come into it. There's been an armistice, a capitulation, whatever you call it. Our appallingly malgoverned country really is trying to change sides, thank heavens, only they're making a mess of it. An awkward affair, at the best of times. You know, begging your enemies, the fellows your armed forces have of recent years been killing thousands of, to protect you from your chosen allies whom you've now decided to betray. Conclude a separate peace, that's the euphemism. Though a combination of massive treachery to one side and unconditional surrender to the other appears to be the real meaning, the real price paid. The Germans are almost certainly beginning their invasion right now and one can't blame them. Unfortunately, rather a lot of them are here already.'

Gabriele spoke as plainly, as lucidly, as tranquilly as he knew how. Like her, he had been touched by the first cold breath of the fear that it was their marriage they were struggling for. Already their experiences of this war had nothing in common. And if now, after this brief chance to love one another again, they were separated for a second time? No, he mustn't think that! Of course they would be all right! All the same, with bitter sweetness he recalled Caterina's early times here, when she'd forever been insisting he explain the politics to her. But then almost at once she'd always giggled and said it was boring. He was to do the understanding and the being right for both of them, please. Now she was twisting and turning before him like a tormented wraith, all the happiness of their last three weeks drained away from her. She kept lifting one hand, in a manner he'd never seen her do before, and making a clawing gesture across her face, as if she'd walked into a spider's web.

'We need to defend ourselves, quite simply,' he said, 'and there isn't a minute to lose. We need a political organisation to combat the Fascists and the Nazis. We need a People's Army, or a National Defence Force, something along those lines, to try to keep the Wehrmacht out. It may already be too late to hold the invasion up in the North. But we must begin to fight back, we'll wear them down in the end. So here in Arezzo we've got to pull our weight, alongside everybody else. Capponi and Di Fano and I are off right now to see the commander of the garrison. We've got some men. Not an enormous number, yet, but good ones. What we need now are weapons, orders, organisation. If we can't hold the cities, we'll be off to the hills.'

'Hills? What hills?' Knitting her hands and with her eyes welling tears, Caterina paced like a caged woman, her mouth become ugly, her mouth working, working. 'Oh it's been like a second honeymoon with you, my darling! Only even more glorious than our time in Antibes, don't you think? Because we'd earned it this time, and because you and I are both deeper now, or perhaps I've imagined that, and – and we've had Lisa with us this time. Oh Gabriele my love, I know how lucky I am to have had two honeymoons with you, honestly I do. I realise about politics being more important than you and me these days too, it's all right, I've caught up that far. And hasn't it been wonderful how Lisa has seemed to know you and love you? How she's accepted you back – well, with a few hiccups – but on the whole.

'She's half you, Gabriele, and she's half me. Fifty-fifty. Did I ever whisper to you that that's still the one good miracle in my silly life? Four years I dreamed and I cried, I wanted you back with Lisa and me. You know how stupid I am – always in tears. And now . . . Of course, we're only women and children, I see that. We mustn't prove unsatisfactory and we mustn't trip you up, that's our job. Twenty days, after four years! It's not very much, is it? Did I tell you I *knew* something horrifying was waiting for us? Clever I am, sometimes. Oh not clear-headed like you – but I know things. Some of those nights alone I knew that something terrible was all around me, was just outside my consciousness, waiting to come in. Only of course this may not be it, because it isn't very terrible yet is it? No, it's probably something else that's waiting for me.

'*Who* do you want to shoot, did you say? Dear God, first Edoardo volunteers to charge off and give the French hell and give my poor old English hell. And now you! Sweetheart, they're your mother's people! You, you *are* German, half of you – have you forgotten that? No, it doesn't matter, I see, I see. But you're a doctor my darling, not a guerrilla fighter, couldn't you possibly . . . ? They'll kill you, I know how brave you are. I . . . But you're through with patching people up, I see that, now it's time for the other thing.'

At last she stood still. Her voice stopped.

'Caterina, I must go now. I hope I'll be back tonight. If not, I'll get word to you. I can't possibly stay here for long if the country is going to be overrun. With my record, they'd pack me off at once to a labour camp or a concentration camp. It wouldn't be a question of working peacefully at the hospital and coming home to you in the evenings like I used to do. You understand that, my love, don't you? I'd have to disappear anyhow, guerrilla fight or no guerrilla fight. We're going to be warred over, here. Well, we've had it coming to us. The old pleasant ways and the old nice manners won't apply much, for a while.

'Oh my darling, oh my Caterina, don't cry so wildly.' He was holding her in his arms. He finished what he had to say, murmuring his words into her hair. 'The whole country is falling to pieces, but some of us don't feel like falling to pieces with it – it's as straightforward as that. We've got to stand up where we are and fight back, on our own if necessary.

'One last thing. No, two things. If the next few days go badly and the Germans *do* succeed in taking over here, it may become essential that there should be nothing British about you. We'll see. A start might be a different identity card, or an altered one. Trouble is, anybody who felt like it could betray you – and we're all in the Town Hall files, with where we were born and all that. If need be, I'll come and get you. Lisa will be all right here, with Mamma and Immacolata. You can escape with us. Ever fancied taking an active part in the war?

'The last thing. And now I truly must go. If life gets really bad in the cities, or if anything happens to me . . . Though you must remember that if I vanish for a while that doesn't mean I'm not fine, it just means I can't get to you. Don't forget the countryside. Don't forget my father. You've got Ca' Santa Chiara.'

They went down the flights of stairs slowly, his arm around her shoulder, her arm around his waist.

Caterina had dried her eyes, and Gabriele was relieved to see that her self-control was back in place. 'So you may be home this evening, but on the other hand I may never see you again,' she said with wry cheerfulness. 'Right, I think I've got that straight. Oh, or you may be going to separate me from Lisa and spirit me away to the hills for machine-gun practice, even though it may prove that you can't get back here to do the spiriting away. Well, that all sounds quite straightforward. And please remember, darling, I think I'd prefer these famous hills of yours to . . . But I dare say the German concentration camps are more comfortable than people say. All the same – don't feel inhibited about galloping up on a grey stallion and rescuing me, will you? Now, have you said goodbye to your mother?'

'I tried to explain.'

'Poor Sonya! I bet she didn't dare give you a crucifix to hang around your neck, like she did to Edoardo when he went off to the war. If your mother has ever had a favourite, it's been

Edoardo, wouldn't you say? I caught him trying to shove the cross under his collar. Very sheepish he was. And he was moved, deep down – but he was trying to conceal that, from me.'

Her brittle voice was like a frozen river, the current still surging along underneath thin ice, which a thaw might start breaking up at any moment. Still, Gabriele told himself, she was trying.

Downstairs Caterina stood in the courtyard and watched through the open kitchen door while Gabriele went in. She saw him kiss Signora Immacolata, who made the sign of the cross over him and then blew her nose. She watched him stoop over Lisa, who was drawing at the table. He kissed her lightly on the top of her head and he said something; but whatever it was did not disturb her, the crayon kept moving over the sheet of paper.

'Well done,' Caterina told him when he rejoined her.

Gabriele faced her, his summer jacket slung over his shoulder. 'Sweetheart . . . If you hadn't married me, you wouldn't be stuck in the middle of this breakdown of everything.' His lips were smiling ruefully. But his summoned love for her was steady in his eyes, and this time she saw. 'You wouldn't be in this danger now.'

'Oh, we English have been getting into all sorts of pickles all over the world,' she told him lightly. 'Honestly, my darling, don't you fret about that. I'd have been sunk with one of the Atlantic convoys, or I'd have been murdered when Hong Kong fell, or – I don't know. Something would have happened to me. You never know, I might still have been hanging boringly around in London, so I could have been bombed in the blitz. Isn't it funny, we still don't know if Canonbury Square has been hit. Or if Giles, in Africa or wherever he – if he . . .'

She again made the gesture of clawing the cobweb away from her face. But then for a minute her eyes met Gabriele's with blazing directness.

'And anyway, my darling, whatever happens I'm dead proud of what we've done, you and I. Even if they shoot us both tomorrow, I'll still be dead proud of who we've been. Now, just give me the most wonderful kiss of all. Let's remember to have that third honeymoon, you and I. Before *too* long. While we're still alive. I wonder where it will be, after Antibes and Arezzo? Yes, off you go. And . . . Oh Gabriele, good luck. No, I'm all right. Just go, please.'

22

—∞—

Despite all the crimes and miscalculations which had already been committed, the last act in the degradation of the country was not inevitable, though it now began to take place.

If the new Italian Government had pursued the armistice negotiations less sluggishly. If they had given the Army orders to hold the national frontiers and stopped the Germans sending more troops south over the Brenner Pass day after day. If Italy had come out fighting while still in a position of overwhelmingly greater strength . . .

Later, when faced with the savageries of a long war being fought in their own streets and their own fields, people with a weakness for speculation were made sick at heart by the myriad chances missed. It was like vertigo, it made you nauseous in your brain, to stare down into the depths of the numberless wrong decisions taken which might perfectly well have been right ones, the innumerable small acts of cowardice here or stupidity there that had mass-murderous results.

If the Rome War Office had fulfilled their part of the armistice agreement to prepare for the Allied capture of the capital that fateful night of September 8th, instead of doing precisely nothing to help the Anglo-American invaders, so that the attack by 82 Airborne Division had to be cancelled at the last minute. Cancelled so late that some of them had already taken off from their bases in Sicily and had to be called back by frantic radio messages.

If the Italian Army had at least been given clear orders to fight the Germans; or if officers and men had obeyed the order which *was* given to defend themselves against all attacks. If German plans for overcoming their former allies had not been well thought-out and resolutely executed; so that in Yugoslavia and in Greece their units repeatedly succeeded in disarming superior Italian forces, in less than a week they captured seven hundred thousand men and a treasure-trove of war equipment, not to mention the thousands of disarmed men they preferred to slaughter.

Then if at daybreak on September 9th the Head of Government and the principal Ministers of the Crown could have refrained from running away. If the King, the Queen, the Crown Prince and some noble courtiers had not given the nation the same example. If the Commander-in-Chief of the Army and the Commander-in-Chief of the Navy had not also run away . . . The whole pack scuttling off south to Brindisi, there to continue their be-ribboned posturing in the convenient, protective proximity of the British Eighth Army, up until that week their chosen enemies, who had just fought their way that far.

Or if Italian commanders up and down the peninsula had not mostly chosen to collaborate with their German counterparts – in other words, for some reason give up without a fight. Or if these military gentlemen had not almost to a man refused to give weapons to the likes of Gabriele D'Alessandria, when in every city in the land the future partisans went to the Army headquarters that night and the next morning to talk excitedly of resistance. But the idea of putting arms into rebels' hands was abhorrent to the officers' conservative hearts, even if the rebels were offering to get themselves killed doing the job of national defence that the Army ought to have been doing.

If those commanders who were made of sterner stuff had not, when they rang up the War Office for clearer orders, been answered by junior officials who said they didn't know anything, every man high enough in authority to take that level of decision having disappeared.

If thousands and thousands of different choices had been made, and thousands of chances had fallen out differently, and millions of individual consciences and individual nervous systems had functioned slightly differently in those particular days and nights. If these telephone wires had not been cut, this command post isolated. Or if Supreme Commander of the Terrestrial and the Spiritual had been General Cadorna, who later was one of the leaders of the Resistance, but that vital night and day outside Rome took his division into successful action against the German invaders. Or at least, he did until the pusillanimous Marshal Badoglio ordered him to fall back to cover his own and the Royal Family's run for it, and then he was ordered to surrender.

Or if – who could know? – the Supreme Commander of the Terrestrial and the Spiritual had been a Pope of a different calibre. If Pius XII had been a man like his predecessor Leo the Great, whose name and dates Gaetano Da Durante had so lamentably failed to make stick in Caterina's memory; Leo the Great who, history or legend recalled, had gone out to face the barbarian Attila at the gates of Rome. Or if the rush to the San Paolo gate by those ten thousand-odd civilians, hastily armed with rifles by the clandestine Socialists, had been the tinder that lit a fire of furious fighting-back in every street of the Eternal City and every town in the land. If that September of 1943 it had worked like it had in June 1849, when at a crisis of the siege thousands of Romans had run to fight at the gates and to fight on the walls, and under Garibaldi's command the foreigners had been thrown back, for a while . . .

That evening when Gabriele disappeared, and the next day when the news was of the Allied landings at Salerno and the tremendous German counter-attack, and then the next day when Rome fell, Caterina had a lot of the vast, cloudy 'ifs' muddled up in her head. But she had a lot of her immediate, small 'my God just imagine ifs' and 'I don't knows' to grapple with too. She had, 'Lisa's got an upset tummy'. She had, 'You know, I think this is worse for Sonya than it is for me'.

Since Gabriele had gone, and in almost every city the garrisons that might have formed the kernels of the national defence had instead from one day to the next ceased to exist, Caterina had realised with a shock how feeble her first response to his courage, his principles and his clarity had been. Why, even when kissing him goodbye she had only just pulled herself together. Now her whole being was concentrated on her determination to live up to him and be worthy of his love. Her spirit, always erratically valiant, was becoming more dependably so by the hour. Twenty days together in four years was so little that it would put an intolerable strain on *any* marriage? Their lives had already diverged? Nonsense! It would take more than a mere war to shake the constancy of a die-hard romantic like her. (That was how she appeared to herself this week.)

So when Gabriele was removed from her by his country's travails for the second time, Caterina went about her life with her head up and her taut mind thinking swiftly but coldly.

Ever fancied taking an active part in the war?

I don't know, darling. Let's see . . .

Even the rumble of the first German tank passing peacefully beneath the shuttered windows of the Palazzo D'Alessandria did not daunt her. If anything, it steeled her spirit. So the years of phoney posturing were over at last, so the fight to the kill had begun . . . Right, then! Let it come!

Echoes rang in her memory. Something Luigi had said about how sooner or later people were going to show up who'd start heaving at the pillars of the temple of this gaudy, fraudulent, charming society, and he only hoped he'd still be alive to watch it come down. Caterina liked to imagine her father-in-law roosting at Ca' Santa Chiara, liked to imagine the glint of dour victory in those melancholy eyes.

Or it might be that old Fascist slogan which came back to her, 'Believe, obey, fight'. She would think that at long last it did appear that folk were fed up with believing and fed up with obeying, praise God. As for fighting . . . Well, at least men might start thinking for themselves before they did much of that – or at least, the pick of the bunch would.

Then a poem she'd read years ago in her college library rang in her memory. 'There died a myriad, And of the best among them . . .' Measured. Bitter. 'There died a myriad . . . For an old bitch gone in the teeth . . .' Good, that. 'For a botched civilization . . .' That had been earlier in this century, in this continent. But it was still going on.

Sitting with her elbows on the kitchen table and her echo-chamber of a head between her fists, Caterina switched the radio off, so that she could listen intelligently, so she could hear. An immense stillness and silence overcame her, flooding into her mind through her wide eyes which gazed at the never-changing stone walls and stone arches, flooding in through her ears which heard the stony quietness that sounded as if it had always been there.

Then suddenly Caterina stretched out her white arms in their short summer sleeves, she smiled delightedly. Under her breath, she began to laugh. Because she'd remembered how when armies were defeated, horrifying casualties were reported and territories lost, Esmeralda's zest for life appeared to quicken, if anything. Yes, she thought, when Sicily was invaded and the Duce's government fell – a government in which for the last couple of years her husband had served as a junior minister, for pity's sake – her excitement was palpable. And now, with Wehrmacht tanks parked in the squares in Rome apparently as well as here; with Wehrmacht armoured cars and lorries patrolling our streets, so that Sonya and I peep through our shutters at them with our hearts pitter-pattering; with their trucks with loud-hailers telling us not to gather anywhere, telling us to be on our best behaviour like the good humiliated rabble it appears we are . . .

How disgraceful! she thought. We've got a foreign army taking over here, and I sit smiling to think of Esmeralda when I haven't a clue what's happening to her, because – oh, because she's always seemed to me more debonair than other people and for some reason I kindle to that. There I go, always thinking the feckless thing.

Caterina sat on at the kitchen table, her mind in the midst of the national collapse darting unabashed from Gabriele's courage to Esmeralda's flamboyance, darting here there and everywhere as undismayed as could be.

Then footsteps in high heels were hurrying closer over the courtyard flag-stones, and her eyes were all dark amber radiance even before the kitchen door was pushed wide. No . . . Yes . . . ! Esmeralda *was* miraculous, you only had to day-dream about her and here she came!

Caterina wavered to her feet.

'Damned parasol, the catch is broken.' Struggling unsuccessfully to furl her exquisite little hemisphere of creamy silk with its tasselled fringe, Esmeralda flung it aside with cheerful petulance. 'Heavens Caterina, don't look at me with those crazy eyes. Or *have* you gone mad? Darling, I can't tell you all the . . . But here we are! Now, you might at least give me an ecstatic kiss or two.'

—ᴡ—

Naturally it transpired that there was nothing miraculous what-soever in Esmeralda's manifesting herself in a shimmery green dress, red belt and red shoes beneath the kitchen's arches. The radiance or the madness in Caterina's eyes had been quite uncalled-for.

If they truly hadn't taught her any geography at that school of hers in London she had only to get out the atlas, Esmeralda told her as she stooped prettily to retrieve the unsatisfactory parasol. Yes, Caterina merely had to glance at a map of Europe to see that if you set off north from Rome heading for the Brenner Pass and Austria it made perfect sense to stop for the first night of your journey at Arezzo, especially if your boring family happened to live there so you could take the opportunity of being dutiful briefly. And if Caterina was so dim that she couldn't work out why Carlo had decided the intelligent place to be next week was going to prove to be Germany . . . She could hear all the commotion by the front door, couldn't she? They were here with the very latest make of Alfa Romeo, with a chauffeur with white gloves and the perkiest little moustache, with Military Police outriders on enormous motorbikes. And Caterina should just *see* their official passes tricked out with sealing wax and signatures and tied around with fat ribbands by Foreign Ministry underlings so that honestly they looked nearly as swish as real ambassadorial letters of credence. Oh yes, these curlicued documents were going to do the trick all right at the frontier – and at Vienna, and at Munich. There was going to be a big political meeting at Munich, with Ribbentrop, with darling Galeazzo Ciano she hoped, with the Duce himself if he could be rescued from his imprisonment in time. Now, they must organise a dinner party. Immacolata must get cracking at once. What did Caterina mean, they hadn't got any food? Always making feeble objections. Immacolata hadn't been able to get here because of the Wehrmacht soldiers on the streets? She, Esmeralda, would dispatch the car with a brace of Military

Policemen to the old dear's house to fetch her. *So* convenient, having oafs with epaulettes and revolvers at one's beck and call, surely even Caterina could perceive the advantages.

That evening the guest of honour seated beside Esmeralda Manzari was an SS colonel; and the Podestà of the city and the Prefect of the province, both now likely to be reinstated as puppets under Wehrmacht supervision, were also once more among the D'Alessandrias' guests. The chandeliers cast the same lovely, glittering benediction as they had over the party when Gabriele came home, and wine from the same vineyard was drunk from the same glasses. Happily the smart Foreign Ministry car had been shrewdly provisioned before departure, so the household's dreadfully plain war-time fare could be supplemented with a face-saving quantity of Roman delicacies. Sonya D'Alessandria, invaded by her own people and switching numbly between her two languages, had the shuttered look back in her eyes. Nobody at the dining-table was so gauche as to enquire after the two sons of the house, or ungracious enough to appear conscious that Signora Caterina's passport must presumably have the words 'Born in London' inscribed in it.

When Caterina allowed herself to think about the danger she was in, her heart battering-rammed her ribs and then it faltered and faltered. But mostly she kept her courage up by being nearly in tears for Sonya. And by telling herself: For God's sake, it ought to be possible to be cool through this. By telling herself: You knew your life was a shameful masquerade, didn't you? Dance, girl! Swirl around! Just remember to *keep* dancing, keep up your false pretences, that's all. That's what Gabriele would expect of you. If you had any spirit, you'd be enjoying this.

Even so, it was a relief when the guests had finished sipping their coffee and had departed. Even the purely symbolic act of locking the front door for the night was a relief. Only then Esmeralda dillied and she dallied, so Caterina was in despair that she'd cry, 'Look what time it is!' and go straight to her bedroom. But luckily Esmeralda too appeared at last to think it would be a fine idea to have one of their late-at-night attic talks, which somehow had never been possible in the Manzari flat by the Spanish Steps.

They flopped onto the dilapidated sofa, just as they always used to. Caterina asked, 'So . . . ?' invitingly.

Esmeralda appeared not to have heard. Then she asked irritably, 'What do you mean, *so*?' But a moment later she slowly smiled, as if in delighted connivance.

'Phew!' she exclaimed. 'Still, I reckon we're all playing our parts with tolerable aplomb, wouldn't you say' – and for an instant she hesitated – 'Kate Caterina? Heavens above – here we are, courteously entertaining our amiable conquerors, while half us hope one day to be entertaining a different bunch of conquerors, and the other half of us . . .' She broke off and her old look of irresolute dejection possessed her face. But she shrugged that shadow off at once, she demanded gaily: 'Now darling, the first of all the vital things is this. You didn't perform too badly at all this evening, and I want you absolutely to swear to me that when I've gone you're going to keep your nerve. No self-pity, no silly panics. Promise me, Caterina. And I won't stand for any self-righteousness either, you horrible English girl. Just remember, when I'm not here any longer to keep an eye on you and tease you. My brilliant husband is going on doing his utmost to keep you safe, so if we're lucky and anyway *some* of his political ambitions work out, or at least full-scale disaster doesn't strike him . . . Just remember to say thank-you to him nice and prettily when the war is over, if any of us are still alive.'

'Oh I think my nerve is holding all right,' Caterina said, smiling. Because the magic of having the front door bolted and the night tranquil was working in her inexorably. Because Gabriele had escaped across the sea and come home to her, and now once more he had got clear away from his enemies, so his great freedom suffused her spirit with pride. Because Esmeralda too had amazingly appeared here for her, and now they were up in the attic in the lamp-glimmer and it was like their old times with all things beneath the moon to chatter about.

So Caterina was already world-beguiled or self-beguiled, and did not notice the mocking laughter in Esmeralda's eyes observing her.

'Now, the second of all the vital things Caterina. I want to know *everything* about how that brother of mine was when he

was here. You knew he came to our flat on his way through
Rome, didn't you? But we were out – and he wouldn't wait,
he was in such a rush to get here and find you. You really
are a quite undeservedly fortunate girl. Still, I console myself
with the fact that he didn't even bother to go and knock on
Cosima's door.'

Caterina had stood up. Most of the attic's windows were
open, but now she unlatched the mosquito screen at one of
them so she could lean out and see the canopy of stars, so she
could breathe the warm night into her head and her chest.

She turned back to her husband's sister, languid with unreasoning happiness, and when she spoke her soft voice chimed
with a victoriousness that was equally without reason as her
joy.

'Oh he was . . . ! If you want to know, Gabriele was magnificent. So even I may behave decently,' she added swiftly to
save herself with diminishment, 'so long as I've got him to try
to live up to. Oh Esmeralda darling, even in the midst of all
these tragedies, don't you think it's magical to be treed up here
together again for a night?'

'Caterina I could almost smack your face since talking to
you is so pointless. Well, I suppose you'd have mentioned it
if Gabriele had been dangerously ill. As for the delights of
twittering with you, I can't remember a word of any of it,
thank God.'

Caterina giggled. 'Oh, we used to talk about what it would
have been like if I'd married that fellow who these days is a
Deputy Commissioner or what-have-you in the Virgin Islands.
We wondered about whether any man was ever going to be
gallant enough to get engaged to you. You used to make me
tell you about the ideas and the stories in the books I'd read,
so you could pretend you'd read them too, or pretend I only
knew about them because you'd told me. And even now, when
by some crazy dispensation it appears that one can be scared out
of one's wits at dinner but an hour later feel – what is it I mean?
– feel magically inviolate for a night, or somehow enchanted . . .
Oh Esmeralda, don't you feel it even a little bit? Surely you too
must dream sometimes that if we're diabolically lucky, or if we
shut our eyes and we hold our breaths, one day this war won't

be here any more, we'll open our windows and gaze and listen
and it will have gone away. Then it'll be like going back by
some miracle to recover the past and we'll live it again only
more deeply now,' she declared with the strength her second
honeymoon had given her. 'Imagine! A new life like the best
of the old peace-time world – like the best because we'll have
learned a little perhaps. I hope so. Modesty, and kindness. A
new peace when we'll —'

'Oh yes, I suppose I remember chit-chat about love affairs,'
Esmeralda interrupted drawling. 'So that's what you dream
about getting back to! *Honestly*, you *have* contrived to remain
a little girl. Though come to think of it, I seem to remember
you behaving in a fairly grown-up fashion in Rome a few
times. But as for peace, if it comes . . . Has it occurred to
you that hatreds don't fade away from one year to the next?'
Her voice rasped. 'Not to mention griefs. Has it occurred to
you that a lumbering great brute like this civilisation of ours
isn't suddenly going to transform itself into an angel in a white
petticoat? That our gullibility and our beliefs, our meanness of
spirit, our contentment with the corrupt and the sham aren't
going to die? A shadow of any of this in your head, eh?'

Esmeralda too was on her feet, she was pacing the shabby
rugs, wheeling around. Caterina stood with her back to the
stars. The teasings and the mockings she knew of old; but this
was the beginning of a voice in Esmeralda that she had not
heard before. Luigi ought to be listening to this, she abruptly
thought.

'So we're going to spread a cloth on the table under the
medlar tree down there in the garden are we, and all sit
down for years of festive lunches, naturally everybody from
the dear old grandparents to the darling children looking bonny
in the dappled sunshine, and the old enemies will sit elbow to
elbow clinking their glasses – and this carnival of hypocrisy
is going to be perpetrated from the Bay of Biscay to the Ural
Mountains in your opinion? I'd think a touch more lucidly
about the humiliation of the defeated and the complacency
of the victors if I were you Caterina,' she snarled, 'and I'd
remember that some of the victors may not be as sweet as
honey *all* the time, and for that matter they may not be who

you think. I'd imagine the readjustment of orthodox versions
and the discreet forgettings and how they'll corrode people till
they die of old age and then vitiate the next generation. I'd . . .
Oh, but I forgot. The blissful past is going to come flooding into
your soul, so that's all right.' Esmeralda laughed jaggedly; but
there was impatience with herself as well as mockery of Caterina
in her voice. 'And of course you're going to have been made a
more profound person by your mild misadventures aren't you,
so you'll know all about fixing yourself up with an even nicer
new peace-time life than the old one, you'll be able to be serene
about that. While I . . . Who am I going to be, do you think, if
I live? No, that doesn't matter. That wasn't what I . . .'

Esmeralda stood still, frowning. 'Sham, Papa said, when I
went to stay a few nights with him last spring. He'd wanted
to whisper that to me before my wedding but he hadn't had
the guts, he told me.' She cocked her head, as if listening. 'So
much of all the thinking and the feeling is sham, Esmeralda my
darling, he said. That's what's sad. That's what defeats you, in
the end. Well, goodnight Caterina. I'm going to bed.'

24

--m--

The collapse of France in 1940 had been quick. But in Italy in '43, it only took two or three September days for the State to cease to exist and the Army to cease to exist.

In Rome, there was no longer any national government sitting there to have imperial pretensions, to make noises about its own grandeur and sagacity to be believed or disbelieved at home and abroad. In Rome these days there was Field Marshal Kesselring, who declared that the place was an open city, whatever that was supposed to mean. Well, it was open to the Nazis and the Fascists. Unfortunately, the Marshal immediately issued another proclamation that said the complete opposite, and this was the one that turned out to be accurate. Rome was war territory, under martial law. Strikers and saboteurs would be shot. And in case anybody still had any doubts, there was also Rome radio – no longer under Roman control, mind you – which transmitted Hitler's announcement: 'the treachery of the Italians will not go unpunished. Measures against them will be hard'.

That was plain enough. But as for what was happening in the armed forces, let alone what ought to be being done, it was impossible to form an accurate picture. And when it came to the phantasmagoria in men's and women's wincing minds . . . Well, up and down the country, lucid, logical fellows like Gabriele D'Alessandria, who these days was lying doggo in a house high in the Apennines with half-a-dozen other indomitable spirits, were trying to jigsaw together the cataclysm they were living through. Chaotic minds with effervescent imaginations like Caterina's were attempting the same thing. Everybody was furiously making shapes with what they saw, what they heard, what they intuited, what they feared, and the shapes were always changing.

Luigi D'Alessandria was sitting under his loggia at Ca' Santa Chiara, glancing out to his orchard and marvelling at how untouched by the national disintegration an idyllic scene like this could be. A grassy slope, trees in their summer foliage in the westering light, magpies, dragonflies – Arcadian! Yes, but if the Allies really had to fight their way up the country, campaign by campaign, sooner or later these hazel bushes and lilac clumps of his would be on the Front Line.

Commonplace enough over the ages for a man who'd lived through the sack of a city or the ruin of a civilisation to want to leave some trace of what it had been like for the benefit of generations yet unborn, or maybe merely so he could try to think of something else afterward, merely to get the sight out of his eyes and the putrefaction out of his nose. D'Alessandria had mulled that over, off and on, writing in his notebooks. Well, the ruin of his people was being enacted with a vengeance now, he told himself, gritting his teeth; and all day long with pen and paper he'd been trying to make sense of the Navy ships that apparently were trying to escape to Malta or to the British North African ports, trying to make sense of the Army units that were fighting back against the Germans and losing a lot of men before they were defeated, the other units whose pride would not permit them to switch suddenly and open fire on their three years' brothers-in-arms.

But now the old man in his threadbare summer suit put down his pen. He relit his cheroot, blew fragrant smoke so it puffed up again off his written pages into the sultry air and the midges. His thin lips twisted. A lot less than a century since a more or less united Italy was founded, but already the foreign armies were back. Perhaps he ought to be writing about his country in the past tense. He tried out the words, speaking to the golden swathes of light on the hillside. 'The Kingdom of Italy was . . . It was . . .'

Then Luigi forgot his writing and in a minute he'd forgotten his cheroot too. He sat immobilised, imagining the army in Greece that by all accounts was disintegrating without a fight, the armies in France and Yugoslavia that had not lost any battles either but all the same were straggling back across the borders. Men who'd been lied to for too long, cannon fodder who'd been exhorted to do this and think that for too long, the habit of discipline no more use to them now half their officers had bolted and the other half didn't know what orders to give. Hordes of disbanded men getting hold of civilian clothes by hook or by crook, forcing their ways onto the last trains running. Swarms of poor devils legging it for hundreds of miles, often following the railway lines because of the Wehrmacht armoured columns on the roads. On horse-back they'd have set off, on mule-back, on bicycles. Hitching rides on buses and carts.

Home! Mother, father. Wife. Sister. The kitchen, the familiar hearth. Home, or into hiding. It looked like it could be going to be the same thing. For who wasn't a deserter now? Not that those men would bother their heads about those outdated niceties, Luigi D'Alessandria trusted. Who of them wasn't a rebel, an outlaw now? Or a momentarily free man who'd a hell of a sight rather stay free than be a prisoner-of-war, or get conscripted into some new ill-fated army.

Luigi sat amid the lengthening shadows and the birdsong, watching the opposite hillside where a neighbour was plodding behind a pair of white oxen and a plough. He imagined the animals' panting flanks and the man's slithering sweat, the poor earth slowly scratched by the shallow plough. And at the same time, and as if at an infinite distance, he saw Edoardo, who if he wasn't already a prisoner must be in one of those mobs of the undefeated but irredeemably lost that were snaking southward and eastward through the Alpine passes. He saw tall, fair, carefree Edoardo, the son whom he'd never really understood much or admired much but whom he loved in a helpless, tender, animal fashion. The lad's long arms and legs swinging along in the dust of that rout. Those blue eyes staring ahead, but hurt and bewildered now.

25

—∞—

In those first days of the Occupation the German garrisons were still small and scattered, and when the escaping Italian soldiers came slipping down a city street, or when they reached a village or an isolated farm, the women met them. The old men and the boys and girls made them welcome too. But above all it was the women who said: You can come in here, if you like. The coast is clear. You can stop here, if you want to rest, if you're hungry.

Caterina had been astonished at how quickly it came to seem normal to her, this going about one's business with a shopping bag in the captured city. If she kept to the back alleys she never met a patrol. On the main streets she'd learned to keep walking steadily with her heart bumping and her eyes down, and so far nothing awful had occurred. The afternoon she saw her first fugitives, she'd decided that it *must* be safe for Lisa to get some fresh air and exercise, and they'd just come down from the cathedral gardens. They had reached their own door, when she saw two young fellows in non-descript clothes trudging toward her and glancing nervously around.

She stood still, jolted by a dull anger that these men had been reduced to this furtiveness in their own land, and when they came abreast of her she smiled at them boldly. Because it had crossed her mind in a trice that despite the war she was neatly dressed and she was framed in the doorway of a distinctly patrician-looking mansion, and they might have good reason to be suspicious of these things.

So she made sure they couldn't ignore her smile. She asked, 'Could you do with a meal? This is a friendly house.' And luckily Lisa seemed to think this brace of bitter-eyed boys looked nice, because she said 'Hello!' and that stopped them, even if her mother's smile and her shapeliness hadn't been going to.

That was the start of the listening, for Caterina. And after a few days and nights of harbouring escapers from the armies, her echoing mind was clamorous with stories, with voices which it seemed that even in her dreams she only half-forgot, voices she awoke still listening to.

'A group of our junior officers went to protest. Peacefully, you know. Those Germans didn't talk. They opened fire right away, killed every one of them.'

'Well what do you think I felt, when I saw a few SS herding a battalion of our fellows along like sheep? My God, they still had their rifles! Trailing them along in the dirt, they were, not carrying them properly. A Wehrmacht sergeant told them where to pile their arms, and counted them.'

'Where I was, women from the town came to the barracks. Our orders were to stay put and wait for orders, don't ask me why. Well, these women and grannies and girls called to us to bolt while there was still time. A few of us did. I shinned down a drainpipe, when the Military Police weren't looking, or maybe they turned a blind eye. But most of our lads . . . Their spirits were broken all right. Know what that means? Seen it, have you? They sat about. They wouldn't come to the windows, wouldn't call back to the girls, not even the pretty ones. Some of the men were crying.'

'I remember a girl on the street grabbed my shoulder. In Rome, that was. "Can't you *do* something?" she screamed. "Make them fight back, make them run away – *anything!*"'

'Of course, at first we'd all been euphoric. Peace at last! It's over! We shouted and danced, we cheered. Men ran about with the news, or started packing up their kit straight away. Right, that's it! we all reckoned. No more murdering and being murdered.

'Then a few of the older fellows started to look pretty miserable and it spread to us young idiots. We began to realise that when you're beaten you can't just forget the war. If you don't fight it, others will. You could holler that word "armistice" as much as you liked, but it didn't mean you were safe and it didn't mean peace had come. Didn't turn out to mean a lot, "armistice". It meant other guys could shoot you without you shooting back.

'It's got a life of its own, a war has, a life that's a lot stronger than yours. We began to realise what it meant, total defeat. What it meant, for Italy not to have an Army, to be defenceless. We were . . . We were what our country hadn't got, and that wasn't a good thing to be.'

III

THE COMING TO LIFE

1

—·—

Gabriele did not reappear in Arezzo and he didn't get word to them. At first, Caterina expected him from day to day. Then, buckling down to life under enemy occupation that autumn, she schooled herself not to get into a flutter every time footfalls came to the house. Those were times when, even when the post and the telephones were working, it was unwise to use them for any communication that might compromise you. Never mind, he would come when he could – she made herself think that again and again, often three times a minute all the live-long day it could feel like.

Edoardo did not come home either. Perhaps when that mob streamed back through the Alpine defiles he had been one of those who slipped away into the mountains with a rifle and a bandoleer. Or perhaps he was one of the thousands of prisoners being despatched north to be forced labourers. But no Red Cross notification that he had been killed or captured arrived.

When rumours came of mass torture and mass butchery in the concentration camps and on the Eastern Front, Sonya appeared to be continually at prayer, and the rest of the time you could see in her eyes that her capacity for even a pretence of inner peace, even a mockery of atonement, was withering away. Faced with her mother-in-law's agony of self-laceration and self-control, Caterina could not pray with her, or for her. She doubted whether either prayer or compassion could have any mitigating effect on the anguish of a spirit of such translucent honesty as Sonya's. All the same, she doggedly tried to keep her conscious love glowing around her, like a nimbus. But then with the Fascist Party reestablishing its power, with the Black Shirt militias out in force once more and brigades of Italian SS being recruited just in case the German SS should require any friendly backing up, not to mention the informers who were rampant everywhere, Caterina began to suspect that in Arezzo she was a rat in a trap – and the idea that she might have to try to escape, she might have to abandon Sonya alone here, made her feel even guiltier.

Courage! Perhaps 'Born in London' was not regarded as an offence meriting a concentration camp. Though if it came out that she was also guilty of a husband who had been a political prisoner and now was with the partisans, who were already beginning to go into action on an insignificant but encouraging scale . . . What did she mean, *if* it came out? Everybody in the city knew all this! If the partisans struck near Arezzo, she'd certainly be one of the first hostages they rounded up. Lisa might be taken too! As it was, in this house they were systematically defying the German garrison's orders not to shelter men on the run.

Caterina had no doubt at all that to have influential brothers-in-law – men who might truly be her friends but might not be – was the kind of frail defence which could cease to exist at any moment. Almost the last thing Gabriele had said to her was that she must remember his father in the country. Yes, and in Urbino the files in the Town Hall would have no trace of her. To be unknown, scarcely to exist at all – surely that was almost to be free! And it was unlikely that General Alexander had particular plans to blow Ca' Santa Chiara sky-high.

Rumours of murdered Jews pitched into Lake Maggiore; of Piedmontese villages burned and civilians gunned down; of a battleship trying to escape to North Africa that had been sunk with all hands – no, some of the men had been saved . . . All manner of rumours, generally recounted in the Palazzo D'Alessandria kitchen by starving run-away wraiths being fed bowls of Signora Immacolata's vegetable broth and hunks of bread and beakers of wine.

Luckily, more reliable news was available from the family's two married daughters. Esmeralda's husband had succeeded in turning to his advantage the fact that he had not been quite eminent enough to be one of the nineteen perpetrators of the July coup, and by a swift reversal had distanced himself completely from his old faction boss Count Galeazzo Ciano, now in disgrace. By October, Carlo Manzari's shrewdness had received its reward. He was appointed a minister in the so-called Republican Government at Salò, where he and the other Italian men of state all had their German minders who really ran the show, an administration which for emasculation perfectly matched the so-called Royal Government down in Brindisi. Esmeralda instantly became one of the stars of that Northern kingless and powerless court, and in their requisitioned villa on the shores of Lake Garda gave galas to which the Fascist and Nazi top dogs and their women were honoured to be invited.

In the South, by the onset of winter the Allied advance had been stopped before Monte Cassino and on the Gustav Line. It was no longer possible for Caterina to bring tears of hope and love and pride to her eyes by thinking of the Eighth Army storming toward her, conceivably with Giles in its ranks. For this year, the battle for Rome had been won by Marshal Kesselring, who thus could continue to go to the Marchioness Cosima's soirées.

This lady's belief in the supremacy of Rome over all other cities in Europe when it came to social grandeur had never wavered. There might be two rival Italian governments in two *horrible* provincial towns. This was a matter, Cosima would let her friends know, of *complete* indifference to her. With the same serenity with which she had enjoyed the society of the King and Queen, and looked forward to resuming this elevating pleasure when in one manner or another they were restored to their true capital, she was now rejoicing in the friendliness of the German Commander-in-Chief.

Likewise, and in common with most enlightened opinion, Cosima refused so much as to discuss the shameful possibility that her native land was slithering into civil war, despite the rather conspicuous facts that a Royal Army in the South and a Fascist Republican Army in the North were getting themselves organised to fight on opposite sides.

In the meantime to have Marshal Kesselring and the cream of his generals and naturally her two or three tame cardinals at her soirées, along with her husband's and her aristocratic friends (their august hostess held strict views about which were the socially acceptable cardinals), reassured Cosima that she was still outshining her sister Esmeralda, whose husband might be a clever fellow but would *never* inherit a marquisate, and who was marooned out there in the backwoods. The price that she exacted from the great Marshal for shepherding him

through her own and the few other unimpeachable drawing-
rooms was fortnightly discussion, at once loud and intimate,
of which Swiss finishing school Carolina should in due course
be sent to.

2

As soon as Caterina's escape from Arezzo had been resolved, she was in a hurry to set off. There were two reasons for this. The first was that, now she knew she was going to desert Sonya, she wanted to commit this unkind act as soon as possible and get it over with, and scarcely let herself know that an unkindness begun was not thereby on the instant concluded. The second reason was that since she had decided that Lisa would be safer in the depths of the country, now Caterina's mind inevitably kept coming up with additional reasons why Ca' Santa Chiara would be a haven of peace, while Arezzo on the other hand was little better than a cell for those about to be executed. Suddenly everything about Ca' Santa Chiara beckoned to her. The birdsong by day and the night quietness seemed irrefutable evidence that the Occupation patrols would stick to the main roads along the valleys, and never leave them for the tracks that wound into the uplands. The lostness of that hillside with its oaks and sheep-bells, even the particular grace with which a cherry branch reached over the garden shed – the most insignificant things murmured to her of an inviolate sanctuary.

For two days and nights, rain thundered down on the roofs of the city. The steeper streets became cascades, up which it was well-nigh impossible to walk, and in the squares the downpour beat up again shin-high. All Arezzo's gargoyles succumbed to fifty hours of continuous vomiting, the whitish grey water splashing and gurgling from the backs of their jaws in such convulsive quantities that when it gushed forth over their teeth it completely filled their widely stretched-apart lips. In the city's gardens, the last dun leaves were stripped off the persimmon trees, so that on bare boughs the ripe fruit hung like reddish golden balls in the sluicing murk.

During the storms of rain, in the Palazzo D'Alessandria it was twilight even at midday unless you lit a lamp. Caterina was trying to prepare Lisa for their trek across the country and their new life at Ca' Santa Chiara with her grandfather. But when the little girl grasped that this involved being separated from her tortoise-shell cat, she let out a wail that jangled her mother's already taut nerves, and burst into furious sobs. 'I hate you, I hate you!' she screamed.

Seeing they had no idea what transport difficulties they might encounter, it was vital to take only what they could carry and Lisa could carry practically nothing. Caterina spent indecisive hours listening to the squalls, and packing and unpacking two suitcases that she hoped were sufficiently small for her to be able to walk carrying one in each hand. Even so, she would not be strong enough to walk any great distance carrying them. Well, they must hope for the best. Next year, Lisa would grow out of most of this year's clothes, so leaving nearly all of them behind would only be a temporary loss. Better still, Signora Immacolata had a granddaughter who was seven, and she produced some cast-offs that were a touch too big now but with any luck would last a while.

Caterina was uncertain also about what to do with her few odds and ends of jewellery. The big-scale power in Italy these days was in the hands of the different foreign forces, some of which were reasonably scrupulous in their use of it and some of which were not. But small-scale power, which could be at least as dangerous to defenceless civilians, was almost everywhere in the hands of the worst of the local pasteboard authoritarians, corrupt officials, militia bosses, and other criminals who did not bother to dress up their true natures with offices and ranks before taking advantage of the breakdown of civil society.

After a lot of dithering, Caterina strung her engagement ring and her mother's engagement ring on a cord around her neck. Then she sewed her few bracelets, necklaces and earrings into the lining of the coat she would wear on the journey. Times might come when she would need to sell them, or use something that sparkled expensively as a bribe to get Lisa and her out of a tight corner.

Troops might be billeted anywhere at almost no notice and a big house was especially likely to be requisitioned, quite apart from being a conspicuous temptation to looters. Sonya D'Alessandria had stowed away her jewellery and the best pieces of the family's silver in the hiding place beneath a bedroom floor that already housed Gabriele's printing press. Now she had chosen a lumber-room up under the eaves which she hoped was remote enough and small enough that, in a superficial search of the house, people might not work out it was there. One of the last things Caterina and she did together in those torrential, dark grey days was to heave up there a few of the most beautiful of the D'Alessandria paintings and pieces of furniture, and the portfolio of Renaissance drawings that Gaetano Da Durante had given Lisa. They hid trunks of bedding and of clothing too, which if the war went on might be at least as precious a resource as a few cases of silver cutlery or a portrait of an eighteenth-century Grand Duke of Tuscany. Then Signor Orazio and the blacksmith walled up the lumber-room. They white-washed the new wall and dragged wardrobes in front of it.

Caterina had never thought of the lovely things in the house from a looter's or an art dealer's point of view. In so far as she had thought of them at all, they had been minute fragments of the civilisation she had come into; or they had been some of the innocent delights of life which after she was dead future generations would enjoy; or – she didn't know, but she knew their significance had not been pecuniary. But now, when it felt as if all morning she'd been puffing up the staircase with a battered altar-piece by an unknown Umbrian master, and coming down again, and trudging up once more with the Marieschi view of the Grand Canal which Gaetano had given Luigi and Sonya for their thirtieth wedding anniversary, she was pierced by how this might be a whole way of life coming to an end.

Downstairs once more, she tried to shake herself free of that chill of the cataclysmic which had breathed on her. In the drawing-room she set to work rearranging furniture and pictures, so it should not be immediately plain that a few things had been removed. But the moment was so poignant that she found she was doing everything more and more slowly. The ceaseless rain seemed to be roaring down inside her skull. Soon she could scarcely haul her limbs about, she kept drifting to a standstill.

How lucky she had been! and so heedless. Flushing with shame, Caterina brought to mind how thoughtlessly she had accepted Sonya's friendship all these years, and had accepted that these altar-pieces and portraits were always going to grace Gabriele's and her lives. (Edoardo was to get Ca' Santa Chiara.) So much taking for granted she was guilty of! But now, with these rival empires slugging it out across the defeated country. Now when she had no idea what had happened to Gabriele. When she herself was about to run away, as soon as the weather improved a little. About to go plodding vulnerably off down the street with her bags, with Lisa lagging and quite likely whingeing. Why did she always wake up to things too late, so that all her perceptions had the odour of regret, so that to perceive and to be sad were one experience?

This marquetry cabinet they ought to have carried upstairs to be hidden with the other things. Well, that lumber-room was bricked-up now.

She stood, softly opening and shutting some of the intricately inlaid drawers of the Florentine cabinet, and it seemed that her finger-tips on the tiny ivory knobs of the drawers were opening and shutting a past that might truly be over and done with now, a past that might not come back, might not endure, however ghostlily. If the Wehrmacht held the Allies and went on holding them – which was perfectly possible. If the heart of Europe including Tuscany remained under the Third Reich. If neither Gabriele nor she ever came back here, if they died in different prison camps without ever knowing if the other were still alive . . . ?

Traces of Luigi's and Gaetano's jokey history lessons had stuck in her head, and she'd ploughed through to the end of more fat books than they'd ever given her much credit for. She had hazy notions of quite a few of the invasions of Italy, and she had no difficulty in frightening herself by imagining cities when they were sacked and palaces when they were plundered. She knew about soldiers taking their revenge and taking their pleasure. She knew too that although afterward the old civilisations were shadows of their former glory, some sort of limping life always appeared to get itself going again; and then, in time, perhaps after many generations . . .

Yes, Caterina thought, but when it happens to you it isn't like when it happens in the history books. When your old assumptions about how this beautiful house was where Gabriele and you were going to live happily ever after these days make you blush. Not a terrific lot of consolation, the vague possibility that in a hundred years' time a great European civilisation may be flourishing. Not much encouragement, for we who stand a fair chance of being the corpses in the ditches right away.

Thinking shakily that even if this Florentine cabinet didn't end up pulverised beneath the rubble of the bombed house, at the end of the war it might very likely be stolen goods in an antique dealer's shop, Caterina opened another of its drawers. Half of them so far had been empty. One had contained a Lalique glass pen, another a pack of tarot cards. In a third had been a photograph of an end-of-the-last-century D'Alessandria shooting party: the gentlemen with their guns and their game-bags and their gaiters, the ladies in a wagonette with a cob between the shafts. And that bonny-looking lad – good heavens, *could* that be Luigi? So fresh-faced, so merry! But this drawer contained letters, and she recognised Sonya's handwriting.

Luigi had tied the bundle with a blue ribband, which was faded now. Caterina stood, holding it, possessed by the girl from the coast of Heligoland Bight who had been courted in Tuscan palaces and gardens by . . .

She conjured up a golden-headed young Sonya in a lilac dress, sitting on a bench beneath a cypress tree. Had that been what it was like, in – oh, maybe 1905 – or completely different? Had she been prompted to that image by some novel or some painting of a generation or two ago?

By adding about ten years to the lad in the photograph who was holding the bridle of the cob, she attempted to bring to life her sallow-faced, caustic father-in-law when he'd been a promising young man, before his war in the trenches. Very spruce in a white suit, reading Leopardi to his Intended, she wondered? Answering her questions about the country, as later Gabriele had explained things to herself . . .

Her fingers trembling, Caterina replaced the letters where they had lain and closed the drawer. After all the wars, half the beautiful things that weren't smashed naturally fetched up in antique shops, but that didn't really matter and anyhow what else could you expect? But how fragile the past was! How vulnerable, when it only existed in our lumber-rooms and in our inlaid drawers with their pretty knobs and in these dying minds of ours.

She thought of the painter of altar-pieces, of whom all that was known was that he had probably worked in Umbria, probably about five hundred years ago. She thought of the painter who had lived only two hundred years ago, and whose name was presumably known although she didn't know it, and one of whose surviving portraits, which happened to be of a Habsburg Lorraine fellow who'd been lucky enough to be Grand Duke of this neck of the woods, was now propped against the altar-piece a couple of storeys over her head where an Axis shell or an Allied shell could easily do for them both.

Those men's talents; their hard work; their intent thought . . . Her blood jolting her heart, Caterina asked: Why had she never met their ghostly eyes, until today? The maker of this marvellous cabinet, too. It wasn't just that she could never master his skill. She couldn't even *imagine* it with any precision! And those who had left no beautiful work, had perhaps left only a bundle of love letters fading in a drawer . . .

Sonya's footsteps were approaching the door. Torn between alarm and inspiration, Caterina swung around, she wavered. Now, *now* she would love her with a comprehending spirit, she would have the right words to tell her everything!

But she could not. She fled toward the far door, but it was too late. She stopped, biting her lip hard. When Sonya came into the drawing-room, her daughter-in-law faced her with bright, miserable eyes.

3

When the bus was grinding along close by the hillside trees, Caterina forgot the freezing wind that blew in through the broken window and fluttered her hair. She let her eyes lose themselves in the November soft orange-yellows, in the grey-purples, in the russet-reds. Then they came out over a wooded ridge. The sky was such an azure dazzle that she shaded her face with her hand which had only her wedding ring on it, and the valley below was a lake of mist with a church tower sticking up clear. Caterina's face at the jagged window was utterly calm. Her gaze was free and happy, as if already she had got clear away, already she was back in Gabriele's and her old, happy, lost places and times that must still be there, the innocence only occulted for a while. Her eyes lit on the shimmering white swathes of vapour, on a rift that opened to reveal a patch of green slope, where in brilliant sunshine cattle stood under an oak tree. Yes, their old freedom and gaiety were somewhere through the sunlit mist lapping that belfry, were beyond those white cattle, were adazzle in the radiant air under the oaks around that old house with its dovecote . . . Oh, whimsy. Or possibly not.

No Black Brigade oafs or Military Police oafs had yet boarded the bus and demanded to inspect everyone's papers. In an hour they would be at San Sepolcro, and she would go to see the D'Onofrio, who were old family friends and with any luck would put them up for the night, and after that she would at once set to work to discover how one got over the mountains these days. Of course, it was quite likely that neither the D'Onofrio nor her father-in-law would have received the letters she had written them, messages couched in such oblique terms that she was sure only their recipients would understand them – but never mind!

Lisa had cheered up, Caterina mused with the same buoyancy. It was true that she had already asked several times when they were going to arrive, and it had been irritating to have to repeat that she hadn't a clue though she hoped two or three days would do the trick; but all the same . . . Yes, and it was going to be good to talk to old Luigi again. Shying away from the petrification of her relations with her mother-in-law, Caterina was suddenly convinced that her father-in-law would be in tune with a lot of the notions that kept flitting through her head. He'd see the images she saw, see what she saw in them. Those *Captives* that Michelangelo had sculpted emerging from the marble they were made of – how they kept coming back to her! Of course, he hadn't carved a female *Captive*, that was a pity. Because today she felt like a woman trying to be born out of the rock she was made of. Yes, that was right – she was the *Captive* which Michelangelo hadn't made, the bound woman wrenching herself free, wrenching herself into being. And honestly, how on earth had it taken her so long to escape from that mausoleum she'd been incarcerated in since the war began? Gloomy rooms and loneliness, old women creeping about, religious quibblings . . . Death! she thought, with hardly a twinge of guilt. Well . . . Just so long as there weren't men in uniform waiting for her when she got off this bus.

Lisa was bundled up in all the garments it had been possible to get onto her, and she was looking at least as adorable as usual, her mother decided, contemplating the woollen hat on the little head beside her. What was more, she was being very sensible about how everything was going to be better when they were staying with her grandfather in the country, and about looking forward to seeing the dogs again.

So far, the child had spoken in Italian, too. Right from the start of the war, Caterina had only occasionally talked to her in English and then when it was just the two of them, at bed-time for instance, and never when they were out of the house. Even so, sometimes Lisa would come out with a sentence in the impolitic language, or start singing 'London bridge is falling down' when you'd rather she wouldn't. However, today so far so good. Caterina didn't *think* anyone had yet noticed anything amiss with her own Italian either, though she knew that if she spoke more than a few sentences she'd betray her foreignness.

Caterina began a murmured conversation with her daughter, all of whose books had necessarily been left behind in Arezzo, and who despite this was being very stalwart about the long journey. But behind this talk, her calm sense of new freedom had disappeared as if it had never been. Her moods were like that, these days. It might be 'London bridge is falling down'. Anything! It might be thinking: Yes, but those carved *Captives* can never really be free of what they're made of, can they? And if she'd taken the wrong decision? With her swings-and-roundabouts moods, how could she trust her ability to think sensibly? My God, if she was abandoning the only half-way reliable refuge she'd had! If Cosima's and Esmeralda's husbands *had* been putting in a protective word on her behalf occasionally, and now she took it into her rattled head to scuttle off into the back of beyond. In this country, if you hadn't got friends in high places . . . Hadn't she learnt *anything* in these years? She, whose very existence was an affront to this régime! She whose every thought was an abomination that any right-minded man in authority might see fit to suppress. And as for all this damned-fool dreaming that after the war it was going to be possible to recover old – old she didn't know what – old anything remotely worth having. Hadn't she *listened* when Esmeralda was rasping at her that night? 'So we're all going to spread a cloth on the table under the medlar tree down there in the garden are we . . . and this carnival of hypocrisy is going to be perpetrated from the Bay of Biscay to the Ural Mountains in your opinion? I'd think a touch more lucidly about the humiliation of the defeated and the complacency of the victors if I were you Caterina . . . Oh, but I forgot. The blissful past is going to come flooding into your soul, so that's all right. And of course you're going to have been made a more profound person by your mild misadventures . . .' Esmeralda might have lived the sham more flagrantly than most people, but she understood it more sharply too.

Naturally Ca' Santa Chiara would still be standing, it must be, and Luigi would be there, alive, Caterina reminded herself nervously. There hadn't been reprisals for partisan attacks in that region, so far as she had heard. No houses burned, no shootings yet.

So many images to fight off! Caterina went on with her low-voiced, Italian version of as much of *The Wind in the*

Willows as she could remember, because these days it was Lisa's absolutely favourite story, but now she kept seeing Sonya left alone in that desolate house. Left to wait for her two sons, who might come home, but might never come home. Left to pray for the unbelievers she loved and whom her Church insisted she would never see in heaven. Yes, and what had happened to all their fine resolutions about not letting the war between Sonya's people and her people mar their lovingness and their openness? Your spirit endured in solitary confinement if it endured at all.

In a throb of all the misery and guilt which two minutes before she had shrugged aside, she saw Sonya walking down the slope toward the Santissima Annunziata, beneath the lime trees that were wintry now. She saw her kneel down in the empty church, before the valiant silvery angels and the lovely mediaeval Mother of God and the goldeny phoenix that she'd always thought had a pleasantly barnyard air. Yes, don't think of that house which is all memories now and all despairs. Think of that cheerful, plump old phoenix flapping up from its really quite comfortable-looking flames.

The bus was bumping to a halt in the muddy village just outside San Sepolcro where the D'Onofrio had their villa. Caterina peered anxiously for men in uniform. Didn't seem to be any, at first blush. For pity's sake! she reminded herself. You're a law-abiding citizen of this country, going to visit your father-in-law. All right? No, it isn't all right. Things aren't like that any more.

'Oh look, Lisa,' she said merrily, 'we've arrived. Shall we see if anyone here will sell us a bun, or something? We're going to have to get extremely good at persuading people to be nice to us, you and I. See that old man over there with a brazier? I bet he's selling chestnuts. Don't you think hot chestnuts would be good?'

4

—∞—

Three days later, they were over the Bocca Trabaria pass at last, and this had caused Caterina's spirits to rise with such effervescence that she'd quite given up trying to be sensibly sceptical about all the reasons she kept inventing for why, once they could only reach Ca' Santa Chiara, Lisa and she would be able to weather the rest of the war perfectly well, which anyhow couldn't go on *all* that much longer.

There had been the D'Onofrio villa with its smashed doors and windows, its silence, its Fascist slogans daubed on the walls – and her own voice saying with resolute cheerfulness: 'Lisa my darling, I don't think we're going to be able to pass a very snug night here. *Not* one of Mummy's cleverest ideas.'

There had been that horrible hour in the San Sepolcro police station, while her papers were passed disapprovingly from officer to officer, and that sergeant or whatever he was had run his eyes over her figure with slow, contemptuous appreciation. So she'd been all in a shake thinking, My God they *are* going to rape me! She'd imagined Lisa locked up, banging on the door and screaming and screaming. She'd imagined herself stripped and flung down, she'd imagined these men taking their time over her, and the sergeant had met her eyes and known she was imagining this. But then the captain who let them proceed on their way had been the quintessence of old-fashioned courtesy, and from the elegant gesture with which he smoothed his moustaches she had formed the distinct impression that he too could not wait for the war to be over, and was probably as heartily sick of the régime he was obliged to serve under as she was.

There had been interminable delays in the dreary village from which the road began snaking up the mountain side through the olive groves, so that honestly she'd begun to be afraid that the winter snow would fall and block the pass before they got up to it. But it had been such fun to be with Lisa, just the two of them adventuring off through the wide world in a way they'd never done together before, that they'd spent half the time in fits of the most unwarlike giggles. To set forth to rediscover the freedom which her heart told her must still exist everywhere behind all the appearances of unfreedom. To take to their heels and bolt like this, with the brilliant intention of going missing, of getting clear away!

The German military convoy had been a sobering sight, and naturally it was essential not to remember the D'Onofrio house and then think of Ca' Santa Chiara. What was more, this must be at least the fifth tradesman's cart they were freezing to death in the back of, not to mention all the talked-about vans and trucks which had never materialised. But all the families who had put them up for the nights had been sweet to them, and she was getting used to plucking up the courage to knock on people's doors and ask for help, and now Lisa was as usual beguiling the other travellers they were jouncing along with. There was a bald-headed clerk, who'd lost his spectacles and was nearly blind without them, and a boy who said he was an apprentice farrier. Then, two sturdy peasant women with hens tied by their legs and rabbits tied by their legs. A fellow who said he was a plumber. Tinker, tailor . . . But luckily not soldier, or sailor – or if they had been, they were keen not to have it known. That was another of the inspiriting things: the strong impression Caterina kept getting that all over the land people were on the move, and half of them were just as intent on not being noticed by the authorities as she was. She wasn't alone, everywhere people were trying to slip through the war and go free.

Each little town along the Metauro river had meant being dropped off from the vehicle they'd been in. Had meant tramping around in the cold and trying to find something to eat; had meant dogged but cautious enquiries about who was about to set off further down the valley, maybe with a waggon of firewood they could perch on, or a cart that wasn't loaded quite full so Lisa and she could squeeze in by the tail-board. When this last cart left them at the final turning, Caterina hugged Lisa for joy. To warm themselves up, they held hands and danced round and round in a jig, kicking out their legs and singing 'It's still daylight!' and 'We're nearly there!' and 'Not far now!' Yes – and buried in this back of all the Arcadian nowheres she'd be safe from going back to Rome. Safe from those necessary, cold satisfactions, with any luck. To finally banish which, she exclaimed, 'Did I ever tell you about the spring night here when Papa and I were out late with a fullish moon and we saw a pair of porcupines? And there's the heron from the Metauro who glides up over the hill, and there are squirrels and pine martens, all sorts of creatures for you to get to know.'

The light was fading and they still had a mile to walk. The track wound uphill and here there would be no chance of getting a lift, unless Signor Gervasio came jogging along with his horse and cart.

Caterina stooped, she picked up her luggage yet again, thinking that even if it was Signora Maria who clip-clopped by on her mule she'd probably offer to have the animal carry these cases. 'Come on, my love,' she said. 'The last stretch!'

Lisa stumped along gamely beside her, still chirruping 'Nearly there! Not far!'

Caterina's shoulders ached, her arms ached. With two or three hundred yards still to trudge, she stopped yet again and grinned ruefully at her daughter. 'Hang on a minute.' She stood in the gloaming among the tawny oaks and the bramble thickets, gently straightening and rubbing her sore fingers, and looking up the slope to the crest that hid Ca' Santa Chiara. Up there among the dim trees, a figure was moving.

'Caterina!' It was a woman's wild cry. 'Kate Caterina!'

Lisa and she must have stood out clearly, dark silhouettes against the pale dirt road. But she knew whose that joyous shout was, and she could see Esmeralda dash out of the wood and come haring down toward her. She may have been the darling of the smart set at Salò most of the time, but today she must be wearing flat shoes to be running like this.

Caterina stood stock-still, her bounding heart suddenly as wide open to love and happiness as it could be. She could hear Esmeralda's pelting feet now, she could see her coat flapping, she could see her wide-stretched arms and see her smile.

The next instant they were in one another's strong grasp, and Lisa was jumping up and down and having to be hugged by them both too, and all three were talking at once.

Esmeralda grabbed both suitcases and refused to relinquish either of them.

'Yes, your letter arrived yesterday – amazing! – so of course we've been expecting you. No, certainly I was *not* looking out for you. Idiot! Lisa, your mother is just as bat-witted as she always was. If you really want to know, I've been up at the farm. They've got an escaped prisoner-of-war there. He's Greek, and if all the Greeks are as good-looking as he is . . . Ill, though. Despite which, he appears to have worked up a most impressive dislike of me. You know, it's quite extraordinary the number of men there are in hiding all over the place. Italians, British, you name it. We had a fellow from Bengal the other day.'

She was striding up the track, her cheeks and her eyes hectic, her quick-fire talk making puffs in front of her mouth in the cold dusk.

'No, Carlo isn't here. I just got bored with Lake Garda and parties, so I came to stay with Papa for a couple of weeks. Yes, really – often it seems like you can't stroll past a vineyard without some fugitive or other sidling out of it and giving you a fright. Then what happens is, they ask would you please let them have a jersey and something to eat. Every time there's a rustle in the undergrowth, it's a man, never an animal these days. Only yesterday I met a badger. Lisa, have you ever seen a badger? Tomorrow I'll show you where he was.

'But the wonderful news, the most miraculous thing – *how* could I not have told you yet? Scattier than you are. Gabriele was here! No, he's gone again. Heavens darling, you've gone as white as a ghost. Oh, Lord . . . Look, I can't . . . Rummage in my coat pocket for a handkerchief, it may be cleanish. Just imagine, Gabriele is the leader of one of the bands of partisans, and a fearsome bunch they are too, judging by the couple of friends he showed up here with. Though awfully nice, of course, underneath all the bandoleers and politics and whiskers and so on.'

5

—⚉—

Caterina had scarcely been aware of how weary she was and how tautly winched her nerves were. But she dried her eyes, and right from that striding over the ridge and down the track to Ca' Santa Chiara, she felt relief surging through her arteries in the beginnings of a languorous euphoria.

Esmeralda went swinging along as if the two suitcases she was carrying had been empty. Lisa trotted beside her, dizzied by the obscure imminence of pine martens and badgers, and asking about the dogs. In fact she had forgotten them, having not yet been two years old at the time of her last visit. But during their journey her mother had talked about them, so now it seemed to the child that she recalled all three animals with great affection and clarity.

No light was burning in the porch, because of how precious lamp oil had become, and because these days the fewer strangers who knew the place was there the better. Caterina peered eagerly ahead through the nightfall trees. But before she could make out the brown brick walls and brown terracotta tiles of their sanctuary, her nostrils knew the house was alive. That first cold tang of woodsmoke, blown to her from the chimney, bewitched her mind with acrid, romantic promises which she didn't understand but she longed for.

A few minutes later, Caterina was warming herself by the fire and sipping a glass of wine which, thanks to her exhaustion and hunger, at once commenced its soothing ministrations in her head. She gazed happily at Lisa, who had at first been alarmed by the exuberance of the dogs which a moment before she had been merrily chattering about, but then had regained courage and asked if the terrier could please come indoors with her. Luigi and Esmeralda had taken the child under their wings instantly and totally, and she was already ensconced at the dining-table with a piping-hot bowl of *passatelli in brodo* and a spoon. Naturally, old Luigi still looked like a death's head, his daughter-in-law thought. But he was an exceedingly dapper one, wearing a tweed suit and waistcoat and bow-tie even here in this muddy and provincial Eden; and he was a manifestly delighted death's head this evening, rallying round to fetch a cushion for his granddaughter, fetch her a glass of milk and a slice of Signora Maria's bread.

Now that they had safely arrived, their journey halfway across the country seemed to Caterina to have been considerably more fraught with difficulties than it actually had been. As for having faced all those perils and overcome all those obstacles – those efforts now produced in her a reinforced confidence that Lisa would be incomparably safer here, and reduced to insignificance the fact that no harm had come to her when they were in Arezzo.

Feeling the warmth of the flames playing near her tired legs, Caterina felt so blissfully lethargic that she made nothing of the first partisan killings of prominent Fascists, and the first captures and killings of partisans by the Fascist authorities which had also occurred, so that her husband and her brother-in-law by marriage were going to have to be regarded as enemies in deadly earnest these days. Why, she concluded in softened, illogical triumph, with Esmeralda coming and going between Salò and Ca' Santa Chiara, Carlo Manzari's protection could be vaguely assumed to extend to Lisa and her here. And with Gabriele and his men armed to the teeth, and the partisan bands by all accounts ranging pretty freely over the hills, didn't that mean they were doubly secure?

The heat from the logs crackling in the fireplace scarcely reached to the table at the far end of the living-room, so the moment Lisa had finished her supper she brought her cushion as close to the blaze as she could get. The brindled terrier, which she had selected for her friendship simply on the grounds of his being the smallest of the dogs, was already on the hearthrug, basking in his evening's privileges and drowsily thumping his tail.

Gabriele had been here! Caterina could still hardly believe that a week ago he had been moving about beneath these oak beams, between the Guido Reni etching and the fishing-rods. And he would be back! Probably not for many weeks, or even for months. She must be sensible about this sort of thing. Yes,

yes – but if he got word that Lisa and she were here . . . This *proved* she had been right to come!

The image of her husband who had been metamorphosed into a chieftain of guerrilla fighters got muddled up in her head with the boy in the truck who she'd reckoned had really been an Army farrier's apprentice, and with the plumber who she'd decided was an Army mechanic on the run. Then, something about a Habsburg Lorraine portrait – what was it she'd been thinking? To be Grand Duke of Tuscany must have been roughly the best appointment Europe could offer, that was for sure – she wouldn't have minded a spell as Grand Duchess herself. Well anyway, now here was dear old Luigi coming forward with a pear from one of his own trees for Lisa, a greeny ochre pear which he'd carefully cut into quarters and sliced the core out of and put on a plate. It *was* rather glorious, as well as amusing, how he was so plainly overjoyed to see his granddaughter once more. Childless Esmeralda too, who had knelt to place another log on the fire with her manicured fingers and was asking her niece which were her favourite stories. What about Sinbad the sailor, who discovered the Valley of Diamonds didn't he, and discovered the Roc's egg, and . . . What was the Roc? Well, it was an Arabian bird, a gigantic white bird which carted elephants off in its talons – had she got that right?

The cold darkness outside and the war outside, Caterina thought, and this miracle of Esmeralda being here. Esmeralda without her husband, Esmeralda almost gone back to who she was before the war. You never knew – were they going to wind up talking all night like they used to in the old days? Well, not tonight.

Caterina yawned. Those dinner parties in the flat by the Spanish Steps might never have been. Only . . . There'd been twitter in the newspapers not only about Esmeralda Manzari butterflying about with viziers and grand viziers, but about that other insect Caterina D'Alessandria too. Even photographs of the two butterflies for pity's sake! And when the Allies did fight their way to Rome, if they ever did . . . How were they going to look, those images of the creature who used to be Kate Fenn sallying forth from some pompous foyer with Esmeralda and a bunch of Fascist potentates, Kate Fenn smiling and waving for the cameras on the Foreign Ministry steps with Count Ciano? There'd been that day too when Esmeralda and she had been among the dignitaries watching from a grandstand while the Duce reviewed a regiment of Carabinieri and then made a speech. The hair on the back of her neck prickling, Caterina remembered the trumpeters, the tramping boots and flashing weapons, the ranks and ranks of men as they saluted. She remembered Carlo Manzari beside her in epaulettes and medals, the hilt of his sword touching her dress, his eyes brilliant with love and pride as his right arm shot up. She heard his passionate shout of victory as it chimed with the roar of hundreds of male voices which rose from the parade ground. That time, she'd understood.

Oh to hell with it, Caterina thought. Glancing at her daughter's bright little face, and looking forward to her own supper before long. Forgetting Edoardo who was missing, and even forgetting Giles. Sipping her wine. Remembering the D'Onofrio house and that she really must tell Luigi about that, and must remember to ask him were they Jewish by any chance, or had they too got a son with the partisans so far as he knew, but not thinking how distressed her news would make him. Remembering Carlo Manzari the last time she'd seen him, when he'd scarcely addressed ten words to her, though those ten had been as affectionate and as could-mean-anything as ever; Carlo talking charmingly to the Prefect of the province on his right and the SS panjandrum on his left, playing his part immaculately; while Sonya and she had just been a brace of twitched marionettes going through the motions. Sipping her wine again, and stretching her weary legs, and thinking: these woods and hills have from time immemorial been so idyllic, of course this macabre invasion of Wehrmacht platoons and Black Shirt platoons must pass away – and anyhow where are they? when I glance around, I can't see anything bad. Thinking: flames in the hearth leaping up. Night trees. A tawny-owl that calls and calls. Woodsmoke . . .

Did Grandpapa or Esmeralda have the book called *The Wind in the Willows*, Lisa wanted to know, eating a piece of pear with one hand and rubbing the terrier's ears with the other. Because it had got left behind with Granny.

Esmeralda had been explaining to Caterina how wonderfully free she felt. Normally if she went anywhere Carlo *insisted* she have a chauffeur and a couple of guards. But this time, on the excuse of just staying tranquilly with her father . . . Had Caterina not noticed her immensely swish car in the yard, beside Luigi's old rattletrap?

Now at the idea of supplying Lisa's literary wants Esmeralda caught fire. *The Wind in the Willows*, was it called? The next time she could escape from Salò she would come with a formidable Military Police escort and with gallons and gallons of Carlo's Ministry's petrol. They would travel by way of Arezzo, and Caterina was to write a list of the books in the house which she thought Lisa would require for at least a year to come.

Next year she might be old enough to be read *The Railway Children*, might she, and *Three Men in a Boat*? Sounded dreadfully English – but write them down, write them down. She herself would provide *Pinocchio*.

You never knew, the way things were going, next year Carlo and she might find themselves facing a British firing squad. What did Caterina think . . . Might she be let off merely with hard labour for years and years, if she could show that she'd been using her Fascist Government car to fetch a little English girl a copy of Belloc's *Cautionary Verses*? She hoped so.

6

—⚭—

After the explosion outward from the home country in recent years, after the Italian armies gone to Spain and France and Corsica, gone to the Ukraine and the Balkans, gone to the Aegean and the Ionian, now there was an implosion. After the armies gone to Tripolitania and Cyrenaica, gone to Abyssinia and Somalia and Eritrea. After the imperial civil servants and the imperial police forces; after the colonists; after the show jumping and the trotting races; after the risky investments and the consolatory adulteries . . . One of the outcomes of all this vainglorious and unprofitable activity, which Luigi D'Alessandria had been chronicling in his punctilious handwriting that unkind souls reckoned showed how crabbed the old boy had become, was that Italy was swarming with half-starved outlaws. And among myriad other consequences injurious to the human race, a young Greek fisherman called Stavros (no one here could pronounce his family name) had ended up in a prison camp in the Po valley, from which he had escaped. Tramping south down the peninsula, hoping to slip across the Front Line and rejoin the Allies, he had got badly undernourished and had developed bronchitis. He was now being hidden in Gervasio's farmhouse, where Maria was feeding him and nursing him.

Esmeralda had been right, it could seem that every copse of riverside willows and every upland oak spinney was alive with men. There were Italians who had escaped from trains taking them to labour camps in Germany; who had taken to the hills rather than surrender; who had legged it to avoid being called up for the new Fascist Republican Army. There were Jews. As for the foreigners, the escaping prisoners, they came from everywhere. The Bengali rifleman with no rifle had gone on southward, after having been put up for the night at Ca' Santa Chiara and fed and given a pair of Luigi's shoes. But Caterina was not long there before she'd tried to help men who hailed from Casablanca to Cairo, men from Vancouver to Trincomalee to Stewart Island and from what could seem like half the points between.

Gervasio and Maria had taken in Stavros the fisherman from the Cyclades unhesitatingly, in the most natural way in the world, though these days for harbouring enemies of the State you could be beaten up and gaoled and have your house burned.

Their son Bruno, safe home from Macedonia, came upon the escaper where he'd crept into an outhouse and was lying on some old sacks, coughing and shivering. Before he knew what he was doing, Bruno had helped the feverish man to his feet and was leading him across the yard to the kitchen door, calling to his wife and his mother to look sharp, there was a fellow needed help.

It was unfortunately plain that the official State was still strong enough to go on administering its injustice, go on using torture, go on recycling bribes. But it was equally plain that an unofficial, illegal Italy was beginning to be in robust health, and Caterina rejoiced in this from her first blissful awakening at Ca' Santa Chiara after nine hours of dreamless sleep. Lisa had also just that minute woken up, and was standing at the bedroom window. 'Look, Mamma!' she cried. 'It's snowing!'

The deep snowfalls did not begin for another month. But that first morning it was good to go out with Lisa into the whitened yard which was criss-crossed with birds' tracks, amidst the trees which were all decked out in soft white fur. Luigi had already been out to the woodshed for a barrow of logs, he had the fire and the kitchen range alight. Esmeralda had laid four places for breakfast and put out a jar of Signora Maria's honey. Now she was toasting bread on a griddle. When they sat down to eat, the snow outside made the room more light than it normally was, with a pale shimmer on the plates and cups and knives. Shards of ice fell down the chimney into the fire.

After breakfast, Caterina and Lisa went out of doors again. They made themselves useful by bringing in more wood than could possibly be burned in a day and an evening. Energetically escorted by dogs, they went down the sloping garden to the spindleberry and picked some sprays with plenty of red berries.

They shook the snow off them and brought them back to stick in a carafe of water on the dining-table.

Then they set off up the track to the crest, to see what the whole landscape and the far mountains looked like. The snow was only an inch deep, so Lisa could go skipping along. They heard a jay's harsh cry and saw its blue and maroon plumage swoop by. When they came out on the ridge, the snow clouds had shredded into veils hanging down the sky, and a silvery sun-dazzle lit up the whole still, quiet, white world, with a farmhouse roof and a smoking chimney every quarter or half a mile. They decided to walk on up the track to say hello to the cattle in the byres, and to Giuliana and her baby.

After her night's sleep, Caterina had reminded herself that of course Esmeralda hadn't really gone back to being her old unmarried self, she'd be off again to Lake Garda soon enough. It was just that she was enjoying playing at being bivouacked in this farmhouse for a few days; she was enjoying playing the game of being her father's darling daughter and her niece's most fun aunt and Caterina's best friend or her only friend. With a pang, Caterina wondered what went on in Esmeralda's head when instead she was playing the political hostess. She marvelled at how she'd only ever been granted flashes of what Esmeralda really felt and what she saw. Her consciousness an endless recession of mirror after mirror – she'd imagined that, one pre-war night. So Esmeralda could strike all the postures she liked before that wilderness of looking-glasses, or she could just stare back hopelessly into her endless eyes. No doubt hearing her own mordant voice: 'Has it occurred to you that a great lumbering brute like this civilisation of ours isn't suddenly going to transform itself into an angel in a white petticoat? That our gullibility and our beliefs, our meanness of spirit, our contentment with the corrupt and the sham aren't going to die?' Esmeralda whose father would not have been disappointed in her if he'd heard that. Esmeralda who'd hurt herself into clairvoyance. Well, at any rate, this morning she'd been *determined* that a present or two for Lisa must be possible, so she'd set off to find out what Urbino could produce, wearing a cashmere scarf and looking very rakish at the wheel of her shiny Alfa Romeo. Luigi had gone with her, and on their way back they were going to stop at the village store and listen to their radio, try to discover how the battle for the Sangro river was going, scarcely a hundred and fifty miles to the south. Also, she would use the village telephone. Without clumsily pronouncing any facts about who or where, Esmeralda was going to tell her mother that the travellers had arrived safely. What was more, in her babble she'd mix in some allusions which would let Sonya know they'd seen Gabriele. All this secrecy of his was really *too* ridiculous, Esmeralda pronounced. And as for his high-minded insistence on not getting in touch with his own mother lest he put her in danger! Just fancy, being saddled with such a stuffy brother.

7

—꿈—

That winter, Caterina knew in her bones that in the country you were safer and freer than in any city – because when you were at the mercy of every soldier you met, at the mercy of every militia brute or SS brute or police brute, the fewer of them you bumped into the better. Like all those fugitives who were trying to turn into ghosts as they made their ways south toward the Allies or north toward the Swiss border, she too wanted to become invisible for the duration, and she couldn't prevent herself believing that at Ca' Santa Chiara she'd nearly succeeded.

Apparently when Gabriele and his comrades had been here, they'd been talking about going to earth for the winter in safe houses in remote highlands, in mountain refuges, in shepherds' huts. Well, Lisa and she would go to ground here, where practically nobody knew about 'Born in London' and about being married to one of the rebel chieftains. Where if military vehicles patrolling the Metauro valley road turned off up this track into the foothills, the alarm would be quickly given from farmstead to farmstead – that was the plan. There was even that cave at the back of the barn, which Luigi and she planned to make into a hiding place.

Stories were rife about how these days you did not have to be a captured partisan to be hauled into a punishment cell for interrogation, hung up by your wrists to be beaten with truncheons. These days, often if a young man did not report to the barracks when he was called up for service in Mussolini's new divisions, they arrested his father and mother, or his wife, or his sister. As for old boundary disputes, family quarrels, feuds over money or over seductions . . . All it took was an anonymous letter, or for some servile soul to curry favour at the police station by *saying* you were a Bolshevik, or you hid Jews, or you hid prisoners-of-war.

Caterina cheered herself up by reflecting that Gabriele had not been captured when the other leaders of the nascent Tuscan

Resistance were rounded up three weeks ago, so the first attempt to organise a bit of actual fighting rather than whingeing and proclaiming had come to nothing much. Then she herself had had that lucky escape at San Sepolcro. Indeed, she joked to her father-in-law, she half expected that admirably courteous Carabiniere captain to show up here at Ca' Santa Chiara and ask if they would hide him till things blew over. So now, with most of the neighbours pulling their weight when it came to sharing everything they could spare and sheltering the outlaws – *all* the outlaws, irrespective of which god-awful armies or which god-awful prison camps they were on the run from. With all the external checks on human behaviour gone up in smoke, here in the middle of a civil war inside a European war inside a world war, so that the bad thing was that the vile people around were showing their true colours and no mistake, but the good side of things was that a lot of different people were showing *their* true colours too. Now that decent folk were showing they had inner restraint, inner dignity, and they weren't going to be that damned easy to corrupt, coerce, degrade. Didn't Luigi think it was rather marvellous, how the old heroic virtues came out? Friendship, cunning, sheer guts. Virtues like that.

They might be in the vegetable patch, digging shoulder to shoulder with a view to planting as many rows of potatoes as they could before the hard weather really got a grip on the land. Caterina might say that, about the ancient strengths that bound a community together, made it work, made it survive.

They'd lean on their spades. Do so thankfully, because the old man and the young woman were both regularly putting in hours of heavy labour and getting tired. Lisa and the dogs would be skirmishing under the fruit trees, and Esmeralda might be there, or she might be away in her villa on the shore of Lake Garda, wearing her high heels and her jewels and her dresses that plunged at the back.

Caterina's mind was racing, these days, and her father-in-law and she were talking a lot as they worked. Times came when it only needed her to start expounding to him one of the cloudy perceptions that were appearing and disappearing in her grey matter, and then she'd be away. At once she'd be telling him what heaven it was to have escaped from Arezzo streets where you were forever walking past armed men in uniform. Where you were always having to pretend there was nothing wrong about you, pretend you weren't dismayed by the sight of them; having to make sure you didn't quicken your pace, make sure you didn't either meet their eyes or conspicuously shrink from doing so. And as for her times in Rome . . . Could he understand how appalling and yet irresistibly exciting it could be to live in a haze of intimations you could never trust, appalling *because* irresistible? God how much happier she was on this wintry hillside where she could talk freely – he could imagine, couldn't he? By the way: it was all right, wasn't it, if she and Lisa perched here till the war was over? She wouldn't even venture down as far as the valley road. She'd roost on this hillside and not exist, please.

Or Caterina's outpouring might be this latest wondering of hers, which was all to do with how she hadn't a clue how much 'one of us' in this hill country she was or she wasn't, and of course she had no notion how spiritually tough or wimbly-wambly she was because she'd never yet been tested. She didn't even know how physically tough she was. But all the same . . . Heartening, didn't he think, those old pagan strengths which people didn't seem to have to *choose*? Yes, she'd been mulling it over, she said. The moral freedom you worked out for yourself was all very fine, but so lousily spectral always. Did he agree? Spectral on account of how nothing in the world corresponded to our idea of liberty, so we *had* to make it up, had to *make* it, which had the unnerving effect of . . . Oh look, there was a green woodpecker! Shh . . . Over there, Lisa, in the plum tree.

Well, give her the ancient virtues that were bred in the bone, give her loyalty, give her endurance – nothing too fancy. Oh, by the way . . . What did Luigi think of her feeling that, after the long-overdue falling to pieces of all the ghastly old theologies and metaphysics, you became the most ridiculous, die-hard romantic? She meant, if you were an incurable moralist like she was afraid she was, and she knew he was, so he wasn't to wriggle. Above all now, with the Old World descended back into barbarity, now when all was permitted, here where no horror was impossible. Come on, she knew he felt it too . . .

That desperate, romantic longing to be faithful to a lost cause, to a shadowy ideal of how you should live.

Caterina might deliver herself of one of her bubblings-over, like that. Standing in their half-dug plot. Shoving her hair back from her eyes with kitchen-gardener's fingers which left mud smeared on her forehead.

Her father-in-law never appeared the slightest bit surprised. He might cheerfully meet her head-on, and talk about what happened when you no longer had metaphysical sanctions for your moral order, and how Walter Pater reckoned that 'not the result of action, not the fruit of experience, but experience itself was the end'. It was years since he'd read Mr Pater and it wasn't likely that those were the exact words, but he hoped he remembered his thinking roughly right. 'The discovery of a vision, the living of a state of consciousness . . .' Something like that. 'A mere disposition of the mind which was the principle of all the higher morality . . .' Which, of course, might account for how tenuous it was. Spectral, like she'd said.

Other times they'd wind up talking about what had gone wrong all over Europe, and Luigi would try to explain his idea, which he'd been roughing out into some sort of coherence in one of his notebooks, that civilisations could die of debauchery, yes certainly they could, of softness, that sort of decadence. But did she not agree that they could equally be weakened by philosophical calm, by ennui, by a sense of fair play, by irony? So then you were scuppered when along came all these lamentably vigorous Nazis and Fascists and Communists, who were signally lacking in a sense of irony and would have been immensely improved by a bit of ennui.

8

—∽—

Luigi and Caterina were getting on famously, and it wasn't just that they both quite happily switched from discussion of the potatoes to consideration of rarefied dispositions of the mind, and with their next breath switched back to the carrots and cabbages again, though this harmony helped. Nor was it chiefly the old gentleman's immediate setting about ensuring Lisa had as near perfect a country Christmas as the war would allow. Nor the grave way in which he listened when Caterina told about Sonya, whose native land had come to find her with a vengeance; Sonya who when a Wehrmacht officer had come to the house announcing that he'd been sent to ask if he might be of any service to her, had replied in German when spoken to in that language, but only to say that she didn't wish for any preferential treatment. And then thank heavens, while the nice young officer had been being stiffly courteous in the library, no old Jewish ladies had come popping out of the concealed door that looked like a section of bookcase, no Canadian corporals had come barging in – the whole thing had gone like a dream. In those weeks, it was above all that Luigi D'Alessandria and his daughter-in-law both loved Esmeralda and were sick with anxiety for her.

It had taken Caterina no time at all to comprehend that, despite the events he was living through, Luigi was in better heart than he'd been for years. For a start, there was nothing lonely about his life at Ca' Santa Chiara these days, and he was invariably good-humoured about all the invasions of his peace, which he undoubtedly would not have been when she'd first known him. He might take an interest in philosophical notions of being rather than doing. But he spent his days doing, and a lot of it was hard work and a lot of it was dangerous. He worked laying in stores, sawing up firewood, breaking the earth with a mattock. Being at least theoretically a legitimate and law-abiding resident of the district, unlike Caterina who never ventured more than a few hundred paces from the house, he went about the neighbourhood collecting coats and boots for escaping men, getting in touch with other households where they'd be safe. In the evenings by the fireside, they both worked making copies of maps for escapers.

But Esmeralda . . . They agreed that it would be churlish to suspect there were real flaws lying silent beneath the swagger of her voice. It was likewise true that they were all of them in danger and you didn't make a fuss about that. But even so . . .

Did Esmeralda realise what a totally double life she was leading, even by the standards of the day? Did she realise quite how easily she might be maltreated, either by her husband's side if they caught her hiding escapers here, or by partisans if they discovered that in her other life she was one of the idols of the Fascist élite? With any luck Gabriele would be able to stop his own comrades doing anything to his sister. But if she fell into the hands of one of the Communist bands in these hills? If they decided that the wife of a Minister of State at Salò counted as an out and out Fascist all right, counted as one of the enemy they were killing as many of as they could? Or if one of their terrorist units tracked her comings and goings in that swanky Alfa Romeo of hers?

The two kitchen-gardeners worried together about these risks, leaning on their spades those November afternoons and December afternoons, and when Caterina was alone with her thoughts she went on worrying. Half the time it was marvellous to have Esmeralda back with her old flaming vivacity apparently unimpaired, have her back almost as if she'd never been married. But at other times . . . There was a wild, despairing glint in Esmeralda's eyes which made you think that she was trying somehow to redeem herself from her marriage. Though she didn't seem to want to run away from Carlo, so maybe that wasn't it. Or you imagined she was longing to redeem herself from her life, from her mind, her self – was that possible? And why was it that whether Esmeralda was at all *happy* was not a question it had ever been possible to answer, or even to ask? As for her battles with the Greek escaper up at the farmstead, her battles of hatred and battles of wits or battles of desire or whatever they were . . . Caterina could hardly believe some of the exchanges she'd heard.

Skeletal, black-haired Stavros coughing on a bed up at the
farmstead, his feverish eyes surveying Esmeralda's lovely form
as she stood before him. 'Half German and half Italian, and
your husband a . . . First one of your damned nations came at
us and then the other.' He could get by in her language, on
account of the invasions and the colonisings and the prison
camps, that wasn't the problem. The problems were that he
was running a high temperature, and that at the provocative
sight of Esmeralda Manzari his grief and anger for his people
strangled the words in his throat. 'Our houses burned. Our
wives and sisters sometimes raped, sometimes starved into
prostitution. Oh yes, my fine lady! Hostages taken from the
villages and shot. Are you still doing that? Working, is it? Ah
God my chest!'

Esmeralda's eyes glittering as she looked down at that threadbare blanket, at her enemy doubled-up by the spasms in his
lungs. Esmeralda in her elegant, tight-fitting coat as she stirred
before him. 'So you don't know which half of me to hate
most?'

'No, I don't.' But his voice had a tinge of a smile. Then he
growled, 'These are good people,' his glance embracing Signora
Maria and her humble room. He gave a rasping laugh. 'They
are good people and we killed thousands of their sons. But the
likes of you! Your flags flying on the Acropolis. Ugly things.
And those of us who ought to be doing something about –
about . . .' Again his illness took him by the throat. 'We're
dead, or we're in your prisons, or we're wandering in this –
in this . . . I don't know. Why don't you tell your husband's
police dogs where I am? Dogs – rats, I should say.'

Not that things got any easier when Stavros was well enough
to totter out into the winter sunshine wearing an old coat of
Luigi's that was too small for him, so his shoulders were pinched
and his wrists stuck out. Not a lot friendlier, when those two
stood up to one another with their bitter half-smiles and their
appraising, disdainful eyes, and he asked her: Would she care for
him, as a member of a subject race, to polish her Alfa Romeo's
headlamps, possibly? When she replied: Polish if you want to.
Yes, why not? Polish, damn you! Or take the car and go for a
spin if you'd rather. Do you think I care what you do?

Caterina found herself haunted by flarings of vision. She saw Esmeralda at Ninfa that summer she got engaged to Carlo Manzari, Esmeralda diving off the garden bridge into the stream – only when she hit the glittering water she shattered into brilliant shards as if she'd been glass. Caterina saw Carlo's white hand with its tiny black hairs holding a cocktail shaker, and she was back in the flat by the Spanish Steps – but then she saw those fine, white, firm fingers handling Esmeralda's naked body, and she didn't know what to think.

9

It was true that when Luigi D'Alessandria brooded on the humiliations his country had been led to, till it had become necessary even for old soldiers like himself to hope for Italy's defeat as the least vile outcome possible, his old anger returned. Then his thin lips would have an unpleasant twist to them. Well what could you expect, his mind would growl, when you were stuck with educated classes half of whom found the Duce an acceptable prime minister and the Führer an acceptable ally, while half the rest of the imbeciles still contrived to take Marx and Lenin seriously as political thinkers so they weren't going to be any use either? This was an age of mass intellectual dishonesty as sure as hell – or did he mean mass superficiality? – and now we'd merely and banally got what we deserved.

However these days his foul moods would quickly pass. It was peaceful to sit after supper at his desk, noting down what he'd heard of the day's events in his province before he went to bed. His granddaughter would be asleep next door. Caterina might be ironing, or trying inexpertly to alter some small passed-on garment so it fitted Lisa a bit better. Or she might be sitting by the fire in a weary daze, wondering when she'd have the strength of will to drag herself off to her cold bedroom.

A log would shift in the hearth and sparks fly upward. Luigi would go on writing down the news he'd heard of a man killed or a house burned. What he'd noticed of the trickle of men making their ways through this hill country up toward Monte Nerone where the rebels of the region were slowly gathering, first fifty, then a hundred, a hundred and fifty. The talk he'd heard of partisans raiding a munitions dump or blowing up electricity posts, and how often they managed to escape back to their mountains so it was the local people who came in for the reprisals.

One of the virtues of Luigi D'Alessandria's old age was that he needed less sleep than he used to. He was regularly up long before sunrise, so he had an hour of solitude or sometimes two.

However horrifying the war news had been the day before, Luigi woke up feeling buoyant. This morning as every morning the fire was still glowing from the night before. Whistling merrily and rubbing his hands to warm them, he got the flames crackling up again, thinking that today was Saint Lucy's day wasn't it and the shortest day of the year – or wasn't that till next week? Then in the kitchen he took the poker and riddled the grate of the stove and stoked it with fresh kindling, remembering that Gregorio Farsetti was staying the night, he'd want some breakfast too in due course.

Luigi brewed himself a pot of coffee, though by this stage in the war the so-called coffee had a lot of chicory in it. Still, they hadn't yet been reduced to making it with acorns, so you couldn't complain. And that incomparable *Saint Lucy* of Tiepolo's in the Santi Apostoli in Venice that Gaetano and he had gone to see; the way when that fat, bald man truly loved a painting he'd stand rapt before it for twenty minutes, his eyes thinking, thinking . . . When would they next saunter together to look at a picture, if they ever did again?

In the cold murk where the pieces of furniture were shadowy mounds, Luigi frugally carried one oil lamp about to illuminate whatever needed doing next. There was no birdsong, these winter daybreaks. Happily he cocked his head and listened, revelling in the utter quiet, and smiling because he knew that when at the beginning of spring the dawn choruses started he'd revel just as wholeheartedly in all that carolling. To each season, its right silence or its right music – wonderful! Then sitting at the table to sip his hot drink, his sleep-freshened thoughts were already playing with the notions he was going to rough out on paper in this blessed interlude before the day began.

Good, the restored fire starting to take this deadly chill off the air. Good, his desk waiting for him by the window in the slowly lightening gloom, with pen and ink ready to be used. Now, he must go on mulling over what Gregorio and he had been saying at dinner about how in upper-class conservative circles the blame for all the defeats had been laid on the soldiers, whereas in their view the fatal weaknesses had commonly been lack of transport and lack of modern artillery, not to mention unimaginative generals and half-baked political leadership – a lot of junior officers and non-commissioned officers and troops, by contrast, often having fought heroically.

Of course if the war had chanced to be won, every historian and every journalist in the land would have been proudly scribbling about the valour of the nation's fighting men; but as it was . . . Yes, and if in the end Germany was defeated too, the courage of her soldiers probably wouldn't get much of an honourable mention either, wouldn't live on all that nobly in the folk memory.

Well, his concern was for the men of his own country, and if he lived long enough his defence of them was going to be the toughest-written essay in his book. What about the Ariete Division's defeat of the British 22nd Armoured Brigade at Bir el Gobi in late November '41, eh? He might start with an analysis of that. Or what about the night when our commandos got into Alexandria harbour and put depth charges under *Queen Elizabeth* and *Valiant*? Men you could count on your fingers putting two battleships out of action – that was the style! Young men, of course, not admirals.

Luigi D'Alessandria did not really believe that when this long cataclysm was over the great truth-telling of which he'd dreamed would occur. There would instead be the usual party-political twists given to everything, the usual skatings over unpleasant facts, the usual face-saving explanations and omissions from text-books. But on winter dawns like this dawn he was so happy that even so he walked over to his desk with a light step.

Carrying his flickering lamp, he sat down eagerly, the old artillery officer in him thinking defiantly of the last battles in the Horn of Africa. Thinking of how at the defence of Keren and the defence of Gondar the beleaguered men had fought on for weeks with practically no hope of relief let alone of victory, and then with truly no hope of relief, and over a quarter of them were lost before the end came. Then there was the magnificent way the Alpine regiments had fought in the Ukraine, one fine day he must get some hard facts and figures about that. And come to think of it, this defence of the fighting man, of the under-dog, tied in rather aptly with another skein of ideas he was developing. This was all about how the upper echelons of the Catholic Church might be being so studiously neutral in this war that they were unforgivable – this argued on Christ's own admirable distinction that those who were not for Him were against Him – but a lot of humble clergy were giving a far more honourable account of themselves.

Notebook and ink well and pen – but this morning he didn't touch them. He sat at his desk, looking out of the small square window at the freezing racks of cloud, his mind dancing from idea to idea. He could reduce these wonderings and defiances of his to some sort of order later, if he was alive. What were irresistible now were his quick, momentary thoughts that kept coming, and the first yellowish grey light breaking over the eastern hills, and the first dour flush of red.

He sat, recalling how everywhere you heard of parish priests harbouring escapers and helping the partisans. Why, right here on the opposite hillside that he was just beginning to make out, at the scruffy little church of San Giacomo, old Don Girolamo was hiding and nursing wounded men. What was it Caterina had been saying, about how splendid it was that these days people were showing their true colours? Well, tiny white-headed Don Girolamo was a man to be proud of, making up his own mind about what was right and unostentatiously getting on with it, without either waiting for good orders that would never come or obeying bad ones. Going undauntedly to and fro beneath his oak trees carrying an armful of hay for his mule, going between his vegetable plots and his rabbit hutches and his outhouses. Coming back to ring his church bell for mass, so the clear note sounded out over the meadows and woods. Or coming in to simmer broth for the wild men he'd got lurking in his parlour.

Luigi heard Caterina's and Lisa's voices. Without the slightest regret at being interrupted, he at once stood up from his desk and went back to the kitchen to warm milk in a pan and cut slices of bread.

After that, all day there were going to be jobs to do. He was particularly pleased with his conversion of the cave behind the barn into what he hoped would be a safe hiding-place. It was a natural cave, which generations of farmers at Ca' Santa Chiara had gradually improved, cutting steps down into it, even white-washing it and making shelves. Time out of mind, it had been a cool place for storing vats of wine and oil, storing cheeses and hams. Now Luigi had carried down blankets, lanterns, water, food. He had stacked firewood across most of the back of the barn, except at the end where the cave mouth was. There he had stored his sheaves of straw, which with any luck would be light and quick to remove and to replace. He had made his granddaughter help him with these preparations. He had explained to her that Mummy and she, and Bruno from the farm because when he'd been summoned back to the recruiting office he'd had the nous to lie low at home, and any escapers who happened to be around, might one day suddenly have to rush down there and be shut in, but she wasn't to be alarmed and she wasn't to cry.

Lisa had taken her own special candle-stick and match-box down to the cave, she'd chosen the corner in which she was going to curl up on her blanket and had changed her mind about it several times. Grandpapa would come and hide with them, wouldn't he? she had demanded.

Luigi had explained that the hitch about this hiding-place was that you needed somebody left outside to rebuild the straw stack, and this had best be done by him, maybe with Gervasio's and Maria's help. They were old, they three, and everyone knew they'd lived here for donkeys' years, so with any luck the soldiers wouldn't be interested in them.

10

—ɯ—

That afternoon of Saint Lucy's day, for the second time that year snow began to whirl down out of a louring, slate-coloured sky, and Signor Gervasio, gutting and skinning a rabbit on the stone table by the well in his farmyard, scrutinised the air and decided it was going to be the real thing this time. He scooped cold innards into one of his hardened hands and tossed the mess to his dog, which at once got its head down and started wolfing. A few moments more of slitting with his knife and wrenching with his fists, and the blood-flecked pelt was peeled off. Blue and pink and sinewy from paws to snout, the flayed carcass lay on the grey stone. Gervasio rinsed his hands in the bucket, sluiced the water over the body and the slab, set the bucket back by the well. He picked up the rabbit and tramped over to the kitchen to tell his wife he was going to saddle Signor Gregorio's horse, because he didn't suppose the gentleman wanted to be stranded here.

Gregorio Farsetti had been one of the half-dozen people in the district who possessed a car; but it had been requisitioned right at the beginning of the national disintegration and he had reverted to his chestnut mare perfectly contentedly. That had been in the days when the German Army was already in possession of the important cities along the coast, but had not yet got around to mopping up all the beautiful, lost hill towns. In Urbino, the Podestà had convened a committee of leading citizens, including Farsetti and D'Alessandria, in order to find out if there existed any agreement about what ought to be done. Soon after that, with German military men calling the tunes and local politicians playing them, this committee's uselessness had become evident and it had stopped meeting. But the two old friends had gone on disagreeing about whether or not it had been a good idea at the time.

Gregorio Farsetti argued that, in those unprecedentedly disastrous days, the attempt to persuade people of almost all shades of political opinion to forget their differences for a while and

unite to maintain law and order, to prevent weapons from
being looted, and to keep the reduced food supplies running,
was simply the community being sensible about organising its
own survival.

Luigi D'Alessandria, who still felt obscurely guilty that he
had only attended the first couple of meetings before dropping
out in disgust, held the opposite view. According to him, all
the blather about the maintenance of public order was merely
the relatively well-educated and prosperous class, the class to
which Gregorio and he both belonged and which perennially
failed to deliver either good government or effective opposition,
trying as always to make sure that there were no undesirable
upheavals in society, to make sure their families continued to
occupy comfortable positions. As for all this determination to
guard the explosives in the dépôt near Schieti, and the howls
of righteous alarm when some defiant spirits purloined a whole
lot of guns and grenades from the Military Police barracks
and decamped with them to the hill country of Rancitella,
where they declined to be at all cowed ... What was this,
in their local town and in all the other damned towns, if
not the enlightened bourgeoisie's attempt to ensure that the
munitions passed intact into the hands of the Wehrmacht?
And anyhow, the officers here who had originally assured the
committee that their men and they would remain at their posts,
and had been thanked on behalf of the citizenry by the Podestà
with appropriate magniloquence about their honour as patriots
and soldiers – these same uniformed gentlemen had shortly
afterward announced that they were going to ... What had
been the slithery words they used? Oh yes ... They were going
to 'take back their freedom of action', that was right. Good, eh?
Well, everybody else had been scuttling too.

Now Gregorio and Luigi were standing in the freezing air of
the loggia at Ca' Santa Chiara and they were still disagreeing
cheerfully. Gregorio was raising each booted foot in turn onto
the low wall, in order to strap his gaiters onto his calves for
riding home to Sant'Ambrogio. Usually when he visited his
friend at Ca' Santa Chiara it was rather like spending an
evening with the last man of God left creeping about in a
half-ruined monastery, or the last grey-headed soldier going

through the motions of garrison life in an abandoned fort. But this time Gregorio Farsetti had taken a manly pleasure in Esmeralda's and Caterina's good looks; he had attended Lisa's supper and bedtime with approval and enjoyment; he had eaten a hot cabbage stew, drunk the best part of a decanter of wine, and one way and another things had been nearly as jolly as they were at his own establishment. As for world-weary old Luigi ... Well, this new buoyancy of mind you couldn't help finding in him was downright miraculous. After dinner they had sat late by the fire, disagreeing vigorously about everything just like in the merriest of the old days, and now Gregorio was still listening with affectionate interest to what his friend thought.

'The good thing you can say about our Podestà is that after that whole nightmarish farce in September he *did* insist on being allowed to wriggle out of public life,' Luigi was saying with robust irritation. 'But at the time ... Every city drumming up deputations of supposedly eminent men to confabulate servilely with our conquerors about so-called public order. Ugh!' Luigi shuddered as if he'd just swallowed some slimy gobbet. 'Select deputations ... Remember how the adjective select always got itself stuck onto the noun deputation and wouldn't come unstuck? Naturally, the Germans despised us. Quite right too. Oh, once they'd been defeated of course the men who'd been the principal servants of the régime were keen enough to urge us all to overlook our differences, but when the bastards are riding high it's a different story. You haven't had one of your sons beaten up and then later locked up by them, but I have.'

Gregorio chuckled. 'What a firebrand you're getting to be in your old age. By the way, if that revolutionary son of yours shows up here again, tell him that even a staid old fellow like me wishes him well with his warring. Only – can we please not have the dictatorship of the proletariat, if it's all the same with him? Had enough dictatorships to be getting on with.'

'God above, I agree with you there,' rejoined Luigi heartily, with an instant's gloom in his voice. But at once his face brightened again, as he glanced out at the white flakes blowing through the gaunt walnut tree, beginning to fret the dead grass with white crystals. 'However, now the snows are coming, Gabriele and his friends will lie snug in their refuges for a while. They're in the high country north-east of Arezzo, did I mention that? You'd better get going, if you want to be home before dark. Well, this looks like being the end of our visiting for this year. Come back when it's thawed. Or I'll get over to your place.'

Gregorio Farsetti finished buckling his second gaiter. Tall, broad-shouldered and still powerful-looking, with his noble forehead and nose that made Luigi think of the prophet Isaiah, he grinned down at his short, slight host. He wound a scarf round and round his neck, tucked the ends inside his coat and buttoned it up. With the same tranquil, good-humoured air, he took out his riding gloves and pulled them on.

'Fascinating what you were saying last night about how according to Gabriele most of the political parties are organising their own partisan bands. Catholics too, and Monarchists of course.' Farsetti chuckled. 'Just imagine, everybody carting their doctrines and their squabbles up the mountain-sides! Still, good what he told you about the bands that refuse to owe allegiance to anybody. Oh, I'm not saying that the Liberation Committees here there and everywhere aren't a good idea – though, you know ... Naturally they all want to bring the Resistance under unified political control, and I suppose it may be a necessary evil. Though I reckon they'll be lucky if there ever *is* a militarily significant Resistance for them to appropriate, and sure as hell those twitterers aren't fighting it. These Communist commissars ... And the other crew, the churchy lot of self-appointed politicians, half of them sitting snug in the Vatican while they wait to see which way the war goes, wait to see what finer people than they achieve or fail to achieve ... Not my kind of men, Luigi. So you see I can't help admiring the bloody-minded fellows who won't obey any political orders, but just keep shooting their enemies when they can. What do you think ... If even dodderers like you and I end up in the mountains with rifles, we'd better join one of the independent bands, wouldn't you say? That'd be the style for us. Well, thank you for putting me up for the night. I like that English wife of Gabriele's. Quite tough, underneath, no? Lucky, that.'

On the other side of the house, the two sisters-in-law came out onto the porch.

'Do you really think it's going to snow for days and days?' demanded Esmeralda excitedly. 'Listen darling, I must dash into town while I still can and send Carlo a telegram. "Snowed up with Papa. Lots of love." What bliss! Or do you think he'll wonder why, if I could get as far as the Post Office despite the snow, I didn't keep driving and come back to him?'

'I should think he might easily,' said Caterina. 'But what fun, do stay!' Meeting Esmeralda's green eyes which were dancing with suspicious brilliance. Wondering if it could truly be Stavros, the Aegean fisherman-soldier, now convalescing at Ca' Santa Chiara, who was the reason for Esmeralda's splendidly disgraceful behaviour.

In the yard, Gregorio Farsetti mounted his horse. Half Luigi's attention was on this farewell. On practical matters too. While they were snowed up, they must keep a path open to the barn so they could fetch firewood and feed the dogs. Whether or not it would prove practical to keep coming and going the couple of hundred yards to the farm was another matter. The other half of him was strangely moved by this soft white downfall that had silently materialised in the sky. How isolated, how peaceful they were going to be, amidst the snow-drifts! It was as if these falling flakes offered a grace, a truce.

'Who knows,' Gregorio was saying, 'next year may bring us to the end of this war.' He pulled his already whitening hat down more firmly on his shock of white hair, he gathered up his reins. 'Oh, by the way . . . It appears that the rumours of Benedetta and her husband rather drifting apart were true. They're living fairly separate lives – I think I forgot to tell you.'

'Peace as soon as next year? Well, you always were an optimist,' Luigi answered distractedly.

The roofs were white already. Snow was gusting through the trees, settling on the bare boughs of the elms and cherries and acacias, settling on the oaks which still bore clusters of coppery crinkled leaves. Snow was drifting across the yard, beginning to ruffle along the windward side of the brick house, making the gutters look as if they had long white feather boas lying along them.

There was a sadness to the snow, Luigi decided, but a sadness which he liked. He imagined it falling all over the countryside, isolating all manner of men and women in the same cold peace. He saw the white benediction falling on the hill cities and the valley farms, falling indifferently on all the beliefs and all the enmities, covering belfries and bridges, covering hay-stacks and fishing-boats. Perhaps the sad, good, quiet snow was drifting down in the South on the two armies facing each other on the Gustav Line, in the North on Venice where it seemed Benedetta had her sad, quiet solitude again. What was her cousin saying?

'Not that the new peace whenever it comes will bring much in the way of glory here.' Gregorio gave a growl of mirth. 'What do you reckon? I guess about the best we can hope for is to be shunted from the German sphere of influence to the American rather than the Russian, naturally without ourselves having ever been anything you could call an influence for good. A pity, when you remember the hopes our grandfathers had when they united this country. Well, I'll be off.' He clapped his heels into his horse's flanks. 'Happy Christmas!'

For years Gregorio had been delivering his grimmest perceptions with a cheerfulness which Luigi envied. But now he seemed to have grown a stoicism of his own, or the snow-storm in which he was standing was still beguiling him. 'Happy Christmas!' he called with a ringing voice, after the chestnut mare clattering away at a trot into the trees and the whiteness.

11

All afternoon, freezing blizzards battened on Ca' Santa Chiara. Shovelling snow away from the outdoor staircase and away from the barn door, Luigi's mind followed the horseman riding through the lanes they both knew so well, his tall burly figure buffeted by the white welter, his mare hating it and laying her ears back.

Shrewd and undaunted, pragmatic without being cynical . . . Yes, Gregorio Farsetti had most of the mental virtues, Luigi mused. And how lucky he was, to have one good friend in the neighbourhood . . . Because heaven only knew when he'd next get over to Sardinia to go sailing with Della Quercia, if he ever did again in his life. As for that vagrant spirit Da Durante, he hadn't shown up here for months so presumably the invasions hadn't yet meant that in this province there were Raphaels going for knock-down prices. And these days even getting down to Rome for a chat with Damiani was out of the question. So really it was exceedingly fortunate, almost enough to make you think well of the world for a change, that there should be that man who looked like the prophet Isaiah riding away through the storm. Ah, so he was absolutely sure that Isaiah wasn't a pathetic little runt with no chin, with knock knees and a squint, was he?

Chuckling as he shovelled, Luigi D'Alessandria imagined snow freezing on the big-boned horseman's coat and trousers, freezing on his gloves and his hat, on his eyebrows, and how he'd ride with his shoulders hunched and his head ducked down. There he went, clip-clopping along the river-side, where the flocculent deluge was vanishing into the Metauro, which ran darkly, glitteringly brown. Then he'd start to climb the final couple of miles of meandering track up to Sant'Ambrogio, past the vineyard, through the fir wood. Horses could slip and come down in snow, especially if the stuff froze caked in their hooves. Luigi saw Gregorio dismount in the white storm, methodically stoop to pick up each hoof, use the spike on his pocket-knife to lever away the compacted snow. Then, what a welcome the man would get when he reached home! That was a house that knew how to thaw out a weary traveller. One of his sons would go to the stable to rub down the chestnut mare and fill the manger with hay. His wife would hang up his coat, which when it warmed up a bit would start to drip. She'd bring him dry clothes to put on, she'd fetch him food and drink.

D'Alessandria knew that all this shovelling to keep a path open across his yard would be to do again tomorrow. Before the winter was over, it would be to do again many, many times. But he was so warmed by the work, and he was so kindled by the vitality of imagining one other than himself, of following him in spirit, that the Sisyphean nature of this digging seemed to him fitting, even dignified. In this weather, it was every householder for himself and quite right too, Luigi thought. Each day, you shovelled the snow of that day. Good, good!

That Stavros the Greek escaper should be moved from the farmstead to Ca' Santa Chiara had been Luigi D'Alessandria's decision. The fugitive's fever might have abated, but he was still mere skin and bones with a racking cough. There could be no question of him continuing southward until spring came, and Luigi was happy that the danger of housing him should pass from Gervasio and Maria to himself. Moreover, the concealed cave was at the back of *his* barn not theirs.

Luigi had told Stavros not to come out to dig in this sub-zero afternoon. Even so he was making himself useful, fetching logs for the wood-basket this evening, carrying the scraps left from lunch out to the three thin dogs in the barn.

A lean time they'd have of it, the dogs, when the snow cramped their hunting style, and what with the food left uneaten after meals in the house often amounting to nothing at all. Well, he wouldn't let them starve. Luigi leaned on his shovel, panting. Stavros made a wild figure, flitting about in the snowy gale, wearing that coat which was too small. The poor fellow was a scarecrow, with shaggy black hair and his neck that looked raw. He must find him a scarf. Fisher-lad turned into a soldier of a defeated army, Luigi thought with a pulse of hot compassion he didn't think he'd felt since the last war. Man of a lost country. Well, this country was lost too, now. Justice of a sort, after the hubris. No, in peace time you didn't feel that throb of unstoppable tenderness for a man simply because the poor devil was a man. Escaped prisoner-of-war, he thought, become a wild man of these backwoods where we're all prisoners of the war. Blizzard wraith with snow-beaten wrists and neck, trudging quickly with an armful of logs.

The ice-coloured driving sky was darkening rapidly. Luigi went back to his digging for a few last minutes, cheering himself on with the promise of a scalding cup of Signora Maria's herb tea. These snow-drifts were already cutting Ca' Santa Chiara off in a makeshift peace, he mused thankfully. Yes, the Nazi-Fascists might be ruling the roost in the towns, but they weren't so all-powerful or so sure of their popularity that they'd venture up these lanes with tractors or snow-ploughs, come hunting for their enemies and spoiling country folks' Christmases. They wouldn't come looking for weapons this month with any luck. For example, come wanting the shot-guns that, according to the emergency regulations, Gervasio and he himself and all their neighbours should have handed in at the police station weeks ago. Well, at least he'd persuaded old Gervasio not to carry his beloved twelve-bore slung conspicuously over his shoulder even when he went down to the valley road.

His good humour giving rise to flights of compassionate imagination without his reflecting on this at all, D'Alessandria's spirit which had followed Gregorio Farsetti on his ride home now ranged farther afield. His arms beginning to ache as he heaved mechanically with his shovel, he saw his wife Sonya in her widow's colours straying about their shuttered house. He watched her pass from empty room to empty room bearing her head with dignity, bearing that urn of her consciousness which had long become one prayer of fearful love for their children – and she brought to him all the echoing houses where women were waiting. He'd heard that in Greece after the massacres it was worse than it was here, in Greece this winter there was starvation, and he imagined an island, a cottage by the sea. He watched Stavros's parents going about the sort of jobs which he himself did here, chopping firewood, digging the vegetable patch, the man and wife who prayed their boy was alive, who hoped someone was being kind to him. Luigi's spirit reached

out to Edoardo, to his younger son who in a city street or a
country farm might have found good people, if he wasn't in
a prison camp or a mass grave. He saw him in a borrowed
ill-fitting coat, carrying logs.

What was it he'd been trying to think straight about? Luigi
came to himself and took his shovel back to the barn. Not
Signora Maria, who always knew which green growing things
should be gathered from which fields and copses, who measured
the moments of the natural year according to the saints' days,
bringing her basket home with wild salads, with herbs from
which she made infusions and salves. No . . . Something about
how if people had got around to philosophical theorising that
meant that any truth there'd maybe been had already dispersed
into vacancy, the fine talk would always be yesterday's words,
when what you wanted were the words for this instant now.
Yes, if truth lived at all it was the song the blood beat momently
in your brain, it was the closest fluttering evanescent thought
which . . . Oh, for pity's sake! Even so, it was marvellous how
Caterina was fizzing with ideas these days. This vegetable patch
of his here was knocking spots off any of the universities he'd
ever taught at. Caterina wanting to know what Pater or Bergson
reckoned about this and Nietzsche reckoned about that – and
what was it she'd burst out with the other day, leaning on
her hoe? Something about desperately trying to hold true to
the ideal notions of ourselves we'd set up in order to bow
down before, and how all this aspiring and kow-towing could
be romantic enough looked at in some lights, but could be
hellish self-destructive too. Well, she was dead right about that.
Even so, it was good too how these days things like planting
potatoes seemed dignified work. Early in the Occupation he'd
despised himself for pushing ahead with practical jobs rather
than getting himself killed taking one or two of his enemies
with him, as other men had in other invaded countries, and
when he'd seen his neighbours at their workaday tasks his
mind had swarmed with rancorous thoughts. Now he must be
getting soft, because these days it didn't seem to him so terribly
contemptible as all that to take in the sick and the homeless. It
was a capital offence, after all. (The latest official proclamation,
distributed all over the province with commendable assiduity,

was splendidly unmistakable, even going in for capital letters: WILL BE SHOT.) No – not so contemptible as all that, to dig earth or dig snow and wait and hope for better times.

In the icy dusk, Luigi bent down by the dogs' baskets to pat their heads.

'Good girl, Furia. We'll get through the winter. Don't you fret about that. Good dogs. There, there. You never know, we may even get through the war.'

He came out of the barn, dragging the door shut behind him to keep the squalls out. In the shrieking air, the grey masses of hurtling snow writhing with chimeras obliterated everything.

No, not quite everything. Luigi's arms and legs tensed, the cold skin on his scalp crept. That phantom was a real man floundering toward him.

Then he breathed more easily.

'Help, please!' the wanderer called in Italian. Then, in English: 'Have I got the right house at last? D'Alessandria?' He slithered, fell down on one knee and one hand.

Luigi could hear the man's chest rasping as he struggled back on his feet. 'Don't be afraid!' he called, first in his own language and then, pulling his wits together, in the other. 'Yes, my name is D'Alessandria.'

They met at the foot of the stairs up to the front door. The escaper was tall, thin, young, and dead beat. He swayed, steadied himself on the wall, slumped down on the bottom step.

'Christ, I've made it. Like looking for a needle in a hay stack, trying to find your house. Bit late in the year, for trekking and all that lark. Not camping weather. Gets dark so early, too.'

Luigi peered down through the blizzard nightfall at the head plastered with snow. 'You can't sit there. Come up, come into the warm.'

'Don't you recognise me?' A grey face was tilted up in the greyness. 'I'm Giles. We're related to each other, you and I.'

'Good God! No, I . . . Yes, of course!' Luigi felt a cascade of blood to his heart, and at the thought of the joy Caterina was about to know he wondered why he'd never realised before how much he loved her. Tears for her prickled his eyes. 'Welcome to Ca' Santa Chiara!' he blurted out rather formally. 'Well done, making it here. Wherever you've come

from, I don't suppose it's been easy. By the way . . . your sister
is here.'

'*No?*' In a flash Giles was hauling himself onto his legs.
'Where? Up these stairs? My darling old Kate? Dear God, this
is more than I . . .'

'That's right. Your darling Kate. Up these stairs.'

Giles bounded up the steps, missed his footing and staggered,
but charged on to the porch at the top. 'Kate!' he called. 'Kate!
How the devil does this latch work? Kate!'

Bored with kneeling by the murmuring fire beside Lisa and
helping her to patch together a jigsaw of the Nativity which
Esmeralda had brought her, Caterina had stood up and drawn
the curtains. Stavros's flaring honesty, that was what was so
miraculous! The way the man didn't pretend he didn't know
that the invasions of his country were gratuitous acts of mass
murder; didn't pretend he couldn't tell right from wrong, as
so many millions of others had been doing for years. This
suffering – *you* caused it. The blessed moral straightness! Just
like when she'd told Luigi the condition in which she'd found
the D'Onofrio house, and his jaw clenched and his eyes burned
and he didn't say anything.

God what a squawking authoritarian hen-coop they'd all
been living in. All the pretending, all the concealing! *Now* she
felt the difference. Shivering in an icy draught, Caterina drifted
back to the fireplace. Yes . . . But what was going to happen
to Esmeralda, now that a few people were kicking holes in the
foetid coop, letting in some fresh air? What was happening *in*
Esmeralda?

'Found it, found it!' yodelled Lisa, brandishing a fragment of
cardboard fretwork.

'Well done, darling,' Caterina responded automatically, guiltily
recollecting all those evenings when she'd played by the hen-
coop's rules; when she'd listened respectfully to grey-headed
pashas discussing the latest reports from the Balkans, from the
Aegean; when she'd taken her pleasure with one or two of the
younger nabobs.

And then she heard it. She heard *him*: excited, jubilant. 'Kate,
Kate!' Then, irritated: 'How the devil does this latch work?'

Giles's voice shot through her brain, was gone as if it had

never been. Her heart crashing, she reeled, she clung to the back of an armchair, for that split second too dazed even to hope.

'Kate!'

She was still bowed with her hands on the back of the chair and her head down, like a woman broken by something. The seas of her blood roared in her ears.

Giles was in the room. His sister stood up with her back straight, her lips parted, her face drained of colour, her eyes wild. She gave a cry, as if he had truly come back from the dead.

The next instant, the snow on his arms was being crammed into her jersey, the snow on his face was crammed against her face.

12

—∞—

Five minutes later, the welcomed and the welcomers were still talking at the same time. The hero of the moment, who had ended up tramping his last few miles in the first snow blizzards of Christmas, and who judging by his initial outbursts of story had an epic tale to tell, stood grinning bashfully by the fire, still shuddering with cold, holding his frozen hands toward the leaping flames and wincing as the feeling returned to them. The heroine was laughing and crying at the same time. She kept flinging her arms back around her brother's neck, hauling his face down to hold it to hers and kiss him again.

'I can't believe it!' she cried for the third time. 'When Gabriele came home, we knew a lot of prisoners had been freed, we were waiting. But now! So you haven't been in Africa at all, or not for ages, you've been in Greece! And here was I, dreaming you were going to win a VC for taking Monte Cassino next spring! *What* did you say about Crete? And you've been a prisoner of . . . and you've escaped and . . . When finally you got near Urbino, someone you asked knew the name D'Alessandria, knew where this house was, and that Luigi was living here. Oh Giles, just imagine if Mummy could see us now!' And once more she burst into tears.

Esmeralda brought Giles a cup of tea, apologising for being such an incompetent handmaid. She believed that she *had* once, years ago, made a pot of tea, which naturally had tasted disgusting, so this brew would probably be vile, but at least it was hot.

Luigi fetched his last half-full bottle of brandy that he'd been keeping for emergencies and tipped a splash into the cup. Then he stood back and looked at Caterina. Yes, he was right . . . You couldn't behold her radiant tear-stained face and doubt that for this hour she was a victrix. Undeserved triumph, perhaps; soon to be followed by defeat, perhaps . . . But for her spirit, for her wisp of moral existence, a terrible battle had just been won.

Lisa stood gazing up with solemn awe at this second legendary man who had reduced her mother to rapturous tears, this miraculous Uncle Giles who had suddenly appeared out of the snow and the war, who was even more a stranger than Papa had been when he came home. After a minute she knelt down at her jigsaw again. But immediately she cocked her head back and went on looking up at her mother and her uncle.

Stavros stood slightly aside from the euphoric reunion, regarding Giles alertly and frowning with attention as he tried to understand a few words of all this English that was suddenly being spoken.

The greatest light in the oak-beamed room came from the big logs burning in the fireplace. It lit the jigsaw on the hearth-rug which everyone was being careful not to tread on. It even played its flamy glints on the polished gun-metal of the pair of twelve-bores in the corner. Away from the fireplace, a few lamps guttered in the gloom. Waverings of radiance picked out the corner of a bookcase, a majolica bowl on the sideboard, one of the pigeon-holes of Luigi's desk.

Giles Fenn wore the tatters of a British Army shirt, a pair of trousers furnished by the Red Cross during one of his captivities, a ragged sweater that a peasant family had given him, an Italian Army greatcoat with a tear in it that he insisted was a bullet hole, and a pair of boots that had adorned the feet of a police sergeant until thrown out as no longer fit to be seen in. He refused to take any of his clothes off, protesting that if he huddled by the fire for long enough he *must* get warm and dry in the end – and anyhow, what did they propose to dress him in instead?

The few garments of Gabriele's and Edoardo's that had been left in the house, and which might have more or less fitted him unlike Luigi's, had all long since been bequeathed to other wanderers, so Caterina had to accept the logic of this. Giles sat on a stool before the leaping flames, and after much cajoling he consented to ease his ruined boots off his frozen and blood-stained feet. Smiling through her blissful tears and repeating 'Oh I'm so silly!' his sister knelt before him with a basin of warm water and a sponge. When he slumped with exhaustion, his eyes went vacant and clearly he barely knew where he was, she gazed at him in an anguish of protective compassion, her sponge dripping forgotten in her hand. Then he jerked back to life with an angry, frightened cry, and he stared around the room as if he hated it.

Luckily Giles at once recovered himself, and didn't notice the glances Luigi and Esmeralda exchanged. 'God what a mess,' he observed cheerfully, contemplating his own feet. 'Haven't had a look at 'em for a few days. Ouch! Go steady, Kate.' The water was not much more than lukewarm, but it scalded him. 'So you got my letter from Cairo? We were in the fleshpots there all right. Great fun, great high-jinks. Could have done with a bit more of that sort of war. So you've been imagining me at Tobruk, at El Alamein. No, my regiment got sent to Greece. Hell of a business and we all got split up, units sent off to all points of the compass. We went up to try to hold the Aliakhmon Line against the German attack – April of '41 that was. Did hold it, for a few days. Remember that particular British defeat? Then we were ordered back and we held them again. Australians, New Zealanders, us lot. At Thermopylae, funnily enough. I kept remembering being at school, all those Greek and Latin lessons. I wonder if Canonbury Square is still standing. You don't happen to know, do you?'

'No, I don't. Oh Giles, Giles! Let's *assume* the house is standing, shall we, until we find out that it's not? And it doesn't seem to matter so dreadfully much, now you're here, now I've seen you again. Yes, yes, don't talk about it! I know you can't stay here forever – but you can't leave me till the snow melts, can you, so right now I'm in luck. Anyway, if the place *has* been bombed flat, we'll find you somewhere just as nice to live. You can live with Gabriele and me in Arezzo, or . . . By the way, Gabriele is a partisan these days, so you're not the only hero I've got to make my silly heart thud. Edoardo is missing, that's the bad news. But you've been missing for years and years and now you've come back to me, so with any luck Edoardo will walk through the door one day too.'

Caterina bathed his cut, swollen feet with infinite tenderness. She kept looking up into his face, and every time she did so the smile came back to her lips and the tears came back to her eyes.

'By the way.' She dimpled. 'If you come to Arezzo . . . *When* you come to Arezzo, I should warn you that Rosalba is *longing* to see you. She's the gorgeously pretty one with black ringlets, remember? Yes, liberating Rosalba from Mr Hitler and Mr Mussolini could have its dangers, or its rewards. So watch out. And of course I'll be match-making furiously. Packing you off for picnics in the olive groves together, that sort of thing. Or if you prefer you can fall in love with somebody else, so long as she's just as fetching to look at and just as sweet as Rosalba. Only another good, beautiful demon like her may be a *little* difficult for me to rustle up for you.'

'Rosalba?' Giles grinned. 'Oh, with a bit of luck I'll find the courage to face her. Listen Kate, I'll do absolutely anything you want in the wide world, so long as it doesn't involve having to stir an inch away from this fire. My God, when the cold has really bitten into you it . . . I suppose I'll thaw out some day. I say, that tea was just the trick, but – is there something I could eat?'

An aberrant muscle in the escaper's left cheek twitched every few seconds, and his blue eyes stared about with ominous intensity. Nonetheless Luigi was relieved to hear him succeed in keeping up the sort of boyish chat that gave Caterina back her lost, innocent brother, gave her back a Giles who had not been damaged.

Esmeralda jumped to her feet and at once began to lay the table, declaring that since Giles was starving, and since it was already Lisa's supper-time, they might as well all dine together straight away. It was dark, wasn't it? What were they waiting for? She set candles in the pewter sticks and lit them. She had arrived for Christmas with a hamper of delicacies which, in war-locked Europe, were beyond the dreams of common mortals, and she had also had the foresight to bring her father enough boxes of candles to see him through the winter. Boxes of soap and boxes of lots of other useful things too which these days were either in short supply or unobtainable – unless, that is, your husband was a successful man.

Luigi poured Giles a glass of wine. Then he came back into the firelight with a hunk of bread and a hunk of salame on a plate to keep his guest going until the pan of water on the range was brought to the boil and the pasta could be cooked.

In the flickering glow, Giles went on sitting on the stool near the fire-dogs, and Caterina went on kneeling before him, the pair of them framed by the stone fireplace. She was gently applying one of Signora Maria's herbal salves to his raw feet, tipping an ooze of the pungent ointment onto her finger-tip and smoothing it on.

'Then I'm going to bandage up both of your nice repaired feet, and I'm going to put a couple of pairs of socks on them or maybe three pairs and you can hobble about like that.'

How extraordinary! she was thinking. Here's Giles, whom I'd been imagining *completely* haywire. Wrong countries, wrong battles, wrong everything! All my stories hopelessly wide of the mark as usual. So – who is he, deep down, now, I wonder? He looks hard, and terribly thin, and not a boy at all.

She gazed at his broken, filthy finger-nails when he picked up his food, gazed at his unshaven jaw as he munched. His roughly cropped hair was wet with melted snow, his hair which was the same hay colour as hers. When he met her eyes, it seemed to Caterina that her love was looking deep into who he truly was, into how irreplaceable and wonderful her brother was. She thought: My heart will skip at *least* three beats, they'll have to straighten me out on the rug and slap my face till I come round. She thought at the same time: I may be half-fainting with love, but I don't know anything about him whatsoever! In all this fighting . . . He must have killed men, I suppose? And that shout when he came to his senses, what should that tell me? Does he have horrifying dreams? Yes, probably he does.

All the same, Caterina decided with swift, gut conviction, he's still my same darling old Giles, only jolly tough these days it looks like. So she asked him: 'I think I've just about understood what you were up to in mainland Greece. But later, in Crete . . . ?'

'Crete?' Giles spat out in a jarring voice. 'After the Battle of Crete was lost we were brigands.' But he recovered, and went on jauntily. 'A few of us managed to slip away into the hills. Best summer of my life, being a brigand. I turned out to have nearly all the right defects of character. Terrific fighters, the Greeks.' He clenched his fists, his voice cracked, and this time he couldn't stop his rising snarl. 'My God those Cretan shepherds knew who their enemies were and knew how to go for them. We killed, and we . . . Christ yes!' Then he glanced around with eyes which had suddenly become vague. He added lightly, as if it hardly interested him, 'Oh, well, if you ask, I . . . We had a magnificent time. Kidnapped a German general, committed all manner of useful crimes. Only I was captured in the end.'

'*How* many times have you been a prisoner-of-war?' Caterina asked softly, into the silence which had lapped back over his breaks and his mends and his lines of weakness.

'Three. But . . .' Giles added in a deliberately manly, off-hand tone through which a chime of boyish pride rang out clearly all the same, 'but each time I've managed to get away, so far.'

Stavros said, out of the shadows, in his own language: 'Good man.' The two escapers gazed at one another, with questioning eyes. 'You were in Greece, fighting alongside my people? Have I understood right? When my country was invaded, only your people came to our aid, nobody else. You fought on the Aliakhmon Line?'

'That's right. Were you there?'

Stavros held out his hand, gripped Giles's silently.

Giles had managed to reply in Greek. Now he added haltingly, 'I was only on Crete for six months. I'm sorry, my Greek is very bad.'

'Explain, please!' Caterina cried gaily, calamity having been staved off. 'What have you said to each other?'

'The Aliakhmon Line, that I've just been telling you about,' Giles said to her, smiling his happy smile from before the war. 'What an ignorant sister you are!' Taking the poker, he quickly drew the outline of Thrace and Thessaly in the scatterings of ash on the hearthstone. 'Here's Salonika.' From it, he drew a diagonal mark running south-west. 'Here was the Line. Only then . . .' The poker rasped lightly as he showed her, bending forward in the fire-light.

Stavros stood looking down over his new friend's head, quiet with passion as the shape of his lost land emerged in the ash.

Giles extended his map southward, he drew Attica. 'Then the rearguard action we fought, Kate, while the rest of our fellows were embarking at ports behind us . . . The action at Thermopylae . . . That was about here, see? Luckily they shipped most of us out too, in the end, so we could be defeated all over again in Crete a few weeks later.'

13

The following day and the day after, it snowed all over the Italian heartlands, on the old duchies and the old principalities. At Ca' Santa Chiara, Caterina watched the drifts deepen; she rejoiced in the colour that warmth and food and rest were already bringing back to Giles's cheeks; she rejoiced in the towns and villages cut off, in this truce imposed by the sky. Soon the rumpled eiderdown of white was knee-deep in the yard, and a lot deeper than that where the wind heaped it against banks and walls, and still it snowed.

When Lisa and she sallied out to the barn, down the narrow pathway which the men of the household took turns to dig clear, they saw how Esmeralda's and Luigi's cars were two indistinguishable mounds. The dogs seemed perfectly happy in the barn where they had their snug baskets and were always pleased to be visited by Lisa because she brought them things to eat. If you stood in the barn door and looked out, all you could see were trees heavily weighted with snow. All you could hear was the snowfall quietness, and now and then, near and far, a sharp crack when a branch broke.

Caterina knew that this truce was not a real truce, that this semblance of peace would not last. Sooner or later it would thaw. There would be boisterous rivulets cascading down every valley. The armoured cars would be able to get along the mirey roads once more. The war would be able to get through to her again even in this remote house.

Giles and Stavros would leave. They were always discussing whether it would be better to head on south and hope to slip across the Line one night, or to go down to the Adriatic and hope to be picked up by one of the British naval patrol vessels which were rumoured to be stealing up the coast to rescue detachments of escapers.

Just as bad, just as painful to the anxious love in Caterina's heart, Esmeralda would vanish away back to her gaudy life in that villa on Lake Garda with all those servants. She would

go where amid the trappings of power without the reality of
government, wearing a sheer silk dress and a diamond necklace,
parting her carmine lips to pout a puff of cigarette smoke she
would . . . Oh, Caterina didn't know. But she was better at
facing the physical dangers looming over her husband and her
brother and Stavros than she was when it came to imagining
Esmeralda back on Lake Garda living out her charade, her
nullity. A corpse was a mockery of a living soul and a lot of
people were getting killed, though you tried to keep your nerve
steadyish about that. But for Esmeralda to become a mockery
in people's eyes while she was still alive . . .

Even so, with this blessing of snow, Caterina had convinced
herself that Giles already seemed calmer, and she was incapable
of feeling cast down.

'In Urbino, they'll be up on their roofs with spades, Caterina,'
Luigi happened to remark.

Her happy mind immediately imagined the hill city crowned
with white. She heard the cheerful voices of men up on their
house-tops with spades chucking down the heavy snow, and the
voices of men down on the ground digging to clear a footpath
along the middle of every narrow, winding street and a path to
each front door. Her mind ranged all over the Italy she loved,
to San Gimignano where the white deluge would be gusting past
the slender towers, to the Mantua fens that would be deep under
impassable snow-drifts now, and the more places she imagined,
the more intense was her joy in this peace that had come for
Christmas.

She imagined the mountain hamlets where the stocky stone
cottages would have nearly vanished, would be white hillocks,
and where the shepherd folk and Gabriele and all the partisans
would be safe. She remembered a famous villa garden near
Florence where he and she had sauntered once, while indoors
Gaetano Da Durante had been negotiating for a Salvador Rosa.
She imagined that beautiful old sanctuary where now it must
be snowing on the cypress avenue and the stone gods and
goddesses, snowing on the wistaria arbour, on the baroque
orangery, on the sun-dials. She saw Gabriele and herself strolling
there once more. Was it now, ghostlily, in this snow? Was it in
some future, peace-time winter, and did that mean they were

both going to survive? Never until this year had this wayward mind of hers *seen* so much, been visited by so many apparitions! There the two of them came, walking arm in arm through the whitened box parterre, reaching the frozen fountain and the portico, laughing about something.

Caterina might be standing at the Ca' Santa Chiara barn door, listening to Lisa and the dogs while they made a fuss of one another behind her back in the dimness that smelled of musty straw, gazing out from below the yard-long icicles to the muffled world and the silence. Or it might be after the little girl had been tucked up in bed, and Esmeralda and she were sitting by the fire to wrap up the child's Christmas presents. But whatever she was doing, in those days of being irredeemably happy because Giles was here, and of longing for peace so he could outlive the harm which had been done to him and the harm he had done, and of being afraid because he was going to go back to the war, Caterina's imagination was delighting in what appeared to her solid grounds for hope, appeared almost to be signs, almost presages.

Even when she was trying her hardest to be practical, her mind kept leaping away. Luigi and she went to the larder, they pitched into a terrifically hard-headed discussion of what the Ca' Santa Chiara commissariat might achieve by way of a war-time Christmas Eve dinner and a Christmas Day lunch. She honestly was concentrating on how best to strike a balance between a suitable festivity and the need to go on eating for the rest of the winter, a calculation complicated by the impossibility of turning hungry fugitives away from your door, and the further impossibility of knowing how many of these unexpected guests were going to show up. In her attempt to be methodical she had even brought a piece of paper and a pencil. She was noting down what quantities they had of this and that, she was scribbling down ideas for possible meals.

But at the same time, Caterina was back in her Arezzo bedroom making slow, glorious love with Gabriele in the hot night shadows, and then lying luxuriously on the cool sheet to hear about his escape from Ustica. Just fancy – getting hold of a fishing-boat and sailing away clean through the middle of the great battles! Sailing agonisingly slowly along from island to island, with the Allies just

over your southern horizon and the Axis over the horizon to
your north, and madly and brilliantly getting away with it, so
you came walking through your own city and in at your own
door. Caterina could not help irrevocably deciding that, so long
as there were men like her husband Gabriele alive and kicking,
this war to liberate Europe was bound to be won.

As for her other adored escaper . . . Well, the adventures Giles
had been telling her were, if anything, even more incredible.
He'd got out of a German transit camp in northern Yugoslavia
by climbing over the wire during a cloudburst with a couple of
other fellows, and had succeeded in walking west night after
night till he'd crossed the border north of Trieste, but then
he'd been captured again, by the Italians this time. He'd got
out of *that* camp last September when all the guards bolted.
He'd set off south hoping that the Allied advance would reach
him and hoping also to find Ca' Santa Chiara on his way. But
that first attempt to get here hadn't worked, because one evening
unfortunately he'd gone to the wrong sort of family and asked
for shelter, he'd told his sister, and the shits had betrayed him
to the police, so he'd ended up at the mercy of the Thousand
Year Reich yet again. After that he'd been in a train-load of
prisoners being sent north to Germany and he'd thought the
game was up, he'd reckoned this time his escaping was over
for this war. But then the train had stopped in the middle of
nowhere.

'Wonderful fellows, some of these Italian engine drivers, Kate.
Even had the sense to pretend to need to get more steam up in a
wood, not in open fields. We piled out of those cattle-trucks,
I can tell you. Italians who didn't want to be soldiers of
Mussolini's, Italians who didn't want to be slave labourers
of Hitler's. All the rest of us wretches from half the nations
you ever heard of, who didn't know what was in store for us
north of the Alps but sure as hell desired to avoid it. Down the
embankment we hared. Into the trees. I didn't draw breath till
I couldn't hear the shooting any more. Don't know how many
poor chaps the guards shot. Quite a few, I imagine, but I was
one of the lucky ones.'

All this, he had told her, without once staring around with
that glitter in his incensed eyes, without his snarl breaking out

even once. And that matter-of-fact openness which Stavros and he both had! Like when they'd all been talking about what shape the spring offensive might take. Esmeralda had drawled something frivolous, and Stavros had shot straight back: 'There are Polish brigades and Free French brigades down there, Canadian and British and American brigades. Don't you think it's quite generous-hearted of those men to come here to fight and be killed to free your damned country from itself? I imagine most of them would rather be at home, you know.'

Poor Esmeralda! In the world she'd been gracing, nobody ever said anything as straight as that.

Caterina stood distracted in the freezing larder, because she had just realised how intermittently her heart loved, in swoops and lapses, so it plainly had little to do with any intrinsic essence which Gabriele or Giles might have, and a lot to do with her own vagaries. It was shameful how she needed to reconceive and reelaborate people in order to feel anything at all. And if her husband and her brother were killed . . . Oh, for a while she'd howl. But in time she'd simplify them, she'd half forget, she'd survive.

Caterina went on standing among the preserving jars, her scrap of paper on which she had pencilled possible Christmas menus forgotten in her hand, being observed with amused affection by her father-in-law.

14

—⚏—

Right at the end of Gabriele's and her three Arezzo summer weeks together, their second honeymoon as she called
it, Caterina had plucked up her courage and given Gabriele
her war-time night scribblings. It had been so awful to watch
him start to turn the pages, it had been so awful to wonder
whether he'd guess the seductions, that she had gone to sit in the
Santissima Annunziata, sit there alone with her abomination of
those heaps of pages which so futilely she had dirtied with her
hatreds and her self-hatreds and her fears, her muddled and
vaporous ideas, her contemptible introspections. But Gabriele
had come to find her. He had sat down beside her, in the pew
where for an hour she had been trembling with misery, and the
compassion and the love in his eyes had started to convince her
before he had spoken a word.

Now faced with her even stranger miracle of Giles, whom she
had been imagining in the Eighth Army but who instead suddenly walked in from the snowy dusk for Christmas, Caterina
had forgotten that she had ever been weary to death of her
abhorrences, weary of hoping and trying not to hope. She had
even managed to set aside her intimations in the larder.

With her brother she laughed about the time in Canonbury
Square when they had decorated their Christmas tree with
brightly painted glass baubles, with blue tin birds and golden tin
bells, and had come down in the morning to find their tree had
toppled over and was lying ignominiously on the sitting-room
carpet with its trinkets smashed. She laughed with delight when
they remembered Mummy taking them on summer Sundays to
Chatham to look at the ships, and winter holidays when the
great treat was tickets to *Swan Lake* or *The Nutcracker*. They
started fizzing with plans about how when the war was over
she was going to visit Giles in London and they were going to
take Lisa to the ballet for *her* Christmas treat.

It seemed that nothing could shadow Caterina's happiness.
She kept rushing into this room or out of that – and if she

did recall Edoardo who was missing, or Sonya who was alone, or Gabriele who was a hunted enemy of the state, she could instantly make herself shamelessly joyous once more simply by listening to Lisa singing 'Once in Royal David's City' as she knelt over her jigsaw with its stable and oxen and donkey and lambs, or by glancing out at the blessed mounds of snow barricading the track, or by deciding that after the war they were never again all going to abandon Sonya at the same time. Then she sat Giles down before the fire with a sheet around his neck and started giving him a rough-and-ready hair-cut with the kitchen scissors, making absolutely no effort at all not to give his head loving little rubs and dab giggling kisses on the back of his neck. He was to go on telling her about how in Crete they'd kidnapped a German general in his own staff car, she demanded. Heavens what dash! Getting him clear away up the mountain goat-tracks; making that night rendezvous with the submarine that shipped their really very nice old prey off to Alexandria, while they turned back to their hiding and their outlawry . . . By the way, in some eyrie of a Cretan village *was* there a beautiful girl he'd had a flaming affair with, and when the war was over *was* he going back to look for her and ask her to marry him?

First Luigi D'Alessandria's wife and then Gabriele's had introduced a few northern European elements into Christmas at the Arezzo house, and now at Ca' Santa Chiara they had stood up a small fir in a tub, though unfortunately they had no tinsel or ornaments to bedeck it with. On Christmas Eve, Esmeralda placed beneath it the presents which even in war time her husband's salary and her own proximity to the shops of Verona had made possible.

Luigi had the happy inspiration of taking down from the walls some of his etchings for Lisa to look at, so he could retell her the Christmas story with the help of his Guido Reni *Mother and Child*, his Barocci *Annunciation*. The others were all busy, some in the kitchen, others laying the table for dinner. But they smiled to see the little girl sitting on the sofa beside her grandfather with the *Annunciation* on her lap (she was particularly delighted by how the Virgin's sensible cat slept peacefully throughout the astounding visitation), hearing about the herdsmen with their flocks who saw the prophetic star, the Eastern kings who set out on their long journey bringing gold and frankincense and myrrh. And it was *also* very sweet, Esmeralda and Caterina whispered to one another, how even during the telling of the most wonderful episodes of the story Lisa's eyes would flick to the silver and red and blue wrapped-up presents, most of which had her name on them.

Luigi was enchanted to have his granddaughter to tell about how unfortunately Joseph and Mary had found no room at the inn, so they'd had to camp in a stable and put their baby to sleep in a manger, though this actually was probably quite snug if there was plenty of straw. Telling her the Christmas story, he was beset by what a powerful legend it was: a child, the Son of Heaven, our redeemer. That overwhelming, terrible hope that this world and this nature of ours might change; that our destinies might be kinder from now on, more merciful, touched by grace.

Luigi did not know if he was more moved by the might of the story and the humanness of the hope, or by the despairing knowledge that life was at least as evil now as it had been nineteen hundred and forty-three years ago. By a fatal instinct, he looked up from Barocci's Angel on his grandchild's knee to one of his etchings which he had not taken down for her. Yes, there was Tiepolo's skeletal Death with his book of all our fates. There were we poor wretches gathered around him, we who wanted to know: And I? And my children? How long, still? What is in store?

Caterina had noticed an infinitesimally altered inflexion in Luigi's voice. She had noticed his bright glance up to the wall, his tightened jaw, and she knew him well enough to guess what his mind's swing from the *Annunciation* to *Death Holding Audience* might mean. But she had also just seen the irritation and the sullen hopelessness reappear in Esmeralda's face, so she at once set her love and kindness to work where they were most needed.

15

Caterina was continually being plagued by remorse because Esmeralda did not have her own good and simple reasons for giving way to joyfulness, and now on Christmas Eve for the twentieth time she resolved that they must have a heart to heart talk. This pang of guilt that she was not loving her friend actively enough had come when Esmeralda had abruptly broken off her flamboyant, faintly flirtatious chatter with Giles and Stavros by the fire-side. In her irresolute shrugging turn away from them, in the morose savagery flashing in her eyes, Caterina with a jolt had known that Esmeralda had suddenly not been able to bear these two young men's cheerful confidence that though there was still a horrifyingly long way to fight, they were in the right and in the end they were going to win. She had not been able to bear the knowledge that she could be as beautiful, as light-hearted, as vivacious as she pleased, but even if Stavros and she declared a Christmas truce – for that matter, even if she decided that her handsome enemy should be added to her conquests – that wouldn't change anything that mattered. That wouldn't redeem her from herself, Caterina suddenly saw, gazing into Esmeralda's loneliness.

The problem was always the same. Every room at Ca' Santa Chiara was deathly cold except for the living-room, so the entire household naturally kept as close as they could to the fireplace and private conversation was impossible.

However, this evening Caterina said: 'Esmeralda, *do* sit up a little bit late with me, when the others have all gone to bed, like we used to in the old days. You will, won't you?' Then at long last she managed to get Lisa washed and into bed, by promising her that Christmas morning would come more quickly if she was asleep than if she was awake. The three men sat talking after supper for a while (Luigi and Stavros wanted to hear more of Giles's stories of guerrilla fighting in the mountains of Crete). But then they decided they were off to brave their freezing bedrooms.

Caterina's eyes followed Giles out of the room, but she turned back to Esmeralda eagerly. Only then, after all her expectation she did not know how to begin.

Restlessly she stood up, she crossed to a window, drew back the curtain. It had stopped snowing. Under a three-quarter moon, the white landscape lay utterly still, utterly silent. Somewhere on the opposite hillside, a dog barked.

Shivering, she returned to the fire. She sat down and held out her hands to the glow. 'So many things I've wanted to talk to you about, and now my head is even more muddled than usual.' She laughed rather awkwardly, and at the same time blushed, for she had never felt this awkward with Esmeralda before.

'Oh well,' Caterina began with an effort at jauntiness, 'I expect I'll remember a few hundred of the questions I wanted to ask you in due course. But there's one thing I've been wanting to *tell* you . . .' In the flickering firelight which made an aureole embracing the two of them, she met Esmeralda's eyes and was taken aback by how coldly they shone at her. Caterina faltered, but she made herself go on. 'There's an awful lot of Carlo that I don't know the first thing about, and there's absolutely no reason why he need ever take me an inch further into his confidence. But . . . You mustn't think I haven't valued how friendly to me he's been, through – through all this.' Esmeralda had cocked one eyebrow, and once more she wavered. 'I mean . . .'

'Good heavens, what did you expect,' Esmeralda demanded in a cool voice, 'that we'd all be gouging each other's eyes out with carving knives? Is it so astonishing to you, that some of your country's enemies should be civilised men? Anyhow, Carlo took a terrific fancy to you right away, don't pretend you don't know that and haven't been playing on it. Heavens, I remember once trying to make him promise he wasn't going to require a night with you as the price of your not being interned in some ghastly camp. I asked him jokingly you know, but only half jokingly. But he wouldn't promise. He just chuckled and said he'd have to think about that.' Esmeralda laughed with exasperated contempt. 'Though honestly I often think there'd be more honour to it if we all *did* take to gouging one another's eyes out. Come off it Caterina, stop being so coy. Oh you're over the moon right now because Giles is here, and I'm delighted too. Rather more to the point – considering what he's been through, he doesn't seem in such bad shape. If the rest of the war treats him kindly he'll be all right afterward I should say, all right enough. Though the rest of the war may hold a fate for him far worse than anything he's weathered so far. But right now if it comes to what you haven't the guts or the wit to ask me, but I damned well know how to tell you . . .'

Leaning forward in her chair, Esmeralda was twisting and twisting a jade bracelet on her slender wrist. Her quickfire mind kept shooting sentences, and she never let Caterina's eyes flick away from hers.

'Don't you go thinking I don't know how innocent I was to believe it didn't really matter having my husband and my younger brother on one side, and my elder brother and the rest of the family on the other, including my damned fool English sister-in-law who . . . that I'd . . . Well, it hadn't actually come to a civil war in those days – but that's what's happening now, that's what's going to get worse. Who was it who said that civil wars were the only sort it really was occasionally a good idea to fight? No, never mind. Papa would know, he'd remember. Yes – thresh out once and for all what kind of country it's going to be. Only they never change, it's only superficial. Well, there went that empty-headed Esmeralda creature, reckoning that all politics were so obviously dolled-up self-interest that they couldn't possibly matter, no one with a sense of humour let alone a sense of style could be seen taking seriously anything so grotesque. Reckoning that you only had to keep on being civilised about things, and at family parties remember to kiss everybody you could lay your hands on, and not fret about how unreal the civilisation was, not fret about how you couldn't kiss all the self-interest away. Only don't you dare think I don't see clearer than you now. Oh yes! But you're all right Caterina, with your eyes dancing and your heart going pit-a-pat pit-a-pat.'

Esmeralda had stopped twisting the jade bracelet on her right wrist, she was feverishly plucking at the gold and coral one on her left. Gazing at her with love and awe, Caterina had a vision of the wedding photograph on Sonya's desk in the Arezzo drawing-room. There was Esmeralda standing between

Gabriele and her bridegroom, with her long silvery veil blown sidelong on a puff of wind. She remembered how a moment before Gabriele and Carlo had been clapping each other on the shoulder and laughing about something.

'You don't see, but I see.' Esmeralda's voice clanged. 'Oh, Carlo knows that if the Axis wins this war Gabriele will be lucky if he ends up in a labour camp – you think that doesn't weigh on him? But he goes on doing what he believes is his duty, he goes on serving the alliance this country chose. I know that if the British and the Americans win there'll be a parliament in Rome again. You never know, it may even be slightly less of a bad joke than the last one. At any rate my husband and yours if they're still alive will be able to get themselves elected to it, they'll both be quite deft at that. Then for years and years they can make the most venomous speeches about each other's gangs, and that will be a bit better than the prison camps but still it'll be fairly revolting. No, that wasn't it.' Esmeralda broke off, scowling irritably. 'What I see when I'm up at the Lake is different from that. I see hatred. My mind jeers all the time, and I see . . .'

Esmeralda jerked to her feet, went striding away from the fire-light into the gloomy room. She came striding back, her sentences tumbling.

'Days come when . . . Well, I have to get out of the house Caterina, to stay indoors would be – oh, unthinkable.' Her defiance of her own unhappiness came out as a rattle of hollow mirth. 'Down along the lake-side I see a subaltern salute a colonel and say something very respectfully, and I think: Don't fool yourself! He can't wait to order you off to be killed, so he can read the despatches all about the brilliant counter-attack he pulled off. I stroll on, I see two little boys being treated to ice cream by their mother. Their fat tongues licking that filthy ice cream are a disgusting exhibition, and across the road the people going into church for morning mass make me want to howl derision. Devils and gods aren't that easy to propitiate, I jeer at them. You think an army going into action has ever been placated by prayer? Inform yourselves a little more scrupulously. Look in your souls, that's what it's impossible to atone for! Naturally I look very elegant as I stroll along the lake with my parasol. Then I see a girl and a young soldier on a jetty, kissing tenderly. Little tart! my mind snarls. Whatever you let him do to you, he won't stay.

'And the nights – my God, the nights! When we have German officers and Italian officers at our dinner table, I can feel their hatred and contempt for each other till I could scream, but I go on talking about how there are never any good films showing in Verona, about how Carlo is working far too hard, I'm scheming to get him away to the mountains for a weekend.

'With this stupendous position on the Lake, the general beside me asks politely, surely it must be possible for the Honourable Minister to get an afternoon's yachting once in a while?

'Oh yes I say, while the autumn was still mild sometimes I did persuade my husband to escape with me on the sloop.

'If he's a Wehrmacht general, he knows I know he despises us all for our servitude to Germany, he despises the charade of our government. He knows I know it would only take another twist in the politics of this nightmarish Axis for them to shoot Carlo out of hand, with or without some sort of show trial. While if the man listening to my twitter is an Italian general . . .' Her snarl rose and cracked and rose again. 'If he's one of our poor devils of generals that the Germans may graciously be allowing to use their soldiers to make roads, because they don't want them doing much fighting thank you very much, Christ no! Any more than the Allies are particularly keen on *their* tame Italians getting into the action, because they've got no reason to trust them either, and God forbid that the wretched turncoats should be dignified as co-belligerents . . .'

Esmeralda choked on her words. 'Civil war, Caterina! Very civil. You wouldn't be so bloody chirpy if it was happening in England, would you?' She stood trembling with the abhorrence in her.

'Hatred I tell you, Caterina! Can you imagine what it's like, living among nothing but loathings and lusts and lies? Living a life in which there's mighty little left that I don't hate? And as for my loathing of myself!

'So of course when our guests have gone I have to escape, I can't wait a few weeks till maybe I'll be able to sneak away to visit Papa. I make a run for it at once.' She broke into ugly laughter. 'Across the terrace, down the steps . . . Carlo lets the coward go, her panic is stronger than he is, he can't stop her. Her loathing is stronger than any love she's ever felt, that's what she's like. Across the lawn she rushes like a woman demented, under the cedars, down to the water. It's beautiful, Lake Garda in the moonlight, why don't you come and see us? Eh, Caterina? Lost your voice? I suppose with the British already in the South, Carlo and I aren't so useful any longer. We could even become an embarrassment, no? Oh don't you worry, you'll be all right. Yes I'm a pariah these days, even you won't touch me.'

Caught fast in the sensation that from the depths of an abyss she was clambering up the infinite air, Caterina swayed to her feet, gasping 'Stop, stop!' In a passion of tears for Esmeralda, she flung her arms around her. She hugged her and hugged her, murmuring she didn't know what, and it took her several seconds to realise that Esmeralda's embrace of her was, if not perfunctory, at best consolatory.

Caterina stood back. Far more wounded by the dryness of Esmeralda's eyes than she had been by anything she said, she fumbled for her handkerchief, waiting miserably for whatever the merry-go-round of volatility might bring next.

'As for this eternal slanging match with Stavros which is so exhausting,' Esmeralda said lightly, gaily, 'and the fact that I truly *ought* to be able to twist him around my little finger . . . Well, I don't know! But whatever happened to that war-time romance one was supposed to have? Though perhaps I've had it, perhaps one of those . . . No, no, they were impossibly dull! Or would it be too much of a cliché, in your opinion? The cabinet minister's wife and the enemy escaper . . . *Do* concentrate, Caterina – I asked you a question.' She frowned, she pouted. 'No, no. It's quite impossible.' But then she cocked her actressy head, her eyes glinted, her mouth curled. 'Or maybe . . .' Once more the whiplash in her voice cracked. 'Well, if it's rank cliché then it'll be about my level. And . . .' Drawling again, she giggled. 'Life *must* have its amusements, I've always insisted on that, Caterina. Which bedroom did you say you'd put him in?'

16

—꿰—

Luigi D'Alessandria was the first person up, although judging by his granddaughter's excitement the evening before he did not expect to be left to his musings for very long. Feeling serene and happy, he allowed himself the extravagance of lighting more than one of his oil lamps, to give the living-room and the kitchen enough wobbling glimmers to make the cold fore-dawn darkness seem like Christmas morning. Feeding sticks into the range and setting a pan of water to boil which he would pour into the coffee pot, the old man rejoiced in how light and active his mind felt. To wonder, to think, not to plod toward extinction like an animal! With consciousness today, death tomorrow or the next day would be fine – nothing wrong with it at all.

Heating up a second pan so that in due course he could shave, Luigi briskly revived his recent ideas for an essay on how one fatal trigger of the European tragedy had perhaps been when Hegel made it intellectually respectable to value collective entities above the individuals who composed them, thus making possible the Nazi, Fascist and Communist worship of the state. Yes, that was it! That turgid man Hegel again! While John Stuart Mill, in his *On Liberty* . . . (In universities where a surprising number of people found it advantageous to write about Hegel with awe, D'Alessandria had cussedly persisted in rereading the hopelessly unfashionable Mill, so naturally the steps to high academic advancement had been blocked to him.) There were those magnificent sentences about how: 'the only purpose for which power can be rightfully exercised over any member of a civilised community, against his will, is to prevent harm to others. His own good, either physical or moral, is not a sufficient warrant'. What would Caterina say to that? he wondered. Well, when all this Christmas rumpus had died down, one grey afternoon when they were digging side by side he'd ask her.

Luigi knelt on the hearth to place twigs against the smouldering logs. He blew into the glow, thinking of how much of the evil he had seen in his lifetime sprang from people deciding they knew what would be good for others. Yes, but there was more to it than that, wasn't there? His essay would try to expose all the craven respect for authority however vilely acquired and exercised, the love of uniformity, the love of regulation, the thinking in formulae simplified for mass consumption.

Flames started licking up through the kindling. For an instant, Luigi D'Alessandria gazed longingly at his desk where paper and pen waited, where soon the window would frame the dawn flush over the eastern hills; at his bookcase where he could take down *On Liberty* to make sure he'd got the quotation right. Just think, if sooner or later he succeeded in getting back to work on his book, before a heart attack or . . . ! Just let him finish it, and then his enemies could shoot him if they wanted to.

For a moment longer he stood, recollecting Esmeralda's wedding day and how in the Santissima Annunziata he had been aware of the impending catastrophe, had been ghostlily conscious of all the couples going to church to be married all over the future slaughter grounds from the Channel to the Black Sea and from Stalingrad to Tobruk. Well, now it looked as if in the next year or two it was going to be brought to a halt, though not by any civilisation-wide return of sanity. By the hideous though necessary business of three Powers uniting to destroy a fourth.

Luigi gave himself a shake. No writing this morning, he told himself, and not too much musing either. Not on Christmas Day, with half a dozen of us already in the house and the family from the farm invited for the midday feast. Now, he must lay the table for breakfast, and as soon as that was eaten and cleared away he would lay it for lunch. He'd polish the silver candlesticks. He'd fetch out that embroidered white linen table-cloth which years ago had been one of Sonya's attempts to introduce a little charm into his austere existence here. That water must have boiled by now. Coffee!

Soon after Caterina's arrival at Ca' Santa Chiara, Arezzo had come under Allied air attack for the first time, although no bombs had fallen near the D'Alessandria house. Reminded of his deserted wife by her table-cloth, Luigi frowned uneasily.

Then a far bell carried to him through the frozen silence and at once his face cleared. At the church and parsonage of San Giacomo across the valley, that was old Don Girolamo ringing his bell for early mass. Luigi carried his cup and saucer over to the window. Out there in the grey and rose dawn murk, over the wastes of snow he could just make out San Giacomo on its knoll among its oaks. The clear bell kept sounding. Luigi imagined white-headed, rickety Don Girolamo at the foot of his humble belfrey pulling on a rope.

He wouldn't get a congregation this daybreak, that was for sure. Or would a few of his pious and able-bodied neighbours come floundering through the thigh-deep drifts to kneel in that shrine where the plaster pattered down from the damp-streaked walls? No, there were places where the snow was impassably deep, most likely Don Girolamo would be alone. Luigi imagined the stooped old priest lighting a couple of candles if he still had any left, standing by his dingy altar to say mass on his own, say it to the icy gloom. No, come to think of it, at San Giacomo lately there'd been a couple of escapers and a wounded partisan holed up and with any luck in this weather they were still there, so Don Girolamo ought to have a modest flock to bless.

Protestants, Catholics, Orthodox . . . He himself had sheltered all sorts under his roof, and no doubt Don Girolamo had too. Buddhists and Sikhs and Muslims too for that matter, though of course you couldn't expect them to come to church. But Luigi hoped for Don Girolamo's sake that any Christians he was hiding might kneel down shoulder to shoulder. He sipped his coffee, smiling to imagine the snow-bound churches dotted here and there among their oak groves on these hills he loved, all the poverty-stricken parsonages where priests hoped that respect for their cloth might save the day when Black Shirts came to the door demanding to know if any traitor around here was hiding enemies of the people. Churches where now lonely men baled in coats were ringing their Christmas bells, which spoke out over the whitely buried land.

Lisa came skipping into the room calling, 'Grandpapa, Grandpapa! Look what I got in my stocking! I got this book and I got this pretty doll – look! And I got crackers, but I'm not going to pull the crackers yet.' She came running to be kissed. 'Happy Christmas, Grandpapa! Look, I got a tangerine and I . . .'

Luigi D'Alessandria admired her presents, he heated her milk, and for the rest of the morning he seemed to be busy every minute and there never appeared to be fewer than two people talking at once. But in the midst of all the merriment, at the back of his mind he was aware of the ideas about Hegel and Mill which were disentangling themselves, putting themselves to rights. He was half-consciously looking forward to when he should have peace and quiet, so he could stand his notions about freedom near a window in a good light and see what they looked like. And might there not be hope, so long as Don Girolamo said mass in an empty tumble-down church because that seemed right to him, and Caterina rejoiced in a godless freedom because that seemed right to her?

At breakfast when Caterina had first seen her sister-in-law, she had been honoured with a flash of mischievous eyes. (There were too many others at the table for any hint of anything to take more than a second.) Taken aback by how flustered she was, Caterina had been obliged to remind herself firmly that she did not in the least envy Esmeralda her adventuring, the simultaneous tingling excitement and languorous satisfaction that doubtless were suffusing her veins. She had busied herself inordinately with Signora Maria's plum jam for Lisa's toast, with a second cup of coffee for Luigi, with her own knife and plate. Though looked at another way ... She reckoned that compared to Stavros's passion for the defeat of the Third Reich and its puppet states, the beauty of some of the enemy women and whether or not you went to bed with them wouldn't matter a damn either way. Or if Esmeralda and he had lain awake and talked, if each had discovered a tenderness for who the other was ... ? Oh, she didn't know! And it was none of her business.

Now Esmeralda and she were kneeling by the Christmas tree on the tatty Afghan rug, supervising Lisa's unwrapping of the shiny golden paper around a brand-new skirt and cardigan, and Caterina's moods were still see-sawing, when she was not hoping that the lunch over which she had laboured would do her credit. Very standard fare in this region, *coniglio in porchetta*, and nothing especially festive about it, except that this winter any meal with meat in it was a rare luxury – but when rabbits were what there were, rabbits were what you ate. And at least Stavros seemed to have decided he liked his seductress after all, or . . . Anyway, he was sensibly addressing hardly a word to her, and when he did the words were cheerful and unimportant.

Esmeralda sat back on her heels. 'You're miles away, Caterina, what are you dreaming about? Adulterous passions, all manner of disreputable imaginings I shouldn't be surprised.'

Then without waiting for an answer she jumped up. 'Now Lisa darling, whip that skirt off so we can see how gorgeously pretty you look in this one. Oh, don't worry about that – but if you insist . . . How surprisingly well brought-up you are! Papa, Stavros, Giles, the young lady is about to change her skirt, so you must all turn your horrible male faces the other way. All right, Lisa? Don't their backs look funny! No, of course I don't want you to take your jersey off, it's far too cold, but you can put the new cardigan on over it can't you?'

Lisa was still being admired in her new blue skirt and russet cardigan, when four familiar figures were spied toiling through the banks of snow toward Ca' Santa Chiara.

The party in the house came out into the porch at the head of the stairway, to call 'Happy Christmas!' to their guests.

Ox-shouldered Bruno was wading forward with his baby boy well bundled-up in shawls in his arms. Giuliana looked very fetching as she clung to her husband, slithering and giggling. Behind them, Gervasio and Maria stumped stolidly in the faintly ruffled declivity which their son and daughter-in-law forged. The whole family were very spruce in the clothes they kept for Sundays and saints' days. Where the trees had stopped some of the snow, it only came to their knees. But there were other stretches where it was a lot deeper than that and even Bruno could be seen to be heaving and slipping.

The sun blazed in a blue heaven. It was a heart of light intolerable to look at, high in the silence. The dazzlingly white drifts criss-crossed with birds' tracks made Caterina think her eyes had never before been so sluiced with radiance. All her mind felt icily and silverly lit.

'Happy Christmas!' she called for a second time. 'Welcome!' Because suddenly and unbearably she loved to see her four neighbours and their carefully carried infant, she loved to have them shoving laboriously nearer under the crisp white interlacings of branches which laid inconceivable intricacies of fine shadow etched on the snow. Here was Bruno who'd fought in those campaigns in Yugoslavia – but this week he'd been telling her about a band of escaped Yugoslav prisoners-of-war who were skulking in shepherds' huts in the uplands nearby and with whom he'd been making friends. Here was Giles who was longing to get back in the war – but right now he was laughing with Esmeralda about something or other. And Stavros . . . Caterina had forgotten all her unease, she giggled aloud to wonder whether he'd already been asleep or had he heard Esmeralda's footsteps, whether in the freezing blackness she'd set her candle on the dressing-table and wriggled under the blankets with all her clothes still on. Honestly one needn't feel *too* sorry for either of them.

'Madonna!' exclaimed Giuliana, who had staggered again, and clutched Bruno's brawny elbow still more fervently.

17

In the thaw the hillsides ran with glinting water and the boggy tracks were open to military vehicles again. The rivulet at the foot of Luigi D'Alessandria's hillside became a bounding torrent that flung up a constant music over the leafless trees. Gradually shrinking mounds of snow lay about the fields where the sheep were back in pasture, and you could hear their bells above the tumbling waters. Lambs were born. Caterina took Lisa to see them, and to pet the sickly one that Signora Maria was cosseting on a sack in her kitchen. Early one moonlit night, Giles and Stavros set off to walk to Sant'Ambrogio where the Farsetti family would house them for a day or two, before they pushed on down to the coast to find out if it was true about the British vessels coming after dark to rescue knots of escaped prisoners-of-war who were gathering on lonely beaches.

Spring came, with its blackthorn thickets in the dark brown scrub suddenly white, its almond trees in blossom, its violets flowering in the muddy grass. From daybreak on the birds sang and began to build their nests. Between the hillsides, the gulfs of air were soft azure shimmer. The countryside came alive with people tending their vines, from field to field you could hear their colloquial voices. Pairs of deer stood at gaze or bounded away. Then for a week there were fresh snow-falls on the mountains, and at Ca' Santa Chiara the apricot trees which had just been beginning to blossom were nipped by the freezing wind, so they knew they would have no apricots this year.

With a flurry of determination Luigi and Caterina dug a whole new plot of flattish ground alongside their old vegetable patch. She had never imagined that breaking earth which had not been broken before could be such defeating work. Her back and arms stabbed with pain, and even in the icy squalls she could feel the sweat rinsing into her clothes. Still, Signor Gervasio had given them more seed, they were going to be rich in cabbages, in aubergines, in courgettes.

Caterina had left all her notebooks in the attic in Arezzo. But now in the quickening, bewildering spring and infused with hope by the Anzio landings, in those mad March days of harum-scarum rain clouds one minute and luminous sun-shot horizons the next, she was writing again. Sitting on the hearth stool after dinner as close to the flames as she could get. Yawning. Scribbling on her knee, by fire-light. Writing for her husband and writing for her brother, in case she was killed and one or other of them lived to come here, turn the pages of what she had been thinking and feeling. Writing for herself, to leave some trace of who she had been. 'It must be abstract, it must change . . .' That echo rang back to her, and she dreamed of the labyrinth of her stories and imaginings, which long ago she'd hoped she might begin to build in her war nights, though then it had degenerated into self-regard and never understanding the slightest thing. 'It must be abstract, utterly free. It must be forever dying and being born and metamorphosing. It must give happiness . . .'

All manner of things that were not greatly connected with each other, Caterina wrote about, from the goose's egg which Signora Maria gave Lisa for her supper, to how maddening it was that with the Anzio bridgehead rapidly established the immediate furious attack toward Rome which must have been the plan just didn't occur and didn't occur. From the rumour that five hundred Jews from Milan had just been sent north of the Alps, to the chives she'd planted, to how unreal the war could feel in your head when for month after month you hid on your hillside and never went down to the Metauro valley road, where the armoured columns passed and the SS patrols stopped in the little towns.

Caterina wrote about how beautiful the pear trees in blossom were, about the wild boar she'd seen, about the endless clayey mud on Lisa's and her boots which drove her to despair. She wrote about one matter which she had decided about very emphatically, after a lot of thought. No, that was a lie. It was the most visceral knowledge. Nothing you could dignify with the word 'thought' had been given to it.

I'm not falling into the hands of men in uniform, that's for sure. I think our system of the alarm being given from farm to farm ought to work with any luck, and there's only one track

to this place so we can't be taken by too much surprise. No,
they won't get me into a militia barracks where they can string
me up by my wrists and get to work with their truncheons, not
to mention rape me again and again.

I remember that ghastly hour in San Sepolcro. Thank God
it was only an hour, thank God it turned out all right. But
the stories you hear these days about the Fascists' punishment
cells in every city, about the passers-by in the streets who can
hear the screams. I remember looking at those brutes with
their epaulettes and their pistols, I remember thinking 'A dog's
obeyed in office', keeping my courage up as best I could by
thinking that. Good mad old King Lear, I always liked him.
Anyhow, it's a question of pride and I seem to have decided.
I rather like pride, these days.

So I'm bolting down into that cave behind the barn like a
vixen going to earth. We've already hidden the shot-guns there.
And if anyone squeals about that hiding-place, or if for any
other reason it's discovered and they pull away the stack ...
These men are my enemies, why should I surrender while I can
still fight? That entrance is narrow and dark. There are a pair
of those twelve-bores and they've got both barrels loaded. It
ought to be possible to do some killing before I'm killed, if
I'm quick.

Then Gabriele walked down the track and into the house,
and her scribbling became a paean of joy, to begin with.

18

—⚬—

Of course, Gabriele can only stay for a few days, but I'm being terrifically brave about that, I don't complain. I'm much calmer than I was when he came home from Ustica, truly I am. Oh I'm quite cool really, I know we'll be amazingly lucky if the war is over by this time next year, almost certainly it won't be. But it's as if some inner victory of my own were in sight at last, some tiny insignificant matter of my back still being straightish and my head still being held up.

First Giles comes back to me, and now Gabriele for the second time! All these miracles! So now I can't help almost knowing that they'll both be given back to me again for good one day. Either that or the more I let myself half-believe in these omens, the more my thoughts lose their last toe-holds in the real world.

It's just like old spring-times before the war when Gabriele and I stayed in this house. Just fancy, we're such hedonists, we even have siestas! But most of the time we go for long walks on the paths that meander from farmhouse to farmhouse along the edges of the fields where the corn is coming up that strong green, as we haven't done since '39. Four spring-times missed, four Aprils when the cherry trees all around here were in blossom but we weren't here to stroll under them. But we're here now, that's the triumphant thing.

Down the rushy hollows where the poplars are coming into leaf, walking hand in hand quite as if we hadn't been married for seven years, it's the maddest happiness. Scrambling from boulder to boulder to cross the brook where it comes tumbling down, getting wet from the spray, holding Lisa tight as tight when we pass her from one to the other and all three of us laughing. Then up the mossy glens, through the broom, into the acacia groves. I never felt so innocent before. The golden orioles have come back, all the migratory birds. The hoopoes too, you hear them calling as you walk. Yesterday one alit on the track a few paces before our feet where Lisa could see it plainly. We talk to people working in the meadows. Sometimes at a farm they invite us in, they offer us bread and cheese and a glass of wine, though it is terrible the number of families who have lost men in the war, or who believe they are prisoners in this country or that, or who know only that they are missing somewhere. But for we who are alive, we who feel free even though we're not, everything seems propitious somehow. Either that, or our selfish delight has blinded us utterly. I know I'm scatter-brained and I may be discovering how selfish I am, but come what may I'll have been happy for a while in the thick of all this and I'll have lived it knowingly, so I'm grateful for that.

Gabriele hasn't been changed by being a partisan any more than being a prisoner changed him. That's what I tell myself and what I half believe, listening to his father's and his tremendous debates about the best constitution for Italy when the war is over. Though then I attend a bit more lucidly to his quick, hard mind thinking through eventualities, working out tactics, and in a cold shiver I know that neither his doctoring nor Lisa and I ever held a candle to his politics; prison and guerrilla fighting have just revealed him more fully, have at last let him be his deepest self. He's dead set on getting elected to the first parliament. Imagine, if I wake up one fine day and find I've got to go in for political entertaining, like Cosima in Rome and poor Esmeralda up at Salò! Well, there'll be time enough to fret about that. Right now the danger is of being hanged in the town square. That appears to be the new policy, and not only for captured partisans either, but sometimes for poor sinners like Luigi and I who hide them. Apparently the dead are left hanging for a few days, so the neighbours get the message. Gabriele told us of a mother who was shot when she crept out after the curfew to try to cut down her hanging son. Dangling by my winched throat while flies swarm all over me. No, give me a useful fight in that cave entrance any day.

Those two hammering away at their politics after dinner, honestly it's just like peace time. Only these evenings it's Resistance politics, so even I can see the point. With dread, flinching – but I see it. Gabriele has been telling us about how impossible it is to get the fighters from the different regions to cooperate with each other let alone take orders, so in a funny and futile sense it's as if the old city states were resuming a phantasmal independence. He's been telling us about his night attacks on barracks' armouries, and what sound even more dangerous, the times when he slips into Florence on his own to liaise with the underground political leaders there. They've been talking about how twenty or thirty thousand lightly armed guerrillas scattered here and there are never going to make much odds either way in the battle for this country, but at least their skirmishing and their sabotaging keep some Axis forces tied down a fair distance from the Front Line. And of course if the Allies get the better of the fighting this year, recruits to the partisan bands will come pouring in, just as if they get the worst of it the trickle of volunteers will dry up sure as hell. Now Luigi wants to know about the stories of partisan units fighting each other, which I can scarcely believe, but apparently it's true. And what about the Communists' ghastly so-called People's Trials? he asks. What about all the wretched men executed by their supposed comrades because they took the incorrect line on world revolution, or on Trotsky, or on the dictatorship of the proletariat or something? Well, the poor devils' political consciousness wasn't anything like elevated enough.

I sit here scrunched up on the hearth stool, tilting my page toward the fire so I can more or less see what I'm doing. And of course despite feeling just as furiously proud of Gabriele as I am of Giles, I still can't keep my attention on his politics for more than five minutes. I cock my head because I think I hear Lisa's footfalls and that girl ought to be asleep in bed, not trotting in here to snuggle up by the fire and be cuddled and told a story. But it was nothing, just the old house creaking in the night wind.

For a minute I go back to listening to the father and son being logical and argumentative, but then my mind meanders away once more, I'm happiest like this. There's what I've been meaning to say to Luigi about how for us with our ideal conceptions of ourselves to try to live up to it isn't so bad; but for Esmeralda? Would he agree that she was clear-minded enough not to go in for ideal conceptions much? This leaving her rather ill-equipped when it comes to having notions to die

*reasonably proudly for, and indeed in the meanwhile notions
to live halfway sanely in the light of.*

*Then the next meander is what Luigi told me about this
hillside a few years back on a spring day of mist changing
into rain, of bonfire smoke and finches. An awareness of his
of time which, if you waited openly for it, or if you listened to
the resonant air with the right expectancy, or if you'd forgotten
all about yourself and it took you by surprise – I can't remember
exactly what he said. But time which could come flooding into
your mind from forever and bring you everything, with no
before and after, no gone forever, no too late.*

*Just think of all those Arezzo nights when I tried to conjure
my good times back to me, when I made myself desperately
unhappy because all I summoned up with my dreams and my
words was the knowledge of how irretrievably you lost every
moment as you lived it, how living and losing were the self-same
experience. What a wretched mistake all that trying was! all that
labouring with images, that building up of vaporous structures.
Because now I've remembered better Arezzo nights when I
forgot my own fortuitous, pokey little self, when I waited for
what awareness might come – illimitable, never complete. And
I seem to sense that nothing is ever lost if you are conscious of
it, nothing ever gets more possessed than that. The labyrinth of
all your possible experience is all about you all the time – that's
what Luigi said. Listen for the echoes, he said.*

*Fine. But why do I have to go on fooling myself in this
cowardly fashion? In my heart's occasional spasms of honesty
I know that my happiness at Christmas was founded on my
not really taking in Giles's lapses into vacancy, his wakening
in terror, his sudden barks of fury, the hatred in his eyes.
Pathetic, how I contrived to convince myself that in my care
he was already getting better. Pathetic, how I hardly took in
Stavros's and his longing for revenge, their longing to kill. The
ruin of them.*

*And now I can't any longer delude myself about Gabriele's
excited, ambitious talk, the political struggle that really kindles
his soul. Oh he loves Lisa, and I believe he loves me. But the
desolation! The desolation of glimpsing how circumscribed and
contingent that love is. Poor darling, he doesn't realise.*

—⚏—

19

Early summer came and Caterina still didn't think the authorities knew she was at Ca' Santa Chiara. Their neighbours in
the hamlets and farms were all proving loyal. Lisa and she still
seemed to be invisible. So now, if their luck would just hold a
little longer . . . And she'd smile to recall her old wonderings
about to what extent she'd ever be 'one of us' in this hill
country. Nowadays you could come from Pennsylvania or
from the Punjab, all the outlaws were 'one of us' and that
was good.

Gabriele who never got word to her; Giles who with any luck
had got south of the Line but could easily have been killed in the
attempt . . . Moments came when Caterina might be distracted
by a dragonfly flitting past, and then it would happen: she'd
stand in trembling rigidity, imagining all the destinies she
couldn't know yet, till it would be the pain in her lip which told
her how hard she'd been biting it, how helpless she was before
time which wouldn't yet condemn or spare, wouldn't yet reveal.
Was Giles back with the Eighth Army, was he already fighting
his way north toward her? And Stavros, who had no Free Greek
brigade to join . . . Had he found other Ionian and Aegean
escapers? Had he peeled off into the hills while still north of
the Line and joined the partisans? Was he astray somewhere in
the South because the Allies wouldn't put a uniform on his back
and a rifle in his hands, astray down there where people said it
was all starvation and racketeering, all whoring and pimping
and theft? Sometimes that bony black-haired young man with
his burning eyes wavered in her mind like the evoked ghost of
all the conquered peoples rising up to take their revenge. And
Esmeralda up at the Lake, Esmeralda with all those dinner
parties and all those dresses and all those servants, Esmeralda
with her mind raging and ravening through the sham of it all?
She'd promised she'd come back, but she didn't appear and she
didn't appear.

Of course no one had yet foreseen the wave of Nazi-Fascist

massacres conducted across the country later that summer and
in the autumn, let alone the slaughters of the following year
when anti-Fascists hunted down and killed thousands and
thousands of their enemies. But there'd already been mass
killings in some of the hill cities not a great distance from
Ca' Santa Chiara and in others not far from Arezzo, in cities
from which guests had come to Esmeralda's wedding, so when
Caterina tried to make light of her own anguish there was little
comfort to be had. In Cortona, thirty-eight people had been
herded into a building and blown up. In Gubbio, forty people
had been shot. Not to mention all the lesser, village atrocities.
And as for Rome . . .

The day she had learned of that attack on a Wehrmacht
column, and how three hundred and something Italians had
immediately afterward been slaughtered, ten for every German
soldier killed the rumour had it, Caterina had pegged up the
last shirt on the washing line, she had stared furiously around
for something stupefying to do or to pretend to do. Oh look,
Luigi had mowed most of the orchard grass but then he'd gone
to do something else, leaving the scythe propped against one of
the pillars of the loggia. Violently swinging the haft over her
shoulder so the long blade hung down behind her back, she
strode off down to the fruit trees.

Luigi had taught her how to scythe and normally she quite
enjoyed it; but that day Caterina went for the feathery grass
savagely, her mind which had found no satisfaction in itself
yelling at the world it lived in. A lousy Pope who hadn't even
got the balls to denounce this crime against his flock, any more
than he'd spoken out when the Jews from the Rome ghetto
were deported. The limp-brained pious who, slaughters of the
innocent or of the guilty or no slaughters, just went on going
to mass and no doubt sucking some sort of spiritual solace out
of that. The rich who went on dining in restaurants, the poor
who went on cowering at home and feeling hungry . . . Oh,
everything was normal. All was as it was ordained to be, she
supposed. And as for the real war!

Weeks and weeks later when she heard that the Eternal
City had yet again changed hands from one bunch of foreign
generals to another, and she ought to have been feeling jubilant

about that but in fact she was feeling venomous because there hadn't been so much as a whimper of an insurrection, just a supine waiting to be reconquered, Caterina was back in the dappled shade among the apple trees and she was hacking her scythe viciously at the swathes, not swinging with the rhythmic motion her father-in-law had taught her. Was she the only mad-woman who thought it was a trifle disproportionate that hundreds of thousands of men from different lands should come here, and tens of thousands of them be killed in battles, merely in order that the place might one day have a slightly different government? And if you cast your mind wider, if you wondered about the greater number who must be killed in other European countries before this capital city and that could have different politicians prattling in them? Oh yes of course, there was the civilised consensus that these abominations were necessary before we could all finally be taught decent table manners or something, that must be it.

Worst of all, they've shot the old fisherman, Caterina thought with abrupt distractedness.

This was an old man from the coast who in days of peace had a couple of evenings each week set off with horse and cart clippety-clopping up the Metauro valley through the hours of darkness with his load of fresh fish, so as to sell to the housewives of these foothill parishes in the morning. Perhaps he had some sort of permit, perhaps the military patrols were all feasting on his mullet. At any rate, even during the Occupation and the curfew the nocturnal apparition of horse, cart and man had kept on trundling up the river valley as his forefathers had done before him, shedding a faint odour of salt-water catch on the willows' fresh-water air. But the old fisherman had not really borne a charmed life. One dawn when Luigi had walked down to see if he could buy a cod or a squid, he'd found him riddled with bullets, cold, slimy with blood, slumped on his boxes of cold slimy fish and his pair of battered iron scales, the shafts empty because his horse had been stolen.

Caterina gave a cry, she flung her scythe away and dropped on her knees. On the cut stalks and the cuckoo-spit, a baby hedgehog which her blade had just ripped into was feebly fluttering its paws.

Icy horror clamped onto her scalp, she gazed at the red drops which slithered on its slashed body. She leaned closer. Those tiny paws! Ah, why couldn't it die? And those were shrill, faint screams she was listening to.

Caterina jerked her gaze around the orchard, but there was no Luigi. With a muddled idea that she might mercifully drown the little creature in the water-butt, she dabbed her shrinking hands down to pick it up, but the spines were sharp. She didn't even seem to have a handkerchief she could wrap it up in.

She scrambled to her feet, she grabbed up her scythe. With her face horribly contorted, she flailed the blade at the hedgehog on the grass. What, still moving? It was impossible! Trying to be more accurate this time, she jabbed downward.

20

Damn all to eat beyond what we grow in the garden; almost no clothes to wear because we've given them all away; the death sentence mandatory for a whole lot of things we do week in week out; no defence except a pair of twelve-bores; Lisa to protect when the fighting reaches us. It's amazing how cheerful Luigi and I are.

Days pass, weeks pass, and sometimes it seems that we're holding our breath, that the waiting can't go on being drawn out and drawn out; but it does go on. Apparently there are not only British but also Canadian and Polish brigades fighting their way into our part of the country, and most people seem to think the end here can't be long now. Or perhaps what I mean is that we only talk to others who like ourselves have longed for it till they've come nearly to believe in it.

In the meanwhile, there are times when the blazing sky and the heat, or the extraordinary peacefulness which surrounds us in spite of everything, or the endless waiting, or – oh I don't understand what it is. But minutes come when I stab my nails into my palms and my head rings because I'm listening for gunfire but all I can hear is a cock crowing from the farm.

Gervasio and Bruno have started reaping their corn. Luigi and I have been helping Maria and Giuliana to bind the sheaves. We've carted, we've threshed. I work alongside nice, stalwart, taciturn Bruno; I remember what Luigi has told me about the atrocities committed in Yugoslavia. It's like when I went with Carlo Manzari to hear Verdi beautifully performed and I wondered about when he was at the Foreign Ministry all day and what policies he supported – while Esmeralda and he and I went on sitting elbow to elbow in the stalls, our spirits thrilled by the music, in unspoken harmony. So now at noon Bruno and I sit companionably in the shade of the farmyard oaks to eat our bread and cheese, and mistily I perceive something of mankind's doubleness or at least of my own; but I don't do or say anything, and I don't know what to think.

On the hillsides the broom is in yellow flower. A field away, you
see deer moving through the uncut wheat. The big fig tree by the
track has hundreds of figs which are coming ripe right now. The
orchard grass is littered with ripe plums, so whenever I can't find
Lisa I know where to look for her. And in this splendidly Arcadian
scene, all the news from elsewhere in the province that reaches us
is horrifying. A harbour town shelled by the Royal Navy. They did
a certain amount of damage to the docks and a lot more damage
to a quarter lived in only by civilians. A market town bombed by
the US Air Force. A little place with no industry, no barracks,
no fuel dépôt. These must be mistakes. But our liberators are not
endearing themselves to people.

As for the other side – the endless announcements about the
new Italian divisions back from being trained in Germany are
depressing. And there hasn't been anything accidental about
the Black Shirt killings in this district recently. Luigi was a
few parishes up the valley, trying to identify other safe or
safish houses. He came home with a nightmarish description
of a lime tree from which some captured partisans had been
hanged. Like that Goya image of a tree bearing dead human
fruit, he said. And this week the Fascist militia stationed in
Urbino shot six poor devils of deserters they'd got their hands
on, after first torturing them to try to make them betray their
friends, though that doesn't seem to have been successful.

The victims were lined up and shot in the evening on that
beautiful hillside opposite the ducal palace, where I remember
Gabriele kissing me beneath an acacia tree when he first brought
me here. Shot rather inefficiently we were told, possibly on
account of the twilight. So a second fusillade was fired to put an
end to the screaming from the men on the ground, and then the
officer with his pistol walked forward to stop the last groans.

These are the events which sicken me with despair, till I want
to howl 'I can't bear it, I can't bear it!' inanely at the sky. In
every region these civil butcheries, and still they go on. You'd
think with the campaign for the heart of the country in the
balance they wouldn't bother so much about torturing and
murdering, but they don't give up. And as for why it's these
peoples that have produced Nazism and Fascism, why these
societies have put forth these blossoms – no one's going to

discuss that for a good while yet, and when they do they'll lie about it.

It's the ghost of the old Holy Roman Empire, Luigi muttered the other evening, with the clout coming from north of the Alps and the posturing from the south, just like before. We are who we are, the old fatalist said. Snorting with laughter. Adding with a swift reversal: No, it's recent. It's infinitely worse. I think it's new. And now I seem to hear Esmeralda's voice: Who was it who said that civil wars were the only sort it really was occasionally a good idea to fight? No, never mind. Papa would know, he'd remember. Yes – thresh out once and for all what sort of country it's going to be. Only they never change, it's only superficial.

While my own mind pleads: We're going to have to learn to outlive this, to outlive ourselves.

Then a few days later . . .

The only problem we used to have with the partisans was the commissars or whatever these Communist rabble-rousers call themselves, the fellows who go around inciting boys who don't know the first thing about Marxism to daub 'Viva Stalin!' on walls by way of helping to free the country. Luigi came upon one of them up at the farmstead. He was trying to convince Bruno that he ought to join the Party, on account of how after the revolution which they were going to be nice enough to organise here, peasants like him were going to have tractors, they were going to have modern ploughs and threshing machines, all manner of marvels, just like those fortunate Soviet kulaks who had Uncle Joe Stalin to look after them.

Exasperating, though not serious with any luck. But the nasty thing now is that some of the men who turn up here and say they're partisans are pretty plainly nothing of the sort. I suppose we might have predicted this, but we hadn't. So far we've given them what food and money we could and got them away from the place. But the prospect of extortion is unattractive. I feel braver when we have escaping prisoners-of-war here, but right now we're alone. Last thing at night we close the ground-floor shutters and lock the doors, but that is pitifully inadequate. I wonder if Furia would go for a man she saw attacking one of us. She might do.

And the last time in the war that Caterina put pen to paper . . .

Gaetano and Esmeralda have arrived. They've been staying with Sonya, and apparently when they walked into the drawing-room, there was Gabriele! Sitting talking to old Count La Marecchia, just like in peace time! Sonya in seventh heaven of course, only she couldn't bear it that he was about to vanish again. And with tears for Edoardo that kept welling up in her eyes. There is still no word of him after all this time, though of course we hope and we hope.

It appears that all across southern Tuscany our enemies are being defeated, there aren't the road-blocks and patrols that we've still got here on our side of the mountains, so if you've got the nerve you can shift about more freely at last. Siena has fallen. No honour to the partisans there, mind you. Not a barracks attacked, not a column ambushed. Sweet silence, from the Sienese. Just the Germans pulling back one night and some Free French pushing forward. So Arezzo must be free any day now and perhaps I should have sat tight there after all. Gaetano and Esmeralda say Gabriele and the other guerrilla chieftains are going to marshal their bands of wild men and descend on Florence to try to fight their way in ahead of the Allied advance if they can, so we'll be able to hold our heads up a bit. And I know that around here a lot of people are determined that Urbino should be free before the Allies arrive. Apparently the story going around Siena was that General Monsabert told his tank commanders they had to take the city without firing a shot, and when they looked rather amazed and doubtful about this he said: Well all right, of course you can fire back if you're fired at, but for God's sake don't hit anything earlier than 1800.

Too excited to think, let alone write, that's the trouble with me. Gaetano's and Esmeralda's stories are nothing if not inconsistent. But it seems they both suddenly remembered she was his goddaughter after years of their having forgotten this, and he and some friends of his had plans for hiding famous paintings so they didn't get pulverised by Allied shells or purloined by retreating Axis staff officers. So Esmeralda offered her swanky car and her government petrol and her official passes, and they've been trundling around the war zone, getting out here and there to go ducking down into palaces' secret cellars with Titians tucked under their arms. Either she won't let him drive because lording it over him gives her a kick, or he won't drive because ordering her to drive him is more decadent and delicious, I can't remember which. Anyhow her doe-skin driving-gloves with tiny silver buttons are quite something. And an improbable and adorable pair they make, pretending he's some millionaire grandee and she's his mistress, or, in his version of the story, pretending she's one of his mistresses, one of the second string. They're going to stay with us for a week while they make sure that all the Barocci altar-pieces for miles around are snugly hidden in all the right basilicas' crypts – or something like that. As for what's been happening up at Lake Garda. Who cares whether that whoops-a-daisy marriage crashes to smithereens or whether it doesn't. Still, I suppose it must have occurred to Esmeralda that if she continues gadding around here and the Allied advance comes through, by autumn Carlo and she will have the Line between them.

It's a hot night, we're sitting under the loggia. The far hillside is a mound of black, but there's a moon so the sky is silvery. I'm closest to the lantern, scribbling. Moths pretty well clogging the air. Everyone slapping the mosquitoes at their wrists and necks and cursing them. Right this minute Esmeralda is lighting one of Luigi's cheroots (she has brilliantly arrived with a new box of these) and is giggling as she puffs it good and hard a few times before handing it over to him. She seems to have shrugged off her despairs all right. And just as miraculous as everything else – when Gregorio rode over here this evening for dinner, he had Benedetta with him on his second horse! Bobbed black hair, slim figure, very quiet demeanour: the fabled and now at last revealed Benedetta. Yes, it appears she decided to weather the rest of the war with her cousins at Sant'Ambrogio. So now Luigi is about ten years younger than I've ever known him, he keeps jumping up to fetch things, keeps teasing us all. Benedetta's and his eyes when they meet – and they flicker toward each other quite a lot – glint with memory, glint with silent amusement at things.

As for me, as for the scatter-brain herself. As for Kate Caterina. It's amazing to think of Gabriele sitting in his own drawing-room, calmly talking to La Marecchia about how the liberation of Tuscany was satisfactorily under way and it was now a question of a partisan action at Florence, a question of coordinating the different detachments, fighting their way into this suburb and that, trying to stop the Germans blowing up the bridges as they retreat. No – after all this time when that scene in that room was impossible, I still haven't made head or tail of it.

Gabriele may still be killed. Taking those skirmishers into Florence will be dangerous work, if it's true that they're going to go in while the Wehrmacht is still there. I keep reminding myself of that. Yes, and ever since the war began we haven't had a clue what was happening between us. For three weeks we were together last year, and for a few days this spring. You make a lot of love, you don't have time to disappoint one another much.

I've just seen a nightjar swoop by over the shimmery trees on those long raked-back wings of theirs, calling churr churr. Luigi and Gregorio, Esmeralda and Gaetano and Benedetta are sitting in the moon shadows under these arches and chatting away, the dogs drowsing at their feet. And I think: this is just like the new peace will be! Which I had not thought before. My spirit flares up and I think: we have come a long way. Almost, almost, we are there. In spite of everything, I will hope, I will!

Then of course my treacherous mind starts wondering about Axis counter-attacks. All these good tidings, the fall of cities, the return of a man to the house he was born in. Signs to delude me, to make me dream dreams.

21

When Caterina started pelting down toward the valley that morning she still had Giuliana's hectic voice ringing in her ears. 'Esmeralda . . . A bomb or something . . . Signor Gaetano . . . Oh my God! Come!' But halfway down she stopped running. The louring sky presaged a thunderstorm before night and she could feel the sweat slithering on her skin. She walked fast down the pale track in the humid, heavy air beneath the trees, looking before her with proud, wet eyes. Thinking, Come! Oh yes, I'll come Esmeralda, I'll come. So it's happened at last, they've killed you, and I . . . *What* did Giuliana say – still alive? But these men don't make mistakes like that, if they think their victims might get up and stagger away they finish them off. To the end . . . Where or when does that ring to me from? Keep some sort of shadowy faith, to the end.

She listened to her rapid tread on the stones and dust. Swinging her arms, she felt the cool wetness of her shirt. Those swathes of blue flowers in the aftermath of that hay field – chicory she thought distractedly, that's what they are. Oh there'll be time for all the anger and all the sadness. But now – this sudden despairing pride that makes me stride with my head up, the arrogance of this love that has got me by the throat and got me by the eyes . . . Proud of Gaetano and even more proud of Esmeralda am I for some reason? Yes, desperately proud! she thought, her lips twisting. How strange, that I never realised it before! How strange, that this should be the strongest passion I feel!

It had not exactly been a difficult or dangerous attack to execute, on that lonely stretch of road. The killer must have waited in the trees and lobbed his grenade into the open car as it slowed down to turn up the track, at the spot where Lisa and she had been set down with their suitcases at the beginning of last winter.

Caterina hurried into the small crowd that had gathered, dimly aware of familiar faces from the neighbouring farms and the hamlet by the river, aware of people drawing back. She went up to the car, laid her hands on the folded-back hood. Flies were swarming on Gaetano's chest which looked like butcher's meat, on his . . . She jerked her white face back without looking closely at what had been done to all of him, she whirled around.

Esmeralda had been lifted out of her seat and laid on the wayside grass. Caterina dropped on her knees beside her, half-hearing voices which said, 'Caterina. . .' 'Oh poor love. . .' 'From Ca' Santa Chiara up there . . .' 'Sister-in-law . . .' Esmeralda's clothes were sopping with blood, but her head which Caterina gently lifted onto her lap was not wounded though blood had trickled from her mouth, and she was still breathing in flutters.

'Oh my darling I'm so proud of you,' Caterina started murmuring wildly. Oblivious of all the world except that beautiful dying head. Noticing the smears of blood on her own hand when she stroked Esmeralda's hair. 'Did I ever tell you how proud, how damned-fool proud? Your eyes are open, can you see me? Darling it's your stupid Kate Caterina who loves you, that's who it is. Once you came running down the track in the dusk calling my name, do you remember? I'm here, I'm here. You're not alone. Can you hear me? No, I hope you're not too conscious any more, I hope you can't feel it too much.'

A sultry gust of wind ruffled the poplars. One of the small-holders remounted his bicycle and pedalled away.

Voices reached Caterina as if she had picked up a big whorled shell and was listening to the sea. 'It'll have been her husband they reckoned to get, that's for sure.' 'Well, whoever he was will have made himself scarce.' 'Fascists or not Fascists, when you see their poor slaughtered bodies . . .' 'Better clear out of here. Patrols all the time, and when word of this . . .' 'What was that about reprisals?' 'Decent burial . . .' 'Leaving poor folks like us to pay for their murdering.'

The woman from the river-side store where Luigi went to listen to the radio was shaking her by the shoulder gently but insistently. 'Come along, dear. She's not for this world, you can see that, and when the soldiers come . . . There, there. Oh don't weep so. Come along with my husband and me, you'll be safer like that.'

'She moaned just now, I know she did! She's alive!' Caterina cried softly through her tears, cradling Esmeralda's head ever more tenderly and kissing her cheek. 'No, I won't leave you my darling. Honestly Signora, you go home. I'm fine where I am, I'm best right here. Look, look, her eyes are moving! Esmeralda I'm here, I'm here. Oh, gently my love, gently.'

The neighbours went away in dribs and drabs. Several people offered to walk up to the church of San Giacomo and tell old Don Girolamo there were two innocent souls needed a funeral. Each of them as they left gazed for one last time with fascinated horror at the fat, gore-beslabbered carcass which had been Gaetano Da Durante, lover of paintings and of women.

More blood came seeping from between Esmeralda's lips. Caterina stayed kneeling where she was. She brushed away the flies. She smoothed her fingers through that soft brown hair, she touched her face. As the minutes passed, she whispered less and wept less. She bent lower and lower over Esmeralda, to hear if she was breathing.

22

When Caterina felt how cold Esmeralda had grown, she gently laid her head back on the dusty grass. She stood up, she looked around – and only then did she realise how deserted the landscape was. No one was working in the harvest fields, or sitting in the shade of a tree to eat their midday bread and cheese. Ever since she had been kneeling here (Caterina had no idea how many minutes this had been, but Esmeralda's dying seemed to her a great sea of time in which she had been drowned) not so much as one mule had come plodding along with an old woman in black knitting as she rode – not a soul!

With the sensation of having been hauled up kicking into the air of life which she was not particularly happy to be breathing again, but where there were tasks she must attend to, and hobbling because her legs had got cramped, Caterina went to the car and opened the boot. Let the dead bury the dead, she heard her mind mutter. Or no, not exactly – I must fetch Gervasio and a cart. We must take them up to San Giacomo, we must organise a funeral. A funeral? Well, they must be stowed in the earth. Jobs to do. Keep myself nice and numb.

There was only one travelling-rug in the boot. She spread it carefully over Esmeralda. 'There my darling,' she said quite naturally as if death had not parted them. 'I'll be back soon. I won't be long, I promise you.'

What could she cover Gaetano with? There were crows in the nearest field, she hated to think of those black creatures jabbing and tearing at him. She waved the flies off the dead man, feeling no horror now but simply pity for his poor savaged flesh. The car's hood, that was an idea!

Caterina loosened the straps, she was wrestling to heave the heavy canvas up and foward when her reawakening mind noticed a cloud of dust billowing up from the road in the distance and she suddenly grasped why the countryside was so empty. Marshal Kesselring's proclamation about taking hostages from districts where partisan attacks were made . . .

That was why everybody had vanished! They'd be in the hiding places they'd prepared, they'd have legged it into the woods. The houses would have been left in the care of grandmothers who with any luck would not be considered suitable objects of violence. Yes, that dust must be being thrown up by a patrol, or by a column of military lorries, or – what else could it be? Lisa, she must look after Lisa!

Caterina dropped the hood and started to run back up the track, but she had only gone ten paces when she remembered that through all that deciding to fetch a horse and waggon she hadn't attempted to start the car. She tore back and scrambled into the driver's seat, not even realising that it was soaked with Esmeralda's blood. The dashboard didn't look too badly damaged. With shaking hands she pulled out the choke, she tried to start the engine. Nothing. Not a sound. She jumped out and set off again.

After running a few hundred yards uphill in the heat, Caterina slowed to a walk. Her blood-stained clothes were clammed to her with sweat. She shoved her damp hair out of her eyes. The dust cloud was reaching the stretch of road where she had been. Gasping for breath she hurried on, running a bit, walking a bit, then running again, trying to reassure herself by thinking sensibly. Even if they did take hostages, Lisa would be all right, they wouldn't take children, for heaven's sake. The vital thing was for Bruno to stay hidden in the cave behind the barn till the danger blew over, and he'd be there already so she didn't need to worry about that, he'd have gone to earth as soon as Giuliana came with news of the attack. Women and children were let be. No, she'd heard of women being rounded up and killed alongside men.

What should she do if she heard engines on the track behind her now? Scamper fifty yards into the undergrowth Kate Caterina my girl, that's what you do, crawl into the broom and the brambles and don't breathe. And just remember, if you do find yourself in undesired conversation with men in uniform . . . There's no Kate in you, that girl Kate Fenn died long ago. You're Caterina through and through, that's who you are. Now, just keep your wits about you and keep calm. It'll be all right so long as none of these Germans speaks Italian well enough to hear anything suspicious in your voice, and as long as they don't ask for your papers. Yes, but if they're not Germans, if they're Italians? A cosy bramble patch, that's the answer.

At the ridge Caterina stopped a moment to listen because she thought she'd heard engines, but her heart was pounding so furiously she didn't know what she could hear. There was dust in the humid haze down there over the trees – but was it closer than it had been or wasn't it? At a jog-trot she descended the slanting track to Ca' Santa Chiara. This last turning looked so nowhereish that maybe no one would think to drive down it, they'd imagine it just led to a field.

As sprucely turned out as ever in a white suit, Luigi D'Alessandria was pacing to and fro in front of his house with controlled agitation. He wheeled around when he saw his daughter-in-law stumbling toward him. Looking very straight into her eyes, he asked quietly: 'Esmeralda and Gaetano are dead?'

'Yes,' Caterina replied, trying not to sway on her aching legs, and wishing she could say it without gasping.

Luigi held her eyes with his own for a moment longer. Then he said firmly: 'The others are all in the cave, Lisa and the whole family from the farm. There didn't seem any point in leaving anyone hanging about unnecessarily. I waited for you as long as I could, Caterina, but then I rebuilt the stack. Sorry about that. Now, you must change out of those incriminating clothes.' As he spoke, he was already lowering a bucket down the well, heaving it up and sloshing water into the two big pewter jugs that always stood on the well-head, then briskly paying out rope and dropping the bucket down again. 'You've got blood on your hands, on your face.'

'It's Esmeralda's blood,' Caterina said. 'I held her. She died in my arms.'

Once more he met her gaze, and it seemed to her that his eyes which had always been watchful and melancholy burned now with a hard brilliance she had never seen before. 'Good,' he said softly. 'You did right. Now, there isn't a second to lose. You must take off that skirt and shirt. Don't mind about me, there isn't time for that any more than there's time to fill a bath.' And then, very gently again: 'There's blood in your hair as well.'

Caterina stripped off her fouled clothes, she stood in her camisole and knickers while he tipped jugs of icy water over her head. She rinsed her body rapidly with her hands as best she could. She lifted one of the jugs and drank shuddering gulps. Then white and glistening she darted into the house.

Luigi picked up the bundle she had left on the gravel. For a minute he stood, holding it in his hands. Then he took it to the compost heap, where it seemed unlikely that anyone would go rummaging.

In her bedroom, Caterina put on fresh underclothes and a dress as quickly as she could. She was tugging a comb through her wet, tangled hair when she heard Luigi's calm voice at the door. 'I speak a bit of German. I may even be able to persuade them not to set fire to Gervasio's house or to this place. But you must clear out, Caterina. Into the woods with you. If you stay within earshot of the track you'll know when the coast is clear. Only . . .' And his steady voice became more clipped as he said it. 'Only we may have left it too late.'

At that instant Caterina too heard the engine. She gave a last yank with the comb, bent to shove her feet into her shoes, fumbled one of them, despaired of buckling them so they'd stay on, and hared out of her bedroom barefoot. In a trice she was through a couple more doors and bounding down the outside staircase, and she was tearing across the yard when a shot petrified her.

She stood, wobbling, her panic-struck head twisted round to stare at the grey lorry with the last of its grey men leaping out of it, at the officer who had been sitting beside the driver and was getting out of the cab more sedately. 'No, no, I'm quite all right,' she blurted out idiotically, as if the shot had been an accident, her brain making no sense of anything except that these men were all around her, these guns were aimed at her. She couldn't make out their faces, they seemed only to have blurs. Her wits made no attempt to guess what their barks might mean. Possessed by some animal instinct of surrender, of begging for mercy, she lifted her hands above her head, and knew how horribly vulnerable that made her breast feel.

Caterina drew in her breath and parted her lips, but no more speech came. Then the crash of the next shot yanked a scream out of her throat. But she still stood, shaking. Did not turn to gaze at white Furia who with a snarl had launched herself to defend her, and now was bleeding to death. Then somebody grabbed her wrists and was tying them behind her back, and her wits must have started unscrambling themselves a little because she noticed with relief that one of the grey men was coming out of the barn, plainly without having found anything interesting there.

In his neatly pressed suit and blue tie, Luigi had walked calmly down the flight of steps from the porch to the yard, his hands by his sides. Now he was speaking in halting German to the officer. But if Caterina had been able to hear she would not have understood, and she kept her fearful gaze swinging between him and the barn because now to her horror some of the grey men were doing something over there. All the same, her heart knew from Luigi's manner what he was arguing for. She knew from the way the officer and he looked in her direction. She knew from the grim respect she began to see on the officer's face.

Now Luigi was walking toward the lorry and she saw his wrists had been tied. 'One person from each household, their orders are,' he called quite cheerfully over his shoulder to her. 'You never know, with a bit of luck it'll all come to nothing. Goodbye, dear girl! And good luck!'

'Goodbye!' Caterina called, her voice a wail. Then her mind changed completely, though not through any willing or reasoning of hers, and she ran toward him yelling 'No, Luigi, no! Wait!' But at the very moment he was being shoved up into the lorry, she saw thick smoke from the blazing hay gush out of the barn door as the men backed away from their handiwork, and now flames were licking out from between the weathered timbers.

Caterina howled 'Lisa! Lisa!' but luckily the crackle of the fire drowned her cry. She ran as close to the flames spreading quickly through the barn as she could get. In her impotent despair she danced a frenzied jig which was made obscene by her wrists being knotted behind her back. The grey men were clambering up into their lorry, which was turning around, but one of them must have been given an order because he ran back with a knife and grasped her and hacked through the cord.

Left on her own in the yard, the maddened woman screamed at the flames to stop burning, she prayed to them to die down. She bolted to the well, bolted back and flung a bucket of water into the fire.

23

All over the parish, smoke arose from houses and barns set on fire in punishment for the attack on the cabinet minister's Alfa Romeo, which was towed away respectfully by the police, who also took responsibility for conveying up to the church of San Giacomo the bodies of the two eminent citizens murdered by terrorists. The sky was still heavy and dull, and the columns of smoke did not blow away but hung ominous and grey, mingling with the dusty harvest haze in the humid air.

Two grey lorries each with a Wehrmacht platoon also converged on the wooded knoll and its church, between them carrying the seven local men it had been possible to capture, and who were considered sufficient sacrifice to keep the neighbourhood cowed from now on. Possibly Professor D'Alessandria's remonstrations with the officer had secured this further effect, or perhaps there was some other reason for it – at all events, no women or boys were among the condemned. The youngest of the men was nineteen, a lad who had run away from the militia but had been cornered hiding in a cottage attic. He'd been bashed about with rifle butts during the scuffle of his capture. When he was pushed out of the lorry in the glade by the church, he was whimpering through a mouth of broken teeth. And from all over the parish other figures too were stealing toward the oaks of San Giacomo, shadows who kept a prudent distance from the grey lorries but came ghosting forward along wooded slopes and thickety ravines, people who knew they could do no good but wanted to be near.

Most of the condemned men huddled together under guard managed to stand with a fatalistic dignity, though with despair in their eyes when they stared at the men in grey uniforms who were about to perform the simple and appalling act of taking their lives. Some of them kept glancing longingly at the surrounding trees, though it was plain that to make a dash for it would only advance the instant of shooting by a minute or two. The boy with the broken mouth had knelt down. With uplifted praying hands he was blubbering to the soldiers.

When Luigi D'Alessandria first found himself standing before the familiar church, he asked, 'May I?' to the officer who had captured him. He stepped over to the humble portico; he gazed for a few moments at the bodies of his daughter and his friend which had been laid there. He said, 'Goodbye,' under his breath and turned away.

Now D'Alessandria was listening reluctantly to a neighbour who'd been a stalwart of what they'd jokingly called their Liberation Committee, that cheerful rag-bag of old gaffers, housewives and adolescents who had gathered to listen to foreign radio stations. This fellow had been a familiar sight for a couple of generations, standing in his high boots in the rippling Metauro under the willow trees to fish for trout. Now in his faded blue jacket and straw hat the poor man appeared possessed by the need to distract himself with feverish chatter.

'Shot in reprisal for the killing of your own daughter, Signor Luigi! Has the world gone mad, or have you?' He crossed himself, muttering a prayer under his breath. 'The butchers! The bastards! Look at them! Oh it's all up with us. Christ above, if she'd only stayed with that husband of hers up at Salò rather than coming gallivanting around here, I could have lived to see my boy back from prison camp. In England, he is. Holy Mary, Holy Mother! But why don't you try it, Signor Luigi? All you've got to do is take your identity card out of your pocket, man, have them compare it to hers!' he hissed. 'Explain to them, Signor Luigi, for the love of God explain! Save yourself! Damned partisans, doing their murdering here and then killing the wrong people. An art historian, eh? Holy Mother, have mercy upon us! Oh God I'm afraid, I'm afraid!'

'You're a good fellow, but – no,' D'Alessandria said to the astounded fisherman, who gawped at him and for an instant forgot that he was about to know several seconds of agony and then nothing ever again. 'At my age, it doesn't matter so very much, and I don't feel particularly inclined to try to save my skin through my connection with my Manzari son-in-law.' Then the old soldier from the last war came out in him again for the last time. He jerked his head toward his executioners and his jaw tautened. 'These men are my country's enemies, they are my enemies. I've been doing what I can against them.' He shrugged. 'What's more – if they let me go, there's the risk that they'd round up somebody younger, or one of the women maybe. Ah, here comes Don Girolamo, and in a fine fury by the look of him.'

After which D'Alessandria stood, looking around at the church and the trees and the men with a twist to his mouth, and with bright, bitter eyes. He stood as easily as it was possible to stand with his hands tied behind his back.

Caterina was not among the shadows slipping furtively through the countryside up to San Giacomo. She was at Ca' Santa Chiara, trudging desperately back and forth between the well and the smouldering embers, her half-crazed mind praying that there *must* have been enough air to breathe in that cave, Lisa and the others *must* be alive. But what about Giuliana's baby, would his little lungs be strong enough?

When Caterina had flung her first bucket of water into the blazing barn without achieving so much as a sizzle, she had sunk on her knees in despair, imagining what it must be like down there for Gervasio and Maria, Bruno and Giuliana who would be trying to comfort Lisa and the baby. But when the fire had burned itself out, and the fountain of sparks towering up had ceased to fill her with terror that the tindery brushwood of the hillside was going to catch alight and the house be burned as well and all of them killed for sure, she had identified as nearly as she could where beneath all this fuming wreckage the steps down to the cave must be, and she had set to work frenziedly emptying buckets there. She had hurried back to the house and finally put on that pair of shoes so she could go stumbling about on the hot ash. Now she had fetched a pitchfork from the shed. Her sweaty legs, arms and face streaked with black, her damp hair caked with ash, she was levering away charred timbers with all her might, glancing wildly over her shoulder at the opposite hillside where she had seen the lorries go up the white dirt road to the church, then bending back to her incensed heaving with the pitchfork.

When Caterina heard a distant burst of rifle fire, she stood motionless, her chest heaving. Her mouth ugly with pain, she gave an animal moan. There was a second crackle of shots. She sank her face in her filthy hands.

Red embers burned Caterina's feet through the straps of her summer shoes. She ran back to the well for more buckets to hurl on, she splashed water onto her face and feet and down her throat. She ran back to her scrabbling in the scorching soot.

And then, out of the smoking ruin, up out of the burning . . .

She who had imagined walking down into the earth to find her daughter dead, heard Bruno's lusty shout. With a gasp of joy, she saw a beam move which she was not touching. Now it was Lisa's cry that was ringing in her eardrums and she heard the baby's scream. Caterina seized the beam and burned her hands but went on hauling. A few seconds later, Bruno had forced his head and brawny shoulders into the daylight, he was lifting Lisa up to her.

Don Girolamo had received the bodies of Gaetano and Esmeralda at his church with sorrow, for he had known them both a little. He had received the foreign soldiery who proposed to use the wall of his church to shoot seven of his parishioners against with rage. A diminutive, ancient priest he might be, but he cursed the firing-squad loud and long in good savage Italian, and he stood in front of them shaking his fist and shouting anathemas in good seminary Latin till he had to be knocked aside and they could fire.

When the lorries had gone, he straightened out the freshly slaughtered men. He knelt beside each one in turn and blessed him. He prayed for each man's soul, before shuffling stiffly on his knees in his stained black soutane to the next.

When men and women emerged from the oaks into the glade before the church, they set to work with mattocks and spades to dig a grave. The ground was stony and dry. It was late in the afternoon before a big enough pit had been dug, and Don Girolamo got ready to conduct the service for the dead.

The party from Ca' Santa Chiara had washed and tidied themselves as best they might. They had walked down to the rivulet and crossed it and climbed the path up the opposite hillside to the church. Then it was time for the baby to be fed again, so Giuliana sat down on a ramshackle bench under one of the oaks and unbuttoned her shirt. It was hot and flyey under the mighty trees and the sunless sky. There were no coffins, so the dead were swaddled in what blankets and curtains Don Girolamo's impoverished house could offer. Bruno helped to lift them down into the pit.

Lisa was very muted after the deaths and her time in the cave beneath the fire. She stood pressed against her mother, and when her grandfather was carried close to the grave she wept inconsolably, not hiding her face in Caterina's skirt, but standing there with her mouth trembling and tears streaming down her white face.

Several of Caterina D'Alessandria's neighbours remarked that she appeared beyond the reach of more passion and more grief for one day. The only minute when she showed animation was when someone objected that Esmeralda and Gaetano should not be interred alongside the other seven, but in a different hole for public enemies if any fool felt like digging one.

Caterina dashed up to Don Girolamo, who was stolidly ringing his church bell. They must all lie together, she cried desperately, they *must*, or this civil war would never be finished, these hatreds would never be forgotten. Caterina choked on her words, she wrung her hands. There was no more or less justice when it came to murdering any more than there was justice in surviving, she cried – and anyway those two were not Nazi-Fascists any more than she was, they'd been killed by mistake or by the wish to kill or by she didn't know what. For pity's sake Don Girolamo, she implored him with sobs in her voice. To dispel all this vindictiveness – didn't he *see*? It must be *one* grave . . .

The old priest heaved on his rope; he listened to this tirade. His one bell's plaintive note quivered above them among the crowns of the oaks. 'Yes,' he muttered grimly. 'You are right, Signora Caterina. It will be difficult to convince some people of this, you understand. But – yes . . .'

So Luigi D'Alessandria had his daughter and his friend beside him, as well as the boy whose teeth had been bashed in, and the old man who had fished the Metauro since before the war before this war.

Once she was assured of this community in death, Caterina at once became calm again. The funeral in the glade commenced, the villagers in their black and brown and blue standing in a semi-circle around the pit. Several of the women whose men were being buried wept quietly.

Caterina stood with her hands on Lisa's shoulders before her. She listened to Don Girolamo's ritual words of farewell; she listened to the turtle doves.

24

That evening Signora Maria refused to go home with the rest of her family at supper time. She insisted on coming back to Ca' Santa Chiara where the ruins of the barn were still smoking and where the white sheepdog Furia still lay in the yard. When Caterina protested that Lisa and she would be all right, Maria said, 'I'm not going home to bed till I've cooked that little girl a hot meal. What's more, I'm going to watch you eat one too.' And she had added, in her gruff voice: 'That's what Signor Luigi would have wished. We were lucky, our family, thanks to him. They would have taken Bruno for sure.' 'Yes,' Caterina had agreed wanly. 'They would have taken Bruno.'

The two women had sat with Lisa at the kitchen table while she ate her eggs. They had stayed by her bed until she was asleep. Now Maria was cooking a vast vegetable stew of which a bowl or two could be eaten tonight and which would also keep them nourished for a couple of days after that, and Caterina had drifted out into the sweltering dusk. Tomorrow she would dig a grave for poor Furia. Tomorrow she would wait anxiously for the Liberation. Tomorrow she would give thought to the living. Try to find a way of getting a letter to Sonya with the news that Esmeralda and Gaetano had been killed by one side and Luigi by the other. Try to be particularly cherishing of Lisa. Worry futilely about her brother and her husband and Edoardo. But tonight; but now . . .

Probably the thunderstorm would not break before tomorrow. Perhaps it would not break here at all, because only a few rolls of thunder faint with distance had been heard. Caterina stood by the walnut tree, she looked across the valley in the gloaming to where she could still just make out the fading silhouette of San Giacomo. She thought wretchedly, in a spent kind of way, because she couldn't not think.

It was plain to her that those partisans who had planned the attack on the car could not really have wanted to murder Esmeralda and Gaetano, any more than those men in grey, who presumably must have had human faces though she'd been too scared out of her wits to focus on them, could have felt happy about murdering Luigi and the other men. Yes, yes – but they'd done it all right. Both the partisans or terrorists or patriots of one side, and the loyal soldiers or docile barbarians or what-have-you of the other. Well – so the war was in first-rate working order, unfortunately. But . . . If we were the war's sole causes and its despicable effects, if our war expressed our inhumanity naturally and perfectly? What would Luigi say if I could ask him about this? she wondered with a quivery smile – and knew the answer instantly. Oh, with his eye and ear for this civilisation's criminal imbecilities, he'd reckon that the meaninglessness of the day's ferocities here had chimed musically enough.

But Caterina did not want these thoughts, she wanted her three dead friends. She wanted Luigi who had been so happy to see Benedetta again. She wanted Gaetano who in Venice had taken her to find Tiepolo paintings and had feasted her on fish, who'd made her laugh with his stories about Lady Marozia and the Popes in Rome. She wanted Esmeralda because then they could dress up as a brace of strapping young Austro-Hungarian archduchesses all over again and sally forth to a dance and forget about the war.

With tears for them in her eyes, she strayed further over the grass beneath the shadowy trees, making herself even more miserable by imagining how achingly she was going to miss them. A buzzard that had been roosting on a bough over her head went flapping off through the foliage. Far away over the mountains, silent lightning flickered. She stopped under a towering elm to wipe her eyes on her sleeve, she watched the hunting bats' crooked flight.

Listen to time, she remembered. Let time lap in you, let the stillness of time come to you and fill you, for its plenitude is always there. Listen to the air, to the voices and their stories.

Yes, Caterina thought, I shall live in honour of those three whom I loved. That, I can do. And although her eyes had at once brimmed with fresh tears so she was going to have to dry them again, she chucked her head up a bit with returning pride. Others will recall them slightingly and then not at all – but I, while I last . . . ! she promised the opaque sky, pressing her lips together very firmly to keep them in order and swallowing a gulp of tears. Esmeralda and Luigi and Gaetano will bring me again the old Italy they gave. A conclave of my chosen spirits, a conclave of abiding injuries and of abiding honourings – that's the only consciousness I want. I shall ring with echoes of their clairvoyance and their bitterness, their innocence and their gaiety, their minding passionately and their not giving a hang.

Of course I shall go on being as muddled-headed as ever. I shall keep on fretting over what this war has done to Lisa's childhood, fretting over what it may turn out to have done to Gabriele's and my marriage if we're both lucky enough still to be alive next month or next year. Naturally too I'll keep on getting waylaid by all manner of contradictory notions, just like I always have done, usually adumbrations so cloudy that nobody else would call them notions at all. I'll still indulge in silly dreams about shoving Giles out in a dinghy with Rosalba and making them promise not to be back till late.

But all the while I shall remember to listen, now and then, in distracted hours. I shall live the stories of my dead as I imagine all the stories and all the times I am living, stories seen and unseen, words heard with the outer ear and with the inner ear. I shall cock my head in the quietness and the solitude as I am doing now; I shall listen to the air, and sometimes it will tell me what I had not heard before.

Kate Caterina wandered on through the hot nightfall.